Born in London in 1962 just 17 years after the end of World War 2, David Jackman grew up against a back drop of sixties psychedelics and seventies terrorism anarchy and punk rock.

Living now in Berkshire the writer put pen to paper in order to leave a legacy for his children. 'Children are our future, the only one any of us ever have…'

To my children.
One and all the children are our legacy.
The only tomorrow any of us will ever truly have.

David Jackman

THE FOREVER XPANSION

AUSTIN MACAULEY PUBLISHERS®
LONDON * CAMBRIDGE * NEW YORK * SHARJAH

Copyright © David Jackman 2025

The right of David Jackman to be identified as author of this work has been asserted by the author in accordance with sections 77 and 78 of the Copyright, Designs and Patents Act 1988.

All rights reserved. No part of this publication may be reproduced, stored in a retrieval system, or transmitted in any form or by any means, electronic, mechanical, photocopying, recording, or otherwise, without the prior permission of the publishers.

Any person who commits any unauthorised act in relation to this publication may be liable to criminal prosecution and civil claims for damages.

This is a work of fiction. Names, characters, businesses, places, events, locales, and incidents are either the products of the author's imagination or used in a fictitious manner. Any resemblance to actual persons, living or dead, or actual events is purely coincidental.

A CIP catalogue record for this title is available from the British Library.

ISBN 9781035882434 (Paperback)
ISBN 9781035882458 (ePub e-book)
ISBN 9781035882441 (Audiobook)

www.austinmacauley.com

First Published 2025
Austin Macauley Publishers Ltd®
1 Canada Square
Canary Wharf
London
E14 5AA

Table of Contents

Prologue	9
Chapter One: Big Wheels	14
Chapter Two: Alone in the Universe	18
Chapter Three: Calling America	26
Chapter Four: Xanadu	31
Chapter Five: In For the Kill	37
Chapter Six: Sweet-Talking Woman	43
Chapter Seven: A Thousand Eyes	46
Chapter Eight: Can't Get It Out of My Head	50
Chapter Nine: On the Run	57
Chapter Ten: A Sorrow About to Fall	66
Chapter Eleven: Across the Border	72
Chapter Twelve: Secret Messages	89
Chapter Thirteen: Midnight Blue	99
Chapter Fourteen: Standing in the Rain	108
Chapter Fifteen: Hold on Tight	114
Chapter Sixteen: Strange Magic	119
Chapter Seventeen: So Fine	124
Chapter Eighteen: Night in the City	132
Chapter Nineteen: Confusion	136

Chapter Twenty: All Over the World	149
Chapter Twenty-One: Telephone Line	156
Chapter Twenty-Two: Secret Lives	165
Chapter Twenty-Three: Ticket to the Moon	173
Chapter Twenty-Four: Easy Street	183
Chapter Twenty-Five: Without Someone	192
Chapter Twenty-Six: Send It	202
Chapter Twenty-Seven: Last Train to London	210
Chapter Twenty-Eight: Tightrope	217
Chapter Twenty-Nine: Honest Men	223
Chapter Thirty: Wild West Hero	237
Chapter Thirty-One: Four Little Diamonds	251
Chapter Thirty-Two: Twilight	268
Chapter Thirty-Three: Your World	279
Chapter Thirty-Four: Tightrope	285
Chapter Thirty-Five: Fire on High	290
Chapter Thirty-Six: I'm Alive	297
Final Chapter Showdown	301
Epilogue	310
Story Synopsis	312

Prologue

He had been scared before, though even fear became a taste you got used to, given enough time and enough practice.

He almost tripped and fell down.

Why couldn't they leave him be?

'Agggh,' he yelled, barking his shin painfully on a rusty post. The boy ran on, limping a little but not daring to slow even one iota, his breathing was ragged and tears ran freely down the kid's dirt-streaked face. It was getting dark quickly and the boy saw the churchyard up ahead. As he ran on he remembered the lessons of the holy sisters, of the power and the nobility of the angels, the salvation that they promised. In a young child's imagination, he saw the brightness of that promise electric yellow in his small mind. For a few seconds, it all seemed so bright as to blind him even to the oppressive terror that his pursuers brought with them.

He wheeled left towards the church spire, a spike in the darkening sky, and he a tiny black darting shadow in that quickly fading evening light. The boy pushed hard, trying not to hear the thudding of heavy boots as the big men closed in on him. He knew he had to run harder than he had ever done in his young life, that if he did not get through the churchyard gate then they would have him. They would hem him in, trap him between them the forbidding iron railings and the graveyard beyond.

The boy was only nine years old, and despite a young boy's imagination, he knew deep down that he could not get over those railings, no way no chance. But if he could just make it to the church…

Well, then the angels.

His thoughts trailed off and tears pushed again at his eyes, pricking and then instantly running into the snot hanging from his freckled nose. Between gasps, he began to pant out loud the lessons he had been taught, those iconic dynasties of the church that he had listened to and then learned so assiduously from the sisters. 'Seraphim…angels of love.' He saw the gates to the churchyard wide open, glistening wet still, damp wood and ironwork from the earlier storm, the very one that had caught him out so late.

'Cher,' he stopped and choked back a scream, a shadow reared up and then fell instantly back directly ahead of him. He realised it was just a cloud moving swiftly across the rising gibbous moon, his tiny heart hammered.

'Cherubim, angels of wisdom,' he continued.

'Thrones, angels who oversee other angels.'

The gate was just twenty feet ahead of him now, but exhaustion was beginning to slow the boy considerably. Had he been listening he might have noticed that the heavy footfalls both from behind him and to the side had stopped some moments earlier.

Ears somewhere out there in the darkness were straining to hear the light and lifting tones of a small boy, trembling terribly as he repeated the lessons taught to him six times a week by the sisters of St Andrew of the Divine Faith, a church house of healing found in the rural lands just beyond Slobozia city. The Monastery was a place whose doors were open to orphans and indigent children cast out from that city, or indeed the wider Romania.

'Dominions, angels of mercy,' the boy's sob-filled recitation continued.

The earlier sprinting was replaced now by jogging and by uncontrollable trembling, equal parts cold, exhaustion, and fear.

'Powers, angels that guide souls.'

The boy wondered if he might have forgotten one, but in that exact instant, he passed through the gates and into the churchyard proper. As he did a veritable army of angels appeared before his young mind's eye, thousands of them. Rank upon rank, all so beautiful and white, all singing God's harmony as they drew together.

He saw generals issuing instructions to lieutenants. Angels and Archangels, and Virtues of course. They were his favourites, a secret the boy kept, unknown to the nuns that taught him. For Virtues, those mighty beings were the angels of miracle, the giver of God's gifts to men, to women and to little boys too. He saw then line upon line, ranked and ordered, fantastical lordlings as far as his young mind could imagine.

And as he pushed through the long-wet grass, uncut for more than just a single season, he gained comfort from the certainty his small heart felt at the coming of that majestic horde.

Now within the yard of the church, he took a wide berth around the tightly packed gravestones, trying hard not to think about the dead bodies he knew lay just a few feet under the sodden ground. Of course, the sisters had spoken of the dead too, those that had been lifted up to heaven, and others of course, those that were less fortunate, those that had not. And all of that had confused a young boy.

'Lifted up to heaven how?' he asked, for people did not have wings, even dead people, he figured they didn't just grow them. In his nine-year-old mind, he had instead configured a plan, a fantasy perhaps, but one that made sense to him. Those good people had been lifted up to heaven upon the wings of angels. And thus, there and then, he was doubly certain that in his time of asking those same winged lords would not forsake him.

His mind switched.

He saw himself sitting upon a chair holding tightly to a pale green nylon bedspread, his feet were swinging, but they did not reach the ground.

He was watching his mama dying.

It was a vague memory, a series of sepia-tone images, dim next to his more recent colourful imaginings of angels dancing and marching. But it felt gritty, more real, and he was unable to let it go. He had felt her hand drop out of his, he remembered that suddenly heavy as the life fell away from her. He had watched as her eyes went glassy, and he had known despite his young years that death came to her then.

Immediately after the preacher charged in. A fat bustling man still buttoning at the white collar around his neck and wiping food from his mouth. And he had said the words that needed to be said. The fat father had turned then to a boy so small as to be almost invisible in a tiny darkroom lit by only a guttering candle. And the religious man said to that boy, 'Sshh young one, hush your crying. Your mama has gone to heaven now, and that's for the best.'

Later the boy came to understand that they always said it was for the best, grown-ups. And he had supposed back then that they ought to know, or maybe they just didn't have anything more, anything better to add.

It was soon after that the preacher ushered the small child out of the room and away. It seemed to that boy in order to allow the angels to perform their ministrations, to remove his mama to heaven where she certainly belonged.

And so, as that same child twisted at the heavy iron ring that was the door handle, and with some effort pushed open one of the heavy oak doors to the musty church interior he smiled at the memory of his ma going on her way to heaven.

Despite the terror of his pursuers and of the green moss-covered grey stone gargoyles that glared down at him from on high, nevertheless, he was reassured by those recollections by the preacher soon after confirming his enquiry that indeed, she had ascended to heaven forever after. For a few moments, the memories had let him forget, in fact just long enough not to be thinking about the dead ones, the people that lay only a few feet away under the wet grass. And the live ones, those others crouched, hidden and watching as he entered the church proper.

The young boy felt with the unutterable certainty of youth at that moment that an army of white was hurtling down to save him, flying earthward on wings from heaven. He was after all in the house of God.

He looked round suddenly as the church door glided back towards its frame, and after a moment slipped closed with barely a whisper and the softest of clicks.

His feet sounded loud, wet leather on stone as he padded his boots down a central aisle between twin rows of bare hard wooden benches, a simple church for a poor community. No golden cross nor stained glass crucifixion scene adorned that place of worship.

Small puddles of rainwater were left on the stone floor where he had trod. There was only moonlight to see by, but what of that to the eyes of a nine-year-old? He stepped slowly, cautiously up that central aisle, stepping on flagstones worn smooth with many long years of kneeling and hard worship. Deep within calm warmed his fears, he believed now he was safe. That here in the house of God, he would be protected from the bad men, and from the dead ones too.

The shadow of those men, that stank of tobacco and of arrack, that had pawed and pinched and hurt him, men that had come in the night. Those recollections sought to assault him, but as they reared up his mind shut out the images. The sudden attack on a child's senses was one he could not quite contend with and did not fully understand, but that made him gasp out loud, nonetheless. Moments later those same senses electrified him with a sudden jolt as the tidal wave of recognition that could not be wholly subsumed shuddered through the boy's nervous system.

The pain and the shame had been too much to bear, simply too awful to know. It had been why he had stayed out long after the peel of the last bell, still out when the thunder and summer lightning had come and lit the evening sky with God's own power. The boy had not wanted to return to his cot, not then, nor ever. Not to those hands, too strong, grabbing and scrabbling, forcing and hurting. Angry and heavy with stink, and the hot wetness on him, and in him too...

'No,' he exclaimed suddenly piercing the silence within the church, his voice echoing and yet sounding very small, barely registering in the darkness.

And after just a moment a voice answered him from that darkness, deep and strong, filled with lust and evil intent, and there was no forgiveness in the tone as the disembodied voice replied.

'Yes, oh yes indeed, little one. Come and pray with us child.'

And in his mind's eye, a small boy saw the white of the angels suddenly recede and just as swiftly disappear. Barely a moment later he found that he hated them, despised them with all of his heart. It was they who taunted him, they who had led him here, and then it was they who abandoned him. And later as hands held him down and proceeded to tear his soul inside out a young boy forever turned away.

The child did survive the hell of that night and in time grew to be a man.

And after many years the boy who became frozen, forever trapped within that man, found others, and he built himself instead in their image.

And after a time that boy became the master of his kingdom.

Chapter One
Big Wheels

He stood on trembling legs, fated, baited, slated, utterly wasted, alone yet not alone in a room that stank of piss and the rancid odour of rebellion. He knew that nobody would stand for him now.

No more running, no more school of life, his time had come, and whether you believed in fate or in a life more random this indeed was his moment, and Jack Silver had known of its coming for a time.

His eyes would not focus, he desperately wanted to look into the face of the matador. However he tried though, he was not able to see outward, and so instinctively at that moment he looked in upon himself, and he laughed.

He remembered a sign he had once seen above the door of a bar. God knew where or when. It had said 'liquor in the front, poker in the rear.' That must have been twenty years back and yet it only just dawned on him right there and then. In fact, he thought, as the craziness came creeping inwards from the edges, it had not really said that at all.

Now he thought of it, *Lick her in the front; poke her in the rear*. Damned if it hadn't. He couldn't see it then yet here, now, right at the very bottom of the shit well, he'd be buggered if it weren't just the funniest thing, and he could see it clear as a bell.

He heard, well more like felt, a rumbling, bass and deep, distant yet ominous, threatening. Oh, how he wanted to look outward, yet something tugged him back…

'Stay. There's more to see, that bar that sign.' He began to understand that things were rarely as they appeared to be at first look, rarely indeed. He thought back to when it began.

When it all began…

There had been nothing, a difficult concept he considered idly, nothing.

But nothing, not having been there, 'And this is where it gets clever,' the voice that would become Caffee spoke up, had not been nothing for any time at all. Because in the absence of anything there hadn't been any time by which to measure it.

And so, after no time whatsoever nothing became something, and when it did so for reasons apparently not important to know and not here explained, it did so violently. White and loud and of a sudden nothing became everything, and in that very first instant everything was measurably forever, and so nested within was born time.

And nothing that had become everything was everywhere, which Silver understood was an inevitable part of being everything. And he saw it was in the very next instant that came the split.

The birth of reality unfolded through its infancy and Jack Silver saw it all, clear as a fresh summer morning, sharp as a drug addict's high.

He perceived the burgeoning reality, which had only moments before become everything, saw as that reality chose to allow regard, and soon after bore the universes and all that was in them.

From gods that would roam all the way down to particles skating beneath the Planck scale, and all that might exist ever after in between for and with a purpose. He saw creation, and he saw also that creation merely became a mirror in order that everything might regard itself.

In that second instant, fulfilling its everything nature, reality began enacting the existence of random possibilities, not some but all of them. All opportunities were created somewhere, sometime, somehow, and though that creation seemed random throughout, it operated within a pattern that was simply too complex, too marvellous for any one part within to ever behold.

Right then, right there Jack Silver saw that truth as it was, and he watched it unfold transfixed.

In the myriad instances that followed laws came to exist both to govern and to be broken, each followed closely by intrinsic structures and elements. And following behind soon after came motion like a gaggle of baby ducklings following a mother duck, energy moving through time space and stasis, flowing and ebbing.

And so, as the Englishman watched these things he spied them as tides. And as they washed up on reality's empty shoreline, so they birthed myriad universes, milky energies that across time blossomed throughout that burgeoning reality, a new garden grown all about.

Later, within those myriad universes came galaxies, and within the galaxies stars, and circling those stars worlds countless and unique, more than numbers could ever hope to record. The laws that were laid down bound them, and the elements built them, and time shaped them. And eventually, across them, commonalities began to appear.

Time was a key in this entire thing for it allowed change to be measured, and with measure random became something more, and so that which grew to regard became with significant inevitability driven by purpose.

Whether by incident or accident or design these infinite galaxies of stars and worlds and moons and dust raced apart, their energies seemingly forever bursting asunder. So it was that all things in a rush moved ever further away, helter-skelter in a mad scheme, an apparent fit to fill the space that lay between, the very space that everything had created in that first instant of being, expanding forever, so it seemed.

Jack who watched this by peering inward saw then many things. Myriad beings that took on individual shapes discovered a type of existence that invited a variated version of regard. He saw sentience as a new and purposed thing, and he saw then also how that which had been previously only watched from without was additionally perceived from within.

These new and purposed things were various, and they were vicarious, lasting an instant or an eternity. Due to time and to the immensity of the garden each grew within, and though many in design and in number, they evolved astonishingly far apart. Rare was the opportunity for any race within the whole of time and space to discover or know of any other.

Whilst one group of tiny things scrabbled in the mists of some gaseous hydrogen ball barely able to survive, struggling and birthing a next generation that would follow briefly before inevitable death. Still, in another instant, another corner of the whole, others evolved and strode out into the darkness of space, believing a life of centuries like to immortality. Moreover, they believed their technologies were enough to make them lords of their reality despite trading only in one small and particular corner. Fastness of that was still new and young everything.

Jack watched many types of life rise and fall, as each lasted their instant, or their eternity, always in the scheme of all things they held a domain that remained a small and pitiable thing when compared to everything, and to all the cosmos, and to all time.

Still, the Englishman saw the small brush strokes made upon the immense cloth that was forever expanding. He spied the marks those things made, and he saw that though tiny, as the aeons passed the accumulation did begin to change how things were, and how things would be, tiny, cumulative, repetitive.

Still, he gazed inward, and on he watched, and after some passage of time he understood that an inevitable thing then occurred. And though it had been long in coming as Jack Silver might have measured things it was in terms of that everything still early in the evolution.

A coming of age as inevitable as night following day.

Chapter Two
Alone in the Universe

Life, like yet not like how Jack Silver might understand life to be encountered by others. And after a period of exploring that other, after some back and forth there began a contest for the mastery.

The contest was not how he might have understood such things to be.

The Englishman spied on one life, a thing that was, in essence, a single entity; nonetheless, that was made up of many parts. A Hive would be as close as he might have understood the entity to be. Yet a thing, a life force, spread across light years of space and existing through aeons of time measured linearly.

A Hive entity that allowed each of its myriad component parts to subdivide all but infinitely. And that, as far as the Englishman was able to understand, saw no reason not to do so in the growing and apparently empty vastness of space.

He saw also that the mind of this Hive emphasised a way of living, evolving a relationship with the environments it encountered, carefully choosing those that invited it to spread, using the elements around and about as well as time and space to provide for that expansion.

The Hive created two specific component subunits and required that they bond with each other in order to allow continuity of the species, and to expand life beyond the energy, each unit was initially imbued with.

Alongside this, the Hive embedded a higher-level communication net. A thing that linked every unit, past present and future, through time and space, in a way that appeared in his mind akin to the form of a series of emotional pulses.

Or as one might understand instinct, or more properly intuition.

This along with the elemental boundary rails that existed as a simple result of the environments the entity settled upon, worlds of gas, liquid and solid, each abundant with hydrogen and oxygen as the growing omniverse's key components. And so, the Hive found growth virtually unchecked, throughout many aeons of time, and across many thousands of star systems.

But, as Silver watched there came a time when the Hive encountered that which would become a force in opposition.

That force, those beings, in the first instant appeared to the watcher more readily identifiable, and yet still very different from anything he had ever known.

He spied creatures that appeared in his mind like gods or even more than that akin to demons. The beings were fewer in number and yet each one held within them a power and lineage beyond imagination. Ancient long before single-celled life had crawled from Earth's boiling first ocean.

These beings were each formed into creation within the heart of a star in the moment of that star turning nova, and so were infrequent if not rare. In the very instant, these things awoke to self-awareness they were birthed across two opposing dimensions. Existing thereafter simultaneously on either side of the black hole being formed at the centre of their birthing nova, accessing either reality through the particular star's black heart within which they nested and grew.

So it was that through a curious elemental quirk, those creatures regarded themselves from two places at the same moment, existing in the darkness of space and in parallel the burning heart of a dying sun. And their birth was every time one of extreme agony.

Jack saw the first moments of life imbued upon each one of those demonic gods as an event that filled their cup with a despising of all things that ever after sprang from this side, his side, of the newborn and expanding omniverse.

He saw a hatred utter and complete and saw also how the duality of their birth allowed for a cold and conscience-free regard across the expanse of time and space that lay before them. Jack struggled with the concept of such cold malevolence, the closest the Englishman could imagine was associating them with psychopathy, a being absent of any conscience. And yet even such a psychopathic individual would be a noble soul when placed next to such.

Time passed and the demon gods grew slowly in both number and in life craft. Turning the energies of their agony, the supernova of birth, the cold of dead space, they bent all things across time with a forceful inevitably towards their cause.

In time, the creatures became greater than the bonds of their birth, and screaming in the darkness, one by one, they flew out into the dead night of black space, setting out to find something upon which to prey. To discover who it would that must pay for the agony of their being.

"The Vistarens" they were named, and though some spread through space in small flocks most went abroad alone, bringing the elements to heel and building huge space-faring machines. This was technology of the highest order in that young reality. Machines that became so complex as to eventually grow independent consciousness, and in time a separate and unique identity.

And those great craft both carried and accompanied their makers.

For aeons, these beings and their great vessels sought, and for "The Vistarens" the seeking was always an act of revenge.

After a long time, as the watching Jack Silver was able to measure matters, "The Vistarens", and their sentient technology began to mismatch. Variations in ambition came about, for unlike the Hive these beings did not evolve with any kind of inherent link. "The Vistarens" neither shared nor provided boundaries to their thoughts nor spread as one group or as several, they simply manipulated and controlled. The machines that they made however useful were forever by definition required to be subservient.

The Englishman saw that whether individual or small sect though akin to tribal and sharing common qualities for the most part each "Vistaren" was unique, growing and changing as well and tide allowed. He saw how fuelled with enough time the paths of each individual development became ever more disparate, and how the great machines they wrought would not, perhaps could not wholly match the hatred of their makers.

They grew in number slowly, nonetheless malice and high evolutionary technologies pushed them far out into the reaches of the expanding reality. Each of the "Vistarens" became virtually immortal, and forging across the expanding sea of space and time they went where they would with immense power at their disposal.

The Englishman watched the slow eddies and understood the coming encounter long before it was revealed to him.

Two races, for that is what he perceived they were, eventually, encountered one another with a dawning inevitability. He understood that though he saw it coming, whatever consideration of the possibility of encountering other life still each race had mostly imagined in reflection only the possibility of other beings like themselves.

In a distant corner of time and space, one "Vistaren", alone but for a great ship of many songs, landed upon a small world circling an inconsequential star. This place that had seemed not special from afar had proven to be the home of creatures who "The Vistaren" learned had some simple but evolving level of self-regard, of awareness.

As it turned out, this was a first encounter and with a relatively small and young enclave of the Hive. That "Vistaren" Silver saw was at first curious, understanding those things were not of its making nor any of its kind. But the residents of that world were apparently sentient, though each seemed puny and momentary. Nonetheless, the creatures had developed somewhat, and in some ways the group essence they displayed, if not quite a mind as "The Vistaren" understood such things appeared capable of deeds. Achievements that given time might scratch at even one such as the spacewalker that had come there.

The Englishman watched and saw then how after a time of study, and without preamble, the visitor who had looked upon the Hive creatures, simply removed them. "The Vistaren" wiped them from that world as Silver might wipe at a stain on a work surface.

Thereafter the being instructed the ship to send out a song upon the winds of space, singing of the puny beings, questioning whether others of "Vistaren" kind knew of them, and if so what might they be.

It was obvious to the spacewalker from that very first encounter that each alone was not a walker among the stars, the small tribe numbered only a few million, and their total output of energy barely registered to "The Vistaren". Nonetheless the beings were different. Each had a self-awareness "The Vistaren" felt, and too something deeper, a connection that lay beyond even the creature's perception.

"The Vistaren" saw that given time the tiny fleeting things might spread. Weeds growing wild in a garden eventually change and choke every other thing.

War came soon after.

"Vistarens" Jack saw, now aware of this new race began to spy in many dark and rocky places, stormy gaseous worlds and raging liquid balls, and they discovered that this Hive had spread already farther and wider than they could have imagined. And wherever they found them "The Vistarens" wiped away all that they encountered.

At times those "Vistarens" acted in concert but most often in small groups or alone. Given the great power each was imbued with nothing apparently could stand in their way.

Conversely, barely aware, and with insignificant energy signatures individually, the Hive creatures were brought together by the onslaught, and in time sought to act in concert. Under constant attack they began grouping, into thousands, and then millions, working together in a common cause, a consensus for preserving life.

As time inched onward wherever "The Vistarens" came they found more, and more, and ever more of that Hive. Silver watched the passage of aeons in moments, his mental landscape brightly lit and sharply focused.

He saw slaughter. And he watched fascinated the Hive developed techniques and technologies, sciences with which they became able after a time to slow the advance of "The Vistarens", even upon occasion to push them back.

At first, the distantly spread enclaves of the Hive had welcomed those visitors from space, imagining them the forefathers of the universe, a fair presumption Silver understood given that each "Vistaren" was imbued with power and even a majesty never glimpsed in anyone Hive member on any world throughout the omniverse.

Still, those "Vistarens" tore the Hive apart. They left worlds numbered beyond count in ruin.

After some millennia had passed, there came a message. What the Englishman perceived as akin to an instinct or a collective understanding, developed and issued far and wide to all corners of the omniverse. This was the Hive communicating, and it was a shared thing. Something which became inherent, and which was passed on through generations.

And that message, that intuition.

'Beware the beings from the outside, beware the creatures dressed in technologies of many hues who walk the starscape. Beware the demons.'

The Hive developed their own sciences, they fought back.

Silver saw flight into the space that existed not between but rather beyond worlds. He saw them touch at the atomic scale and create weapons of enormous power, to mimic and to rival eventually the energies of the stars that lit the worlds on which they lived. To Silver's watching mind other designs were still, more akin to magick, trickeries that would blind or disable their opponent forever, or at least for a time.

As he watched the Hive begin to have successes, the scales started to return to balance. Though never yet did the Hive recapture the foothold in the omniverse they once had.

"The Vistarens" were born with a vengeance as a purpose wished only to wipe out all of the Hive, and that had not proven as straightforward as any had expected. A final solution was sought, a plan to destroy every soul throughout all the dark reaches of space, and to that end, each ship of song was tasked to remake itself. Each song craft remade to be a universal weapon of planetary destruction.

"The Vistarens" born in agony knew only one pathway to the removal of the Hive. Hurt dialled up to the maximum, one step at a time, until each and every creature in each and every world in every corner of space would be wiped from history, and though it looked sadistic beyond reckon to the watching Silver he also understood that the creatures acted according to their nature and nothing more.

The wanton genocide renewed "The Vistarens" who consumed the destruction of their opponents with relish, though Silver spied and understood that the sentient craft they had created were less enthused. But time had changed other things too, and the Hive in some places had become both innovative and resistant, as "The Vistarens" worked on their plan, so the Hive were not idle, and defences were contrived of the great redoubt.

There might be no hope of defeating the unbending menace of the spacewalkers, or their mighty machines in a direct confrontation. The Hive instead worked upon magicks, arcane arts outside the sciences of particles, quarks, and atoms, gambling instead on a different route, an outcome unseen by malicious opponents. The Hive's intuitive consciousness prepared to give up almost all of itself, to retain only an essence of that self, hidden. A seed with which to begin again, to flourish anew once threat passed.

Those seeds were sent forth minutely and in great secrecy. Embedded deep into the amniotic elements of worlds not to that point ripe for life, and so hidden in the darkest corners, wrapped in the deepest mysteries of molten worlds, wreathed in poison gas and frozen tundra.

And when the Hive saw that it had done all it might in order to perhaps come again it took the remaining core of itself to another place, a farthest corner in the growing reality, becoming nothing more than a memory for any that might come after, both a wish and a warning.

"The Vistarens" came, and for millennia they wiped out everything they found, scorching worlds like torching insects burned from nests, visiting terrible destruction both mental and physical, until at last the spacewalkers perceived their great plan fulfilled.

They had become the dealers in death their agonising birth and subsequent nature had made them for, and as Silver watched, they gorged on the kill, until at last "The Vistarens" were consumed and complete.

They too withdrew, and the omniverse was quiet for a long time as both of its noisiest children appeared gone, or at the least asleep.

The omniverse grew back unchallenged and for many millions of years no living thing appeared anywhere, though the elements roiled and clashed and changed as they crashed about randomly, the universe flourished, but the garden remained for a long time absent any consciousness.

The Englishman drifted.

He understood that a long time passed even when measured against this history of everything. Then slowly, without fanfare, in one or two backwaters of that new quieter everything life did again begin to sprout, poking itself out like moss filling in cracks as spring comes.

Enclaves small in number, began to grow and spread, started to fill in once more the rocky promontories on which each had been given root. And as that slow evolution began once more to take hold, far away un-glimpsed by any, unknown by all, sentries posted millennia past were stirred to waking.

In that instant, Jack Silver saw the sleeping dragon slowly awoken from slumber in distant treasure caves far afield.

In a small galaxy away from the centre of everything, far out into that sector's spiral arm of stars a rocky world circled a small no-account star.

The watching Silver felt a frisson of excitement as upon that world life began to flourish, and with some slowly gathering momentum watched as that life began to spread. Till it covered that world, became integral to the pattern of the things of that place.

A species of creature stepped forward from the myriad of life that grew there, a biped that stopped crouching upon the ground, and that found awareness for and of itself, learned and grew, discovered science and magick in different measure, and built itself a civilisation with towers to rival those which nature had placed on the rock and water garden of Eden.

Jack Silver understood that those beings had no knowledge of how quiet was the omniverse, no understanding of what had gone before. He saw the myriad energies that emanated from that world with neither guard nor care. Saw no person yet on that world with any knowing of the others that came before. Saw a race believing themselves alone, the pinnacle of all things across the far reaches of space.

The human race stood up on its legs and began shouting out into the darkness. And Silver saw how after a time they would become the centre of things.

Jack Silver, the Englishman stood alone, broken and facing his final demise. And in that place and time, he did not care what had passed, nor what was to come, only what was.

He looked into himself ever more deeply, and he remembered…

It had been eternity, millennia beyond count that the thing had lain dormant, resting and free of encumbrance. Peaceful in the utter black and the cold vastness of space.

Chapter Three
Calling America

The year was Nineteen-Ninety-Eight, and the world was vibrant.

Thousands of life forms living in on above and under one rock spinning around a small yellow sun. Among all the living things on that world, that Earth, is the race of humankind.

After the rise and fall of many things came a period of calm, and across a few million years a frail and short-lived biped developed, began to grow and adapt to the environment, to discover sentience, and to multiply. Time passed, and these bipeds stood up upon their legs and took a grip on the world.

Nevertheless, by their own frame of measurement at the beginning of the third millennium, the race of humanity had woven itself successfully into the fabric of the Earth that had made them. And too had developed some flourishing technologies with which to grasp the essence of the greater reality they inhabited.

Around that time one nation came to the fore technologically, a republic much aided by a self-sufficing land mass that had invited a less empirical approach than the dominant predecessors of their history. This nation built great edifices of concrete and iron and moved people en-masse into cities, great human-built homes with shared geographical infrastructure, akin to Hives.

At just the moment when by looking out humankind might have begun to see a greater universe, in significant part through a history of war and divisive conflicts the people of Earth looked in. Energy signatures were thrown from that small world into space with no knowledge of the galaxy-spanning war that had taken place, few gave any thought as to what such loud unguarded calls to the universe might bring in reply.

Once again Jack Silver saw this all playing out, his mind's view like a hawk looking down from great height. He saw the world, and more particularly spied on the west coast of the United States of America, and there he looked down on a city called Las Vegas.

The Englishman saw Las Vegas translated to "The Meadows" though saw no meadows in the illuminated stone city he then looked upon. In the heart of Clark County Nevada, on the plains of the High Mojave Desert, he saw a city of a million people where temperatures topped out at forty degrees in summer.

As he looked more closely the Englishman closed in on one block of that city, and then one street, and then there amongst all the myriad souls on that one street finally he spotted one man.

Lennie was thirty-four years old; he thought his rubbish cart might be older than he was. He was pissed today and figured it was because his foreman had kept him late, moaning at Lennie about that bastard Billy Dodd. Lennie knew Billy Dodd was a lazy piece of work who never got to the job on time, and it seemed like recently just about every fragging day his boss took to leaning in on Lennie and telling him what a layabout Doddsy was. And yet he thought that boss, well he never did any damned thing about it, leastways not so far as Lennie could see.

'Juss keep on moaning an making Lennie late. And the thing is, if Lennie is late out then Lennie is gonna be really late gettin back, an damn it all to hell if it doesn't get blistering hot,' the man mumbled to himself.

Lennie understood life was hard. After all, he'd had polio for as long as he could remember, his right leg was pretty screwed up, and his other leg was swiftly following suit. Every day he swallowed a cocktail of medicines that would've knocked over a buffalo.

Jack Silver looked at how most folks turned the other way when Lennie approached, especially when he was in his city uniform and pushing his dented dirty city cart.

Yeah and the job was crud, and yeah it barely paid minimum wage, and even that was before union dues. He had to spend half of the rest of his dwindling few dollars on buggerin medical insurance, and that meant he had no luxuries. And that was a damned joke, in the world's premier capital city of luxury and excess. So ran the thoughts of the small man pushing his metal cart.

Lennie considered the damp condo he had left an hour before, considered the empty wallet in his back pocket, the meds that were making him bilious. And worst of all he considered for the thousandth time the fact that not only would life never get any better for him, but it was entirely certain that all the plans and checks and balances he put in place would not stop the reaper from taking him one day.

And by the looks of things perhaps real soon.

Yep, he thought, today's not a good day. Inside his mind the watching Jack nodded in agreement.

And yet despite all that Lennie had risen at 04.30 as he did every morning. Had a meagre shower and then climbed awkwardly into a stiff and unyielding nylon uniform. Despite every impediment the small man had then left the warm and damp condo, careful to switch off anything that might suck power and so incur cost. Walked then ten blocks into the city proper, in significant part just to get his legs working.

And when he had got there that bastard Billy Dodds and his boss both had once more done all that they could to ensure Lennie was late out onto the streets.

Trouble is he considered, pushing a litter cart around and picking up the trash the rest of humanity left lying about wasn't perhaps the hardest job ever made up for a man to do, and he knew that.

He also knew he wouldn't get anything better.

And most of all he knew that once the traffic started to build, and once the civvies, the people woke up and started hitting the Strip, and the sun climbed up onto its perch bleaching the shade offered by the concrete hotel monstrosities. He knew well enough that then Lennie's cart would get in everyone's way, and all of that, well that would make him late.

Jack carefully watched the man Lennie running behind time, saw the morning growing already really hot, saw how the man's legs were just that tiny bit extra painful as the limp became more pronounced. People were out, ambling up and down the wide concrete boulevards busily looking the other way, those few that even noticed a small black man with a nasty crook in his back and an evil limp on his right side. Few truly spied the man with a head bald as a cue ball and pushing a stinking and dented litter cart around a city that both he and the watching Silver understood stank to the heavens of success built on the back of misery and failure.

Lennie had a look in his eyes, that look suggested his view of reality, that being pissed at everything was probably what kept him going. Many years before the small disabled man had concluded someone of his ilk had only two "looks" that might command him any space in the world. He figured as quickly that the world's beautiful people had myriad faces, from disgust to grace and a world of subtle hues in between.

'All the world's a stage, and all the men and women merely players.'

He had seen that written down somewhere a long time ago. And as some things do it had stuck, though he had no idea from when or where the words had come. The look you proffered was key to the part you would play.

Lennie believed he had but two. Pissed, and that was his reliable proposition, and not too hard with three million dicks wandering blindly about his city at any given moment. And that didn't include Billy Dodds. There was always someone to be pissed at. The other look he had was as close as Lennie ever got to offering insight to the rest of the world about how he felt, about the truth of it all. The way the small street cleaner figured things everyone had to have one honest look, one undeniable face, one only that occasionally peeped above the wall of subtle deceits that every person he had ever encountered wrapped their lives in.

Lennie understood that the likes of him had limited alternatives. Pissed on the one hand, and very occasionally when his guard dropped, the other look the one he had no name for. The small man had learned down the years of his life to watch "the stage", to spy looks upon the faces of others.

He believed he might have seen a million looks on the people he moved among. In fact, he had long since decided he was a damned expert in spying on people's artifice, from shitty lies right through to blank-eyed evil. If Lennie were to name his true face, his honest player, to self-reflect at length, he would most likely have come up with haunted, the result of a lifetime chase by the twin devils of polio and isolation. Living in a city where the world came to the party had taken its toll and had left one Leonard Garfield Ambrose Richards with a truth that was undeniable, and a look that reflected that truth.

On a white heat morning on the Strip, just in front of the half-built Parisienne Hotel and Casino in Las Vegas Lennie was walking as quickly as his legs would take him, and he was feeling mighty pissed at the world. He reached a corner, hauled his cart to a halt and found himself waiting for the crossing light to turn from red to the yellow countdown that demanded he cross. The small bald dark-skinned man looked up. It was something he had done less and less in those latter years, and across the street, he saw a man.

Scrawny and unshaven, hair tousled, long black wool coat incongruous in the desert heat that already was rippling the air in the early morning. The wool-coated man looked close to a life on the street if not already there. And yet something in his stance showed Lennie the fellow was not a street creature at all.

The man looked across the space between them, and Lennie with a compulsion that emanated from somewhere deep inside, he would later call it intuition, in the same instant looked up and directly into the scrawny guy's eyes.

Lennie whimpered quietly, no one would have heard the sound even if they'd been standing within two feet of him. The cacophony of street burble, the sounds of construction, the honking horns and casino noises combined more than enough to mask one small man's whimper.

Good god thought Lennie the man he stared at was wearing his true face. The man stared back at Lennie unblinking, and Lennie thought he seemed to be asking for something. Help connection, he was not sure. In that moment, Lennie understood his own look, and ever after was to understand the difference between haunted and hunted. To understand what it would be like not to be pissed at the world, but to be untethered from it.

The small street cleaner plagued by polio and much bad luck besides looked into the man's eyes for maybe two seconds, and there, he saw more fear and more pain than he had ever dreamed possible in his whole life.

And the woollen-coated man looked back.

And he saw everything, and he saw nothing.

Within the thing were components of self-awareness that if sparked into life would be beyond the match and mind of all the gods and builders that in those latter days walked abroad in the omniverse.

Chapter Four
Xanadu

Jack was daydreaming, he was thinking about a better time and a better place. He had only recently come to Las Vegas.

In fact, he had been there for only a single day, and given a choice he would be gone before another passed. Jack Silver was an Englishman, a London boy, whatever that meant. As he stood there balanced on the balls of his feet, right at the edge of the kerb, waiting for the overhead sign to tell him to walk he stared across the busy intersection and saw a small dark-skinned man holding on to a battered cart and staring straight at him. He wanted to nod at the fellow, but something stopped him.

His mind wandered, and he found himself thinking of London, of a sunny day. Of walking across the Millennium Bridge over the River Thames. The great thing he thought about summer in London was that a warm day was rarely too warm, crowded was rarely too crowded, and loud was rarely too loud. The recollection was beautiful, relaxed, cheerful.

As Jack stood there thinking of distant shores a cab honked its horn, and instantly he snapped into another London. It was night, and on a shadowy street electric neon glinted in black puddles deep into an alleyway out back of a Soho restaurant.

He, Jack Silver, stood in that alley, listening as the rain pattered lightly onto a corrugated lean-to. This was not a warm London, rather it was cold, and he was not dressed to be outdoors. Yet in his recollection that man on that street had thought things were ok really, hadn't he? His date had run out on him, and he was a little drunk, but what of that? He remembered that those things had not been bothering him.

Then of a sudden once more in his mind it all began again. Three men turned into the alley which had led off from Berwick Street near to the west end. Three men, each one with shoulders hunched, night-time lights behind them had made it difficult for Jack to see clearly. He remembered how despite alcohol having been taken he became immediately more alert. There had appeared some intensity, some menace wrapped around those men, apparent in a way not quite visible even later upon recollection, but instinctively discernible, nonetheless.

Jack Silver was alone, and of course, it was late at night, and he was in an alley in London's seedier heart. It was right that he had ramped up his attention, proper that he had become a more wary watcher.

He had slipped out of the restaurant after visiting the toilet, it was amazing how many pretty-fronted London cafes and restaurants had ugly and dirty washrooms stuffed down the back end of cold and badly lit passageways. There by the toilet Jack had seen the door and read the words "Fire Exit" in silver on green. He remembered feeling hot and stuffy, how a minute outside had seemed appealing. The Englishman had only realised the fire escape door had no external doorknob once he'd gotten outside and on the far side of that handless door.

So, there he had found himself in a dark alley late on a rainy night with no quick route back into the warmth and the light. And three shadowy men, "*Shadowmen*" for company, and walking directly towards him.

The Englishman remembered how he had thought that those men looked intent on mischief, but how could he have actually known that? It was dark and where he stood he could barely have seen his hand in front of his face, and in his mind, he recalled how a voice had spoken up within his mind, and it had been contrary as the voices in Jack's mind invariably were.

'Didn't you just think about running, without paying the bill? Back then when the door clicked shut. So, who exactly is intent on mischief?' And as they had continued to stride towards him Jack had answered that voice in his head.

'Yeah, but these guys, well there's menace hanging off them, I'm one of the good guys don't you know. These bastards look mean.' As they had moved closer Jack heard low muffled voices, though unclear from thirty or forty feet away. He had pushed himself back as far as he was able into the shadows, he remembered becoming more nervous by the second. One of the voices had appeared terse and angry.

He remembered how a car had turned at the head of the alley, and for a second, headlights had shone stark white light onto the three men, Silver would have gasped except he had been holding his breath already. The three men actually looked exactly like he would have dreamed hoodlums to appear, castoffs from some ancient 1930s gangster movie. Humphrey Bogarts in long trench coats, two with collars up the third, smaller in height and build, with a white scarf hanging loose around a buttoned wool coat, and that one had looked to be in charge.

In the seconds of light, Jack had seen that white scarf was in fact the guy talking, the fellow with the agitated voice, and as he had tuned in Jack made out somewhat of what was being said.

'What the fuck are you talking about, if my brother says do it, then you fucking do it.' Jack hadn't heard the next bit, something had popped, an exhaust backfiring perhaps.

'Listen I don't like it any more than you do Dickey but Stevan's the man, an he says cut her, and he says kill her, so you gonna fuckin cut her, then you gonna fuckin kill her. And if you love that bitch then you better pray she goes to heaven. Cos one way or another she's gonna die tonight.'

Jack had gone cold. The men a few dozen feet from where he was hiding in the shadows of a restaurant's back exit were casually discussing murder. One of the big men answered, his accent had been heavy with Scottish broadside, and he had sounded as if he was getting angrier himself.

'Aye, but Rosie didna mean no harm, Cedric. She just got it wrong was all.'

'Don't matter,' white scarf responded his own voice raising the temperature further. 'Stevan told you, my brother told you, and now I'm telling you, Rosie's time is up. And Dickie it's you who screwed her, you brought her into Stevans world, so you're gonna fuckin take her out,' the one named Cedric had spoken and that seemed an end to it. Though he had then added in a mollifying tone.

'And it'll be for the best, and you know it has to be soon Dickie.'

The man called Dickie had not answered, and Jack whose night vision could see a little more by then than the dim outlines of previous minutes looked on, holding his breath still, trembling as the cold of the night seeped in and fear grabbed hold. He had watched as the one who hadn't spoken whatsoever to that point began to slide slowly around and behind the man called Cedric, stealthily taking a position immediately behind the white scarfed man, and so outside of his eye line. And as disconcertingly to Jack Silver that man had moved closer to him also, and in that instant had moved not more than ten feet distant from the hidden watcher.

Cedric the man in the white scarf, the one who had appeared to be the leader of the particular pack of jackals, had then appeared to calm down a little, and when Dickie hadn't replied, still in his more mollifying tone he had spoken again.

'Look no one's saying Rosie isn't a good girl, but she can't run off at the mouth like that in front of the punters. She's gone an brought this on herself. She must have known my brother would find out. An surely it's better you do it than someone else. Some other fucking amateur slashing and gouging her, that don't seem right Dickie. You cut her and then you kill her, cos if it is one of the others Dickie then you know they're gonna have their fun first. Look at it this way, you know Rosie's gonna die. This way you control the how, the where and the when.'

It had been at that exact moment, and with no discernible signal as far as Jack could remember that the silent one had pulled a long blade from inside of his coat. That steel blade had glinted off electric light from some nearby night-time window, and Cedric the scarfed man who was completely blindsided had not seen it coming, had no warning as the quiet one had stepped up behind him and thrust the blade deep into his throat quickly and professionally three or four times. Jack remembered how he had heard distinctly a gurgling sound, and the voice of Dickie in a whisper as he had said.

'Ye should've spoken up for her Cedric, I can't kill Rosie, but I can kill you ya fucking dumb wit.' The man called Cedric had dropped to the ground in a heap, and Jack Silver remembered the voice of the third man as he had spoken for the only time he heard.

'We mustn't stay round here; Stevan's gotta think Cedric was on his own.'

Dickie had peered at the killer through the gloom, and from the shadows trembling almost uncontrollably Jack Silver had watched them both talk calmly whilst standing over a quickly cooling corpse.

The illuminated sign changed to walk and returning to the present Jack started across the road, treading quickly and dodging the sad-looking guy pushing a beat-up cart. The Englishman spied him for a moment, the cart and faded city uniform barely registered, and the beady eyes that had peered at him from across the road were now downcast. The twisted body that limped and battled with both it and the trolley he pushed, none of that really arrived for Jack. And yet nevertheless, right at the edge of his thoughts, like some cloud briefly covering the summer sun on that English summer day way off in the recess of Silver's mind he heard a voice warning, and some intuition knew the voice was that of the bin man.

'Watch out fool, the safer you think you are the more dangerous it will be.'

'They are coming. And they're going to kill you when they catch you.'

And as Jack and the bin man moved further apart like two old-time sailing ships moving ponderously away cannons fired, so too the message faded. The thin man in a wool coat hunched his shoulders and walked a little more quickly. Part of the problem Jack realised was where to go, it was all right running, hell he'd been doing that for months now.

'Your whole life,' a small voice whispered deep down where the bugs crawled.

Throughout his escape, Jack Silver had little idea exactly where he was going. Five months before his life had been just like everyone else's, plodding along he supposed.

'Well, completely stagnant in fact,' his new mind counsellor added cheerfully.

Then suddenly, no preamble, no indicator, and there he was accused of murder, and of murder by a man who, even if he could prove he didn't do it was likely going to kill him anyway.

After first hitching and running up and down the length and breadth of the UK, finally under cover of storm and darkness, the terrified Englishman had crossed the short stretch of water to France, and in the days that followed travelled by land to northern Spain. And then seemingly almost inevitably now he reconsidered he had drifted, apparently invisible, to the United States. Jack Silver could not think of the last time he had not been scared.

'Well, that would be five minutes before you were introduced to Stevan Cipher and his merry fucking gang of Stormtroopers, so say we all,' came the cacophonous mental retort to his recollections.

As he walked past yet another glistening concrete edifice to wanton waste he was surprised to find himself hungry and in need of a drink. He did not wear a watch but guessed it not later than seven in the morning, and so he wondered why any licensed establishment would be open to sell alcoholic inducements this early in the day, what kind of customer might they hope to attract, even in the twenty-four-hour hedonism city that was Las Vegas.

One of the things nevertheless that Silver had discovered early on was that alcohol remained one of the few things that helped dull the fear. He sensed himself become like a First World War trench rat, understanding how a few tots of the hard stuff might carry him better through the coming hours.

As he walked past the hotel, a passage that took several minutes due to the monolithic size of the establishment, and thence across a parking lot, he saw with no surprise whatsoever a helicopter liveried with stars and stripes, blades turning lazily as it sat at rest in the tarmac parking lot straight ahead.

Impervious to outside influence, waiting…

Chapter Five
In for the Kill

A few moments later he strolled past the resting flying machine, and then up to and pulling on a creaking glass door through which he walked into an utterly average American diner. He blinked at the change from bright sunlight to dim electrics, and somewhere inside felt as if he had stepped through a time portal. The place was in fact brightly lit considering, though nothing could be as bright as the desert blaze climbing into the jet blue sky just beyond the establishment's tinted windows.

At first, Jack could not see a soul inside, to the left of the door he had stepped through was a singular and grimy bay window looking back out onto the main drag populated by a growing stream of what he thought of as casino rats, venturing into the light and moving busily back and forth.

Staring back out he was glad to be inside, away from the chaos.

He spied two dozen booths covered in mats and ancient glass ashtrays, running down in a row to his left, and then opposite a black onyx counter running the length of the establishment upon his right.

Silver sat himself down in a booth at about the midpoint, unbuttoned his wool coat and pulled out a sweat-dampened pack of Marlboro, placing them carefully down on the table. He did not smoke and had not since that night in Soho. And anyway, what he needed was a drink.

He had kept the increasingly crumpled pack of cigarettes as a matter of habit. During his months of running, he had discovered that in any bar in the world whether a pub in London or a Tapas bar in Spain, if you settled down at a table and looked as if you were in for the long ride; generally speaking, the staff on site would be just that bit quicker to your service. And so, he put down the cigarettes. Having nothing else they were simply a signal to draw attention.

The Englishman took another look around him, this time a little more slowly, he rubbed his hands together chilled by air conditioning units he deemed set on ice-cold, and in that instant, he realised that barring his hands he was in fact quite warm, and that was due to his wool coat. He shucked the coat off onto the leatherette bench seat though it was colder within than the early-morning desert sun of the Indian plains he had worn the coat since getting on a plane in Spain and heading to Lax and then onward to Las Vegas. He could not recall when last he had taken the coat off.

The crawly voice team from down below offered "fetid and sweating" and Silver frowned and tried to ignore the anxiety he felt bubbling up inside him.

After a minute or so, eyes adapted to the electric neon lights, he found himself drawn to the bar. It was black and highly polished, with no marbled swirls to mess with the deep inky night-like hue, and the surface was buffed to perfection, with not a whisky ring in sight.

A huge mirror sat centrally bolted on the wall behind the bar, taller than a man and running the length of the counter, reflecting the light back from a range of multicoloured half-empty optics. At one end sat a huge chrome-plated coffee maker, an artwork of glistening silver and blood-red. The big mirror covered a nicotine-stained wall, and to Jack, it all felt entirely in keeping with the establishment, stale yet somehow as artistically unique as the chrome and the optics colour work.

At the farthest end of the bar, Jack saw a picture, well actually upon second look a poster embedded in a black wood frame. The image drew him in with a bright dandy of colours, and it was emblazoned with bold words. He spied a circus tent with prominent red and white candy stripes standing forth below a star clustered and navy dark night-time sky. In the picture, he saw the smudges of many folks, apparently dressed in gay summer finery, all walking up towards the great marquee, in ones and twos. To him, it appeared a quintessentially perfect scene from an English Victorian summer evening long since passed.

'Roll up roll up good people, just a penny buys you miracles and magic. Step inside and come see the world of the circus.' As he stared, Jack thought he could even hear the voice of the ringmaster earnestly entreating anyone within earshot.

In black and gold lettering stood out tall against a deep blue night sky filled with the pinpricks of a thousand stars read the sign:

O'Shaunessy's Circus

Featuring Jonathan the Strongman,

and then a line below in only slightly smaller lettering,

And starring The Great Bezanto.

At that very moment, a voice spoke up, and as Jack refocused, he saw for the first time there was a man standing behind the bar.

'Where the hell did he come from?' the internal debaters queried, anxiety tingling at the enquiry.

'Top o the morning to ye kind sir.' The newly appeared barkeep chirped in a heavily Irish accent.

'Oim guessing it's a bit on the warm side out there?' he continued.

'So, what might I be gettin for ya?'

Jack looked at the man who had spoken. Balding, apron pulled tight around a girth which carried a dozen spare kilos, a damp rag slung across one shoulder and a freshly polished pint glass in one hand.

'Good morning,' Jack replied carefully. 'Yes, it is warm. Beer would be good though it is early.' He spoke wanting to smile at the barkeep but finding himself uncomfortably wary. The barman began to slide down the bar, a marvellous feat for one so large Jack considered, and as he did, so he replied.

'Like the Guinness advert says sir there's only two times that count where a pint is concerned… Light o the clock, and dark o the clock, so oi would be pleased to pour your fancy.'

Jack found himself fidgeting and after a few seconds without glancing up changed his mind and said in response.

'No, actually, I think coffee. Yep, coffee will be fine, black with lots of sugar.'

If the Englishman had looked up at that exact instant, he would have seen a moment of wild fury move swiftly across the barman's features. What he heard instead was a loud noise as the pint glass the other had been holding banged firmly down onto the black polished bar.

Jack was nervous, something was wrong with the whole set-up.

He had only got off a plane a few hours ago. There was no way they had tracked him down this quickly, who were these damned people anyway. Yet he found himself in urgent internal debate, his amygdala already dangerously close to pushing the panic button.

He could not understand, could not put his finger on what was wrong exactly, but his instincts told him he needed to leave the place, and so he stood up suddenly. Knocking his leg against the table he leaned instinctively, nimbly, and grabbed at the heavy glass ashtray that was suddenly sliding from the impact of his leg off of the Formica tabletop towards the floor.

As Jack sought to step away from the leatherette bench, he sensed and saw in the same moment a hulking figure that closed quickly on him. He turned and ducked in one motion as the barman came at him, and all he saw was a manic frenzied face and a small fire axe in one raised hand swinging down in a deadly arc.

Jack Silver had no time to think. Had thinking time been allowed he would likely have thought himself into a coffin, but instead, he instinctively and wildly swung, blindly, and as fate, or fortune would have it he was holding still the heavy glass ashtray he had grabbed at a moment before. Chopping in an upward ark across his body his arm swung straight up into the madman's face.

He felt a sickening impact as heavy glass settled with a heavy thud into bone and soft tissue. A half second later he heard a guttural scream, and then just as quickly the barkeep folded over. The cry stopped just as suddenly as it had begun replaced with a breathless choking gurgle.

The thin man turned and ran and just had time to register the small fire axe embedded in the Formica of the table top he had been leaning on only seconds earlier. As he battered his way through the diner's outward swinging door with a loud crash the heat of the day hit him like a wall.

At some level he was aware that he had been in a heightened frame of awareness for several moments there, sometime later he decided it must have been brought on by overwhelming panic. Right at that moment he was still in the terror space, and so without looking back he ran madly across the bleached white concrete apron and headed blindly towards the Bellagio hotel and its array of fountains.

Each second he ran, each meter he moved further away from the diner he expected to hear the doors slam open behind him, even whilst running he waited for the sounds of rage and screaming. And then after a dozen more paces he thought that he must surely hear the sounds of sirens, the police would surely come, something, anything.

And thoughts of the mad barkeeper's face drove renewed energy into his pumping legs. Had Jack Silver been a fly on the wall in the diner he just left he might have been astonished by the sight presented to him, almost as much as by the events of only moments previously.

In the diner sitting sat in a booth, crying quietly into his hands, an overweight middle-aged man was smiling through blood and gristle as he sang to himself, 'Happy birthday to me,' between gurgling and small sobbing sounds.

In the mind of Andrew O'Malley, he was back in Kilkenny waiting to blow out the candles on his eighth birthday cake. And from there he was never going to chase Jack Silver up the Strip, nor was he ever going to be anything more than an eight-year-old child for the few weeks of life that remained to him.

The thin man though was not a fly on that wall, and so he ran on into the desert heat.

It was several hundred meters before he finally stopped running, the heat touching thirty degrees wilted even his panic, and as his heart rate slowed he decided finally that he really did need that drink.

He walked on and thought about what had just occurred, trying to get his head around the fact that a guy had just come at him with a fire axe a minute after he had walked into a diner. He tried to rationalise as the voices rose up within him once more.

'You know what's weird, Jack; you knew that was coming.'

The voices were small and insistent, marching back and forth at the back of his mind, just about loud enough to pay attention to. He had been in Las Vegas for less than twenty-four hours having run halfway across the world in an attempt to escape a madman and his crew. Inside his head he was trying desperately to figure out whether what had just happened could possibly in any way be connected, and if so how.

A minute or two later Jack reached the main drag once again. Traffic was starting to build, and the sound of horns, the gaggle of people which before had seemed to him intrusive was now reassuring, he reached into one trouser pocket and was relieved to feel the solid weight of his wallet. He had thought a minute earlier the wallet with credit card, cash and passport might have been in his coat pocket left on the seat of a diner he would never frequent again. But no, he'd travelled to Vegas light, and now he was a little bit lighter.

'Less one topcoat and one half-empty stale pack of Marlboros.' He figured. There was no way he was goin' back, but the wallet in the city of Las Vegas where the buck was king, he decided might still buy him a few hours of anonymity.

In the distance, the Englishman heard a police siren howling cat call, no one looked up, a drunken couple leaning heavily on one another tumbled recklessly onto the road and laughed as they stepped back only seconds before the cruiser screamed past a few feet away.

Silver had jumped at the sound. He realised he needed to get off the Strip. To his left was a walkway back into the main Bellagio concourse, the building he had run past only moments before, the new grand hotel on the Strip opened only weeks before. And so without further thought he stepped on and let the travellator carry him soundlessly away from the heat the murder and the insanity.

Elsewhere out in the darkness lay another. Small, created to offer no perception of value to any who might stumble upon such, one amongst myriad. It was placed, left to grow and shape to fullness as the universe cooled slowly from the heat of so great a conflict that all its corners had been scorched.

Chapter Six
Sweet-Talking Woman

Rosie knew she shouldn't have been saying it, she was Dickey's girl, and Stevan Cipher definitely did not like his girls having too much to say about company business. She knew that but Mr Mainwaring, well, he wasn't filth now was he, so what was the harm? Just a sad old man who drank too much and stank slightly of his own piss underneath that cheap cologne.

Now, Mr M, he'd been stickin' his half-soft cock in her for, well blimey, the best part of a year. A once-a-week thing, she giggled as she thought how it was Kinda like going to church. Like religion on a Sunday, except this was always on a Thursday night.

Rosie smiled to herself and thought, *There weren't no copper gonna do that an stand up in court, was they?*

She was a little bit drunk; Mr M had bought her several very large cocktails before retiring them both to his small windowless inner room at the Grand Corinthian, a place that she thought was not that grand at all. She felt sure people knew what was goin on, course they did. What with him being old enough to be her grandfather let alone her father. But no one was gonna do nothing, nobody would speak out, not knowing as how she worked for Mr Cipher, not knowing as how she was one of his girls an all.

'No, see, Mr M, I only does you as a special now. I have other duties for Mr Cipher these days, what with Dickey moving up to being his brother's right hand. N me n Dickey being very close an all you understand. See I run to the bank, an' I take all the letters over to them legal people. An' sometimes I even welcome Mr Cipher's overseas friends see. But for you Mr M. Well, I don't mind. You are one of my specials,' at which Rosie grinned widely.

'And as I know what goes on in Mr Cipher's rooms well ain't nothing he gonna say is there?' Rosie smiled as she burbled on, drunk and stood naked in front of a bathroom vanity mirror and downlighter.

Outside the sky was black marked only with the tiniest twinkle of red and white lights as an intercontinental flight stretched its wings and inched across the night. Rosie admired herself in the glass, her pale white sixteen-year-old skin, unblemished by tattoos and piercings, very important if you wanted to get into Mr Ciphers employ.

Pert breasts that she knew drove the boys wild in the loose tops she favoured with her tight blue jeans. Small blonde fuzz downstairs, and not an ounce of fat. She did a bit of coke and knew that neither Dickey nor Mr Cipher would approve. But what they didn't know and all that. No marks on her arms, no needles, just a bit of coke to liven it up with these poor sad old men she tossed and turned. *C'mon*, she thought, *I'm young, and I gotta party.*

Rosie had no idea why Mr Cipher even bothered to stay "on the side" with an old fool like Mr M. Who was the old boy anyway. She frowned for a moment then remembered. That's right he'd been "a senior planning officer", whatever the heck that was. Rosie could think of no reason why Mr Cipher would even notice such a man.

But still...he was always gentle, and anyway, he never took too long, well sometimes he never got there at all. Rosie might only be a teenager, but she certainly understood the concept of persuasion. And she knew full well that beyond the enticement of her tight white flesh were the photos safely locked up in Mr Ciphers vault.

As Dickey often said to her, this was Mr Ciphers world and the rest of us.

'Well, aye we're just his guests.'

And Rosie understood that was just about right. Maybe not the whole world, not yet at any rate, but in this little corner for as long as she had known Mr Cipher had called the shots. And in the main, though he was hairy scary alright, and she didn't ever wanna be in his wrong book so to speak. Well, like as not she had seen some of those folk as didn't do right by him.

She had a room all of her own in the big house, and she didn't do the streets no more. Rosie had good gear and as she brushed her long blonde hair and stood naked in front of the mirror, she was sure a bit of coke and a natter about Mr Cipher with silly old Mr M. Well, what harm was there in that?

Alex Mainwaring lying naked on the bed smiled briefly and looked at the pert bum that until about five minutes previously had been bouncing around on top of his admittedly ageing carcass.

'So, when you say, Mr Cipher has you doing more important things, Rosie, is that?' He paused and scratched at his crotch before continuing laconically, 'Is that like a routine thing for you? Say like do you go to the bank every day?'

He asked that last a little more carefully trying not to be too obvious.

'Nah,' said Rosie. 'See Mr Cipher he has stuff moving all over, n I don't just mean money,' she continued giggling. And had she turned her head right then Rosie might have wondered at how intensely Mr Mainwaring now appeared to be listening to their idle chatter. And had she seen that her young senses might have sharpened right up. Just might, and she might then have just shut up right at that second.

But Rosie was a bit more drunk than she realised, and over the next minutes, she let go of what she knew, which wasn't much to be truthful. But notwithstanding it was all about the inner workings of Stevan Cipher's crime syndicate. And it was to a sad old man who unfortunately for her happened to be a retired CID officer from Truro in Cornwall.

More importantly, an officer handpicked and painted into the backdrop in order to get inside of Cipher's henchmen. Rosie, guileless and young, sealed her fate the moment she started to talk out of turn. And for that matter, the teenager sealed the fate of a world of other folk too just for good measure, including her ageing punter, though she would not live long enough to ever know that.

In some places, it was understood the garden would cool, new life would nurture and grow. And the thing of no worth was harvested as had been foreseen and carried then in secret for millennia, by guardians appointed only for that task. Unbeknown to any that artefact had a task appointed, and so watched and waited...

Chapter Seven
A Thousand Eyes

Jack sat at the bar and stared gloomily at a third large whiskey in an hour. In another life, a trip to Las Vegas would have been a dream fulfilled, but as it was Jack was trying to figure out what had happened a little more than sixty minutes before in a diner not a mile distant. What if the axe man was one of Stevan Cipher's had they found him so quickly? The Englishman had not come to Vegas to fulfil a dream.

Indeed, sitting in a coffee shop at Malaga airport, it had come to him that Vegas was just maybe ironically the most inconspicuous place in the world he could think of, as he had sat brooding over a different waning glass of amber liquid. Fuck a duck a million people all partying twenty-four-seven, he'd figured nobody would find him there. And even if by some miracle they did well compared to some places he'd been in recent months surely it wouldn't prove too difficult to, well just melt away.

But all that had gone pear-shaped, firstly because some nutter who didn't on the surface seem a likely candidate for Cipher's Stormtroopers had merrily tried to kill him for what, daring to order breakfast? And secondly when he had subsequently walked up to the counter and asked for a room from the pretty coffee-skinned Hawaiian girl whose name badge announced her as "Cookie – Reception staff" well hell in a hand basket why hadn't he thought things through, of course, they would want a bloody passport; of course, they would want a damned credit card swipe, this was Las Vegas.

A city once run by gangsters for gangsters, but which was now run by bloody accountants for multinationals.

'So just bigger gangsters eh.' Silver mused mumbling out loud. He sat at the bar, looking up every minute or two wondering who was watching him and feeling about as inconspicuous as any tourist could make themselves, or at least that was how he felt.

The Korean barman at the other end of the counter hadn't appeared to take too much notice of Jack, which might have been down to the miserly fifty-cent tips he'd been leaving. Or on the other hand, perhaps he was watching without looking. Trouble is Jack figured how did you bloody well tell.

What he needed was a room and a sleep, some escape from the Las Vegas crowds which he understood would build, and build even more, as the day progressed, but as he sat at the bar Jack couldn't see a way. In a city with half a million beds, he couldn't find a way to one of them without putting his head above the parapet, and after that morning's pot shot he didn't think he was ready to try that.

The barman, or "Vietcong" as he had labelled him began to glide down the bar to Silver's end, and as Jack was mulling over whether the guy might decide to pull out an AK47 and open up on him if he sat there for too much longer, based on recent events this seemed at least plausible, the barman spoke.

'Hey, buddy, you need a refill on the JD?' he asked, his accent all American, his tone belying the downcast expression sat on his Asiatic features.

'No, I'm good thanks,' the Englishman responded looking at the ice and straw-stained beige by the remaining rye in the bottom of his glass.

'Say what,' said Vietcong, and for a moment Jack wondered how it was that the cousins across the water, a loose term he supposed for seemingly a son of the far east. How was it that the bastards never seemed to understand what he was saying? He felt himself growing mad and knew some of that was down to the cocktail of jet lag, fear and tiredness.

'Sorry,' said Silver suddenly asking brightly, 'Can I get a coffee?'

'You want cream and sugar with that?'

Jack thought right then about his earlier coffee order but knew instinctively that this guy was straight up.

'Black with lots of sugar will be great.'

'You waiting on someone,' the barman continued, seemingly just making time for a dime but perhaps also a little curious at the slightly bedraggled and pale man who sat looking for all the world like the devil was only a pace or two behind him.

'Well, no actually, I've just flown in and somehow I seem to have mislaid my passport,' said Jack, lying half idly, but fishing.

'Hey, don't get anything in Vegas without ID,' said Vietcong with a hint of disapproval in his tone, perhaps wondering whether this wasn't just another down-on-his-luck bum.

'Oh, I've got ID,' continued Jack, on a roll, pulling out a battered leather wallet with a flourish and flipping it open to show a British driving licence with a photo of an engaging angular young man in his early thirties, a shock of dark hair slung across his face and forehead like some Manga comic hero. Vietcong eyed the wallet and, more than the licence noticed a clutch of credit cards, Visa, MasterCard, and Amex all in attendance.

'No, the problem in truth is that it's going to take a couple of days for the embassy to sort my damned passport, and I'm dying for a bath and a kip. Seems I can't get any kind of room at this glitzy hotel without my passport…Great huh.' Jack wondered if he had said too much and wondered what he was hoping for exactly. Nonetheless, stranger in a strange land and all that, Yanks were supposed to love the Brits he thought.

The barman had moved somewhere along the counter and finished pouring his coffee, slipped a couple of paper sachets of white sugar onto the saucer and lastly stuck a straw in the steaming black brew. Jack stood up and moved up to the bar to collect it.

'I'll bring that right over sir,' said Vietcong the beginnings of a smile at last starting to warm his features. Perhaps the English dude was o.k. His story seemed plausible, though how he had lost his passport he hadn't said.

'You know I shouldn't say it cos they pay me an all, but the Bellagio ain't the only watering hole in town.'

Jack looked at him quizzically as he put the coffee down in front of him the bill on a separate saucer for company.

'Yeah, hey, if you need to get some shut eye just go down to the Motel Six out by the airport. Ask for Danny at check-in and tell him your story, tell him Jason sent you. I'll be back for that in a bit,' the barman finished flicking his eyes down towards the bill. Jack thanked him and smiled warmly the passport safely hid in his back pocket.

Jack thought that on balance he had not really expected a solution, had not believed something as straightforward as this barman offering him an intro would present itself. Silver waited then long minutes till the barman was turned away and dealing with a couple of giggling twenty-something women doing their level best to get noticed. He slipped his hand into his pocket pulled out a twenty-dollar bill and slipped it under the tab. He was up and gone before Vietcong had even looked back.

Disappearing was an art, and Jack was becoming a real Rembrandt in that new art form. Moments later, he strode quickly through the hotel conscious the flow of humanity was building and feeling eyes on him as he walked purposefully away from the bar through the flower-strewn lobby area and out past reception, where myriad folk continued the steady flow of checking in and checking out. The Englishman exited hastily out of the air-conditioned nirvana and into the scorching heat of a full Las Vegas day…

In the darkness of space scale, that is the measure of all things from minuscule to enormity, is too great a thing for any one entity to comprehend.

Chapter Eight
Can't Get It Out of My Head

Well, there hadn't been a Danny on at Motel Six, but the mention of his name and a shortened tailored version of the lost passport had got him a room. Only well the whole lost passport thing hadn't stopped them needing his credit card to charge the room to and Jack had got to thinking that it would be as easy to find him from a credit card slip as from his damned passport.

In the end, the need for rest and the simple wish to get away from people had tipped his hand.

The Englishman showered long and hot, looking carefully at an island chain of bruises down his left side picked up whilst running away from a bar fight in Spain. Soon after the self-examination he had lain down on the bed without removing nor climbing under the covers. The air conditioning was humming on full to provide a glacial room temperature and bumps all over his still-damp flesh. The whiskeys earlier in the day had left him fuzzy, and the need for sleep soon overtook any urge for room service that had been pushed into his brain an hour earlier during check-in.

Jack drifted off soon after into the peaceful darkness of sleep, except that sleep proved not quite as peaceful as he hoped.

He understood intuitively he was dreaming finding himself in a house, in a place he did not know, though he felt certain he knew the type. Print wallpaper and patterned carpets, ornaments and pictures covering every free inch of space. An olive-green faded three-piece suit that had seen better days and took centre stage in a lounge reminiscent of his Auntie Bessie's place.

The lights were switched on though Jack noticed it was not dark outside. To his dreaming eyesight it simply appeared the heavy net curtains draped across the large bay shaped front window swallowed up the natural light.

He found himself stood in the centre of the room yet somehow did not feel as if he was really interfacing with the environment. Something felt to him more like a ghost in the machine feeling.

'What you mean like a dream,' a pedantic voice spoke up in his mind. This dissociative view of his presence became conclusive when two people walked into the room paying no heed whatsoever to Silver's presence.

A woman walked in first, tall and elegant in a decadent way. Dark hair and something a little Adam's family about her that Jack couldn't quite put his finger on. The woman seemed to be standing where Jack had thought he was stood only seconds before.

'I am dreaming, aren't I?' a different Jack voice asked, realising in that dreamlike way that rules weren't the same as in the waking world, that moments did not always run linear. The Adams family woman had a dog with her, and Silver drew in mentally at the sight. He never liked dogs, didn't really trust the scavenging bastards he thought. And the dog was a brute, that sort of bodyguard dog that gave meaning to putting off burglars, dream burglars or real ones would make no difference to a monster like that he thought to himself. Jack didn't know names of breeds but thought it was a bit like the police dogs he had seen back in London, sniffing out drug dealers at Heathrow airport, and the IRA's Semtex up in the ring of steel back in the early nineties.

So, he was Mister Invisible, there was a big bastard dog and a weird Adams family character for company, and Jack began to recognise this was not gonna be one of those dreams about cookies and cake.

The woman was irritated and seemed to be waiting on somebody, the Hound of the Baskervilles sat down watchfully beside her. On the wall, a large oak clock ticked loud and sombre, a sound that was disquietingly real as it echoed inside of Jack Silver's head.

The room appeared to have got larger as the dream progressed and Jack now found himself stood behind a tall leafy palm, watching the tapestry unfold in the illumination cast by a dull yellow electric light stood in one corner. He realised he was now hidden within shadows cast by the plant's wide splayed leaves, and that felt to him somehow marginally safer despite his new invisibility power.

The only door into the room stood diagonally opposite the Englishman and was closed. As Jack looked on fear coursed through him, a sudden tightening in his throat that restricted his breathing. He felt like an asthma victim on a bad day, and this in turn triggered a trembling so bad he thought he felt the warmth of his own piss soaking into his underwear. For a dream, Jack reflected it all felt damned real, and for that matter, he didn't like it at all.

His fear ramped up another notch when he saw that his ghostly presence had begun to attract the attention of the wolf companion, the dog was staring at the Englishman unblinking. Thank Christ dogs can't talk he thought to himself, and then all but fell through the protective foliage when the dog appeared to clearly mouth something quietly to his mistress.

With what looked like perfect articulation the animal said, 'He's in here, right now, madam.' And Cruella leaned down and without looking away from the door herself even for a moment, but with equal calm responded, 'I know, I believe he is supposed to be here, leave him be.'

She looked at the animal knowingly and then finished with "for now". At that exact moment, the door to the room began to open with what the watcher saw as unnatural slowness. Jack had time to consider how it was a Georgian period door. A once smart piece of carpentry, eight panels each of which appeared cracked with age or wear. He thought the door would creak, based on age and general condition, so he was surprised when it opened silently. Fear continued to throb in him, running up and down his frame like an electric current passing through him. The Englishman couldn't move even though he could feel one of his feet going numb as the blood pooled. His heart was hammering in his chest he was barely able to register any longer whether and what might be real or imagined.

To Jack Silver it all felt very real, and he found himself both petrified and intensely curious as to who would walk through the door in to the ancient post-war sitting room which had grown in grandeur and size as various occupants had arrived.

Jack was momentarily distracted and found himself paying heed to a bone-china figurine. It depicted a lion and a lion tamer, and the ornament sat atop a mantle above a low burning fire, a fire that he was sure had not been there only a moment before. Silver looked back where he had been previously waiting in the door and there standing, framed by that now open door was a small and somewhat dapper man. He was dressed in a dark suit, the man had a slightly receding hairline pulled back from stark, perhaps one might consider even mean features. Jack's immediate thought ran something like.

'Adolph Hitler, Poll Pot, Xiaoping, Idi Amin fuck who is this guy. Fuck I'm scared. I was frightened before; I'm really fucking scared now. Who is this bastard? Fuck I don't want to be here. Fuck. Shit. Fuck. Fuck.' And on and on, it went in his mind as panic dialled up. And in truth Jack really knew that the man in fact resembled none of those nightmare dictators of humanity's recent past, indeed the small middle-aged gentleman framed and backlit by soft and slightly sickly green light shining from somewhere down the passageway that ran into the distance behind him was the kind of unremarkable man that most people might just walk past in the street in the real world, more likely to be your accountant or your dentist. But in that place, at that moment, the man seemed to exude a power, evil appeared somehow to bleed from every pore of his being, and like a fly caught in the lair of a spider Jack Silver found himself completely unable to even look away, let alone think about leaving that room, that dream, that nightmare. He tried to think clearly but found his mind babbling almost incoherently in fact he decided the guy looked more like a picture he had once seen. An old black and white dust jacket image in fact that had depicted the evil Doctor Crippin, a most famous Victorian English murderer, a serial killer, back when serial killers weren't even popular.

'Hadn't he liked going to the circus?' one of those small irritating parts of Jack's mind asked himself, an enquiry he dismissed instantly as the man moved through the doorway and into the room proper.

Unlike the Hound of the Baskervilles and Cruella De Ville the dapper man did not appear to notice Silver at all, stood as he was busily trembling behind an oversized pot plant in the corner diagonally opposite the rooms entrance. The dapper man walked over to the woman, who was probably the best part of a foot taller than him, his steps were small and delicate.

'Mincing,' an unhelpful voice whispered inside Jack's head. In a small but perfectly clear voice, the new entrant to the room said, 'why aren't you two at the front of the house?' The dog looked awkwardly down between his paws in some kind of obvious deference to his mistress who seemed for a moment uncertain how or whether to answer. Instead of responding directly she looked half over her shoulder pointedly to where Jack was stood shivering, turned then back to the dapper man and said in a deep and luscious tone, 'He is here already, and I don't think he came in through the front of house. 'That's no matter, that's not your concern,' continued the small man. 'I want you at the front to keep those idiots from murdering each other, in fact from killing my whole operation, comprendes.' And it was obvious to Jack that the small man was in charge despite the fact that the woman, and even the dog, looked on the surface as if they would be far more imposing characters, and Jack reflected on how strange it was that throughout history so often it had been the small or the weedy ones that had grown into the world's greatest despots. Not a hard and fast rule he decided but nevertheless it was amazing how often cruelty and power over people was born out of some hybrid mixture of self-loathing and desperation to escape some perceived physical or emotional or mental flaw. His thoughts were interrupted as the small man continued.

'I know he is in the house.' And then looking directly at Jack. 'And now he knows I know. So now you listen to me very carefully both of you,' the small man said aimed at the dog and the mistress.

'See I want two things from you, just two, so that shouldn't be too hard, one thing, plus one other thing, yes.' And the man paused though the question obviously needed no answer as moments. Later, he continued, 'First, I want you in front of house keeping the punters where they need to be. And second I want you in front of house keeping the killers ready for my order…right?' And before The Cruella de Ville woman could answer, the small man continued, 'And there are also two things that I don't need from you,' at which juncture, the woman seemed to cower just a little, to shrink down so that most of the twelve inches, or so she had had on the dapper man disappeared in an instant. 'Firstly, I don't need you telling me where Jack Silver is. And secondly I don't need you telling me how Jack Silver did or did not get here.' A moment later the room resounded to the sharp crack of a sudden and vicious slap delivered to the woman's face and followed a bare instant later by a small whimper, 'I'm sorry sir,' the once tall woman retorted in a husky whisper. 'I just thought.'

'And I don't need you to do too much of that either.' The small man said with a finality that brooked no dissention. The woman turned and walked quickly from the room and the dog trailed along behind, both as it were with ears down and tails between legs. The man took centre stage and Jack found himself holding his breath like he had done once before. The tall woman had closed the door behind her, as silent in closing as it had been in opening. The small dapper man was turned away from Jack and yet he had made it quite clear a moment or two before that he knew he was there; indeed, he had looked right at him. 'Through me,' Jack thought to himself. He wanted to stand up straight, but he couldn't and wasn't sure whether it was fear or blood numbed legs that kept him down. Instead, he just looked at the back of the man, at his narrow shoulders, his hair neatly clipped and sat just above the collar line, and he felt then more than heard as the man faced away from Jack started to speak in his light and flighty tones.

'You know who I am.' And then without waiting on any answer, 'I am going to catch you Jack Silver…and when I do I am going to hurt you, and when I say hurt I don't mean hurt, like in the movies, or in books. I mean hurt you like you cannot even comprehend.' All of this was said without any anger or even any real emotion, yet somehow it was more dangerous, much more frightening to Jack for its simple sincerity. 'You think that you can hide from me, but you don't know yet what dance this is we two-step together.' And after another thoughtful pause, the small man, still turned away, added, 'You will.' And finally, then after another moment. 'Hide where you can Jack Silver, whilst you can, our time is appointed, you will pay for what has happened, and your price will be high, and its payment will be slow, and at the end you will despair completely. And perhaps then when you are utterly defeated and when everything appears lost to you, maybe then I shall show you death, and we can find out if you embrace it.'

Jack woke suddenly, cold and yet sweating, the day was electric bright and crawling round the edges of the blackout curtains, he had indeed soiled his underwear and even more surprising he had slept through the whole of the previous day and the night too, so advised the digital day and date readout on the bedside cabinet, god knew it did not feel that way to Jack.

Although the dream was quickly fading he knew still in those first waking moments that he had just seen Stevan Cipher, chief of the Shadow men, and apparently the architect of his doom. Jack stood up, removed his underwear and stepped into the bathroom to clean himself up. A few minutes later and as he returned to the room to dress himself the dream had faded to nothing more than a nagging sense of fear and danger, but for Jack Silver a sense of danger lurking around every corner was something he had got used to during the past six months. Cleaned up, kind of rested, and dressed in clean clothes, Jack knew intuitively that once more it was time to get out of Dodge, time to run. He realised that Las Vegas had been a poor choice, in fact instead of allowing him to disappear in a sea of aimless souls the city had in fact proven to be a nest of a thousand spies, a place where everyone could be the bad guy, and whilst hatchet the barman might just have been a nutter, and god knew Jack had seen his fair share of those these past few months, he didn't think so, no that guy had had a Stormtrooper sleeper worm in his brain. 'What the fuck are you saying?' his mind whispered urgently and added, 'He was a bona fide due paid-up member of the Stevan Cipher lets murder Jack Silver club.' Of that, he had no doubt, and that meant that Jack wasn't safe in this place. Silver had learned to follow his instincts; they had kept him alive more than once now and so that just left how to get out and where to go next…'

An hour later, Jack was on the road heading north out of the city of Las Vegas, map in his lap, a paper bag full of supplies on the rental car's front passenger seat, and Elton John crooning Rocket Man from the radio of his midsize Chrysler.

In one dark corner far from the roiling heart of the omniverse, a backwater quiet for so long that sound no longer existed except as a concept. And despite the hard vacuum that surrounded everything of a sudden came a noise. A single click so quiet as to have not been audible even had ears been listening, and yet that click far off in time and space would change many things. A click that signalled awakening…

Chapter Nine
On the Run

Jack had been driving for six hours when the hitchhiker stepped out in front of him and nearly got them both killed. He had been in that state all motorists find themselves in from time to time, lulled by long straight stretches of black top, girded by rugged but somehow uninteresting terrain on all sides, and interrupted only by an occasional trailer trash encampment. Jack thought he was in control, figured instinctively that he was appraising every little thing that went on around him, whilst at the same time his speed had climbed slowly so that he was touching seventy on a fifty-five, all the while drumming his hands on the hard plastic steering wheel to classic Steely Dan and then equally bullish Lynard Skynnard, mentally wandering through the pleasant nondescript garden that was his life prior to the dramatic incidents that had precipitated all that had happened to him since that previous November night.

Suddenly, Jack caught a flash of vivid red and green, in that instant it seemed it might have been a hat. *A cat in a hat…groovy*, he thought as, in what felt like super-fast motion, he slammed on the car's brakes jammed the steering wheel around to a full right-hand lock and slid off the tarmac onto the gravel roadside. Silver actually felt quite calm as he cracked the door seal and let in the scorching desert heat from outside, some part of his mind was stacking up how he might deal with things if he had suspiciously begun to think he might have just run somebody down. In fact, in spite of the sudden unfiltered sunlight and sweat instantly exiting every pore of his body, the first thing that Jack took in was that he could not see a sign of human habitation in either direction, he couldn't think of the last time that he had seen a trailer park or roadside refill and diner now that he came to consider that fact, then as he came around the Chrysler, the free bird track rising to its crescendo from somewhere safe and cool inside the cabin, the engine ticking like a clock slowing down as it too exited heat now stalled at the road's edge Jack heard, 'Hey, dude, good of ya to stop,' and there walking up the opposite side of the dirt to where his Chrysler had come to a halt perhaps as much as sixty feet away was a guy, no older than twenty-one or twenty-two, sneakers and blue jeans, a tatty rust coloured shirt which appeared buttoned incorrectly and a strange red and green leatherette sports holdall with a picture of a big cat on the side slung over his shoulder, all of which had seen better days. The guy was smiling and as Jack walked towards him he could tell that his words had held neither malice nor sarcasm. The guy had a shock of hair that might have been mouse blonde, but even at that distance Jack could tell it was full of desert grit and dust which only sought to accentuate the young man's bright blue eyes, Jack returned the good cheer with a smile and said, 'Hey, there, I'm glad you're ok… I thought I might have clipped you back there.' And as he spoke he thought of how much the fellow reminded him of Shaggy, the one in the original Scooby-Doo cartoons. Not so much in the face, his mind urged but more in the lollops way that he was walking towards him, and what Jack would call Texas drawl, although in truth he knew little enough about accents, it could just have easily been Greenwich Village Manhattan. His mind's voice was persistent continuing, 'And not that movie Shaggy, or even the later one on TV when Scooby appeared as smart-mouthed as many of today's teenagers, bloody talking dogs.' No, this young man was a bona fide first series Shaggy Jack decided. 'So how come you are out here? I haven't seen another person in ages?' Jack asked cheerfully as they drew together. 'You English?' the guy asked the distance closed now to just eight or ten feet. They both began to answer at the same moment, looked at one another, laughed, and in that instant, they became travelling companions, and maybe even friends, because in the real world, these judgements come from instinct, that higher-level intuition that can befriend you, or as every horror movie ever made will attest can just as easily let you down catastrophically just when you don't need it. Jack understood this and more than most folk had been tending very much towards caution in his human interactions during recent times, but truth to tell he was lonely, he was in a foreign land, and if he was any judge of people at all then he could see not an ounce of ill will in this young man, and so he put out his hand and said, 'Yep, English I am, Jack Silver, good to meet you.' 'Wow, man, like in Long John Silver,' the guy replied.

'That's a real unusual name; I bet you must be related. I'm Keith Kirkcaldy, but you can call me Caffee cos in the end everyone does, so how you doin?' he said this all whilst pumping Jack's outstretched hand vigorously.

'How long have you got?' Silver retorted with a wry grin. 'Hey, man, you give me a ride I can listen all day long.' 'Do you drive?' Jack asked a plan beginning to take form in his mind. 'Ain't got no car man, but hell yeah I got a licence,' Caffee replied. 'Then I guess I've got myself a driving buddy… How far you looking to go?' 'As far as you wanna ride with me,' Caffee said as they both walked toward the car. Twenty minutes later, they were on the road and busily putting the world right.

'So, yer heading for Canada, and you've bin in the good old US of A for just a couple of days, an I have to say you don't strike me as the travelling touristy type.' 'I guess that there is a question in there somewhere,' said Jack, enjoying jousting with this latter-day eco hippy, and pleased to actually be talking and at peace with another human being, it dawned on him that it had been a while.

'Yeah, well I guess my question is who are ya running from, and you know I'm only asking cos I can be doin with avoiding anyone thas gonna get me into trouble.' Jack laughed again, Caffee had been only a little more forthcoming than he himself and had hinted without saying that he was running away from his own little pile of problems. Though Jack guessed that unlike he who was running for his life, Caffee was much more likely to be running in order to ensure his freedom. When Jack had suggested that he was heading for the Canadian border, a crossing that was the best part of a thousand miles north, and that he would like to consider turn and turn about driving to keep them moving he had been pleased and surprised when Caffee answered affirmatively.

'Hey, listen, Jack, I don't mean nothing by askin, I'm young an its just my way,' continued Caffee and then tried a different tack. 'So, what did you do back in London?' And before he had given Jack even a moment to reply, with his infectious youthful enthusiasm he continued. 'How is it that your damned country's got so many names, do you figure you come from England, or is it Great Britain, or the UK or what man?' Jack thought about the question for a moment and then said with all seriousness, 'Caffee, I am first a citizen of the world…and I trust that my place of birth does me no disservice throughout this world wherever I touch down because it's the only one I know, as to what I do, or more to the point did, most recently I put my waning talents as a writer to work and have been somewhat prosaically selling myself as a personal biographer. 'In other words, I have been showing old ladies how boring and full of farting their lives have been, and then writing that down for them. As to England and the rest I have to say we Brits are a bit less inspired by our empire than you Yanks, so I don't care for names one way or the other, and come to think of it, are you from the US, the USA, America, the United States...need I say more?' Thereafter, they fell to talking about Las Vegas where surprisingly Caffee had never been. He had "swerved that nest of vipers" as the young put it instead finding himself on Highway 97 heading north, all after some months of dodging the law, and an interested ex-employer around San Diego and subsequently Los Angeles. Eventually, heading inland on the back of a truck bringing parts in to a firm that serviced the Hoover Dam. Jack had been surprised to learn that Caffee's first love was poetry; although this had been tempered in Jack's mind by the young man's love of a rap artist called Eminem, who he called the lyrical genius of the twenty-first century. By about the same margin, Caffee had been surprised when Jack had said that he had not put even one quarter in a fruit machine, seen not one show and barring two reception staff, two waiters, 'Only one of who had tried to cave his skull in with a fire axe,' he reminded himself, oh and a car rental representative, well Jack Silver had moved through Las Vegas and not spoken with another soul. Caffee had quoted Samuel Taylor Coleridge, and whilst Jack had never quite got Kubla Khan, he listened, smiled and nodded. 'In Xanadu did Kubla Khan a stately pleasure dome decree, where Alph, the sacred river ran, through caverns measureless to man, down to a sunless sea.' That verse rang true and somehow symbolised his brief but polarised view of the world-famous gambling capital, so much so that long after Caffee's demise, that moment, that verse, came back to haunt Jack Silver time and again.

So as the miles rolled by this middle years Englishman, and his new companion a youth of modern America talked of many things, from who were the world's great despots of yesteryear, and then of today, to who were the world's great singers, of yesteryear, and both agreed less so today. And from the best places to eat, to when the world would likely end, and as day turned to night bond and circumstance, alongside humour and simple attraction made these two firm friends.

'It's getting dark,' Jack said. 'Perhaps the next time we see a diner we could stop and fill up.' 'You mean gas,' Caffee replied.

'I mean us and the gas tank. It's going to be a long night on two packs of Lays potato chips and a coke,' Jack said looking sideways at his companion. Caffee looked doubtful for a minute and seemed to be striving with some internal debate, then after a moment. 'Jack, truth is, I ain't got but five bucks to call my own, thas why I'm hitchin, an I don't wanna waste that on some skanky meal,

Lays look great to me.' Jack laughed and then halted immediately apologetically as he saw the look that crossed Caffee's face.

'No, no, I'm not laughing at you,' he said. 'I just spend my life, well, spent my old life to be more accurate, surrounded by people that would jump at a free anything, and yet consider themselves the spirit of modern nobility. No, it would be my pleasure to buy you dinner Keith Kirkcaldy. Young man you are my friend and moreover my travelling companion, and nobler by far than most of those fools back in Blighty. Furthermore, if you're doing the driving tonight I need you fresh and fed, so I won't take no for an answer, and I am not sitting awake all night listening to your guts rumbling.'

Caffee looked sidelong at Jack for a long moment, then nodded, reached across and shook his hand.

'Hey, ya know what, maybe the old friends across the water ain't so far from the truth, thanks Jack you're all right, that's real good of ya.' Twenty minutes later, they had pulled off of the main drag following a signpost onto a dirt track side road that said.

Motel, Gas, Best Food in the state, One mile East. And sure enough, dead ahead they pulled into a trim little dirt car park surrounded on three sides by diner, motel, and gas station, and furthermore by a run of pretty cacti in white pebbled borders. Walking into the diner the sky had darkened to full night and was lit by distant flashes of lightning and the first rumbles of thunder.

'Gonna be a storm,' Caffee said distractedly looking for a sign for the restroom. Jack asked a portly lady for a table and wasn't surprised when she gestured around at the empty interior and said, 'Hey, honey, hep yerself.' Jack sat down in a booth looking out through the window and back down the dirt track they had travelled, the red vinyl creaking as he slid across the bench. He ordered coffee for them both feeling sure that if Caffee didn't drink coffee then he would drink for two, and a moment later he watched Caffee amble back in and sit down opposite him. Shortly after, the two ordered a mixture of tacos, burgers, onion rings, and a peppered salad with two ice-cold light beers, and Jack was further pleased and surprised to find minutes later that the food was pretty good, and that he was ravenous.

During the time that they ate the storm closed in on them and was, Jack guessed quietly counting elephants after a flash of forked lightning, not by then much more than ten miles distant. 'Honey, I can't see as how you two is going nowhere,' the portly waitress whose badge announced her as Dolores said, looking pointedly at Jack and at the dishes with the meal as yet unpaid, the bill sat atop the Formica table. 'See that storms in for a few hours, and we is deffernetly closing up in a half hour. Seems as how you twos need to get under cover,' she finished. Jack got the drift, pulled a roll of twenties from his jeans pocket placed two of them on top of the bill and said, 'Madam, why don't we get this bill out of the way first?' And he was rewarded instantly as the server relaxed visibly and smiled as she thought about the possibility of a fifteen-dollar tip. 'We saw the motel sign out front,' continued Jack. 'My friend here, and I wondered who we might be able to speak to about obtaining a room, you know, at least till the storm passes.' The waitress Dolores with dollar signs dancing responded immediately and enthusiastically. 'Well, I can do that for ya honey.' And then after barely a second. 'Twenty-eight bucks, another five for fresh towels, plus tax,' she said this all without hesitation all the while eyeing Jack's roll of remaining twenties hungrily.

'Well, you go right ahead and organise a room...plus some towels, and my companion, and I would like another beer to be going along with during the interim,' Jack replied grinning widely. And so as the waitress come Dolores of all trades walked away, a bounce in her step, Caffee looked at Jack and said, 'A room?' frowning questioningly. Jack looked back shook his head and said, 'Listen Caffee I have no wish to stop any longer than I have to.' And in his mind's eye right at that moment, a picture of three heavyset men bunched up together in a black sedan hurtling down a freeway appeared unbidden. 'But that storm is coming right this way, and I see no way that either of us is gonna drive through that, so what say we make use of the facilities, god knows I could do with a shower,' he spoke looking pointedly at Caffee's own bedraggled appearance.

'And we'll make some miles when the storm has passed. It's your call Caffee.'

'Hey, yeah I guess I see you right Long John,' Caffee said laughing and downing the rest of his beer.

In the end, the storm closed right over them and then settled in, thunder and lightning appearing to rip the drab and dimly lit room apart every minute or so, something which both Caffee and Jack agreed seemed more than vaguely disturbing. But Jack persuaded his new friend that alcohol was a reasonable cure for all ills, and so it was that after each had showered, something which seemed mildly pointless to Jack in Caffee's case as he climbed straight back into to the road dust dirtied clothes he had been wearing before, nonetheless they settled down to decimating the contents of the drinks fridge.

As the storm eventually passed, some three hours or so later, Jack realised they were both far too drunk to drive even somewhat competently, and at night on unlit blacktop, and that was irrespective of what the law might do the two men if they caught them, and so they agreed to stay till early morning. And so, as the evening ran into the night, and the drinks fridge in the room was replaced by beers from the dollar and dime cooler both men's tongues were loosened by alcohol, and so they both began to open up.

First of all, Jack Silver looked on as Caffee started by opening his curious green and red sport holdall and with great care pulled out two faded photos of two small boys each one flanking a pretty twenty-something woman with a big eighties hairdo. Jack listened as Caffee related the story of how his mother and his kid brother Anton had been walking back to their apartment in Austin Texas after school one hot October day. That day Caffee had stayed on at school late in order to help with the Founding Fathers presentation for the upcoming Thanksgiving Day.

Caffee was told that a police cruiser that had been responding to a 911 officer down call had failed to stop at a crossing and had run down and killed them both, his brother dying instantly, his mother a day or so later in the nearby Mercy Hospital. It seemed that nobody had taken Caffee to see his mother there at the end, and no one thought to explain to him what had happened, then or after, and so at seven years and three months old people that didn't care had taken him into care, and the boy had become another statistic, his future irrevocably changed by a tragedy almost nobody noticed he was even a part of. Two cops had died that day, many things it seemed had not gone according to plan, and so with no one to stand Keith Kirkcaldy's corner the whole thing had been swept under society's big dirty old rug, and that child had begun ten years of being shunted from place to place, person to person, of growing up disassociated completely with the world in which fate had decided he must live. The cops who had killed his family, well perhaps they might have bad days Caffee didn't know, but he was sure that they never faced justice, as he grew older he went back and checked the public records, and surprise surprise no case was ever brought. And for him worse even than that awful dismissal, neither they, nor even anyone from social services had ever come to see him, had ever from that day to this ever made the smallest effort to visit a child, an orphan, and to explain what had happened, how, why. On the back of one of the photos had been a small verse in what Jack recognised as a child's spidery hand.

'What's that?' Jack asked, and Caffee handed the photo over wordlessly, tears glimmering in both eyes.

Wait and see Mama said
Wait for me I heard instead
Do as you're told papa said
Back off I'm old I heard instead
The man said learn then go get a job
When I asked why he spat cos you is a yob
Freedom of speech freedom to choose
Now as ever the old folks ruse
So come to the circus roll up if you dare
But the acts are the same as ever they were.

'You write that?' Jack asked looking up from the words straight into Caffee's bright blue eyes. His tears had cleared, and he looked directly back at Jack. 'Yeah,' he replied simply, 'I was only seven an I still miss 'em, worlds bin a pretty wired place since, I guess.' Caffee added unscrewing the top from a Jim Beam miniature he had found rolled under the bed. 'So, you spent time in institutions, or were you adopted?' Jack asked. 'Both, but I got labelled as difficult, an I guess I was difficult for a bit, but heh you know, don't no one ever talk to kids an ask em why they're getting into trouble time n again, especially when stayin out of trouble seems so much easier. So I guess I sank low, and I only climbed out long enough to write for a tiny bit. Life ain't always great you know Jack, but I'm twenty-four years old later this fall an I'm still alive, I don't do drugs barrin a bit of puff back a while ago, and I try not to hurt no one, though I must admit more than a few seem to wanna hurt the likes of me.' Caffee finished then leaving further explanation unsaid, he chugged the remains of the Jim Beam turned to Jack and added as an afterthought. 'OK, Long John Silver, you ain't no pirate I can see that so, nuff of my story what's your tale?' Jack stared at Caffee, wheels turning inside of his head, fighting the latest in a long line of whiskey fogs for long moments he wondered about saying anything, but he knew that his new travel companion had taken a leap of faith in telling his story to the Englishman, and Jack had got the impression that he had told him this unvarnished. He was also pretty sure that he had not told it to many other folks during these past thirteen or so years, and so after a moment longer he looked down at his sneakers, crossed on the floor, and said.

'Do you know how many people go through their day without ever looking up at the sky?'

Small of no apparent value, passed from keeper to keeper. Kept close and protected from the vagaries of chance, despite chance being companioned down times winding road. It had a name now and the name had a meaning close in fact to the thing's true worth. It existed only as a possibility, just in case. An instant in which one thing might change and so chance becomes purpose. If so, this small thing would discover a new direction...

Chapter Ten
A Sorrow About to Fall

Steven A. Cipher stood at one end of an ancient oak long table that would not have looked out of place in an Arthurian castle, it ran twenty-five feet and dominated the room. Cipher was a small man, slight of build and a little indistinct in a black expensively cut suit with equally black hair, oiled and heavily parted atop a pale-skinned unsmiling face. He looked down from the head of the table at the three men who stood in front of him, and a stranger walking in at that precise moment might have wondered at the trepidation that surrounded each of the three. Cipher spoke in high fluting tones, clipped and precise, quick and even words.

'Let me understand what it is you tell me...exactly,' he began, his accent almost perfect Eton but just unable to mask completely a hint of brogue Edinburgh.

'I tell you where to find him. I give you all the resources that you might need, I advance you a rather significant proportion of a handsome reward, I set you free to undertake this frankly rather straightforward task. And today instead of coming here and bringing me this, this Jack Silver,' and at this point his voice rose another octave.

'Instead, you simply advise me that he has slipped through your fingers. Like I'm fucking custard, or at least he is.' Cipher looked in turn at each of the three men, and he slowly walked round to their side of the table lowered his voice to little more than a whisper and said.

'So you come back to me, and you ask what it is you should do?' The smallest of the three men towered over Cipher was stood at least six feet and two inches in bare feet, and yet each of the three looked at one another and none of them spoke, Cipher said it again.

'So what is it you would have me do?' Long moments passed, and the atmosphere hung filled with fear and menace, until eventually, one of them spoke, gruff and diffident, almost mumbling. 'Mr Cipher sir, we came to tell you he ad gone. It wasn't meant to go down like that, but it was like, well it was like he was suddenly covered in invisible dust. We were watching him at the airport, two on and one off as you instructed, he seemed to have just given up. He sat there for hours, didn't even get up for a piss, just kept on ordering one coffee after another, musta had at least ten, he knew we wouldn't take him in there with them cops all around.' Cipher was staring intently at the speaker, not even a blink of his eyes to betray what went on behind them.

'We would've snatched him right and then but like I said there was rozzers everywhere; so we figured we would wait. It wasn't like he could just vanish, Mr Cipher sir.' The gruff mumbling man gulped, visibly sweating, and it seemed to take him some seconds to reconstitute before he then continued.

It happened at twilight… I think it was Marshall and Victor that were changing over. I was looking at 'I'm, and it was that time of the day, you know, people were everywhere, and then, just like that he wasn't there anymore. And I have to be truthful Mr Cipher, I haven't seen anything like it, not ever, he vanished. We checked all over like I said he was boxed in, the bloke was in a corner, a real bind, he had nowhere to run, I still don't get it…' He trailed off his voice little more than a whisper and those onlookers all could sense growing panic creeping in at the end. Cipher did not speak for a long moment. Inside, he was thinking about how he had seen this play out inside of his head. Somehow at some deep instinctive level, he had watched the whole drama his henchman had just described play out inside his mind, and yet until he had heard it in those gruff mumbled tones he did not appear to know that he had known, and that bothered Cipher considerably. He was a man of extraordinarily tight control, physically, mentally and most of all emotionally, it was not in his nature to let anything slip. Six months ago, Cipher would have questioned these insights that were so uncharacteristic in his world, so alien to his view of reality, he had always been a pragmatist and so somehow this was new, this was outside the periphery, and at some level he recognised that masked by the fog of his growing fury many things were slipping, changing, drawing to a head. Even more surprising to Stevan Cipher was the fact that not only had he seen the drama at the airport three days previously, played out as if he had been a character on the set, but he also knew where Jack Silver had gone. At some deep intuitive level, he even thought he recognised why, what was driving the fearful renegade. Deep inside of himself a part of him he did not fully understand yet showed Cipher images of Silver sitting in an eatery, a man dirty and bedraggled, to Cipher he seemed to be sneering, and he could feel a rage rising in himself, felt that the man's sneer was aimed at him, at Stevan Cipher. And as the images passed across his mind's eye Cipher watched as Jack Silver suddenly without preamble jumped up and ran, it was almost as if the man in his mental stage was showing, almost as if that man could feel Cipher's anger and so had bolted in the face of it. All of this roiled like a storm in his mind, yet despite the turmoil outwardly, Cipher remained utterly impassive. Putting both hands down on the table, he instructed the three men to sit, and remaining standing himself he smiled witheringly as he said, 'You appear to want me to tell you what it is that you should do, and so I shall. Silver has flown out of the airport right under your noses, and he flew to Las Vegas in Nevada.' And yes you sad little crew of miscreants he walked past you all, and no he is not a magician, but that bastard is the man that killed my brother. So now you three will fly out there, and this time you will find him and bring him back to me. Cipher paused and looked at the three nodding donkey heads. 'I am going to give you each a choice, and it is an opportunity that is quite simple, return to me with Jack Silver or I will have your hearts, one and all.' And after a moment. 'Do we understand one another?' The three shadow men looked uneasily at one another when Stephen Cipher made a threat then you did well to heed it as a promise, their previous failure had resulted in no more choices for them at all it was to find Silver or die, that was what Stevan Cipher wanted and so that was what Stevan Cipher was going to get. They each nodded and one and all deep down wondered how it was that Cipher had known where the prey had flown to, they each thought about how much their boss had changed since the murder of his brother. He had not been there at the airport, indeed he had been more than five hundred miles away at the time as far as any of them knew, and so did the man have watchers watching the watchers. The thought chilled each of those three hardened killers to the marrow and each of the men left the room minds filled with concerns, swirling around like Indians hollering war cries as they rode around the circled wagons of each man's sanity.

As preparations were made to depart Cipher sat alone in a darkened room elsewhere in the huge baronial castle in Scotland where the meeting had taken place. He closed his eyes, and in the darkness, his mind lit up and in that mental illumination he was able to see each of his henchmen, their focus and their fears, and more interesting to him still he was once more able to see Jack Silver sat alone in a tawdry motel room many thousands of miles away. Cipher no longer questioned why he could see these images in his mind, it had proven to be both a curse and a gift in recent times he considered, on the one hand allowing him to see his prey, and yet by the same token allowing him to watch that prey slip through his fingers now on more than one occasion. Stevan Cipher had himself changed much in these past months, he was not consciously aware of those changes and that in part was pragmatism, and in part, the Machiavellian nature of the man, but in fact in some ways he had grown, or perhaps mutated, and was now more in many ways than he had been months before, more connected, more intuitive than when he had first "felt" the sight and dimly become aware in the moments as his brother died many miles away from him in London. As he sat in his darkroom, he pondered the changes that he felt more than saw in Jack Silver, and it might be that these were in some ways a mirror reflection to those he was unable to register in himself. Cipher was concerned that Silver was changing, he perceived that he had become wilier than before, more able to survive than the character he had first encountered running recklessly through his mind and escaping his men by the skin of his teeth some five months previously, that was a man who had escaped the grasp of his men barely. And so, Cipher was beginning to feel like there were bigger things taking place than he was entirely able to comprehend, but this failed really to compute for a man who did not imagine that there was not anything that fell within his awareness compass. Consumed as he was by white rage and by a wish for vengeance against the man who had killed his brother Cipher was therefore for the most part blind to all of these changes and focused instead on that revenge. His mind wandered, and he thought again about the moment he had known that his brother was dead, images unbidden in his mind, his brother's bodyguards apparently blindsided in some filthy back alley in London, the face of his murderer twisted in rage, a long blade jammed into Cedric's neck time and again, blood spurting in gouts onto the cold stinking stones and the puddles of rainwater atop them in the alleyway as the life ebbed out of him. Dear Cedric, Stevan had always loved him, he was the only one that had ever really got even somewhat close to him, the only one who had been able to calm the rages of his brother's youth, and the only one who had been able time and time again to keep all of the crap away from him.

At times looking back Stevan knew that he had been cruel even to his brother, and in his mind then those cruelties came back to haunt him, to tighten the noose of pain that he felt even more tightly around his throat. Stevan remembered how in the days after his brother's death, driven by grief and the loss of control over the universe a soul like his could not comprehend that he had lashed out at those images. In a frenzy, he had taken hold of the fifteen-year-old girl they had foolishly sent to his bed; he did not remember doing any of it, and he believed it was their fault, not his, why did they send her? And after they had taken the body of that young girl away, and they told him some time later that they had been forced to burn it, that was all they could do she had been so badly beaten and disfigured that a fifteen-year-old child became another missing person because they did not understand how he hurt.

Cipher wondered then, later in the Scottish castle how this could have happened without his awareness, he thrived on control, but the emotions that boiled in him in those moments had had to be released, and well, he shrugged, what was one more wasted teenager, weren't all teenagers a waste of something in the end, to him the world looked like it was a little too full of them.

Time and again his mind returned to the image of the killer, to Jack Silver to when he had travelled to London to retrieve his brother's body had gone to that place, seen the alley, looked deep into the electric reflections in the rainwater puddles. His people had questioned the staff at the eatery where Silver had lain in wait, and after little coercion, a credit card imprint had served to provide them with all of the information he needed.

Suddenly Cipher snapped back to the present moment as the phone rang. He picked it up still sitting in absolute darkness.

'Yes.'

'Ready to go now, boss.'

One of his men had said, it sounded like Dickey, although in recent days Cipher reflected they had all become the same thing, the same person, just so many chess pieces, yes just like chess pieces he thought to himself, and then considered that he needed to check mate Jack Silver, and so far that man, that worm, had avoided his pincer moves by the skin of his teeth… Well no longer, times up buddy a voice whispered malevolently deep in his mind.

'Good, you leave now,' Cipher continued a newly discovered vigour now in his tone.

'And remember, when you get there no standing around in Vegas watching the local talent, holding your dicks, playing the fucking slots, you get on highway ninety-seven and catch that murdering…' he trailed off.

'Boss?' The voice at the end of the phone asked hesitantly.

'Just go get him and bring him back to me...it is your last chance,' Cipher finished replacing the hand set and returning the phone to its cradle.

Following the click, measured in terms we might understand as micro fractions of a millisecond, energies were drawn in from everything within several light seconds around it. And this thing used those energies to amend its form. Constructing itself in a new image and building itself a fortress, as it knew it must.

Chapter Eleven
Across the Border

Jack knew that he was drunk, not utterly but enough. Caffee's story had reminded him for the first time in a long while that there was a world out there, a whole existence that operated beyond his own situation, desperate though that had proven to be in recent times. Caffee was a decent enough young fellow, funny and talented, bright, and a curious mix of shy and bold that seemed to sum up so many of this new century's teenagers Jack mused. It seemed the poor sod had been striving to climb out of the hole he found himself in, and to find a better life, for years now, converse to Jack Silver who appeared to have jumped straight into a vast black maw, and in his case from a life that prior had at best been, well nondescript he figured.

Nevertheless, Jack saw a commonality between them, it seemed to him that they were both dealing with their respective life issues by running away. And so it was that before Jack really understood what he was doing he found himself telling his own story, a potted version granted, but this was something new, and so he heard his own voice recalling the events of the past months for the very first time; finally, he was talking to another human being, sharing what had happened to him during five and some months of hell, and in speaking he discovered bringing some kind of order to his understanding of those events, something that till that time he had not found in the turmoil of run and chase.

'So, I don't really understand any of it,' Jack said slurring a little, gazing past Caffee as the last echoes of thunder and vague lightning splashed and danced their patterns lurid beyond the drawn curtains.

'I witnessed some guys; hoods I guess you'd call them,' he continued. 'Murder a man.'

'Wow, I mean double wow,' Caffee said.

'Double wow?' Jack said looking at Caffee quizzically and actually smiling.

'Well, yeah wow, you saw a guy getting tapped, and double wow you actually think all Americans call bad guys…hoods. So double wow.' They both laughed.

'Well, anyway, I saw three men take a fourth, another man, who I think might have been their boss. Take him and stab him in the neck in an alley behind a bar, a bar that I'd just left. I saw it all, and I saw them leave him for dead.'

'Hey dude that's full-on shit but how come your running? It's not your crap, not like you killed anybody.'

'Well, that's just the thing,' Jack continued his senses clearing a little as the details came back to him. 'This man, the one that got stabbed, well as far as I can figure it he has a brother, turns out that brother is some kind of big shot gangland crime lord. And you know, I don't know all of it, but so after it happened. I was right there you know.' Jack was not aware he was repeating himself and his ire was rising as the memories returned with interest. 'I'd stepped outside for some air, and it happened. I was in the shadows ten, no less than that. I was like eight feet away. Anyways they did him, all of a sudden, no warning, after it happened they just dragged him, I don't even know if he was dead at that point, but the three of them dragged the bloke half of the way back up the alley, puddles and rain and all. 'And then as I looked on, I was bloody trembling all over I can tell you, they just kind of pushed and then rolled his body behind some dustbins. And then after that, well then they just left, at least I thought they had…' Jack trailed off, took another tug and then another on the miniature he ha had been holding onto like a tiny life raft as his tale unravelled. So, what had happened Silver thought?

I witnessed a murder; (First mistake) I went to check on a dead man (Second mistake) I picked up a murder weapon (Third mistake), and then best of all, covered in a dead man's blood, my fingerprints all over the blade that killed him, I went and walked out of an alley and straight into the arms of the men that did foul murder (Biggest mistake). After a minute or so of ruminating silence, Jack began to explain this as best as he could to his young companion, he struggled to articulate the stupidity and so after a further moment just said, 'Let's just say that in the minutes that followed the deed I made a mistake, or several, and now, well, it's like the whole damned world is after me.'

'Worst thing, Caffee,' Jack said.

'What's that?'

'I did commit a crime that night… I never should have just watched Caffee. I should have tried at least to stop them, but Christ I was so scared. I had never been so scared in my fucking life, they would have killed me you know, I knew it right then, and ironically, I've been running from them ever since.' Jack Silver paused and sucked in a long anxious breath, and then finished with, 'And you know what they're going to do when they catch up with me…and they will.' He offered cryptically.

'Yeah, I think I can guess. Listen man I sympathise I really do, an I don't wanna sound like one of them movie geeks, you know asking all the real obvious questions just to make sure the viewer gets…What do ya call it…Perspective,' Caffee replied trying to impose something positive into the conversation, 'but what about the cops man, people must know you ain't the murderin sort.'

'The police, well looking back I think that was where I figured I was going when I walked out the end of the alley,' Jack replied.

'I went to cross the main road at the top of Berwick Street; actually, you know I never thought of it at the time, but I was only a few minutes' walk away from New Scotland Yard. But I can remember I was cold, and as I said I was really shaken up. Whatever I had drunk that night, well in fact whatever I had drunk in my whole bloody life up to that point I was suddenly one very sober drunk. 'So, I knew where the all-night police station was, and I knew there was pretty much no chance of finding a copper on the beat, no one seemed to be about, which now I think it is a little strange so close to the centre of London, but still, there wasn't anyone around, and certainly no coppers. I put up my collar and started to hoof it towards Piccadilly, and mmm.' He paused nodded to himself and then continued. 'After a minute or two, I kinda realised that someone was following me, actually as it turned out three somebodies were following me.'

'No fuckin way,' Caffee exploded. 'They musta knew you were there.'
'Yeah, I have been thinking on that one in the months since.' Jack continued, 'But actually, I have come to the conclusion that they were just sitting there figuring out the options when I came waltzing out of that alley with victim lit up on my head in bright bloody neon.'

I think now, looking back, that they just followed me to see where I might be heading, you see I got as far as the top of the rise where the city police station sits, and of course (mistake number five), the Englishman thought, *I suppose that told them that I had seen, or found, or knew, well something. And then based on the time frame, the blood-stained clothes and so on probably both. In the end, I* reckon they just looked at me and saw their alibi written all over me in bold script. By then, I was shitting bricks, so when I got near the station, and by now they weren't hiding the fact they were on my tail. It was like… 'Did you ever see a film called *The Warriors*?' Jack suddenly asked. 'I might a,' Caffee replied.

'Classic teen gang movie, Sol Yurick book,' said Jack. 'The good guys spent the whole damned film being stalked by various tripped-out gangs of dressed-up psychopaths, tempting those "Warriors" at every turn into making a move, into standing and fighting, and anyway, that was how it felt, they were waiting for me to make my move.' I mean they could have killed me right there I guess, but then how would a dead man a mile away from another one prove to be the killer? At least that's how I figured it. 'Anyway, I got to about two hundred yards from that bloody police station. I think I could smell it, and all of a sudden, they pulled up right across the road from me, screaming brakes and smoke everywhere, two doors open and these two guys. I mean fucking hell I recognised them straight off; both of them got out of the car, a big bloody BMW I think, and in that instant, two things went through my brain simultaneously.' Silver was on a roll, almost babbling, but Caffee listened carefully and let him continue uninterrupted.

'First, I did not think I could outrun them, you know, to the cop shop, the police station, and as I said it was amazingly quiet, bloody spooky now I think about it around the west end that night, and second I already got to thinking by then, what if the police don't believe me?' Silver paused and chugged on his drink, coughed as it went down the wrong way and then offered.

'I mean I was covered in blood; I was full of booze; I had been alone. And so, for about half a second I think I persuaded myself that if I walked away then the murderers would disappear, and it would all just go away, like the proverbial bad dream I s'pose.' He paused then and shook his head back and forth with a look of regret-filled remembering.

'The police would undoubtedly find the man's body, at least that's what drunk me told scared me, and I would save myself a whole heap of trouble, oh and quite possibly my life, or at least getting bummed in the Wormwood Scrubs.' He paused and then added, 'Sorry, that's prison mate.' This all came out of Silver in a rush. It appeared like releasing the poison, and Jack Silver found that he felt himself glad to be saying it, albeit that even tipsy it all sounded contrived, faintly ludicrous actually in the cold light of day, as he heard himself speaking. Nonetheless, after a further suck on the booze pill, he added, 'So I ran. That's what I decided, or maybe I didn't decide or maybe I just crapped myself, and then I just ran, up and down side streets, in and out of one-way roads, sucking in air, sobering up real quick, without stopping for what seemed like a month, but I guess was maybe for about a half an hour. And then eventually, when the panic subsided, and I convinced myself that no one was following, oh, and I couldn't breathe anymore I found myself near Oxford Circus, and so I caught the tube.'

'What's that, man?'

'Sorry, matey, that's… London underground, trains.'

'Oh, OK, right gotcha.'

'So yeah, I caught a train back out to South Kensington and got back to my place. I never turned the lights on. I was still cacking myself, but you know drink, adrenaline, after a little while I, well I guess I just crashed out. And see they didn't follow me, at least not right away.' He paused, or perhaps he was done, Caffe could not tell, but it seemed there was more, and so he prompted. 'Right, so it didn't end there?' he asked. Silver looked at him and found a reserve of enthusiasm for the tale though Caffee saw the tightness around the other man's eyes, and he understood he was struggling with the retelling. 'Well, for a few days, yeah, I guess all was quiet. I suppose I tried to blank it all out, stay in the moment kinda thing, keep to the routines and let time pass between the first then and the second then, but then came the third then, and well that's when the real crap started, the weird stuff,' Jack almost screeched that last sentence and pulling the tab on a Pepsi said smiling.

'Gotta drive tomorrow,' Caffee grinned sheepishly and at the same time frowned at the soft drink.

'Yeah, I guess you might say I started running that night outside of the police station, but the following week, well the following week all hell broke loose, and that's the third then, and that's when I really knew I was running, that's when I knew I had chosen poorly.' Jack petered out a few seconds later, and although Caffee had proven an attentive listener, a realisation came over the Englishman that he had said over much, more than he had planned, and to a guy he really did not know so well. In the back of his mind, a voice whispered that a day or two previously a guy he had not known so well had tried to kill him. Jack considered this for a few moments and though he saw nothing like that in the amiable young man nonetheless citing the long drive to come he had not so subtly invited the conversation to wind up, and so after a little while longer each man lay down on one of the two rather sparse double beds, and he slipped into a few hours of uneasy sleep.

Silver awoke to blinding white light streaming through unguarded windows, the smell of hot coffee and a thudding base beat marching a two-step with some slow ponderous rapping tune all coming from somewhere close. The Englishman realised it was all emanating from the bedside clock radio, and furthermore that it was positioned above his head as he lay prostrate and still fully clothed on the motel room's floor. He thought he remembered laying down on a bed and had no recollection of how he had come to be on the stained carpet of the motel room floor. His head thudded dimly, but actually, he thought as he struggled into a sitting position on balance he felt a little better than he might have done, than he deserved a voice spoke up in his mind, considering what he had drunk the previous night. Black coffee sat in two polystyrene cups on the dresser between the two beds.

'Hey, Jack, I hope you don't mind, but I kinda borrowed two bucks for the coffees,' Caffee said smiling as he walked in from the bathroom obviously considerably more awake and refreshed than Jack, and apparently not the worse for wear from their escapades of the previous evening.

'No, your fine,' Jack replied and continued.

'Storms cleared up then. It looks like we might get some miles under our belts today.' He was gazing squint-eyed at azure, blue sky and early sunshine, and so any evidence of the previous night's storm was it seemed a distant memory.

'Yeah, looks like,' Caffee shot back. 'You want me ta drive, Jack.'

'Maybe,' Jack shot back. Felt a vague uneasiness, he could not quite put his finger on, though he had learned the hard way to listen more closely to his intuition in these past few weeks.

'Let's have the coffee and see where we're at.' An hour later, they were on the road heading north, Jack had taken the wheel again but had explained to Caffee that they would change later in the day, instinct told him that he needed control, and this time, he listened, though of course shared none of that with his young passenger. They made good progress, and the cheerful low-key banter between them was only marred by the growing sense of unease that Jack felt, an unease that made it difficult for him to lift his mood and rediscover the brief optimism he had encountered at their first meeting the previous day. He was increasingly aware that on two or three occasions in the previous twenty-four hours, brief images had come to him. Those images, first of three men in a black sedan vague yet somehow disturbing, then more explicit, three men and some scenery visible through a windscreen that rather alarmingly was not unlike the countryside scrub and desert he remembered actually driving through the previous day, exactly around the time when he had picked up, well run down to be fair he thought, the hitch-hikers hitchhiker that was Caffee. But those images did not stop there, because then most recently he found himself gazing internally at the clear image of a man, a big heavyset brute who was asking at a rest stop if the server had seen somebody. The brute had a picture held in one huge meaty fist.

Jack had not been able to see that picture in his mind's eye, but each of these fragments, each one of those images had proven increasingly disturbing, and although the voice of logic in his mind reminded him that he should know very well it could not be real, nonetheless he became increasingly paranoid that he was being followed, his amygdala was telling him a very different story. The black tarmac sped beneath the wheels and Jack Silver pressed on, and Caffee noticed after an hour or so that Jack had fallen into a brooding silence, dark and thoughtful, He watched him for some minutes as the wide expanse of road inched on and on and then eventually enquired a little gingerly. 'You OK, Jack?' There was a pause, no music playing and the whine of rubber on the tarmac was the only sound at play, after perhaps a minute Caffee was rewarded.

'Yeah, I think so. I think last night's just paying me back,' Silver replied. The young man thought about that, and his doubt was perhaps somewhat evident when a moment or two later he offered. 'Listen here, Long John, I've got five bucks. We need to stop and get some coffee. What do ya say?' Jack glanced across at his passenger, then looked at the needle on the dash which was inching around seventy, his hands felt clammy, and he was holding on tightly to the wheel. After a few moments, he said, 'No, listen, Caffee, it's probably just stupid, but I really feel we need to keep going, did I tell you that someone tried to kill me in Las Vegas?' Jack spoke without inflection and Caffee who might otherwise have laughed and taken this last as a joke realised instantly that his driver was deadly serious, he said it all with his eyes staring straight ahead, and so Caffee, trying to take any tension out of the cabin simply said.

'Listen you're the boss, Jack, if ya wanna tell me bout Vegas go right ahead, if not I understand, you got a lot going on appears to me.' Jack drove on and did not speak again for several minutes, and then just when Caffee thought that perhaps he hadn't been listening, or more likely did not wish to expand, again without taking his eyes from the road. The Englishman said, 'There's a lot I could tell you, Caffee, but I'm not sure you'd believe me, to be truthful I am still trying to work my way through things myself. Do you remember I asked you last night if you knew how many people look at the sky? Well actually, more to the point what I meant was how many people don't. Almost nobody looks up at the sky Caffee, and do you know why?'

Caffee did not answer immediately but looked across at Jack quizzically, his eyes still fixed on the long straight road that lay ahead.

'You see the thing about the sky is that it's always there, always has been, maybe always will be. But the thing is you see the sky, well it's not like the roof of this car, or like the ceiling in your room, you see those things protect us, cover us up, keep us safe from whatever is going on outside. But that old sky, well she is a different animal entirely. Here, we are, you n me, all of us we all just wander about under it, like it's some great big blue roof over our heads, and yet in truth, it's not a roof is it, it's a bloody window. We don't look up mostly though because if we did we might see the bloody great comet that's heading this way, that comes crashing down on our heads.'

'What's that gotta do with murder?' Caffee asked.

'Well, nothing really,' Jack replied. 'But then perhaps everything. I know that I am being hunted down for a killing I never did. Well, actually, you now know that too I guess, but then wherever I go, wherever I get under cover, seems I don't get to be safe. I can't figure it out, cannot get a handle on it. How it is that somehow, in the past five months, I have been nearly stabbed to death in a Spanish bar fight, I've been literally chased from a pub in a village in North Wales, they run me right out of town, a mob that just went friggin mad, I felt like that Bella Lugosi in bloody Frankenstein.' Silver paused, all the while never looking away from the endless road, but then added, 'Anyway, let us just say there have been other moments too.' He stopped then and the two occupants of the car listened in silence to the whine of tyres, finally after a few more miles were added to the odometer he spoke again, as if no time had passed between his next words and his last.

'Then I get here, well Vegas, close enough for government work. I walk into a diner for a beer, you know earlyish in the morning, what is that now two days ago.' He shook his head at the recollection and still did not look away from the road, then continued, 'Well I change my mind, and I order a coffee, and half a tick later, some Irish bloody psychopath, well he comes at me, and he tries to cave my fucking head in, with a mini fucking axe thing, what do you call it, a hatchet.' Caffee looked hard at Silver. He was some years older than Caffee, but he had learned that age was not a prerequisite to wisdom, not in the world that he inhabited, and neither was it an assurance of the truth. Yet somehow Caffee knew that Jack Silver was not lying, he knew instinctively that man was not even guilty of exaggerating. Nope, however bizarre it all sounded, and it surely did, the young hitchhiker realised that Jack Silver was most definitely at the bottom of one hellish deep dark hole.

'So OK, Jack, it's the understatement of the century to say that yer in a run of bad luck, and I get it that yer running from some real bad folk, but all this other shit, well unless the guy that's chasing yer is F.B.I. then there ain't no way that all the other stuff is connected surely.' Jack slowed as they passed a group of forty or so brightly coloured cyclists in racing nylon, the first road users barring them that either had seen in twenty minutes or more, he half turned in his seat and said.

'More like Mafia.'

'Sorry,' Caffee said.

'I said more like the Mafia than the F.B.I. but yes I grant you it's an impressive network to chase me all over the friggin world like this. And yeah I thought all of that too, but you see the only thing that has been constant in all the places I've been has been the bloody sky. Just like some spooked UFO spotter there am I looking up every place I stay, and there's the sky all blue and sweet and pretty, and I reckon that however unlikely it seems perhaps all of this is linked cos if it ain't then not only am I fucked, but I'm crazy to boot.' Again another minute passed, the whining sound of rubber on black top, Caffee had nothing to offer kin reply, and then just above a whisper he heard the driver utter, 'Maybe there is nowhere I can go.' And then after a moment more, 'I figure the sky isn't a roof over my head, more like a window into my mind. Cos if nobody knows where I have been going, mostly because more recently I haven't known myself. And I know this will sound nuts, fuck I think it sounds nuts, but these people, these different people that have attacked me. Well, they had a look in their eyes, a, you know, a village of the damned type of look. 'And yet besides, you know, wanting to kill me, well they were mostly just ordinary people. I really didn't notice it right off, why would I, but I think this has been going on right from the off, it's been there all along. These people aren't just following some trail I am leaving, there ain't no bread crumbs my young friend, so however crazy it sounds, I think they're following my mind.' He finally looked across at his passenger, and Caffee spied an intensity in the driver's gaze he found rather discomforting, but as Silver seemed not yet done je masked his own angst and listened still.

'But best of all?' Jack went on. 'If anything, I think it's getting stronger.'

'No riddles eh, Jack,' Caffee finally volunteered lamely.

'I mean I can feel them getting nearer, I can feel them seeing me more clearly. I know it all sounds nuts but that's what goes round in my head, that is my sky, Caffee.' Jack trailed off finally and having safely negotiated the cyclists and by then many miles of road he saw a sign ahead that lifted his spirits but a sign that raised another series of questions.

Border 312 miles

During the rest of that day's drive, they batted back and forth, swapped driving and exchanged bits and pieces of each other's life stories, and throughout men did their best to dance around Jack's revelations. The Englishman could see that although Caffee struggled with much of what he had heard he did believe what Jack had told him, or at least he believed that Jack believed what he had told him, and this in turn it seemed had given Jack himself a lift, perhaps given all of the insane events just a little more credibility in his own mind.

But too, Jack Silver could also see that some part of Caffee wanted not to believe, and Jack could understand that also, the young man wanted not to believe, and even more the young traveller wanted not to be involved. Caffee had asked one interesting question though, and Jack had found himself returning to it over and again as the day drew on. If all this village of the damned stuff was true, and if in fact, all sorts were trying to kill him, then how was it that Jack had hooked up with Caffee. Why hadn't Jack just kept on going, why wasn't Caffee trying to strangle him, or some such? Jack went round and round that, thinking back to Las Vegas hadn't he known something was not right in that diner, and equally hadn't he known Caffee was all right, straight off? And so over and over he asked himself, how did that work then? And the reply came back into his mind, too many questions, no answers. And so, after ruminating Jack turned to Caffee and broached the other biggie looming in his mind. 'Canada?' Sometime later in a small-town diner. 'Osoyoos State Park?' Caffee asked questioningly.

'Listen, I need to get across the border. I don't want to go through passport control, do you know a better way?'

'Hey, Jack, I ain't never been this far north, not ever,' Caffee said.

'But yeah I guess it can happen, just park up in the grounds, and we hike across. I figure we juss have ta be careful as to whose looking on the other side. I like it, Jack, that you are a thinking man,' Caffee said. Jack looked at him and then down at the beer and fries that sat untouched in front of him on the Formica table of the roadside diner they had parked up out front of forty minutes previously.

'I am not convinced it's a good idea we both go,' Jack continued.

'I mean look I have no idea what's out there, I can risk my own neck Caffee, but I don't want to be responsible for yours too. Not only that, this is going to be really slow, we have just travelled a thousand miles in what two days?'

'And, well, I can't say I've been big on hiking these past few years. And I told you that I think they're getting closer. I can't be responsible for you Caffee, and anyway, I like you too much.' There was an intensity that passed between them for a few moments before Caffee replied.

'Listen, Long John, ain't no one bin responsible for me since they took my mama. Don't you see I bin running too for a real long time? And I bin thinking since you broached Canada that it would be sweeter maybe for me too. So, which is my favourite word, so, I can always walk behind you, or a half mile up the track, but seems as like we ought both go together, and we'll see how the cards fall eh Jack.' It took two hours of to and fro, but in the end, Jack knew that he liked the idea of Caffee's company more than he liked the idea of them going their separate ways.

He had got better at the whole outdoors thing, but he knew he was by no means a woodsman. He bought them a torch each and a couple of hunting knives along with some water and a few limited supplies at a tourist outdoors shop, he looked at the hunting rifles but felt a churning in his guts that might have been an "English" thing, or it might have been a "the bad guys have the guns" thing, but anyway, he was a foreign visitor and Caffee was a bum, apparently, so a gun did not seem an option.

Sometime later, they dumped the car in a car park that was about half a mile short of the park gates, then loaded their few bits into small backpacks also just purchased. The weather felt oddly warm, and rain had fallen once more, and frequently as they had driven further north. Wet a little bedraggled, and they both appeared a little lightweight for the trek ahead in sneakers and two-dollar plastic rain capes, one with a small pack and the other with a red and green holdall that bore no little resemblance to the cat in the hat. Still, once loaded off they set, Jack with a compass and a small rainproof map showing the final US state park on that side of the border with Canada, and more specifically, British Columbia. As they departed the sun was going down quickly and whilst the days were late into springtime nevertheless as they had travelled further north night-time still came, both suddenly and soon enough, and with it came a variety of sounds that signified to both Jack Silver and Keith Kirkcaldy that they were no longer wandering through the domain of their own kind. Out there things were closer to nature, everything was a little more wild, a touch more edgy and both men felt the thrill of reconnecting, of something akin to fear, that nervy buzz that people get when they step outside of their comfort zone. The two walked late into the evening and as they walked once more they talked.

Caffee, after a time recited some poetry, both of his own and from a variety of poets that were favourites. Jack was impressed that someone with Caffee's background had proven to be so well read and by comparison felt something of a literary dimwit. Eventually, at around ten o'clock, they found a dry ridge under a knot of evergreen trees and decided to settle down. Caffee had some lighter fluid deep in his colourful bag, and Jack did not question why or what for, but in the short time, they had gathered some various logs and twigs soaked a couple in fuel and had a comfortable blaze going surrounded by a ring of small stones.

The night was cold enough that the fire was of real benefit to them both, but the ground was springy and as they had steadily climbed it had dried out, a gibbous moon shone intermittently among the trees and though the swiftness of their departure had precluded thoughts of sleeping bags or real camping gear, along with the fire the crisps chocolate and water in fact supplied all the fuel that either man then required, and as evening drew into the depths of real night-time so Caffee took to talking openly about his hopes and ambitions. Jack as suggested had been much impressed at Caffee's knowledge of literature, and especially poetry, and he guessed that had been true right from the off, and then throughout their time together, but, as he listened, inclining his head in order to hear his friend talk of finding a place, seeking out a community of like-minded people, Jack guessed that although Caffee did not say as much explicitly he was lonely, and his road had become increasingly tough. He understood as he listened in the moonlight just how young, and how naïve, Caffee actually was.

Earlier in the day his new acquaintance had hinted at dark moments in his adolescence, exploitation, probably sexual the Englishman guessed, and also likely at the hands of adults in whose care the boy child Keith Kirkaldy had been placed. Jack had listened to those half-hinted tales and wondered at quite how Keith Kirkcaldy had turned out to be such a balanced, engaging and stellar young man. A young man who quite evidently had had little contact with women, other than the matronly sort that inhabited social services, and this, Jack had understood was simply a natural reaction to losing his mother all those years ago. Yet in all of his tales spoken Jack had not heard Caffee speak even once of a friend he had made, or even a friend he had lost, and perhaps having been running away for as long as he had that too was not so unusual Jack thought. Moreover, as he ruminated, perhaps in that regard at least he was seeing how his own future might map out, should he live long enough.

It was just as Jack was contemplating quite why Caffee had been so accepting of Jack, a man who was at least twenty years his senior, and by no means putting out his best presentation when the wolves began to howl. Yeeeoowl echoed into the night and then from closer a returning howl, the two men looked at one another in the crackling firelight. 'Shit me and call me Julie Jack I think that's bloody wolves,' Caffee said. 'Yeah, I think so,' Jack replied, 'but I don't think we've got to worry too much, especially whilst the fires burning, there's lots to eat out here other than me n you.' As he said this, another howl pierced the night, and this one was rather closer, and so in spite of his confident assertion, Jack reached into his backpack and pulled out the two hunting knives that he had bought earlier in the day, both large seven-inch blades, one side serrated for sawing flesh Jack's mind whispered, and handing one to his young friend, Jack felt a little reassured at holding a death-dealing weapon in his hand as it gleamed in the fitful moonlight.

'Well, my friend, I guess we must be the only people in America without a gun, but I guess also though that we do have these, go in kid, take it… Just in case.' Caffee looked at him for long moments not blinking, and then reaching out wordlessly took the knife. He was scared Jack could see that, but then Silver was a little scared too. In daylight hours, the walk up into forests of pine seemed like fun really and more so perhaps with his friends along and the lovely green spruce in springtime for company it had been an adventure, one with a lemon twist of being out in the wild. Out here at night though and as the moon shone and the shadows drew long each one of those shadows took on a different connotation, mysterious, demonic, and wolves, well a hungry wolf isn't a trifling thing.

'They're like dogs, the bastards are always hungry,' a voice spoke up inside his mind, and Jack thought grimly, well yes a hungry wolf with maybe a few of his buddies for company was a prospect that did not endear itself to Silver actually any more than his companion. He walked in circles around their small camp for a while, the howling thank goodness having ceased. Of course, this did not quell the nerves and so both knives could be seen by the light of their small fire, gripped tightly by both of the hikers. Jack spoke after a minute or two more boldly than he felt, in an attempt to allay his friend's fears. 'Nothing to worry about, Caffee. We're a couple of desperate men remember; I don't think wolves will attack the scent of two healthy men.'

As Jack spoke he fervently hoped that he was right, he leaned forward and stirred the fire's embers into activity, suddenly it was imperative to ensure that there was no chance of that fire going out any time soon. Ducking under the branch of the particularly gigantic tree that formed the backdrop to the clearing they were in he then stepped a few feet away and clear of the light of the fire was able to look out into the night and find himself standing under a now clear starlit sky, the moon obscured by the great cone of the spruce. He looked up in silent contemplation for a long time until eventually, turning to Caffee, he said, I can't see anything, I think we're gonna be ok. Listen why don't you get some sleep, for a few hours at least, if I hear anything I'll wake you.' Caffee looked at him with scepticism. 'Sleep?' he said.

Nevertheless, he hunkered down, and then pulling his jacket up round his shoulders he slid the knife blade down into a pock et of his hold all and laid down on his cat in the hat bag a comfortable distance from the fire his hand resting seemingly casually over the flap where the knife was secreted. Surprisingly Caffee's breathing quickly settled into a rhythm, and Jack realised after little more than thirty minutes that the young traveller had indeed drifted off into sleep. The wolves it seemed had gone completely silent, and as the Englishman sat there leaning back into the shadow of the tree he noticed how utterly still the night had become. Not a puff of breeze disturbed the night-time around him and as he sat there Jack strained to hear any sound being carried on the night. He was still a little nervous, though somewhat more relaxed than he had been an hour before. And so it was that after a little more time had passed that steady young man's resonant breathing, virtually the only sound on the still night air finally took its toll on Jack, and he too fell into a deep and dream-filled sleep.

***

The wolf was grizzled and ancient, he had been a hunter his whole life, the alpha male though having no concept of such things, and until only one season past had held sway as the pack leader for many cycles of the moon. Humans did not scare him, even men with the big sticks that fired flame and death. He was though wary as he padded silently around the two sleeping humans, sniffing the ground, and then the air, remaining just outside of the firelight cast around their small camp. They stank the humans, all humans reeked and often the smell of fear would intoxicate the younger pack members. The wolf's thoughts turned, and he knew intuitively that the pack pursued him. Presently, he was still too quick for them and inside he was content for he could run for at least another season yet. But yet something had compelled this timber wolf to turn aside from his check and run game with the pack, that howling scampering group he had once led, some imperative coursed through him, and it was strong yet despite that below even instinct, and that imperative had taken him from the trail to the edge of this camp, to the two humans that slept like naïve wolf cubs.

The fire burned low but remained red and intense, and a tremble shuddered through the creature for fire was every woodland animal's greatest enemy, and this wolf had encountered its might before down his long years. He saw also the glint of steel, sharp amongst the men's kit. He watched awhile, and once certain that they were both sleeping he lifted his head as if to howl, and then sniffed the air once, and stepped silently from behind the tree line.

The wolf's eyes glinted green in the starlight. He walked up close and towered over the two men, ordinarily he would have been driven by his nature to piss on the ground and so mark his mastery, but the compulsion that had taken him persuaded to him act outside of the nature he had honed during long years. Instead, the wolf walked around the edge of the camp three times, stopped by the young one, sniffed briefly at the hem of his trousers and then looked up as the other, the older one stirred and mumbled. To the wolf's perception, a faint halo appeared to hang in the air around this other one, though this was a wolf, an alpha predator, and so it did not see in that precisely the way that humans do, colours weren't quite within his perception, instead that sense of sight was supported by a range of scents, different shades and strengths, the visual range mixed at source with the nasal range, and so he saw the older human with a curtain of these scents and energies, something far beyond what any human might see coruscating around any human, a sensory energy never still, moving constantly with a myriad of tiny eddies that appeared to come from within. It was late in the spring and nature was abundant at this time of year, the hunt was easy, and the hunter was well-sated and for that reason alone felt no need to attack these two. The animal was mighty and yet still would have had to be very starving indeed, perhaps even facing death, before attacking two adult humans. The creature felt something akin to confusion, uncertainty as to why exactly he had stepped off his chosen trail, left behind the scented path he moved along and trod so carefully around and about the encampment, the animal was even more confused by the aura that surrounded that older human, here was a thing that spoke to something beyond the wolf's comprehension. Finally, certain of his mastery the beast walked up very close to Jack Silver, then sat down, with his nose perhaps no more than three feet from Jack's upturned face, and from that vantage point the animal watched curiously as Jack tossed and turned in the throes of some dreaming place. To an onlooker the sight would have looked most strange, had either man awoke most terrifying more likely, and yet the wolf stayed like that, unmoving, for several minutes. Then suddenly without preamble the heavily furred four-legged creature simply stood up and silently padded back off into the woods.

Much later a distant howl was answered by another, also many miles away, neither disturbed the sleepers, but the call's would have offered an experienced tracker a clue that the old timber wolf had drawn the pack to him again, but even that tracker would not have appreciated that in so doing the forest knight had ensured those humans peaceful passage for many a mile.

The morning came, it was crisp and took some time before the rising sun added any warmth to the day. Jack and Caffee with little to pack set off quickly, both settling quickly into a comfortable routine, the night fire had died into black charcoal and the night fears were similarly banished at the rising of the sun. The two men walked all of that day and on till late into the night, and then after building a bigger fire and eating junk food and speaking junk talk both slept another night without further disturbance or incident. By the end of the second day, the two men had walked across a wide swathe of fairly heavily wooded land, needles and moss underfoot, great spruce tree canopies in clutches overhead, the sun was warming, the climbing created a weariness that conversely seemed to free something in both men. And during that time, they came no closer than a distant hail to another human being, and yet unknown to either one at some point during the following days, their third since setting off on foot they had stepped across humankinds invisible border between the United States and into the ex-British colonial country that was a chunk of a continent in its own right. Many people travelling between these two countries have encountered fences and gates even at crossings far off of the beaten track, and yet for reasons unknown, these two encountered none, and would never know if that were some magic, twist of fate, and a general probability of somewhat. It was equally true to say that neither one had any frame of reference, no opportunity to compare when it came to the crossing of borders, and so they just kept on walking.

In those early moments, the thing's designers believed their construction to be at its most vulnerable to forces external. Great care was taken to allow it every opportunity to maximise all capability to protect itself. Random chance might bring the thing forth in the heart of a burning star, or the midst of a time dilation, black impenetrable and heartless. This thing was the product of the combined minds of the great race that had built it.

Chapter Twelve
Secret Messages

They walked out of the Great Woodland National Park into a semi-rural area and after a time began to spot one or two people here and there and then after another hour of steady trudge came across a rest stop and shop, and there they picked up refreshments at the service station shop and shortly after they took it in turns to clean themselves up in the ice-cold water of the fuel stops rest room. Jack had treated them each to a fresh T-shirt, his emblazoned with "Canada Dry… No need to ask why", Caffee had chosen "Camp Coffee drink of champions" and had then proceeded to ink out the "o" in Coffee and replace it with an "a". Jack had laughed at that, and by now, the two were completely at peace with one another, and had they only known it firm friends. They had chatted while in the woods and whilst both agreed they were on the run they had come to the conclusion that with a little more preparation they might well disappear into the Canadian countryside and become invisible for as long as they wanted, the great outdoors was doing its thing and both men felt freed from many of the binds that had tied each one down. In fact, Jack's trail of suspicious mental images had faded from mind and from memory, and to them both their respective past lives had grown somewhat dimmer. Partly, through the security they found in one another and more because of the miles that they had put on during the few days they had known each other, and the bright azure blue sky, often cloudless for great stretches of the day, the crystal-clear water of fast running mountain brooks, the grasses and mosses and heathers that put a skirt around the great conifer and spruce forests the two marched steadily through.

They decided between stops that at the next outlet. They ought to buy a tent, and beyond that more appropriate camping supplies, a Gaz cooker and a bibby and mugs and bowls. Jack explained to Caffee that whilst his cash was far from endless, and whilst he would only use his credit cards from now on in an absolute emergency, nevertheless, he was happy to pick up the tab, and then made the suggestion that later in the season the two might both be able to obtain some casual work when a bit more settled and that this could allow Caffee to pay his own way if he felt compelled. At first, Caffee appeared uneasy with this arrangement, but as the days passed, slowly at first and then with increasing confidence the young man's unease allayed, and so too did any remaining niggling doubts that Jack might have had about Keith Kirkaldy being a straight shooter. So, in the end, they had agreed, and Jack had gone on to the next small watering hole and bought two sleeping bags, water containers, a small and easy-to-set-up tent, fire lighters, pre-packed food, and two pairs of sturdy walking boots along with a range of blister and sore creams. Once again, he saw the array of weaponry, guns and spear guns and knives twice the size of those he and the kid sported, and once again he discovered that the sight of these implements merely rose a bile of sickness in his stomach which took a long time to pass.

They walked for two more full days and as spring headed towards summer, and spruce towards grasslands each step that they took seemed to move each man a little further away from their respective anxieties. Late spring in British Columbia was and no doubt is a beautiful time, and Jack and Caffee avoided well-trodden paths aimed for the many vast tracts of land in between communities. The weather got warmer by the day, the grasses got longer and the fish began to jump up out of the quick-flowing waters as their own spring dander rose. And like Frodo Baggins and Master Samwise those two men walked, packs hoisted high on their shoulders they both visibly grew fitter and healthier, and frankly as Jack at one point admitted, as the days passed by they simply got better, in mind and body and a million other ways too.

At one of their replenishment stops, Jack Silver had stood in front of a liquor display in a simple small-town general store for such a long time, unmoving, that Caffee had begun to think he had fallen into some kind of trance. In truth, Jack had been in the midst of a raging debate concerning the buying of a couple of bottles of strong rye whiskey. In the end, the "Leave it be" argument had prevailed over the "but you'll need it" retort, and now as Jack walked with Caffee eyeing the stunning woodlands tucked neatly under puffy white clouded spring blue skies climbing mountains that seemed to reach out far in the heavens towards those clouds, he thought back to that debate and was pleased.

He saw more clearly the period before, the months when he had run to a bottle at the end of each and every day. Finally, now he was beginning to realise that the drink had only been playing into the hands of the chasing pack, he was beginning to see incongruities in the chain of events that had bought him to where he was now. At moments during the past few days, he thought he was living out the script of some kind of slightly unreal movie or perhaps it was a play, he didn't share these thoughts with Caffee. Whilst Caffee was in many ways a very mature young man, he was nevertheless a young man, and much of Jack's thoughts were little more than instinct, glimpses or moments of enlightenment that often faded before taking any real form, such fragments were not for sharing, and most times to Jack seemed more an invitation to the paranoia club. The Englishman remembered walking home from school more than thirty years before; he had been listening to his best friend back then Michael Pacey talking excitedly. Mikey as he remembered things had told him about an idea he had had for a science fiction movie story. A "what-if" kind of idea that he recounted as the two of them had dawdled home, dragging school bags along the pavement behind them; and the story had gone something like.

What if...you looked round suddenly and unexpectedly one day, just a regular and not particularly special day, just a regular and not particularly special look around? And what if you had not then seen what you had expected to? What if instead of seeing the cars parked outside the butchers shop you had just walked past, the small poodle yapping and pulling at the lead tied to a railing outside of the florists next door.

What if instead what you had seen was, all the people, in fact all living things frozen in place like caricatures, birds hung in mid-flight, cars utterly still and yet seemingly held in a state of motion. What if you had seen a corner of your reality peeled back and revealing a completely different scene beyond. And what if that whole revelation had revealed itself for only a fraction of a second? After that second, who would you trust, where would you go, and how would you conceptualise the consideration that the whole world was not actually real? In fact, what if it were just something akin to a stage set, nothing more than an experiment to see how you would react in the set of circumstances put before you? Suddenly you specifically become both a god and the slave to your own private ecology that would equally be your own private hell, and if all of that were true what would you do? Jack shook himself mentally as they walked onwards, and he then thought to himself that they had done that idea in Hollywood at least twice in recent years. Both the movies "Matrix" with the mysterious Keanu Reeves, and Jim Carrey's The Truman Show had taken the premise of false realities and then placed their lead characters within the particular dystopian alternate sets. But the point his mind busily conjectured was that ultimately in both cases there had proven to be somewhere to escape to, an off ramp once those reality walls had come tumbling down. Jack reflected that Mikey's theory had been a little bleaker. In his universe, there was no escape; you found out something, a thing which ultimately you would have been better off never having known. In his universe, you found out that your life was a complete falsehood, and furthermore, that you were managed from without, and worst of all, that said management were offering no alternate venue, and no new tour dates, and this information could only serve to harm you, except perhaps in the absolute last moments before you died.

'What you thinking, Jack?' Caffee interrupted his thoughts. 'You look like you seen a ghost.'

'Ah rubbish really,' Jack responded. 'Guess, I'm just figuring how nice and.' He paused and pushed out a wintry smile. 'Well, how nice and comfortable this all is. For the first time in forever, I don't really feel like a bloody fugitive right now if you get my drift.'

'Oh, yeah, buddy, course, I get your…drift,' Caffee replied cheerfully. 'Fuck, man, I haven't been this chilled for the longest time, Jack. Most people just treat me like a punk, so you, you're the saviour, Long John. It's all down to you, big man. I owe you large. You know I don't tend to mix with older guys, but you, well you're I'll tell you this. In my humble view, you're almost cool, even with that freaky accent.' They chatted on easily like that and had covered nearly another thirty miles that day, legs growing strong and the spring into summer climate invoking a kind of ambling merging with the natural surroundings, and it was long into twilight before pitching their tent in the lea of a small tree covered hill. As they sat in front of a small ringed fire Caffee recited what appeared to be some aimless rhyme he had run back and forth, so it seemed to perfection.

'Men with bare arms, bear arms, shoot bears, so arm the bears, and see who stares, and see who scares…and put your guns away.' 'What is that?' Jack asked, after Caffee had repeated it half a dozen times growing it into a pleasant sing song rhythm. A voice answered, but instantly alarming it was not Caffee's.

'He juss working up his magic,' the voice said, and there came walking towards them from between the trees a little man, at a guess probably of West Indian origin if the accent and the ebony dark skin was anything to go by, both

Jack and Caffee jumped to their feet in an instant, all relaxation gone in an instant, electric tension hung in the air.

'There there settle down you young'uns,' said the man, who looked to them both ancient and incredibly worn, and yet impervious and durable as he stood passively just within the ring of flickering light cast by the fire.

'I is no threat to two fit young fellas, though thinkin I'd be minded to sit awhile if you'd have me, and warm me self on dem flames,' he said. 'Courtney's ma name, so said ma mama, an that was sum years ago though she bin dead more an many a life now.'

Jack And Caffee looked at one another and the expression that passed between them was doubtful, after all they had spent every waking moment of their time together reducing to an absolute minimum any interaction with strangers, indeed with anybody, and here they were miles from anywhere and in significant part that was precisely to avoid such encounters. In the end, though oddly upbringing prevailed, and so Jack after some moments held out his hand in greeting, and said, 'Sir, you are a long way from anywhere out here, you are of course welcome to sit with us, but I would ask you to share your story, how is it you come by this place?'

Courtney the ancient man came then close to the fire, closer even than seemed comfortable, and although it wasn't cold that night colour seemed to rise in him as he sat down between where they both stood, and the old man had proved far more nimble than either man might have expected. Caffee joined him, then finally after measuring the dynamic for a moment or two longer Jack squatted down on his haunches next to the old man flanking him on his other side. The Englishman felt a little strange, he might have considered that he was light headed or giddy, and yet somehow if he had been able to articulate he would have offered that actually he felt clearer sighted, more balanced, kind of mentally stood up on the balls of his feet, and in a way that he had not recollected since he was a much younger man. He didn't though have time to think on any of this because within seconds of sitting Caffee had poured the old man a tin cup of steaming black coffee, he himself had then chugged back half of a can of Pepsi, and as the man rolled a cigarette from an ancient tin he pulled from his inside pocket so the trio had set to talking with the intensity of lifelong friends.

'What was that you said I was doin?' Caffee asked without preamble.

'I said you was working up yoh magic. Seein you rhyme those words and roll em round tryin to find their deeper meanin, thas magic,' the old man replied drawing long on his hand rolled smoke.

'You see where I come from they'd tell you that you're a wordsmith young fellah. And if you listen fella they'll tell you too that words is one o the old magicks.'

Caffee looked a little perplexed but pleased also at what sounded at least like some kind of a compliment, albeit wrapped in an old mans winsome chatter, he didn't question the old man. Jack watched the interaction all that while the old man's head was turned away from him, Caffee's eyes glistening with intensity in the firelight stared unblinking, and when he was sure the man had finished responding to his companion he leaned in and asked once again.

'Courtney you say, and sir we are without doubt pleased to make your acquaintance, but I have to ask again, we have hiked many a mile to this place and barring a few wild rabbits and a goat a ways back we have not seen another person in.' He paused and looked again at Caffee. 'What do you reckon Caffee, twenty miles or more?' But Keith Kirkaldy wasn't listening, in fact he had returned to mumbling his little rhyme to himself over and over, whilst avidly watching the blue smoke rise lazily from the old man's rolled-up cigarette, and he seemed significantly separate from those other two. 'Ayum, guess you could say I live up the trail aways,' the old man replied without much apparent interest. Jack persisted, 'Well, OK, but we haven't seen a house in many a mile, and I mean no discourtesy to you, but you look, well hale and hearty that's for certain but perhaps a bit old for camping out, are you alone or do others wait for you close by?' The old man squinted back at Jack in the fires flickering light the smoke of the cigarette drifting between both men. 'If I told you where I was from you wouldn't believe me, so let's juss say I bin places you wouldn't dream, and places you couldn't dream, and still yet you know already, that few things in this life are precisely as they first appear. See I have floated down the great river that runs its banks up to Babylon way back in the morning of the world, an I have swung through the trees of the deepest jungle on a dark and moonless night, and I have looked too into a blazin noonday sun in the hottest corner that this world has to offer. And son, I done all these things just to fill the time, waitin for you to get here right now Jack Silver. And let us be clear young mister there are still deeper and darker paths than all of those that I have ever trod.' Jack was astonished at the words of the old man, images conjured and fell away, he found himself desperately thinking of the where and the how this man had come by his name, whether his origin was embedded in that name, whether the story was named in the lineage. These were strange and alien thoughts and Jack found himself about to ask without actually knowing why, but before a word had escaped his lips the strange ancient creature that was man and was much more beside, had started to speak again.

'You have questions. I know that, but as you can see I really am tremendous old. Truth is I am probly the oldest thing you ever gonna see. So now we is both here Jack Silver you best ask what it is you really wantin to know cos fate has made our time here terrible short.'

Jack wasn't keeping up, one part of his mind screamed that this old fellah was mad as a March hare, but fucking hell how in all the gods names could this octogenarian know his bloody name, and for that matter what in Christ's name had happened to Caffee, he was sitting not six feet away bumbling to himself like a simpering idiot. Jack watched suspiciously as the old man, who had introduced himself Courtney finally finished his rolled-up cigarette with seeming relish, followed it up with a slug of black coffee, burped hard, and then finally looking up hard at Jack said. 'Old Jack was right as he strode along the path, but now, he's just as dead as if he were wrong. Do you see, Jack Silver?' 'I haven't got a damned clue what you are talking about,' Jack said, finally finding his voice. 'And how in fuck old man do you know my name? Who are you really, are you here to kill me?' Jack said building up a head of steam, and at that the old man looked at him long and hard his eyes wide and unblinking by the light of the fire.

'As to who I am Jack lets juss say that for conjectures sake I'm not rightly sure, Hows I know your name. Well, I don't really know that neither, such things ain't carryin much weight where I bin walkin as they do here. I am a vessel that gets filled with what it needs. I don't rightly know if you is s'posed to unnerstand these things or not, thass not my reason for bein here see. I juss know we is crossin this path for a short time, and maybe I can help you see some things. Maybe…if you is willin to look that is, but as to killin you, I ain't got no handle on that fer sure.' The old man quieted then and stared unblinking at Jack Silver, estimating, calculating what impact his words had had.

'Damn it, old man, what are you telling me?' Jack asked, 'and what are you not telling me? Who are you exactly, a witch, an alien, some super whiz scientist time traveller? I don't understand any of this.' And then finally the Englishman added in a high-pitched voice, 'Did Cipher send you?'

'Everything ain't what it seems Jack Silver, old men in the woods aren't always juss old men, and yes I have walked paths you will never understand, and yes I am shortly gonna be free to choose my own path, and you, well you follow still the destiny that is set out before you, and I have a message for you about that destiny. I suppose in the end you could say I am a little like the mail man.'

'A message from who?' Jack asked. 'Well, actually from where that I figure might be a better question,' the old man responded after a second or two, and then burped once again as the coffee seemed to settle on him, he smiled a little self-consciously and then continued uninterrupted.

'I ain't never bin too sure where these things come from, these tit bits of information, but I gets to carry them little bits an pieces for people, an I kinda know that they is important to the people that's hearing, but in't my place to know no sender, happen though that I have wondered how these things come to me, an p'raps where they comes from. See you know cos I told you that I bin to more places than many, an I ain't never seen no clue as to where this stuff arrives at me from. I guess I know when I gotta delivery, all kinda deep down inside, an you, well you're like my last errand Jack Silver, an maybe my best errand.' Jack was by now both completely confused by the old man's rhetoric but still perhaps surprisingly found him enigmatic and curiously believable, albeit that he did not really feel that the man had yet said one word of real substance. He inched himself a few feet further back from the man, enabled himself to take in the sight of that other fully, and then he leaned forwards back towards the man called Courtney and said to him.

'So old man tell me, what is this message you bring. You won't, or you say cannot tell me how you know who I am, you speak in riddles about yourself, so tell me then if you please what it is you came to say?' The old man looked curiously then at Jack Silver leaning forward from the waist up himself, drawing the Englishman's gaze back in. 'What I got to say ain't the issue, nor is it the message I gotta be givin, but I give this to you in all conscience Mister Jack Silver. You ain't gonna figure out where it is you are, or where it is you goin, not till you know where it is you bin, an you need to figure that out quick, I'm thinking you know already that the time is runnin away from you…' The man looked ancient in the winking ebb and flow of the light from the travellers small fire to Jack he looked at that moment like some Indian tribal leader, perhaps one that had crossed the border northward a couple of hundred years before. The cadence as the man had said his piece had calmed Jack Silver acting like some kind of verbal balm, and so then he found himself filled with an innate sense of well-being, indefinable but there.

'Who are you really?' Jack heard the question but had not known he was asking it. Time passed, though he could no longer measure such things and unexpectedly the old man answered, and Jack understood some sense of that reply, just a feeling really, that he was being given a glimpse of deep things, ancient and monumental things that until then had remained beyond his imaginings. He sensed majesty and kingliness, and a lineage of such proportion as to humble him. He felt held within a single moment and in that moment this old man, this ancient king of the elementals was moving around him, through him, above and below him, the word "Swirling" came to him, and it seemed right, a creature distinct in one instance then less so the very next existing with him and only him within the bubble of that single moment. Caffee had faded to some shadow of himself, and Jack could see in the hands of the swirling man a gleam of white, he spied some kind of a soft glow pulsing through the old mans gnarled hands, a soft white light that danced in time to the swirling motion of the man, the woodland sprite that moved in and out front of him. A voice audible and yet not came to him within the moment, asked him to reach out, entreated him to play along and so Jack watched as his hand did indeed move, after seconds it closed with the old mans, and the swirling force of nature gathered it all in. And when after an instant longer those hands separated Jack felt that he had lost something, and yet gained something more, he could not have articulated any of this had he been asked, but as he looked down, he saw a small white object sat in the palm of his right hand, and like the centre, the sternum of a flower, it was more beautiful than any petal that surrounded it, and with it the moment he had spent eternity within was gone and that moments would never walk abroad in the world again.

In Jack's hand, the object, this new gift, felt distinctly warm, and somehow, it felt heavier than it ought to have for something so small. And whilst the glow that had affected his vision had dissipated and Jack could now see that what he actually held was a white pebble a polished smooth stone and not much more, still deep down inside himself Jack felt a change and the thought came to him.

'If not now, when.' Somehow, he felt that he had moved on, unexpectedly and unbeknown to any except himself and some strange old woodsman, and perhaps that movement had been without his tacit acceptance, of that he really wasn't sure at all, but the step had been taken nevertheless. Deep in the night many miles from anywhere he had ever called home Jack Silver had stepped off of the path that his life had been taking for as long as he had lived, the path that for decades had been ordained as his, and if there had been any doubt left that too had gone in a puff, there was no turning back. He wondered vaguely as the thoughts drifted like dream mists around him about the significance of the stone, pretty though he felt it to be there was something, some attachment, some future Jack Silver that would wake to a different understanding. Right then the exchange with the old man faded quickly and Jack was left with a sense that something dramatic had happened but without being precisely certain what. All of a sudden he felt deeply tired and looking up to see the old man grinning at him from a toothless mouth Jack wanted to stay awake, found himself battling suddenly to even keep his eyes open, but damn he had a million questions, and he knew that he ought to ask, 'If not now,' and Christ in a fucking bread basket, he was on the run. And yet despite all of that somehow as the old man grinned and the dull embers of the fire warmed him he drifted swiftly into a deep sleep that took him over quickly and completely…

Within a fraction of a fraction of one second the thing was all but impervious to any force or energy that might be released in that universe, and that was exactly as the builders had instructed it to be. Protected from without it opened its senses and began to rove.

Chapter Thirteen
Midnight Blue

The fire had burned down at some point in the intervening hours and had been replaced by the morning warmth of early summer sun, a blue sky clear of clouds greeted the opening of eyes and Jack awoke to the sound of birds singing and Caffee, still snoring deeply. Much of the previous evening had faded to a dreamlike state, and like dreams all was fading quickly in the different realm of wakefulness. Jack looked down at his clenched right hand and saw that in it he held a small white pebble, a stone, and not an especially exciting stone at first look, but Jack reflected somehow this new treasure, well it "felt" exciting, it seemed to him that whatever had happened the previous evening with that strange old man, his thoughts stopped short.

Suddenly prodding and poking at the young man he fairly shouted, 'Caffee, wake up, wake up.' As Caffee yawned and stirred, 'Do you remember that old man last night?' Jack asked, and the stone for the moment was forgotten though slid determinedly into the Englishman's jeans front pocket. They talked over fresh coffee, and both agreed after some debate that there had in fact definitely been an old man with them for a time the previous evening. After that, the two found it more difficult. This was much because he had seemed to each of them a figment of each man's night-time imagination, and god knew where he had gone. The visitor seemed to have come and then left in the deeps of the previous night, touching each man uniquely and subtly, although as Caffee had said at one point.

'What was such an old geezer doing out in the Canadian woods late at night anyway.' Who knew, and then as he considered he added even more suspiciously a question. He asked Jack what they should do if they came across the old man's body later in the day. Neither one of them appeared able to quite recollect the man's name, or his features exactly, and Jack said nothing about the stone in his front pocket, or how he felt...changed by the events of the previous night despite some uncertainty as to what exactly had taken place. He simply felt he was driven now by an imperative, something new, and different than simply running away. And though he did not quite know what he must do, the previous evening had for reasons he could not explain, even to himself, changed him from a man on the run to...well a man running towards something. He didn't know what exactly, but he intended to figure it out.

They set off within the hour and walked in companionable but sperate silence for some time. After about four hours, they crested a wooded rise in the heat of the late morning sun, and descending the far side found themselves headed into a small town that sat at the foot of a daunting range of mountains that stretched snow-capped into distant mist beyond the town and before the two travellers. Jack Silver looked on at the conifer forest growing close knit as far as the eye could see in a one-hundred-and-eighty-degree arc. Caffee had become more animated as the small outpost hove into view but somehow Jack who had been a little more circumspect that morning had begun to feel that their time together was drawing to a close. He had begun to think that perhaps it was time that he got onto a plane and returned to the UK and time to face up to his destiny, whatever that might be. But yet still he felt guilty, he had led Caffee throughout with the idea of disappearing into the Canadian wilderness for a season or perhaps for many, and now he planned to dump him and go, leaving this man that in truth was only little more than a lad many hundreds of miles from anywhere he knew and from anyone that might offer a fellow like him succour or aid. And worst of all Jack Silver knew that he could offer no cogent explanation as to why, other than the obvious that it would be much too dangerous for the young man to be with him when he got back to England, even assuming that he had a passport. Jack bought them both a lunchtime breakfast at a quaint diner, and they both ate steaks and bacon with mash potato and runny grilled eggs on the top with relish, along with iced water and the inevitable black coffee all banged down by a portly female who appeared disenchanted to be disturbed by these two ramshackle travellers.

It seemed that both men had toughened up during their outdoor experience, and Silver considered it was remarkable how quickly human beings learned to cope without home comforts, and yet they attacked the meal and were profuse with their thanks to the kindly couple that both owned the establishment and prepared food for their customers. Jack tipped the waitress generously, though in truth it was her employers that ought to have derived all of the credit for fine sustenance. Jack had intended to use the break as a preamble, allowing them both to discuss the immediate future on a full stomach, but as they had waited to pay the tab he clearly overheard a conversation that chilled his blood.

'Well, yessum, pretty sure I saw two of 'em, Australians mebbe.' Silver saw that this all had been said an older man, local by the look of him, though to whom had not been clear from his vantage point. 'They bullied poor Harry, inside the damned barbers shop, I mean they pushed and shoved at him in his place of work, that in't right. See I heard him, and he said he didn't know of no Englishman up here this early in the season, and he said that right back at them when they asked him. But I could tell, Harry was real sacred, and later I heard him say so. And he wasn't lying now was he, cos we haven't seen any tourists to talk of too early in the summer, too late for the winter.' The unseen man with him mumbled something Jack didn't quite catch and then cocking his ear he heard, 'No, I think the sheriff's due in tomorrow, but they're up at Ma Timpson's lodge. I reckon there's two, or mebbe three of 'em, and I don't think that they're up there for her muffins… These are definitely baduns, certain those that I saw were.' It was then just as the infernal waitress returned with the bill that Jack heard the other man say, 'Do you think maybe someone ought to go up and check on the old girl?' Soon after, Jack Silver settled up and left quickly, with Caffee in tow, and he realised that if he was the English man about which enquiries were being made, and his mind reminded him that nothing indicated that had to be the case, barring instinct of course, well then having Caffee with him turned one mildly interesting English hiker into a pair of totally invisible walkers passing through. Jack tried to think about what to do and could only think about getting back above the tree line. He had told Caffee that they needed to talk but now decided that would have to wait. 'Caffee we need to get out of town.'

'Why?' Caffee replied.

'I think that maybe some people here are looking for me,' Jack retorted his voice taught. 'Let's go then,' Caffee said. He had learned to trust Jack Silver's instincts increasingly, or perhaps in his position he had little option. But surprisingly Jack replied, 'No, no we need to go, but we're gonna need to stay gone this time for a while, so like it or lump it we'll have to get some supplies before we leave or we're buggered.' A single tarmac road ran through town with a variety of gravel driveways and parking areas off of it at regular intervals. At the very edge of town, Jack and Caffee found a general store with the usual selection of food and camping gear alongside fishing equipment and, for the first time sparking an interest in Jack's mind, a selection of hunting rifles hung in the shop's main window. The noonday sun was by then bright and hot and as Jack and Caffee walked up to the store's main entrance the Englishman felt incredibly vulnerable, obvious, caught like an insect out in the bleaching white gaze of that sunlight. Looking back out in the countryside, shielded by trees and various outcrops of rock and tuft, well somehow Jack had felt considerably more secure, although as the arrival of the mysterious old man the previous evening had proven, any safety had been purely in his mind. 'Caffee, you wait outside, I'll be just a few minutes,' Jack said. 'Outside.' 'Yeah, I think we need to keep an eye out, and I have the money.' 'Yeah, buddy, but what am I looking out for?' Caffee asked sounding petulant and perhaps with an undertone, Jack could not tell whether there was fear or some angst in the young man's tone.

'Anyone that looks out of the bloody ordinary. You see some big bloke with a gun just holler, OK,' Silver replied. The tension he was feeling slipped into his own tone. Caffee looked back at him sullenly, nodded and leaned onto the porch railing making it evident to any onlooker that he was none too happy. Jack stared hard at him eyes unblinking for a second or two and then mumbled out loud, though more to himself than anyone else. 'Kids, they're all bloody prima donnas when all's said and done.' He instantly regretted his words but rather than turn and apologise he walked quickly up the three steps into the shop proper and in so doing saw his companion alive for the last time. As soon as the Englishman walked in he sensed that something was not quite right, immediately he looked at a prim woman of about fifty or so, a solid grey bun of hair sat atop creased but homely features, he smiled at her despite the emotional turmoil he was feeling, and he noticed that she was tight, the woman was reigning in some upset of her own. She stood beyond a wooden counter that ran across the width of the shop and furthermore that acted as a boundary between the shop floor and a number of shelves and storage bins behind. Jack stood front and centre between cornucopias of product on shelves and on display, and as he looked down momentarily he noted a light dusting of sawdust which softened and masked the worn wooden floorboards, a voice piped up "slip hazard" in his mind a little unhelpfully. He was about to voice a greeting when he felt, for the second time in less than twenty-four hours, his senses sharpen almost preternaturally, to ramp up in an instant into some kind of sensory overdrive. In that heightened state, he saw dust motes moving lazily through the air, beams of sunlight cutting through the shops dusty atmosphere, he smelt fear and stale body odours, he felt the eddies of the air in the room. The stone in his front right jeans pocket had perceptibly warmed up, and he was aware of that too though he hadn't thought of it at all since that morning, and yet now it instantly came back to the front of his mind, connected to him as it were, and he was again minded of the words of the strange old man. 'You got to figure out where you bin before you can figure out where you are, or where you goin.' Jack was just wondering whether running back to the forest was his best move when a number of things happened all pretty much at the exact same moment. The door he had walked through only half a minute or so previously blew inwards as an explosion like a crack of thunder accompanied his friend Caffee who came flying through backwards blood tissue and glass spraying into the air. Jack found time to half turn and dive sideways instinctively seeking cover. Out of the corner of his eye, he saw a man with a shotgun step out from behind a screen that led through to the back of the shop, and the same man jam the fire stick nonchalantly into the side of the shop assistant's head. As Silver continued his roll across the wooden floor of the shop, scrabbling in the sawdust and broken glass another crack rang out, and Caffee, who Jack couldn't see but realised had been screaming at the top of his lungs for at least five seconds, suddenly stopped. Jack Silver twisted his head at an awkward angle to catch sight of his friend and what he saw told him instantly the young man was dead, half of his face seemed to have fallen inward, and blood pumped across the whole mess pooling around him on the shop floor, bits that alarmingly resembled bone and tissue were spread around the mess and Jack was no more. A second man then strode through the remaining scraps of the door and pointing his own shotgun at Jack said in a strong east end London accent.

'Get up you cunt...or I'll fuckin toast you, like I just done yer mate there.'

Jack stood slowly and as he did realised that tears were streaming down his cheeks; somewhere deep inside himself he hoped that they were for his friend Caffee, but thought that they were also for himself, and he knew that he was very frightened. He heard the woman behind the counter whimper and then heard but did not see as the gunman beside her smashed her hard in the head and barked a screeching laugh as he did. Jack guessed she had been hit with the butt of the gangsters gun, but the Englishman didn't turn away, he looked straight ahead staring through tear-filled eyes at the big man standing just inside the doorway of the shop, and at the moment, Jack found he couldn't turn away.

'Mr Cipher has sent us, Mr Silver. Come with us now or die here. It's your choice you killing motherfucker,' said the gunman with a curious mix of courtesy and venom. As he walked through into the store proper, he stepped disinterestedly over the corpse of Caffee and walked up close to Jack Silver. He reeked of tobacco and cheap stale aftershave, and something else, testosterone he realised. The man was pumped up by the maiming and killing.

At that moment, a vehicle pulled into the gravel frontage immediately outside and the man who had murdered Jack's friend looked at the other shooter behind the Englishman and said.

'Deal with the fuckin bitch. She's seen your face, and more importantly, she saw these beautiful features. This bastard's goin nowhere,' he said pointing with his free hand at his scarred and entirely un beautiful face. In an instant, Jack realised in exactly that second that he had maybe one chance, his heightened senses seemed still to be on point, or perhaps back for an encore a section of his thinking offered. He saw that the gunman walking towards him had been standing in a quickly spreading pool of his friend's blood and around it all the layer of sawdust he had spied perhaps five minutes previously. The guy behind him appeared to be dealing with the shop's other occupant, and Jack realised that with the first gunman standing so close to him, the other guy probably wouldn't risk getting a shot off, and deep down in his mind, he thought, *They won't kill you. Cipher wants you alive... You know that he's gonna do you himself. That's this guy's thing.*

Jack suddenly shoved out, clumsily pushing at the gunman who had momentarily dropped his guard. As he hoped the gunman slipped in the tacky but ever so slippery puddle of blood and sawdust spreading and soaking the wooden floor, he was a heavy man, and he went over landing heavily with a howl. 'Get him; grab that fucker; don't let him get away.' Jack heard no more as he charged, nearly slipping over himself as he crashed through the badly damaged doorway, he saw momentarily a huge truck with MACK emblazoned in chrome across the radiator, darting behind it panting he looked at the tree line perhaps fifty metres up a fairly steep slope. Moments later he heard a shot and then another and was grateful that the truck whose startled owner still sat in the driver seat, was between him and Cipher's two Stormtroopers. He ran as hard as his lungs would let him arms pinwheeling in a desperate attempt to gain any ounce of additional momentum, and he reached the cover of the conifers without further incident, but just as he charged through into the shady cover afforded by the trees he heard the sound of sirens approaching. Jack thought of his friend lying almost certainly dead on the shop floor, and of the poor woman god knew whether she was still alive, and he hoped fervently that his deepest fears for them both weren't realised. He wondered momentarily about going back but then remembered overhearing the conversation back at the diner, the sheriff was due in tomorrow, two gunmen and one early sheriff, and those two "Shadowmen" did not look like they would stop even for a second at one more sheriff. Silver knew that if he went back then everyone died, no witnesses and as he eased into the shadows he had no doubt of that reality. If he ran then perhaps they came after him and however unlikely perhaps they left the others alone. And so, he ran…

Further into the forest, the smell of spruce and the deep shadows a stark contrast to the smell of cordite and blood, panting and running until his breath and his legs would carry him not a foot further eventually after what seemed a lifetime of ragged breathing and watery legs he flopped down at the base of a huge tree and immediately sobbed through the racked and broken breathing. 'Caffee, oh, Caffee, what have I done? I told you it wasn't safe.' He wailed to himself and to the world at large, as gradually his breathing slowed. 'Caffee, they killed you.' He stayed like that for several minutes, curled into a foetal ball unmoving barring the shaking of his sobbing frame caught between a couple of huge tree roots. It was after quite a time before he found himself able to get up and so move on. As he set off he realised that he had cut his face and also his left leg quite badly, he was not sure whether it was the broken glass in the shop or something from sometime after, but then realised due to the bits of bark around his torn jeans that likely he must have crashed through the undergrowth with no regard for himself, and he understood, as some sense of rationality began to return, that only luck had prevented more serious injury.

Jack Silver stumbled deeper into the woods, still racked periodically with desperate tears for his lost friend, for himself, and for the world. He was completely lost in every sense and by the time he realised this it had gotten dark, and he was a long way from any other human being. Finally, he collapsed beside a swift running stream, and without any clear thought the Englishman fell into a dream-filled tortured sleep that chased him deep into the night.

Many hours later he awoke, and still battling the recollections of earlier events found himself wailing deep into the darkness, with only a quarter moon glimmering dimly between the thick canopy of trees. In his mind's eye, he saw Caffee flying through the door backwards, gouting blood already flowing from a huge wound that had removed a good part of the young man's face, and the image came like a rerun movie reel over and over. In the instant when these events had taken place, Jack had been desperately trying to save his own life and so not fully realised that his young friend was in fact already mortally wounded from the gunman's first shot. Caffee's screams had in fact been his dying words and the impact of this reality slammed into Jack Silver's mind over and over with a dawning dread that somehow hit harder even than the awful shock of his death. After a little time, he awoke fully and then he sat and with a monumental effort calmed himself, and as he did this, he began to take in his surroundings. He had run blindly and so took nothing with him when he made his desperate bid to escape Cipher's men. In spite of the sorrow, he felt at some core level that he needed to take stock of his situation. He felt in his pockets and found the small pebble that he had come by so mysteriously what seemed now about a thousand years ago, in that same pocket nestled next to the stone he found a disposable lighter and five sticks of gum.

Silver remembered not wanting to offend Caffee and so one day after repeated offers had said yes to a stick of gum, though chewing was not his thing, and like so many kindnesses it had ended with him hiding one stick after another in his jeans pocket, the memory bought a prick of tears to his eyes yet again as he thought back. He counted out the sticks and placed them on the ground in front of him neatly placed beside the lighter. He had cash in his other jeans front pocket and by the roll estimated at least a thousand dollars still. All of the camping gear had been in the rucksacks and so left far behind, and barring the sticks of gum, lighter, and a battered candy bar that he pulled out of his back pocket plus a thousand bucks that was of no use to anyone where Jack now found himself he had nothing, a voice countered, 'Except your life… And you're seeing stone.'

After some time, he scrabbled around in the dim light cast by the new quarter moon and managed to pull together a bundle of twigs and bracken, and a few larger branches which lay dried out on the ground. He sparked the lighter, but as hard as he tried, he could not get even the smallest of the dried undergrowth to catch. He remembered a TV documentary that included advice on stripping bark from dried wood to persuade it to flame on but still to no avail. The lighter was of a clear mauve plastic, and in the dim light, he could just see that the fuel was quickly running out. He paused and thought for a moment and then remembered the roll of ten and twenty-dollar bills. And so, after a brief mental debate he reached back into his pocket and pulled two notes out, lit them both rather nonchalantly and dropped them into the centre of his small pile of brush and twigs. Within moments it had lit, and Jack casually threw another two bills on just to get the whole party rolling. Before long he had a roaring fire going, as he did all of this in a whisper he said to himself. 'Fuck it, fuck it all to ass-kicking hell.' It was some time before he fell into a dream-filled uncomfortable sleep, the fire slowly burning down the fevered thoughts within burning hotter and hotter as the night drew on, and all was death…death…death and that was how he awoke in the early light of predawn. A short while after Jack scrambled down the bank near where he had lain and crouching down scooped water from the clear running stream that had tinkled away throughout his tortured sleep. The water was incredibly cold and as he threw handfuls over his head and washed at the cuts on his hands legs and face the coldness of the water brought with it a sense of reality and perspective that appeared up to that point to have been missing from Jack's night-time carnival.

He realised that having crashed and banged his way this far into this Canadian spruce forest there was in fact little chance of anyone finding him, were they of course to be still looking, but equally the Englishman knew that he was hellishly lost, that he had no provisions and no camping gear and no way to protect himself. He threw himself down on the ground in front of the fire which he had reset with a further clutch of twenties before dousing himself and thought about his predicament. He had sat moving between waling and sleep for hours through the night listening and drifting as small creatures entertained his fears with indistinct scratching and pawing. He had rolled his own fears around his mind and mingled with them every moment were images of Caffee, and of another man, a man murdered in London what seemed then about a million years before. Jack was exhausted both physically and emotionally and as the pre-light grew towards full dawn he fell again unwillingly into a sleep, but this time drew him down quickly into steady breathing, and a relaxed body and another place…

The artefact, for as years had passed so had it become, did not look forth nor about. It was changed and that change allowed it to know what purpose it now sought, and to that end, the artefact recognised that soon enough it would pass to one only amongst all in the clamour.

Chapter Fourteen
Standing in the Rain

Jack stood absolutely still in hammering rain; he was completely soaked. He looked around him and had absolutely no idea where he might be, he felt a bit fuzzy and somehow detached, also he felt a biting wind that blew across the damp clothes that clung to him and that rubbed the cold and the wet into all the wrong places. The light was dim but not night-time, Jack Silver looked around and noted that he was in a built-up area, there were blocks of flats that towered above him on all sides, and beyond those in front of him, he could just make out dozens, maybe even hundreds more towering off into the distance. The cold wind was whipping between those buildings, and Jack found himself squinting as grit repeatedly slapped his face, and ground into the corners of his eyes, the whistling sound that accompanied the gusts had a vague malevolent undertone, and the air did not smell cleaned by the wind but rather dirtied by the intrusion. He pulled up on the collar of his wet woollen coat, a gesture that seemed to him instantly pointless and then similarly pointlessly kicked at an empty plastic carrier bag that blew up around his legs, boy the Englishman thought it was foul weather. As hard as he tried Jack was struggling to remember how he had gotten to this place, yet he felt uneasy, below the sound of wind and rain he thought he could hear other sounds, noises not common to his mind's ear, human voices perhaps, heavy machinery definitely, but underneath that pastiche of sounds was some kind of vague and disquieting screeching, barely within his earshot, in fact only just even within his auditory range at all, but carrying a distant sickening undertone that worried constantly at the back of Jack's mind. He began to walk towards one of the buildings randomly chosen, the wind was at his back now, and it pushed him forward so strongly that was now gusting. As he moved closer to the building he saw that the concrete it had been built from was pock-marked and broken, in fact, it looked like something he had seen on news footage of

Beirut years before, and at that moment, 'You're in a war zone,' he heard clearly inside his head as his mind's voice decided to join in. After a minute or so of wandering uncertainly, Jack walked under a concrete overhang and then began to stride down a tired and dirty concrete ramp which quite clearly appeared to lead to an underground car parking area. Initially, he was simply glad to be out from the cold wind and the driving rain, and so as he walked into deeper and darker gloom descending the ramp he shook himself out of the long woollen overcoat and dragging it off felt about forty pounds lighter. The Englishman's eyes grew quickly used to the gloom, and he peered around, just in front of him was a metal mesh grill that ran about two meters high by perhaps five wide, and this blocked his progress any further down the ramp. Rubbish had blown up against the steel barrier in sufficient volume to suggest that it had not been opened in some significant period of time.

Silver looked right and left and spotted there, about three paces behind and over his left shoulder there was a small doorway, not quite full-sized, almost a service hatch he thought, and in the gloom he spied dim electric light bleeding out from around the edges of the door, escaping from between it and the ill-fitted frame the door sat in. Jack walked over to the door, and he noticed that his footfalls echoed in the closed concrete space, he tried the handle, it felt cold to the touch yet he clearly felt warmth emanating from beyond the closed door similar to the light that warmth bled around the edges, the door was locked. Yet that door didn't look up too much he considered and so as Jack was thinking of putting his shoulder to it that was when he heard voices, this was not the undercurrent of noise that he had picked up outside, which now he thought about it had receded as soon as he walked down the ramp, no siree these were proper voices, they were male at there were at least two speaking, and worryingly to Jack they were getting steadily louder. He was not sure in that first instant from where the voices came and so as he looked around he realised he was in an especially vulnerable position. 'Like outside the back of a restaurant,' a kind yet sarcastic voice piped up in his mind, and then was added, 'Well, buster why exactly should voices immediately suggest threat?'

This time, the speaking in his head began to sound remarkably like his young friend and travelling companion Caffee doing the asking. He did not know the answer to his mind's questions, and he just felt that if the approaching voices were connected to folk who were up to no good then he was going to find himself stuck halfway down a concrete ramp with a steel barrier in front of him the wide-open asshole end of the world storm waiting behind him and Christ knew what beyond the door immediately in front of him. He turned and was just about to run back up the ramp when of a sudden the voices stopped. Jack Silver instantly stopped too, he listened intently. After a moment, he began to feel and then to hear quite clearly his heart thumping loud and fast in his chest, he heard the wind and additionally the heavy rains and distant steady thunder. The Englishman was frozen on the spot, he found that he could not move, and still, he wasn't sure where exactly he had heard the voices coming from, but even so, something compelled him at that moment to stand absolutely still, not to move even one single muscle, he realised that he was even holding his breath, this was a repetition of another night standing still, breath held, rain pattering. At some level he understood that he was waiting, everyone, indeed everything was waiting…but for what? And that was when the broadcast began. Standing there, Jack all of a sudden began to feel weak, and quickly, this grew to an overwhelming sense of being broken and terribly afraid, and this sensation was not so much physical. At some level, he remembered feeling these things before physically, but no, this was more a thing deep inside of him and though he had felt all of these feelings he had never felt anything in his life to that point quite so… Literally.

Seconds later, tears began to course down both cheeks unbidden; he dropped to his knees, and he was no longer afraid of men's voices or afraid of anything in fact in that dark concrete place "graveyard" the Caffee voice helpfully offered, afraid of nothing barring that feeling that assaulted his mind and his spirit. He began then to visualise images in his mind, and they were myriad, some flashing past at the speed of thought, yet others that appeared like movie-tone reels seeming to last for many minutes each, and there were people dying. In every image sequence, there were people being killed, in fact, murdered, butchered battered and killed stone dead in any and every hideous manner imaginable. In his mind, he saw then men taken to dark places and beaten to death, and others stabbed, and others still clubbed, or choked, or men shot in the back of the head in the cold of early morning. And he saw women stripped of their clothes, their dignity, their pride, women made to beg and never once gaining a modicum reprieve and so having throats cut, eyes cast asunder, limbs even on one occasion a woman had her womb chopped out. And lastly and possibly most horrific of all he saw children and even they were similarly slashed, and others were pelted with rocks as they ran from inevitable doom to an even greater doom. Jack wanted to wail as vision after vision assailed his quailing reeling senses; but hard as he struggled in this place he then found himself, nevertheless in his mind there was no off button. He wondered at some deeper level that somehow remained detached still whether he was witnessing reality or whether this was some awful dreadful figment of his mind, and without any conscious thought at that second he slipped a hand into his jeans pocket and that hand closed round a small hard object. In an instant, he began to improve, to feel better, yet above at a conscious level the images continued to pour across his mind like a tidal storm, but now since clutching at the small hot stone some part of him appeared able to look at those images at least somewhat more objectively. The fear and revulsion were dimmed, and even if only fractionally that had let something else into his mental picture. So, the imagery continued, and he looked on as a woman was casually garrotted, then as a man was beaten and butchered with a sledgehammer until he looked like nothing more than blood and bone pulped. In the Englishman's mind, he understood that these images were real, that somehow he was picking up, tuning into if you will, on some kind of sick evil broadcast, and in his fractionally improved mind as he watched image after image fade in and then out he began to ask himself Who? Who was it that was doing these terrible deeds to one person after another, after another? 'Sending out such pervasive fear-inducing horror, Jack, and why? Yeah, you know the answer to that one Long John,' so said the Caffee's voice that had most recently taken up residence inside his head.

Actually, he thought to himself Jack believed he was beginning to figure things out, and far more clearly than he might have wished. When he had run and the assault ceased Jack had begun to reconstruct what had happened, if not exactly why. And as the memories flooded back once more he dropped onto both knees and appeared vomited on the wet coat that he had been carrying since removing it some time before. As he crouched there his stomach griping and retching a voice in his mind enquired, 'Exactly how long before though, Jack.' He was just climbing to his feet, still feeling more than a little nauseous when a strong pair of hands grabbed him under the armpits and lifted him up and onto the balls of his feet. 'Whoa you OK there, fellah?' said a male voice. Jack turned and saw an ageing man. He guessed instantly at seventy or more but not with any assuredness. He had always been poor at identifying age. The guy was definitely wrinkled and had a marked lack of hair and florid red skin that might have implied ill health, evident to Jack even in the underpass's dim light, and yet he had been strong, easily able to lift the Englishman back to his feet.

'Thanks,' Jack replied rather dubiously. 'Yeah, I'm fine, just came over a bit sick is all.'

'What you doin down here?' the old man asked looking at Jack through a pair of round wire spectacles that were taped across the bridge. 'There's troopers out ya know,' the fellah continued disengaging his hands from Jack and then leaning in and peering at him closely.

'You got yer I.D.C pass?' he asked, and Jack began to wonder just exactly how lost he was, he didn't have a clue what the man was talking about.

'I'm sorry sir,' began Jack. 'I think I'm still a bit mixed up, where are we exactly?' he asked, 'And what troopers?'

'Look, fellah, I don't want no trouble. You ain't gonna be trouble, are you? This is building number nine, and I have to get back to my boiler room, I just came down here to check out on the noises I heard, and now I have seen you I figure my checking out's done. Anyways fella who were you talking to before, I heard their voices.' The old man stopped talking and turned back towards the small-lit doorway that he had entered through. Jack knew he was about to lose the old man to the boiler room, and so found himself right back at square one, do not pass go do not collect two hundred he thought, and he admitted to himself that he was still feeling pretty ropey, and so after a few seconds he shook himself down mentally and said. 'Listen sir my name is… Jack, Jack Gold.' The voices immediately cackled and said in his mind, 'Now, why'd you go and do that then.' Once more, it did sound alarmingly like the voice of Caffee speaking inside his head. He returned to the moment and heard himself saying, 'And I heard voices too. You know before, but I haven't seen anyone barring you, and I'm grateful for what you did. Now, without wishing to burden you, could I perhaps come inside and warm up, maybe just for a bit? It's mighty nasty outside.' He finished and pointed at his wet clothes and especially his filthy and sick-stained coat lying on the floor. The old man half turned and looked back as he shuffled towards the doorway, and Jack was convinced at that moment that he intended to say no, but instead after a moment he just grunted and nodded once, and Jack moved as quickly as he was able shot through the door and into the brightness beyond.

As it evolved and looked about this thing explored itself, tasted the different facets of its own being both from without and from within. At first cautiously, as this was how it had been designed to move forward in all things, and then with increasing relish. And after the passing of some time, it came to understand that if it wished it might win the mastery of a good portion of all things.

Chapter Fifteen
Hold on Tight

Jack awoke and instantly shouted as he opened his eyes and found himself face to face with a small stoat-like creature that snuffled around no more than two feet away from him, the wisps of the dream were immediately forgotten, and he groaned loudly as he tried to pull himself up to a sitting position and in doing so found muscles all over his body that were screeching their anger at the temerity of movement. The small fur-covered animal disappeared into the undergrowth quickly at his yell and Jack unable yet to quite force his muscles into a standing position settled for squatting on his haunches. The sun was up, and it was warm, and he figured it might have been as late as eight o'clock from its position in the sky. Silver had taken to not wearing a watch at some point in the past six months and at that moment could not exactly remember why, whether a decision or a circumstance nonetheless he felt grateful at least that the weather was warm and fine because he had… His thoughts froze as the previous day's events came flooding back to him. He was able to acknowledge that he felt a little calmer than he had been, but he shuddered nevertheless and saw again clearly a vision of Caffee, half of his head spread across that store's wooden floor. Suddenly the aching muscles were overcome, and he scrambled awkwardly down the bank to the fast-moving stream and drank his fill of icy cold water. He then proceeded to wash his face and hands before rolling up his jeans leg and wiping carefully at the wound that had got crusty and was scabbing over, it was a nasty-looking cut that ran forty or more centimetres up his left leg, and he winced with pain and stopped when after a minute or so the wound began to weep at his swiping and rubbing. Jack stood upright and urinated beside the stream being careful not to colour the water. Though felt himself more rational than he had been the previous night still he found he was at a loss to know precisely what to do next. He struggled to comprehend how devastated and responsible he felt at the death of

Caffee and guessed at the probable murder of the store assistant too, he was very lost and very alone and seemingly wherever he ran these people were able to find him. He doubted his courage, he had always believed himself a wizard of Oz lion, and after the previous day's events, he seriously doubted his own ability to carry on.

Nevertheless, somewhere below that angst, deep down inside of himself where maybe survival instinct lived he knew that carry on he must, even though to what end he could not know. Down there in the deeps, he had begun to believe that there were things at play not clear to him, beyond a man's reckoning. And, at that an example, floated to the surface of his thinking. He could think of no possible way that any man, whatever his network of connections could find him in the way that Cipher had, in fact, he doubted that the god damned FBI would've found him as often and as quickly as Stevan Cipher was managing to. Jack acknowledged to himself that he had seen plenty of weird shit during the past few weeks and having run all over the world perhaps he ought not to have been surprised at a couple of hoodlums turning up in some store in the back of beyond.

'But it doesn't make any sense,' he mumbled out loud and then debating internally considered once more that he did not believe he was leaving any kind of financial trail, genuinely thought he was inconspicuous enough to be nigh invisible. And yet they kept on finding him. Once more his mind slipped back to the coffee shop in Vegas, and he wondered yet again about the attack by the bartender. Down deep where the instincts did the navigating he felt rather more than knew that he was being followed, more ephemeral than physical. There had been moments during the last weeks especially when he could almost feel the tickle, the faintest brush of another mind reaching out to his own, crawling around the edges of his feelings and thoughts, casting a shadow of malice which now that he thought of it seemed to be growing imperceptibly day by day.

Jack saw all of this but struggled to apply logic or context to the various thought constructs his mind presented him with. More curious than much of this to Silver was the small white pebble in his jeans front pocket, a stone which sometimes felt warm in a way that it ought not to, and furthermore a little heavier than such a small stone might have been. But most mysterious of all to Jack was the sense he had when held tight in his left hand as he squatted in the dirt by the crisp fast running cold Canadian stream…well, he just felt a little better.

As he pondered he had no clear idea where to go but felt an urge, or perhaps it was instinct, like a whisper in some deep recess of his mind, that told him to look for the sun and follow its passage across the sky, follow the sun, walk westwards, and as he had no idea whether this would prove good or ill and certainly no better plan he went with it, he followed those instincts.

At first, the going was fairly easy he was hungry but other than that the walking itself was not unpleasant. Jack found himself debating with the council of voices within his mind. The Englishman supposed everybody heard voices in their mind, but mostly he believed that he ignored them and gave the noise short shrift. 'Yep, you didn't listen,' one spoke up. He considered and realised that he had always told himself these were just a reworking of his own voice, his own opinions, his own thoughts but with occasional subtle variety of depth and perspective that maybe otherwise was not immediately obvious to him, but as he walked through fragrant pine forest Jack began to notice that the voices in his head were different, new. That part of his mind he considered to be him admonished him then, well it cannot be because this "voice" sounds different that would be stupid, the voice is in your head it can't sound like anything. No Jack mused as he walked on this was more some variation on a theme, a mental speaker that seemed to hold court, and that compelled with its own choices and reasons, and these all seemed to him outside of that essential "Jackness". And Silver was damned if the voice did not seem to become minute by minute more like his memories of Caffee speaking and that was what freaked him out the most as he pushed on through the wild outdoors.

He walked like that for three days, and for much of three nights, generally only sleeping in those dead hours late at night in the last dregs of darkness before dawn, panicked and wary, starving and weary of his constant companions. He was lucky that the night-times were clear, and the moon was moving towards full steadily lighting his path deep into the night as pine woodland steadily levelled out into sparse forest and then less steep ground that was full of early summer grasses with occasional colourful clutches of flowers that Jack didn't recognise. As the Englishman walked he thought, driven for the most part by the odd sense that he was boxed in by events, and despite the fact that during this period he encountered no other human being whatsoever. He still wanted to run and hide but in his isolation found himself wondering whether in fact this putting off of something inevitable might in the end just worsen whatever the climax to this whole thing might prove to be, the voice of Caffee reminded him often of his self-view that he had always been akin to the lion in, full of gruff and growl but lacking in simple hard to dig up the courage. And he thought of Caffee often and carried the guilt that if he had faced his pursuers head on then perhaps his friend Keith Kirkcaldy might still be alive.

More disconcerting though even than the recollections of Caffee and all that had occurred were the stormy dreams that chased down Jack Silver each night when sleep did finally manage to pull him back in. Dreams where he revisited time and again blood-soaked images of death and depravation, each time the Englishman returned to the same concrete underpass, spoke with the same old man and encountered the same vile imagery. And each time when he awoke the dream was quickly swept away from his consciousness leaving behind a growing gnawing doubt, a confidence-sapping shadow of other bigger things that apparently were beginning to happen just beyond the grasp of his mind.

Physically Jack was starting to suffer too, he found enough water to meet his needs, but he had no craft for the world he found himself in, and so the finding of food had for three days proven beyond his measure. He knew little of country ways and like most city dwellers found almost all of the things he encountered in the wild significantly unsettling. So far hunger pangs had not quite driven him to desperate measures, but he knew that time was against him. Jack found himself oftentimes walking pretty aimlessly and talking, or more properly debating, sometimes internally and other times quite vocal with that part of himself that had simply grown into Caffee. And throughout, his hand was thrust deep in his pocket where it clutched tight the small white stone. He did not understand how the stone somehow allowed him some measure of control over the roiling images that swept through his mind with ever greater force and rapidity, both the conscious and the unconscious. So as Jack Silver grew weaker by the day, even by the hour nevertheless somehow he also became more lucid, more in touch with the mental storm that was massing. Mentally he grew stronger in equal measure to his physical deterioration.

On the fourth night, the moon sat nine-tenths full in a clear star-strewn inky night sky, and as it reached its peak in that sky Jack found himself crushed by exhaustion, hunger and isolation beyond the point of continuing. The ground was now open and rolling grassland, the small hills had dwindled some way back and if Jack had only known such things the beginnings of crop plantations sat within a mile or so of where he found himself, but he didn't know, and he fell in a faint to the ground and drifted deeply into uncomfortable vivid dreaming.

Its own energies grew unchallenged and exponentially. Already it had peaked at a point beyond any other living entity in those latter days. But that was not its purpose, and it turned aside from that disinterested. After a period, the construct found something new. For the first time, the evolving creation tried on and tried out malice.

Chapter Sixteen
Strange Magic

The old man looked at Jack through the bleary and creased eyes of one who has been broken by his world and stays only because he is more afraid to go.

'Me names Albert, not that it matters much no more. Nuthin matters much no anymore, whole world's breaking down anyhow.' The elderly man continued to watch as Jack huddled down beside the thrumming boiler that cast out enough warmth to satisfy them both. The Englishman was confused, it seemed somehow he was a part of this world, yet something was wrong, some things were off, and it didn't quite fit him. It all seemed a bit like a coat that was too big, though at that moment he was not able to put his finger on exactly what that meant, but nothing felt quite right.

'What did you mean earlier about IDC and troopers? You may have guessed, but the truth is I'm not from hereabouts.' The old man gave a short laugh and after a second or two in reply, as much to himself as to his visitor, he said.

'Not from hereabouts, not from anywhere about seems more likely. If you don't have an identity card then the Shadowmen gonna reel you in like a carp. Ain't gonna matter to them where you came from.'

Jack snapped upright, as he both heard and in the same instant felt the term "Shadowmen" in his mind. It seemed to be vying with him in some other time and place. Somewhere, somehow he understood that these, Shadowmen were bad, and he knew equally well that they were very much trying to reel him in. With a nod towards the old man, Albert Silver draped his damp coat over a scorching hot iron pipe sticking out at right angles from the main boiler. The old man continued to watch him warily as Jack crouched down on his haunches, a series of audible clicks emanating from knees and ankles both.

'Ain't got no food juss tea,' said Albert which Jack accepted eagerly and with copious thanks. They sat and talked for a time, and he learned that Albert

Simpson was the janitor for building number nine. He had formerly been the same for buildings eight and seven though it seemed they had both fallen into disuse some time before. Albert's primary function as a janitor had been to ensure that the boilers kept working. Once upon a time as he told things his duties had been more widespread. But over the years, according to Albert, everything had changed. Elevators, doors and windows, lighting had slowly failed. Following the changes, he alluded to, well at first engineers came promptly, and for a time things ran like clockwork. But then came a time when engineers took a little longer to show up, or perhaps those engineers had no spares when they did turn up. And then steadily over months, and then years, the engineers changed, and the new ones became increasingly unable to fix problems. Instead, engineers showed up, and they just made, and then broke, promises to return. Until in the end those engineers and repairers simply just did not bother to show up at all. And so, when the phones had finally packed up there were simply many things that were beyond Albert's limited scope, and most had already broken down beyond his ability to repair anyway. And so maybe he was the last man in the telling, but then Albert too like all the other engineers began to not bother, with the long walk into the town proper in order to report breakdowns nobody would attend to.

He grew old and as the years passed his hair greyed and then began to fall out. It was long since the maintenance man Albert had given up on anyone ever showing up again. Albert Simpson barricaded himself into an ever-diminishing space and let the world carry on spinning without him.

And as that world decayed and drifted towards damnation Albert paid the price, like that of all of the people that remained in those later days. That cost it seemed had been to surrender control of his freedom. To let the barbaric into the world and into his mind. And when he gave up the fight as Jack was to discover his soul was passed over to the butchers.

Jack then knowing little of these things asked the old man why he stayed. Particularly having learned that almost no one lived any longer in that strange city of numbered tower blocks. Albert had just shrugged his shoulders looked down at his hands clasped tightly between his legs and told Jack, 'Ain't got nobody see. Not anymore, everyone's either gone or dead. Don't you see yet boy? The world's gone to hell in a handbasket since Cipher took it all fer himself.'

Jack looked up sharply. 'What did you say?'

'World's gone to hell in a handbasket,' Albert repeated quizzically.

'No-no, who. Who did you say just then?' Jack asked impatiently.

'Cipher, Stevan Cipher…'

'Don't go messin with an old man. Everyun knows who's boss.'

'He's in your head ever' bit as much as mine now, ain't he?' the old man replied tartly.

'And you're definitely running from them Shadowmen. I seen that in your eyes already.' Jack didn't reply immediately. Mentally, a huge chunk had just dropped into place like a great shelf of ice slipping noisily into the sea down the side of an iceberg. Silver understood intuitively this was not his world. No, perhaps that was not quite right, perhaps it was his world but not quite the same how, or when, or where he usually found himself.

Somehow he figured he had washed up in some other kind of parallel, or perhaps it was nothing quite so outlandish. Perhaps he had just fallen asleep like Rip van Winkle, awoken to a future from a nightmare. Or maybe they had got him, fed him a cocktail of drugs, and this was the far side. When Albert had mentioned Cipher Jack had, at an instinctive level, ratcheted the internal anxiety meter up a couple of notches. He reached into his pocket and caressed the Shaktar stone.

'How do you know that is what it is called?' a familiar voice asked in his head, Jack mentally shrugged. He felt unable to stay focused in this "Other World". Find somehow touching the small stone offered some easement.

If the place really was some kind of pseudo-warped reality he wondered how it was he could not simply grab and hold of images of his world, the real world, the one from which he had come.

Dorothy had clicked her heels three times to get back home, and she always knew what Kansas looked like. He recognised many everything was wrong, but he could not see and was unable to remember what should have been in its place instead.

'Don't try and cross the streams,' the familiar voice in Jack's head told him, and somehow, he thought instinctively he knew what the voice meant. This world and his world must not bleed into one another. His mind spoke up, suggested if that happened then both would be changed, and that would be bad. Jack Silver did not like change, no way siree. He smiled tightly and thought, Seems I'm somewhere where I don't belong. Now guess I best figure out why. Then perhaps how to Dorothy my way back home?

During his long minutes of mental conjecture, Albert had grown fidgety and so Jack turned to him and said, 'Oh, yeah, of course, I know Cipher and his Shadowmen. Like I said before, I'm not from around here. We do it a bit differently where I come from.' He figured he needed to keep Albert talking.

'So I heard voices earlier, just before you came. And before the other thing.' He offered then trailed off. Memories of the vile images stirred again despite the vale he had been able to draw by clutching the Shaktar stone, still held tightly in his hand. 'Shadowmen, it's gotta be,' Albert replied. 'See no one lives here no more cept me and the rats. And well, they mebbe boss the place them rats, but they don't talk much, Leastways not yet.'

Jack looked at Albert and thought perhaps those rats weren't quite the bosses of this little empire just yet, and that Albert Simpson knew them a little more intimately than he chose to let on. Jack wondered if he pried deeply enough whether he might find that rat casserole was a regular on the menu at Café Albert.

'These Shadowmen where will they be now?' Jack asked.

'I don't want to bring you into any kind of trouble on my account,' he added hoping this might help soften the pathway.

'Ayup, they'll be getting undercover as darkness comes. Most do, don't think you gotta worry bout them till mornin. You'll be wantin to stay I'm guessing. Juss the dogs and the deadens after nightfall. And you won't be wanting to play with them now…will you?'

At that, the Englishman considered how many blanks he still needed to fill in. His stomach turned sharply as he thought again about rats on the dinner menu, and by Christ, he felt hungry. But something told him the old fellah was right, and he absolutely did not want to be out after dark, with just "dogs and deaduns" for company. And so he enthusiastically accepted what he hoped was an invitation to stay, and sought to engage the old man by busily asking more questions as the world outside slunk into the darkest night.

Sometime later the older man, bored or perhaps looking to fulfil some private plan made his excuses. He gave Jack a nasty-smelling blanket, a finger wagging and a severe warning the boiler would go off at eleven.

The old man appeared oblivious to the complete lack of time-telling devices in the boiler room. Neither were there any on Jack's person let alone Alberts wrist. And so the old maintenance man took his leave and left. And as he walked away he looked more sprightly than at any time since Jack first encountered him.

The Englishman was in a fix. And as the night drew to its circadian fullness tiredness took him. It began to dawn on him that was not some storybook wizard of Oz. He was a long way from anything he recognised or understood. Worse even than being lost was the sense he had no plan, and so absolutely no idea what he would do next. Eventually, as midnight ticked unseen he slept…and after a time he woke, to screaming.

The small rock carried back and forth to many places within the growing expanse and tried to foresee every possibility. When the artefact felt forces abroad unanticipated it drove onwards swiftly investing a great part of itself in that carriage. Searching for one only amongst all the clamour.

Chapter Seventeen
So Fine

Jack opened his eyes suddenly and looked around in alarm. He felt disoriented and for a moment in that confusion could not understand why he was surrounded by a copse of conifer trees and long grass. I was in a building he thought but as the scream echoed and came again that thought faded like a morning mist caught in the first rays of the day's summer sunshine.

A scream came to his waking ears again, this time a little more distant. A child's scream Jack thought as full consciousness returned. What Jack really thought was "a human scream". Fading though then only moments after, like thunder as a storm eases into the distance.

Nevertheless, Jack said to himself, a scream usually meant danger. And after recent events, the Englishman was cautious in the extreme, and in no mood to give himself up easily. He stood up keeping close to the protection and covering the bough of the nearest tree provided. He had no idea which direction the sounds had come from, but as he scanned the horizon in all directions no further sounds availed his senses. In fact, he was aware of how still everything was. Neither a puff of breeze nor an insect chirping, nor the thrumming wings of a bird disturbed his senses.

After a brief time, he grew a little more confident and so stepped away from the tree that he might look about him, though acknowledging that he would become visible. As he did so at the same time he was preparing himself to run back towards the more wooded area from which he had earlier come, still nothing stirred.

Jack called out, 'Hey, hi...hello.' Then after a pause and more loudly, 'Hey, is anyone out there? Can I help you?'

Nothing, Jack had woken still bone weary, he was thirsty, and he was starved beyond any experience in his life to date. And to top it all he had been living on his frayed nerves for a long time. Perhaps that was why he found himself completely nonplussed and lacking any idea what to do next.

He stood where he was for several minutes and simply gazed out towards the horizon, first to the left, and then to the right as far as he could see. Voices in his head doubtfully debated what might be a good next move for him. After some time stood like that his hand strayed to his pocket and closed around the Shaktar stone. And as he did a clear thought sailed into his consciousness, like some galleon of old appearing through the fog which till that instant had been clouding his mind.

'You gotta move, Jack, or you're gonna die. You can't avoid the human race forever.' 'Oh, you paragon of virtue and right choices,' he considered drily.

Silver began to walk.

He wasn't aware of picking a direction, merely that he walked away from the more wooded areas and further into the grasslands. One foot in front of the other, slow and steady. The scream and rush of adrenaline that had awoken Jack faded and was soon replaced by dog tiredness born of hunger thirst and grief, mixed with nerves stretched taut for too long. If he could have stepped outside of himself and looked down what he would have seen would have shocked the formerly middle of the road safe and sensible Jack Silver.

This version of him resembled some latter street tramp that existed in every major town back in England right then. Shuffling slowly over the uneven ground, occasionally mumbling to himself, clothes crumpled, a man dirty and matted with bloody stains on both cloth and skin. But Jack saw none of this his whole world had become polarised, step then step then step then… Deep in the Englishman's mind, he was he was ruminating on how far he was able to go before just sitting the hell down and giving up, when all of a sudden he glimpsed something ahead in the long grass. Something which should not have been there.

Given the condition he was in it was no small feat for Jack to identify and recognise the small iPod for what it was. It was pink, a bright colour incongruous in the long spring green grass, but of more immediate concern was the small dark-skinned hand that lay unmoving across the gadget. Jack moved forward more quickly but still cautiously, in the same instant he swiped away the images crawling around the edges of his senses, of Caffee lying dead in a hardware store. All at once he stepped between the tall grasses that had effectively shielded the space between him and…

A young girl, no more than nine or ten Jack estimated, perhaps eleven; or maybe only eight he thought after another look. Christ he was shit at that sort of thing. The girl lay unconscious, or asleep, it was not immediately obvious to Silver, and almost certainly he figured she was the cause or at least the issuer of the earlier screams he had heard. Jack saw no one else around and having been brought up in a big city environment he immediately worried about the prospects of a strange man invading a young girl's space. But equally, he knew he could hardly leave her where she was, and she couldn't have got too far from people he figured, and so he was faced with yet another quandary. People would almost certainly mean food, shelter, and refreshment, but his mind told him with some aplomb that based on recent experience it would equally likely involve police, Shadow men, and the nightmare his life had become.

The girl stirred, and Jack looked down, his wayward thoughts disappearing in an instant. She had a nasty-looking cut on her face and some puffy bruising around her left eye he had not spotted before, but despite that the child was pretty. As she stirred into complete wakefulness and opened delicate cornflower blue eyes Jack thought to himself that she looked like an angel. In all his years, he had never even got close to having children, having always pretty much been a loner. Girlfriends sure but the C word, hell no, he hadn't minded a bit of occasional Saturday afternoon west-end shopping, but there were limits, and family had certainly been one of those limits. That was the old Jack Silver, the life that had been his, but he figured if fatherhood had ever grabbed at him then this coffee-skinned blue-eyed girl that looked unblinking up at him, would be exactly how he might have imagined it.

'Are you OK?' Jack asked carefully, crouching down onto his haunches in order to bring himself to her level.

'I think so, Mister Jack,' the girl replied, her voice high, clear, and ever so smooth. 'He tried to get me under his spell. I didn't want that, and… I fell down is all,' she continued, climbing up into a kneeling position and brushing herself down. Jack looked at her quite confused, once more not really understanding what she had said but half of him figuring that was the way with young children, and all the while the other half wary at being addressed as Mister Jack. He was not a parent and so guessed his translation skills might take a little longer.

'Did somebody try and hurt you?' Jack asked. In response, the girl reached out and placed her small and delicate hand into Jack's dirty and scabbed right hand. 'People always try to hurt people, you just have to learn not to let them,' she said and stood up, her hand tugging at Jack to do likewise. 'Will you take me home now please?' she asked in her best Sunday school voice. And Jack with no idea what else to do said that he would.

'I'm Molly,' the girl continued as they began to walk, Jack noting once again that he had made no choice of direction as they set off, he just followed the child's lead.

'I'm ten years old, and we're gonna be best friends, Mister Jack,' she said.

'Why do you call me Mister Jack?' Silver asked.

'Cos you are Mister Jack.' hen after a moments consideration, 'Aren't you?'

'Well, yes… I guess. In a way… I am,' Jack stammered a little taken aback by the girl's confident and direct approach. After all, he supposed if the truth was told he was the most likely Mister Jack within some miles. As they walked the Englishman looked sidelong at the youngster. Faded khaki dress and an only slightly newer looking pair of white high tops only sought to enhance the girls simple pretty features, as did her hair which was long and straight and pulled into a pony tail tied with a pale blue ribbon, that near as dammit matched her eyes. Molly bounded along as they walked, seemingly unperturbed by whatever had taken place earlier, but equally completely unwilling to discuss it with Jack. She remained impervious to his questions on that topic, and he figured that as the cuts and bruises did not appear to be bothering her perhaps the job of debriefing needed to be left to her parents, "or the police" a stern voice spoke up. Jack turned to other topics and found out that the girl lived on a farm.

He also discovered that they were in fact now close to many thousands of acres of wheat farming country. For reasons, which did not appear clear to Molly, but sounded like separation to Jack, she explained that she was "working" spring and summer on the farm with her aunt and uncle whilst her mom and dad, and she quoted her uncle at that point "resolved some issues". She explained to Jack that she had her own room in "the big house" and that as long as she was back by sundown each day and did her chores in the morning, then pretty much she had free rein.

Jack figured there would be hell to pay. As far as he could figure Molly seemed to have been absent throughout at least one night, they had been walking for some time already with no sign of getting to wherever they were going yet, and Jack nervously had to admit into his imagination roving search parties out combing the countryside for her. It appeared to him that as spring had turned to summer this feisty young girl so confident and certain of her place in the world had ventured further and further from her home from home, at which his stern mentor offered, 'Isn't that always the case with young children? It's us adults that slowly drain life's certainties away.' The Englishman guessed that in the end she had stepped a yard too far, and perhaps barring his timely arrival may have had a lucky escape. 'But from who, or what?' spoke up the Caffee voice surprisingly quiet up till then. 'Does that hurt?' Jack asked pointing at her face. 'No, it's fine,' and then after a moment, with no embarrassment or apparent forethought, she exclaimed, 'I'm a kid… We always get cuts and bruises. You should remember that.' She looked at Jack and smiled dazzlingly. He smiled back and deep inside him knew that she had been right before at the beginning. They were indeed going to be friends. As they walked Jack found himself telling Molly little snippets about the awkward situation he found himself in. Not discussing the meat and bones of it all of course but pointing out that he was trying to avoid people, and that overall, it might be best if when he got her back to the farm or somewhere approximating that he just slip away. Molly seemed to take all that the Englishman said in her stride, unperturbed and unquestioning all of his vague assertions. She appeared wise beyond her young years and for the most part to look at him knowingly, and after listening patiently to his garbled recounting she merely responded.

'You'll stay in the barn. It's not time for you to go onwards yet.' Jack was perplexed but acknowledged that he felt a calmness around Molly that was beginning to insinuate and so calm his shredded nerves. They walked over springy yellow and green tufts of wild grass slowly. After a while, Molly began to talk of small things, sometimes naming small spring flowers or pointing out tracks that to Jack seemed all but invisible in the long spring grasses. At one point during their waling his stomach groaned loudly, and Molly chuckling asked him if he was hungry. Jack thought for a moment and realised that his hunger had completely vanished, well at least from his mind. Nonetheless within fifteen minutes she had bought them both to a short, stunted hedge from which small white flowers protruded, and there just on the other side sat a small red lunch box, like the earlier iPod, wholly incongruous in the pretty country setting.

Inside lay what appeared to Jack like a veritable feast, and much more he thought than any ten-year-old girl might consume at one sitting. Molly pulled out four wrapped sandwiches, the grease paper crunching with crisp invitation, an apple and a pear, a packet of salted crisps and a small box of raisins, plus the inevitable chocolate bar. Jack thought as she lay it all out on the ground upon two napkins that if he did not know better she had prepared this all for them both, and for precisely that moment. The feeling was exacerbated when he a moment later enquired about the lack of anything to drink and was greeted with the news that a small stream ran not a hundred feet distant.

Soon after they sat opposite one another, and both ate. Jack examined properly Molly's cuts and bruises and satisfied himself that there would be no permanent damage. He also enquired how she had got to know their surroundings so well in such a short term, according to her comments only one season on her aunt and uncle's farm, but the question seemed to fly over Molly's head who instead told Jack that they had "quite a long way still to walk". He was staggered that she had come so far from her home, but he continued to find himself becalmed in the face of her steadfast certainty. After a time, they walked again, and as they did Jack asked carefully who might be out and about looking for her. Molly didn't seem to understand this question either and when pressed just said that everything would be fine as long as she was back at the farm by sunset. Jack just shrugged, and so they continued their unusual trek through beautiful Canadian countryside watchful as it slowly began to give way to more arable land where they discovered occasional dykes and hedges and eventually even fences to navigate as the day drew on.

Late in the afternoon as far as Jack could tell they happened over a rise, and suddenly without warning there in front of them both lay a sprawling farmhouse with a mixture of outbuildings and two somewhat weary looking tractors all sat no more than an acre or so of what Jack took to be a fledgling wheat crop across from where they stood. It was the first manmade structure that Jack had seen since running from the hardware store, and he was immediately wary. Crouching down onto his haunches and tugging at his companion he noted in that first instant that there appeared to be no activity. Molly sensing his unease took his hand in hers and said, 'Don't worry, Mister Jack... They're all out working, never back before five... Come and see the barn you like it.' Jack didn't reply but wondered how she knew whether or when five o'clock was. She wore no watch, and the iPod he had found her with had lacked any charge whatsoever upon investigation. After a few moments, Jack allowed himself to be led down the slope, and after several more minutes of toiling around the edges of the closely knit crop they finally arrived in the dust bowl of a yard which stretched perhaps a hundred metres between a main house and two barns, one of which Molly then led Jack over to. The Englishman noticed that close to, the property that had seemed worn but somehow picture-perfect from atop the hill, upon closer inspection was quite a lot more than just worn, and in places in need of quite extensive repair. He felt oddly comforted that the owners of this place, presumably Molly's uncle and aunt were real working farmers with a real working farm, this seemed reflected by the "used" nature of everything that he saw around him, and somehow Jack figured that such people would be more reasonable to treat with than some other folk might be, when the time came.

Molly led him into the barn; it had no door to speak of; many of the timbers of what at one time had been a set of double doors were long since gone. Another red-painted tractor in greater disrepair than those in the yard sat inside the door and as dust motes hung still in slanting late afternoon sunbeams the barn was lit like some old-time chapel. Jack stood just inside the entrance, a little bewildered by the simple beauty of the rundown structure and then all of a sudden a quick darting movement towards the barn's dim rear caught his eye, followed moments later by a deep throaty growl. Suddenly, an animal grizzly with black fur leapt out, and in the same instant, Jack dived to his right pulling Molly down with him protectively. In his mind's eye, he saw and thought in that instant "WOLF", and so was amazed a second or two later when Molly, pulling herself free from his grasp laughed with delight and threw her arms around the creature's neck.

'No, no, Tully. This is Mister Jack. He's the one I told you about,' she spoke excitedly as she petted and hugged what turned out, at least to Jack's untrained eye to indeed be a wolf, but a trained one. He knew little about dogs and generally had liked them even less, but notwithstanding the dog in front of him was as much a wolf as he might ever have thought possible and would have given Shere-Khan a run for his money in a straight-out punch he felt sure. The creature now wagged its tail effusively and licked busily at Molly's face as she laughed and ruffled his fur. After a time, they both came too and Jack who had stood up again came forward at first gently and then more enthusiastically, and so they met one another proper. Molly explained patiently to Jack that Tully was her friend like he was, and Jack understood more clearly why her aunt and uncle worried little when Molly was abroad in the rolling lands about the farm. Apparently, Tully had usually gone with her and Jack saw visions of the two of them running and swimming and climbing and hiding out that somehow made him wistful for his own lost youth. 'Lost Jack Silver, where did you lose it then?' that inner voice asked him. And although Molly offered no explanation as to why the dog hadn't been with her when Jack had found her that same voice said to him 'She didn't want to frighten you off Jack.' He heard this and dismissed it in a moment, not yet ready to give himself over completely to the magicks of a ten-year-old child, however absorbing she had so quickly become.

Sometime later, Jack Silver found himself settled atop the barn, in a roof area still sound albeit little more than a machine storage loft. He heard rather than saw in that night's full dark Tully padding around in circles below as he too found his place to rest. Molly had proven as good as her word, both in satisfying her uncle as to her welfare as well as in keeping Jack's presence a secret, and incredibly just before night closed completely she had sneaked out with further supplies that included a hot tin mug of strong dark looking sweet tea, along with fresh bread and cured fish, all of which had seemed like manna from heaven to Jack. Guilt rose in him at the girl's complicity in his hiding and of her stealing from these good folk, but he pushed the feelings back down, wondering again at the roller coaster his life continued to be "more like a train wreck than a roller coaster buddy". Caffee piped up. But he consoled himself with the fact that he no longer had the slightest clue what else he might do.

And so as Molly left him, snug and secure with his protector below, for that was how he certainly felt, Jack drifted into sleep and thought astonishedly that the day had turned out to be the best that he had had in a long while…

It found hate…exactly as it was supposed to do.

Chapter Eighteen
Night in the City

Jack Silver was uneasy, he had awoken minutes before shivering with the heat all gone, the boilers stood down as Albert had promised, and so he had looked around distastefully at the room "cage" he found himself in. The old man had not returned, and whilst this had not surprised Jack he realised, nevertheless he had awoken partly because of concerns that were surfacing about the man's intentions. Something about the old bastard wasn't right thought the Englishman as a nasty little cackle went off like machine gun fire inside his head.

Jack Silver had heeded the old man's warning, and he had no doubts that to be abroad on the streets would most certainly not be in his interests, and might very well lead to his undoing, but increasingly he realised so might remaining right where he was. He needed information if he was going to survive, and for that he needed to move away from this buildings boiler room.

The decision taken Jack gathered up his meagre belongings and drew the long coat close around him, whilst still filthy it had at least dried earlier in the evening to a cardboard-like consistency on the room's heating pipes, Jack reflected on small mercies as he set off.

He followed the direction that he had seen the old fellow take, initially down a small poorly lit corridor almost exactly opposite the entry point they had come through earlier from the underground garage. No corridors led off from the main walkway and again Jack was pleased that he did not yet have to make any decisive choice. Up two flights of litter-strewn stairs, I must be at ground level now Jack considered, but as yet no windows just rubbish piled up in every corner, everything was dust-covered and appeared long undisturbed all around him, his footfalls echoed loudly, or so it seemed in that closed in the concrete stairwell. The Englishman wondered if Albert had in fact access to some other exit, one that somehow he had missed in the poor light. At the top of the second set of stairs, the electric light bulb was gone, and so it was that Jack was upon it before he realised there was a door that stood closed directly in front of him. Now a choice Jack thought, and carefully by god. 'Paranoia will be your bedfellow from here on in if you want a long life,' said the Caffee voice energetically. Silver put one ear up close to the door and in the same movement lay his hand flat against the cold laminate, and so both listened and felt…

Nothing he thought after a few seconds, but then he stayed there, motionless for at least a minute longer. Eventually and slowly, every sense extended out to its maximum, sweat pouring from all corners despite the night's cold, Jack reached for and grasped at the door handle, moving infinitesimally slowly. 'I'll just run back,' he told himself, and every part of him felt tense, his innards coiled like a spring on the verge of dynamic release, though for what exactly he didn't know.

'Ah fuck, it'll be locked anyway,' he mumbled twisting at the door handle and aware immediately that he had been wrong as it clicked once, and the door began to swing open.

'No need for locks in Cipher's new world. He's unlocked all the doors already,' a new unrecognised voice spoke up inside his head. Now, for it, he thought letting the door swing open inwards into the room and remembering in that moment the old adage *Fire doors push out.* Which he reflected later saved his life about two minutes after the odd thought came to him.

The room appeared dark, the tiny glow from the receding light of the stairwell now behind him and disappearing in an instant as the door swung shut silently. Something about that door scratched at the recesses of Jack's mind bothering him but not resolving into clear thought, but as his eyes grew quickly used to the gloom he realised that in fact the room was lit, albeit dimly, up ahead and to his left was a window, and through it even from where he stood ten metres distant he could make out the light of distant stars in a clear night sky and thoughts about the door receded. 'Well, at least the storm has passed,' he said to himself, at which point a number of things happened at almost exactly the same instant.

The Englishman had stepped a couple of meters into the room as the door had swung shut, and all of a sudden from behind him he heard a shuffling sound, an awful inhuman scraping noise that sent his shredded nerves back into overdrive, in the same moment he became aware that the room stank and his senses placed the smell, or an approximation at least, sweet and yet putrid, "rotting meat"…he thought in alarm, the gag reflex pushing at his oesophagus, by then he was already stepping blindly away from the noise and so further into the room proper, and in the next second like a train pulling in arrived the thought about what had nagged at him, about that door. It had opened silently, in this place of refuse and disuse, shit and shinola, the damned door had opened. 'WITHOUT A SOUND,' Jack's mind, the whole mental assembly, suddenly screamed at him.

'It's in use. The fucking door is silent because someone or something comes through it, often, that's what keeps the fucking creaking away.' A trap Jack thought, as he did stumbling and banging on some hard fixture unseen on the floor, tripping he barked his shin painfully, and as he went down he let out an involuntary grunt, and as he sucked in air a curse. Pushing up from the ground a second later he felt before he saw the heavy killing blade that arced through the air, and that missed him by maybe two centimetres.

Instinctively Jack pushed himself back to his feet. In a blind panic, he was instantly scrabbling and driving across the floor. He heard a loud crash right behind him, and his mind knew that his attacker had swung again and missed. Jack had time to think that the room's darkness whilst drawing him in had saved his life then at least twice in the last ten seconds. He was heading low and fast towards the room's only light, the window, and as he scrabbled and pushed on wildly he had a fraction of a second to recognise the second exit. As it resolved into his night vision he saw a door, stood closed right beside the window.

Fire doors open outwards, he thought crazed and flying on adrenalin as he flew straight on crashing into and through the door just as something cold and clammy grasped at his leg. *Oh god in his fucking heaven, not like this*, he thought at the grasping touch, having no idea what that deathly contact had been, but the revulsion touched at something deep in his psyche. And in the same instant, he realised he was outside, and he ran on into the night a demented lunatic charging helter-skelter away from the asylum.

Had Jack Silver looked back he would have seen a pair of eyes, lit as it were from within, moments before the possessor of those eyes had reached for the Englishman and the two orbs had been filled with malice, sinister and intent upon deadly harm. But had he turned his head and looked back at those two eyes now as he moved away he would have spied them simply staring vacantly, and then after a moment or two longer they would be gone, like a match extinguished. Jack Silver did not look back, nor in that moment did he consider that had that door opened inward rather than out then he most assuredly would have fallen prey to the malevolent thing lying in wait. He ran, wildly, into the night, and into a scene from Mephistopheles's kingdom.

At last, it found the one despite being hidden within the entire clamour, it had been supposed to do. But it felt late time had run onward.

Chapter Nineteen
Confusion

Jack awoke early the next morning his clothes damp with the sweat of faded night-time dreams, but he was awake instantly drawn to consciousness by the sounds of laughter and industry. Carefully from his vantage point atop the disused barn the Englishman, rubbing sleep from his eyes, looked on as Molly, Tully, and who he guessed must have been her uncle, plus an additional two teenage boys, men Jack corrected himself feeling momentarily old, went about what he took to be preparation for a farm days work.

Of the two youngsters, one was an exceptionally tall and thin black-skinned lad, basketball stature thought Jack to himself, and arriving with him into the farmyard on a noisy exhaust popping and incredibly beat-up motorcycle, the opposite of that tall farm hand in the form of a stout pasty-faced lad of perhaps nineteen or twenty, the bike's rider a mirror of opposites to his passenger.

Jack watched as chaos resolved itself into order under the barked instructions of the older man, who was indeed Molly's uncle as Jack later confirmed, he had no idea that in that space a pattern was beginning which would resolve itself into a period where he would be able to recoup some part of himself lost in the long chase.

During the next few days, he watched from his eyrie; the chores seemed to take around an hour, eventually culminating each morning in the Uncle, "Isaiah" Jack later learned, leaving that yard with Chad and Stan in tow. Jack never did quite get it clear who was who, let alone what rural tasks awaited them out in the hundreds of arable growing acres wrapped all around. And each day the three did not return until so close to sundown that the moon lit their path back as much as the fading sun. Same story every evening, seven days out of seven.

The English urbanite Jack Silver learned quickly that life on a farm was no picnic for these people. He also learned that Molly's aunt, "Missy" who had not appeared that first morning, generally remained in the house and invisible until around seven thirty at least forty minutes after the three men had left for the day. And so, another pattern would prevail. This time, she drove off in a small badly dented Nissan a few minutes after eight each morning Monday to Friday, and again on a Sunday though a half hour later dressed in her finest she would take Molly and make that same journey into town but for prayer rather than work.

These were good god-fearing people Jack learned and Missy's job as a library assistant took her to the same place as each Sunday's worshipful Thanksgiving. A small church hall with a district library was built onto the side in the equally small watering hole that was called *Pullet* a hamlet that was about five miles due west of the main farmhouse. Each morning Jack waited until all this activity had passed and then cautiously, like a ferret emerging blinking into daylight, he would step out and wash himself with icy cold water from the hand pump that fed directly from a well to one side of the yard.

Molly bought food and Tully, and an eternal optimistic spirit of adventure that on most days took them far abroad from the farm, she running and climbing with the hound in two, Jack walking, and both talking and with laughter, it seemed without end. So was growing a burgeoning friendship between them that quickly took on, for Jack at least, an almost worshipful quality. The Englishman learned early on that in Canada school summer recess was a long-drawn-out affair spread over ten weeks and as he had encountered Molly only three weeks into that break time appeared on their side. He thought back to his own four- or five-week childhood school breaks, a time which, after the death of his father, he had despised. Jack recalled being left, the unwanted wretch at the orphanage, the same deal for three years. And then as he grew older and more independent instead of wandering the streets pockets empty of anything resembling cash, pushed around various foster homes, so much for his older years he considered.

Jack was an urban rat and had never understood quite how fantastic "*clean*" living might be. As the adolescent had grown into his adult life he had eschewed modern technologies, calling himself out as a rebel for avoiding owning the burgeoning new mobile technologies, barely using e-mail or even text messaging. The truth he admitted was that he had seen these devices as a bright light upon his low popularity rating. But here he watched and learned from a ten-year-old girl about the simple pleasures of being alive, you didn't need the tech, you didn't need the people, you just needed to get out there and live. Day after day, he awoke and thought, *Wow*. Out there on that farm, with Molly's boundless energy, her dog, a walking stick and a whole world to explore Jack learned over and again how the place in which he had lived both internally and in the city, all of his life, was somehow just a shadow kingdom to this oh so much more real world. His life he decided had lacked reality, had been another fool's errand blinded by the constant reminder to be a useful provider to the wider society, when in fact he had merely sold sand to bloody Arabs.

All those things he had held up to the light as "the important things in my life".

The glitzy bars and clubs, the lightweight romances doomed to failure and sat comfortably alongside cheap sex. The TV, the pornography and the mortgage payments. And his pride and joy, a bloody lifeless hunk of metal, his Mazda RX7 sports car forgotten for so many months now.

He understood that life had been a prison, a modern society prison that he had walked into like a smiling idiot.

And whilst the city he called home was well decked out with glitzy curtains and coloured lights for sure, it was a prison, nonetheless. And the more he thought about it the more he concluded that that life was an ethereal unreal thing, that the connection between the external and the internal had got turned around, too much attention to the outside nowhere near enough to his internal landscape.

As he looked out from his eyrie, in a strange contradiction, like some latter-day Ann Frank, he became increasingly certain that the previous world would henceforward only be other people's prison sentence, no longer his, that was his epiphany, or so he thought during those long hot summer days.

And as his love for Molly, and for her clean and simple life grew, down in the deeps of his heart, so it became easier for Jack to stay in that place, to deceive himself, and to simply hide away from the terror and horror combined.

He began to tell himself, that he had come this far precisely in order to find someplace in which to hole up and hide away, he was running for his life, and this farm had been put there, a final reward, the perfect place at the right time Jack figured, until the eye of Stevan Cipher, and the stamping boots of his men passed by and moved far far away.

Molly was a balm, like something from a fable or fairy tale.

Jack learned that her life though had been through change, also was different from the life she had previously had, but she referred to that life and to her parents very little, artfully avoiding the Englishman's enquiries and dwelling each day instead of the small doings of field and farm, brook and tree.

Jack learned many things, from gathering honey from bees to river fishing, climbing trees to drinking nettle milk. He was amazed and wondered often at how this knowledge had come to a ten-year-old girl who floated around like some wood elf of the countryside. Gliding over, under and through all of that domain at each coming day's whimsical request.

In all twenty-three days passed, and never once during that time did Jack hear or even sense any foreboding, any looming danger.

Each day the weather proved to be fine, the food and passage of time simple, and the companionship wonderful and calming. Helping, though he did not realise it, to get Jack at least past if not at peace the brutal murder of his friend Caffee.

Caffee's voice still spoke occasionally to him inside his mind, although less often in that period, instead, it seemed Caffee and the remainder of his council of the wise were content to leave Jack Silver to the ministrations of Molly St Etienne. Hours turned to days, and days to weeks, and Jack got better, physically stronger, and spiritually back to a place where he felt in control.

Eventually, a time came when much recovered Jack Silver began to question what he must do next. And at that enquiry confusion and doubt returned immediately. Jack just like during his long walk through the Canadian forests found himself bewildered, wondering how he might bring an end to the bad that pursued him and release him to the goodness he now understood awaited. He felt more able to cope than during those dark days before, but at the same time, the good life that surrounded him gave him something to shoot at in a way not previously envisioned.

Over a few days with dawning awareness, he began to look about him, and he realised with some initial shock that whilst he had felt at peace he had lost sight completely of the fact that he had no right to burden these people, not any longer, probably never ought to have at all, even should his previous torment have garnered him some forgiveness for the risk he placed upon them.

He now understood that though he, rather than Molly, had in fact been the victim when first they had met, he was sufficiently recovered now. It was time to move on.

Time to face his destiny without further ado.

Jack lay in the loft of the broken-down barn, it was a hot summer night, and he looked out on a clear moonless ink-black sky pierced by many thousands of bright white pinpricks of light, the universe lit his thoughts. Below him Tully stirred and growled quietly at the back of his throat, perhaps hearing, or at least dreaming, of some wild creature beyond the range of Silver's senses.

Jack sat looking out and wondered at all that had happened, and at the strong tug he felt as he told himself over and again that it was time to go, time to tell Molly.

'Thanks, but I have to go and face the world again.'

He knew it would prove a difficult thing to do, but he knew also that he would not this time sneak away in the night like a thief.

'That's your problem, Jack,' he told himself. He had sneaked out of a restaurant all those months ago. Sneaked away from telling his date.

'Sorry, ma'am, this isn't working for me.' He had sneaked away from a murder, too avoidant to walk into a police station, 'Where had that got him?'

Jack understood that he had been running away for his whole life, and that hadn't really worked out.

Here though, in this place, he had grown to love Molly St Etienne with her assured self-belief, her confidence in simplistic fate, so unlike his own battered belief system.

Jack considered that the young girl appeared to have no voices in her head, nothing contrary, filling her with doubt and delusion. To him, she appeared always clear about who she was…who he was, and where everything was heading, a powerful mix beyond his imagining.

Looking back Jack thought that since that first day, Molly had never once referred to the moment they had met, or what might have taken place prior to that meeting.

Jack had wanted to question her further but the easy "people-free" routine that they had settled quickly into had so suited his needs, the pattern of his recuperation, that as days passed it got easier simply to shelve questions and replace them with living.

He considered then though, in the dark, that he had shelved his own responsibilities for long enough. The time to move on had arrived, and he determined to tell Molly. In the morning, he would tell her that he was going into Pullet to seek a greyhound or railroad or whatever else would be close enough to set him on his way and to figure out how with his dwindling supply of cash he might undertake the journey home.

He wondered if she would figure out his plans before he got around to spelling them out. Jack knew that it was cowardice, laziness on the part of his mind, but he adored Molly, and despite allowing her to be complicit in their strange and somewhat unreal deception he thought that in fact, their friendship had proven to be a good thing for them both.

In all the long summer days, the child had not spoken about another soul, appearing to have no friends in either this life or her previous life, barring the dog Tully. The Englishman believed she had benefited from his companionship too, although he admitted to himself he knew little enough about the ways of ten-year-old girls, well children at all in fact.

Eventually, as night grew towards glistening dawn, he fell into a restless sleep, and dreams of another world, and the council of voices inside his mind settled down and waited for the time for truth.

The next day dawned extremely hot and close, Jack figured a temperature in the upper seventies by the time that the farm had emptied. As he doused himself and drank from the still chilly well water Molly skipped across the yard to him with Tully, tail wagging, inevitably close behind. 'Hullo, Molly,' Jack said smiling.

'Hiya, I got us some apples for breakfast,' Molly replied with no preamble, handing over two buffed red and green apples.

As Jack bit into the first of them offering the other back to his young friend, Molly continued, 'I thought we could walk that way today,' pointing and looking at Jack inquisitively. Jack knew that Pullen was in the general direction that she had pointed, west, although he was unsure quite how far.

Once again, he felt undone by the girl's innate ability it seemed to read his thoughts. He just nodded his head and said through a mouthful of apples, 'Let me get my boots,' and then after a pause said, 'Some more of these apples would be great, for the walk.'

Less than an hour later they had set off, Molly as full of infectious enthusiasm as ever, in fact so much so that Jack managed to forget all about the conversation he had planned then for the next several hours as the three of them climbed fences and tramped steadily through more cultivated areas.

After some miles, the Englishman queried the cropped nature of the route they walked, and Molly admitted that after forty-five minutes, or so they had left the boundaries of her aunt and uncle's land, but she seemed confident that the cultivated fields they walked through were unlikely to lead to any troubling encounter with other folk. In fact, Molley suggested that as these crops were early in their season they needed sunshine and water to grow, and little else besides. Jack had got used to the young girl's wealth of good sense, her wisdom had generally proven beyond reproach, and so he simply walked relaxed on a scorching summer sunshine day with little troubling his conscious mind.

It was maybe one o'clock if the sun was a guide when Molly suddenly said 'Look you can see Aunt Missy's car.' 'Where?' said Jack looking towards where Molly pointed suddenly upgrading his alert status.

'There, tucked between the tree and the end of the hedge,' Molly replied.

The Englishman looked, and though he did not spot the battered Nissan immediately he did see that from their perch they peered down onto a small and tidy community that was nestled in a gentle downslope between fractured fields of pale green and gold. The sky shone the brightest blue and as he looked out and downwards from their vantage point, at a wooden church steeple in the centre of a huddle of white-painted buildings, he thought how fantastically pretty the whole scene looked. And then a word from Caffee, 'Pretty and safe Jack heh, remember last time,' and then for god measure.

'Be careful.'

Jack though in truth needed little warning, and furthermore he had no intention of walking into that village however picturesque it might look in the golden summer sun, not just then at any rate.

Nevertheless, he peered keenly around the community in order to spot and mark shapes, and to note them upon the general horizon in order to allow him the best opportunity to return later that night under cover of darkness. 'Molly could we find somewhere quiet and go sit and talk,' Jack spoke up. 'Sure fire, Mister Jack,' she replied the sunshine expression on her face darkening just a fraction. They walked over to a copse of trees away from the picture-perfect village, and so out of sight of any possible passers-by. Both sat down and simultaneously bit into two more of the apples that Molly had begun their day with. 'What's up doc?' she said grinning.

'Did you want the last apple?' and then with barely a pause.

'Do you like Pullen?'

'Yes, Pullen is very pretty, Molly. It's…well, it's just how I imagined it would be,' the man replied carefully.

'I'm glad we came here today, and now, you can have the last apple. I wanted us to have a bit of talk if that's OK. I've been thinking,' Jack Silver promptly trailed off. In a little under three weeks, this young French-Canadian child had stolen his heart, and in truth from the outset had seemed able to read his mind. 'You've been thinking that it's time for you to go, haven't you, Jack?'

For the first time, the child was using his first name properly. Jack looked at her for a long moment too wrapped up in the magick of the girl to question her natural insightfulness any longer.

'Yeah…you understand don't you that,' he stuttered. 'Well, that I'm not supposed to be here. Your life's here, Molly; you and I are different. You seem…' Another pause, 'Well, to fit this place, whereas, well, I guess I am finally starting to realise that I've been running away from my life, my whole life. There is a world I should inhabit, and I think it's time for me to go back, to stop running.' He looked steadily into Molly's eyes.

'Do you understand, kiddo? Am I making any sense?'

'Mister Jack,' Molly said standing up. 'I don't think it really matters whether I understand or not. I think you made up your mind already. But actually, I think I do know what you're telling me. You've decided to stop running away, haven't you?'

Molly had her hands on her hips, and her eyes blazed with an unknowable energy, and in that moment, she actually seemed many years beyond her age. To Jack Silver, the young girl appeared more like some wise old sage. Perhaps that might sit behind the throne and whisper to him, the recalcitrant ruler of the kingdom of his actions. He sat on the ground, and as his eyes looked at Molly his mind drifted and memories flooded in, an overwhelming cascade of memories sparked in him for the first time in many years.

His father ebbed away, in his mind he saw himself eleven years old, and yet as he sat among the small copse of trees and remembered, he was, in fact, viewing his parent through the world-weary cynical eyes of, well how many summers was it now? Thirty, forty, a thousand, he did not know anymore, and in truth that part barely registered. He saw himself like his father had been, right there at the end. Sat in a room alone, everything around white and esoteric; the bleeping machines fading to beyond hearing, his eleven-year-old legs swinging loose between chair and bland carpeted floor.

A nurse had left a television on for him and told him not to feel embarrassed. She had given him instructions that he should talk to his father because according to her he would still hear him.

Jack knew that was rubbish, he didn't hear anything anymore, not him. But then had he ever heard anything Jack said he wondered with bitter cynicism?

He did not hear the commentator talking over a rubbish South American soccer match, nor the bleeping of the various monitors he was hooked up to.

No, his father was busy; he was in death's waiting room, buying his ticket and counting down to departure.

His father was checking out, and was internal now, ensuring that everything was in order, shutting down the redundant bits and turning off the lights before he left.

And although an eleven-year-old Jack Silver could not free up his tongue to speak, to offer even a most paltry farewell to his father, somehow he did not think that the dying man would really care, not anymore.

He was busy, he had always been just a bit too busy, and even at eleven years and eleven days old Jack Silver had known that.

As he sat there remembering he wondered curiously, had he known that?

How many of those memories were nothing more than thoughts that he had placed carefully into those selected memories of his childhood like the advert said, 'How can you tell which one is real when they both have such a buttery taste?'

He did clearly remember being in the room right at the end, and yet he could not remember the actual moment when he had gone. Looking back, he did not know whether he had been there or not, and so how might he be so sure that his memory was any clearer near the end than it had appeared to be at the end?

The records testified that his father had lain dying a slow drug-induced death, in a hospital bed for seven long months. Those same records indicated that he'd been only 10 years old when the man he had called dada had been taken into that terrible hospital.

He had felt uncomfortable being there, he remembered that. He didn't want to bed there, and he didn't like that nobody felt sorry for him. 'Little orphan Jack,' a nasty voice spoke up perhaps from then, perhaps from now. He was an unwelcome intruder. But also, as he latterly remembered he had felt bored.

At the end there at the hospital he had been eleven, and at eleven life tended to roar at you to get on with it, and…he stopped, and his eyes widened as he thought back and clarity arrived with a bump.

He had known instinctively, in that way that children always do, that his father did not care whether he was there or not, not any longer.

He had known that he ought to have felt sad, thought he probably should have been crying. As he then recalled, he had not been crying and though he had felt a bit sad, he could not see clearly whether it was because his dad was going to leave him, or rather that he could see out of the single window and honestly, well it had been a sunny autumn day.

When he had arrived the boy was pretty sure that the tree that swayed gently in the afternoon breeze by the room window was a conker tree. To a boy of eleven that simply meant he might be missing a king conker, and when at eleven that's important stuff.

As he sat in the long grass on a Canadian summer's day and remembered it seemed to him that he had been in that room, and on his own, and he had existed like that forever.

Right next to the bed was a side cabinet, and though by then his father had slipped into a coma, a long, long sleep to an eleven-year-old, Jack had felt too guilty to reach up and drink any of his father's apple squash, though he had been really thirsty. No grown-ups had been in and checked on him for some time, and he did not suppose his dad would care.

Grown-ups' rules seemed stupid to him then, and Jack admitted to himself those rules and conventions, of the folk that had gone before, they still seemed stupid to him thirty-odd years later.

Mind you Jack reminded himself with a wistful smile, a year before the end and his dad would have clipped him round the back of the head if he had even thought to pick up an adult's drink without first asking, and so he had told himself that was why he had not taken a drink back there at the end, when he had been so thirsty, and so itchy to be anywhere else.

Nobody had come, and two goals had been scored in the really bad soccer match...

And so after what had seemed a long time the boy Jack had started to sing a song, mumbling the words to himself, but the song had developed and evolved as it rolled along.

'Two little boys had two little toys; each had a wooden horse...'

He had not known that he knew so many of the words, or that the song was usually sung by an Australian painter whose name was Rolf Harris, or even that the particular song had been a favourite of his father's many years before, or that it turned out the painter was a child abuser, Jack had known none of those things, but he had known the words.

An even more ancient memory came then. Jack's mom, who was dead now, had been carrying his brother, who was dead now also, his father laughing a lot, holding a young wife's hand, and a song about two brothers that had seemed quite right. A father is certain that his wife and he and their two boys were in it for the long haul.

Then of a sudden two were gone, and just Jack and his father, a pale shadow version of that man, no longer singing, no longer smiling, smelling of cigarettes and whisky, new additions to the sensory range of a boy alone in the months following the destruction of a family.

But the Jack Silver of now understood one thing that he knew he had not back then. When you are a child you have had no practice in life, so you do not have a frame of reference. The boy Jack was lonely and afraid but simply did not understand how devastatingly bad other people saw his child's life had become. Or indeed the sweeping and tragic rage that coursed like tides through his father in the months and years that followed, eventually to consume and take him also.

At eleven years old then, just three years on he had no more frame of reference for Rolf Harris's Two Little Boys than for the life taken from him, and so he sat there, and he sang quietly to himself, in his father's death room.

Jack guessed that at some point a nurse must have come in and rescued him as the memory lost colour. He guessed he knew his dad had loved him but somehow he had never been able to fight his way back from losing the remainder of his family. Jack had not been a demanding child. He could not have known back then that might in fact have been the only thing, which might have saved himself and his one remaining parent from slipping over the cliff's edge of tragedy.

And so his father had smoked and drunk and lost jobs and friends too scared or too angry to treat with him. And in the end, his father had contracted bowel cancer and eventually discovered the release he desperately sought.

So it was that Jack had become an orphan at eleven years, and as he remembered that day had for the most part found himself thinking about conkers and marbles, rather than orphanages and dying parents.

As Jack thought back he realised that what is important when you are eleven is mostly a matter of perspective. He looked at Molly who he loved. He knew that he would leave her, but he decided that was ok, his father had left him, and he had survived.

He did not know then that she might leave him first!

They walked back at a gentle pace that afternoon, the heat of the day slowed their pace and both of them dragged their feet, hanging out their remaining time together for as long as they possibly could.

They held hands as they walked, Tully sometimes wandering with them and other times charging off after some unseen challenge. Had they been spotted things would have looked strange indeed, but if any watcher had come close enough to hear them speaking, Molly admonishing Jack for shortcomings in his plans, Jack toiling in the afternoon sun with a smile interspersing short breathy replies, both of them laughing often…perhaps a little too often, an onlooker would have spied a caring parent and an energetic child.

Molly had found an additional supply of sweet summer apples, and so they munched, smiled, walked, and both tried desperately hard not to think about the fact that in a few hours, Jack was going to walk away from the barn where he had made his home, and most likely they would never see one another again.

That afternoon Molly had seemed to Jack as much like just a ten-year-old girl as he had ever seen her, little about her offered any insight into the magic and maturity that had appeared to swirl around her since first they had met.

There was much about the girl Jack did not understand, but he smiled inside and told himself that in the end, she was just a kid, a wonderful innocent kid, as yet untouched by the bitterness and pain life would eventually undoubtedly bring to her.

As he walked he found himself drifting from Molly to the self-pity he had become embroiled in for weeks before his arrival in the United States. Jack thought for a while about giving Molly the stone that he kept in his jeans front pocket, never yet mentioned, and quiet during their time together.

He did not have much to pass to her, and he felt deep in his heart that he would not see Molly again once he walked away from the disused barn that had been his home for the best part of three weeks now. The stone seemed to impart something, unseen, appeared to have something surrounding it that was perhaps similar if not the same as the magicks that he considered drifted around Molly St Etienne.

During the long dark nights in the barn, Jack had had much time to think on the unusualness of both the stone and his young friend, as well as coming to terms with the loss of Caffee Kirckaldy, who had also been young vibrant, and his friend.

Jack had not been able to figure out anything concrete, but it tugged away at him night after night that all of these encounters had a taint of something hidden, some secret in the fabric of events surrounding them. A thing which all of his mental prying had not yet allowed him any insight into. So many nights he had lain there clutching the Shaktar stone in his hand gazing out at the sea of white night-time stars spread across the backcloth of ink-black space.

He felt events hurtling to some unseen conclusion far away whilst he sat atop his broken-down timber throne and took a time out from the world. None of this had seemed necessarily wrong to him, but as time passed and each night drifted towards dawn, he found that he had to look away, to blank out those stars seething against the smooth black of the universe (omniverse), and so find solace in the simple cool white stone, worn smooth by who knew how many years of slow wear and tear, unseen and unnoticed.

Jack walked back hand in hand with a ten-year-old child who in three weeks had become more important to him than anyone he had known in his life. He thought that he wanted, in fact, needed, to give her something to remember him by.

'But no that's not right,' his mind told him, in a voice, no not a voice just a tone, indistinct and harsh. 'Nope, not to remember you by, to protect her with.'

Jack did not though attend to the harsh screeching warning that sat fractionally below his own more prosaic thoughts. And so instead after a melody of other thoughts he decided, rather than giving her the stone to alternately resolve to break with that self-sorry vision of never returning, and so instead to come back, in spite of the odds. The Englishman felt empowered by the thought, began to persuade himself that he would survive his encounter with Stevan Cipher, and so why would he not come back, we should he not build a life here? London held nothing for him now, in fact as he thought about things it never had.

He was no longer the person that had left that metropolis, and so as they walked he pushed back against the fear and the melancholy and promised himself he would return to this place, and to moment in time, and watch Molly grow.

Hell, that was so much more of a gift than a bloody magical stone Jack told himself as they wandered back to the farm in the sunshine.

Appointed to a programmed destiny the entity evolved to become a great engine of awesome destructive power, consuming and in turn spewing forth energies. Given an instant of two possibilities, without thought for the discarded choice that entity sent a tiny part of the whole outward seeking just one other being in all the universe.

Chapter Twenty
All Over the World

Jack ran from nightmare into nightmare. He didn't look, back but as he ran into the night what confronted him was a world like nothing he had ever known. And despite the close shave Silver forgot all that had happened only moments before in an instant and found himself quickly drawn into what he saw all around him.

Fires burned unchecked, the air stank of gasoline, and of other things more putrescent. No electric light burned anywhere as far as he could see, in fact, there was no evidence of any manmade power sources at all, and in that murky black shadows moved to and fro just beyond his sight, the night was lit by the lurid dancing light against the dark of the flames.

Deep wailing sounds assaulted the inky night, and were pierced by periodic screams, and less often but more ominous came occasional howls deep and filling Jack with a terrible dread as he ran on as hard as he could.

Despite the stench, Jack Silver was glad to be out of the stuffy building's interior, and as he ran, his footsteps lit just about by starlight and the sickly orange glow all around him, he breathed in deeply the icy cold night air, and felt the chill breeze blowing onto his bare skin.

A space appeared directly in front of him clearer ground than on either side, less fires, and covered with a thick layer of what appeared to be ash, a grey layer forming a skin atop a variety of unburned waste. The Englishman sensed more than saw the outline of what seemed like a road, bisecting the tall dark monoliths that reached up and touched the sky around him.

His pace slowed to a jog, he was by then a thousand meters from the exit he had stormed through three or four minutes before. His amygdala was calming and so simultaneously he began to believe he was perhaps then far enough away from his attacker. And whilst he had no intention of stopping and every intention to keep moving he trusted his instincts just enough to slow to a watchful walk, all the while staying out of reach of the darker hulking shadows formed by the tall buildings all about in that new night-time hell in which he found himself. Caffee whispered then, 'Yes, but when you stop Jack, what about when you stop?'

No time to think Jack answered in his head and strode on, trying as he might shut out the distant howling and other associated sounds of the night, trying to clamp down on his terror, all the while clutched tightly in his left hand single small white pebble, a thing he had no recollection of bringing into this place, a thing that felt hot and weighed heavy when perhaps such things should not have been possible.

Jack was trying hard not to think at all about what was and what was not possible in that place. It seemed to him that if he did that then he would pull up with a jolt, sit down and give up, only madness waited down that particular path he thought grimly.

Time passed, and Jack found himself moving down the dust-covered track between several towering blocks and heading towards the gap he had spied towards a more open area with fires less in number, Jack reflected there seemed less there left to burn.

By now, he had been moving for an hour, his pace slowing imperceptibly by the minute during the past quarter of that time. Finally reaching an open space, about an acre or so, covered by scratchy short grass and scrub weeds under his feet lying atop a covering of uneven ground, spying it the best vantage point he had yet discovered Jack Silver made the decision to stop.

He was winded and so came to a halt by a large lump of wood he spied lying in a patch of slightly longer grass. 'A weapon,' a voice whispered inside his head in the exact instant a howl set off somewhere in the near distance, guttural, wolflike.

The Englishman figured that now he was a little away from more built-up areas he might be safer from whoever the predators were, those that he imagined as the cause of the repeated noises that assaulted the night. Looking all about him in a three-hundred-and-sixty-degree arc, despite the dimness of the night, and hefting the large piece of hardwood in one hand he felt his heart rate begin to slow, just a fraction, and decided that if he could he needed to find his bearings. The Englishman understood he could not just keep running, he had arrived in this place from somewhere, somehow. And so, he determined to find some clue, some recollection as to his whereabouts, if not out there then somewhere within his mind.

If he could figure out where he had come from, well then maybe he could figure out where it was he was trying to get to.

'Hah,' he barked into the night all of a sudden, his voice sounding weak and reedy.

'I haven't got a damned clue.'

Everything felt wrong to him, it was as if reality was just out of alignment, and without that reality frame of reference he was struggling to nail down particular thoughts in his mind, barking expletives here, and there seemed somehow a route to some small sanity by which to anchor himself.

His shouts though died quickly on the cold night air.

He did though feel a little more confident with what had turned out to be a well-worn example of a teak table or perhaps chair leg in one hand he conceded. It seemed to fit just right, and he swung it back and forth like a batter walking to the plate. After another minute or so, his breathing continuing to slow he crouched down onto his haunches and then with some care replaced the now cool pebble into his front jeans pocket, lodging it deeply where it too seemed to fit just right.

Crouched to the ground he decided to work through what he did know one step at a time.

It seemed to him he had arrived in a big city, an urban concrete landscape, that much was reasonably clear. He felt rather than knew that there were people there about, albeit none that had evidenced themselves directly to him thus far. Fear and death permeated the atmosphere of the place but so did other sounds and other odours, and humankind was he believed an undeniable presence however well hidden. He conceded then that it felt most likely the majority were under cover of night through fear, it was a fairly awful place. Nevertheless, his senses suggested something else to him, he thought that the city felt emptier than a place that dense with high-rise housing ought.

He could not put his finger on those things, but it had become increasingly obvious to him that in that place his wits and his intuitions were the only things he had that might keep him alive, those and a rather sizeable chunk of hardwood.

'Aint much good in a gunfight,' the voice of Caffee offered somewhat forlornly.

He thought back to the attack he had endured earlier in the evening, and again he wondered at how everything appeared fractionally disjointed, marginally less right than it might have been.

'In my world,' the thought began, and that brought him up with a start...

'In my world, well, what bloody world is this then?'

He thought for a few moments and realised that he "knew" somehow. He acknowledged that he understood himself as an interloper in that place.

'Well, that's something new,' he considered. 'Now, I need to know why. And as importantly, how in hell do I get back to where I do belong?'

Another deep and wailing cry broke his thoughts and got him moving again. He stepped over the debris clutching tightly the teak table leg in his right hand. He moved further away from the tower blocks but could see in the night's gloom that more buildings squat and one or two stories lay directly ahead. After a minute or so of treading through soot and rubbish, with occasional unwelcome squelching sounds from further beneath Jack found what seemed to him unequivocal evidence that he was in fact in London, England.

He came across a street sign at waist height, covered in soot and fire burned, visible only dimly in the night-time gloom. The sign announced that he was in fact in Pedesloe Road, N6. Jack had no idea what or where Pedesloe Road was but the name, the style of the road sign, and the postcode he recognised. The sign was butted up close to the low brick wall of a long-terraced building that may once have formed part he considered of a chain of small shops. The whole place was burned out and sat menacing and eerily silent, windows broken, cracks spread like a network of spider webs through the brickwork and beyond. The street sign in itself of course offered no evidence as to when or how the building beyond had last been occupied.

Silver walked past the low wall through a hole not made for a gate, walked up and stepped through what appeared once to have been the entrance to one of those buildings, the first one he came to. Inside it was dim, but Jack thought to himself a little less so than it had seemed an hour or so earlier. Moments later, and the tread of his feet must have woken the night as he stepped noisily onto a mixture of glass masonry and rotting and burned timber, all of which cracked and snapped loudly in the silence. Jack hefted his wooden club again reassuring himself and peered deeper into the interior.

He saw nothing and was just proceeding to step backwards and so to leave, retracing the steps by which he had come in. His head was turned looking back over his shoulder, and so he almost didn't notice the smallest of movements from the farthest reaches at the back of the space.

But Jack did spot the movement, and in the moment suspiciously tightened his grip on the wooden table leg.

'C'mon then, you bastard,' he whispered.

'You can't surprise me now.' And after turning his attention fully back towards the dark recess, he hissed, 'Get the hell out here where I can see you.'As Jack spoke, he readied himself for the attack that he expected at any moment. He reflected a little nihilistically that he felt oddly pleased to have survived as long as he had, death having chased him out of the tower block. Silver had expected since then nothing but death all of this dark night; nevertheless, he had decided a while back that he wasn't going down without a struggle, and the movement whilst momentary had seemed a small thing, perhaps some feral creature rather than another hideous full-sized "Zombie" attacker, thanks Caffee he thought a little wildly. 'C'mon, you bastard. Cos sure as eggs are eggs you're coming outta there.' He growled his hackles up. A second or two later Jack heard a strange mewling sound, and he frowned. His rage and fear receded as suddenly as they had reared up, and a moment or two later again came the strange mewing cry. Jack realised in fact the sound was a sob, a human sob, and so crouching down a little he looked more closely into the darkest corner of the building's interior. Slowly as they grew used to the dimness it dawned on his eyes, and on his mind, that half buried in the soot and charred rubble crouched the figure of a person, a child.

And as Jack looked two eyes opened, cornflower blue and glistening a brilliant white, ignominious beyond belief in all the desolation that surrounded. The Englishman's demeanour changed instantly.

Relief and concern washed over him as he said.

'Heh, it's OK. I'm not going to hurt you, you can come on out.'

He held out his free hand and carefully placed the wooden table leg that he had brandished as a weapon only moments before down onto the ground.

Again he heard a sob.

'I won't hurt you I promise,' he said, his voice now gentle and soothing. And as he stared at the two disembodied eyes, the darkness slowly resolved into the figure of a child, maybe nine or ten years old. It was impossible for him to tell if the child was a boy or girl so black with soot and dirt were they, but a hand stretched out towards Jack's and as he closed his hand around that one outstretched hand, a memory triggered for just a fraction of a second in his mind.

The small warm hand in his took him away from that place, but only for the briefest instant. A sudden boom another instant later instantaneously seemed to fill the world, and the concussive noise brought him violently back. Jack ducked bringing his free hand up and over his head, though he did not let go of the child's hand with his other. The sound lasted for perhaps ten seconds, but so deep and powerful did it tear through the night that it seemed to him to last for far longer.

He guessed the sound was how he might imagine a missile explosion would sound and seeing as the surrounding area looked somewhat like the Beirut of a quarter of a century previously, well at least in Jack's world, it seemed to him a sickeningly reasonable assumption. After long seconds, he became aware that the sound had ceased, and in the moments after the follow-on reverberations died down.

He still had hold of the child's hand, and then looking down he saw eyes filled with terror. Jack held his arms out and gathered the shaking body of the child into a tight, and he hoped reassuring embrace. 'Don't be scared,' he said. 'We'll be OK now.' The Englishman had no sound reasoning for the statement, but Jack had found someone apparently far more vulnerable than he himself was in that nightmare place, and so for him at least the terrors of the night had to be tempered by the needs of this other new evolving dynamic. A voice spoke up, surprisingly strong from deep within the folds of Jack's mouldy coat and crossed arms.

'I'm hungry. Do you have any food?'

'I don't,' Jack replied after a moment's thought, believing from the voice he was probably addressing a boy.

'But I'm hungry too. Perhaps we can find some food together,' he replied and then said, 'What's your name? Mine's Jack.'

'Robbie,' the boy said tugging and disengaging himself from Jack's embrace but not letting go of his hand. 'I'm really hungry is all…and thirsty too.' And then after a second, he added, 'But they got all of the food, you never get none from them, no one ever gets none from them.'

Jack had no idea what the boy meant, but he seemed to know things that the Englishman figured he needed to learn. He stood looking down at him thinking for long seconds and then after a minute or so said as chirpily as he could manage.

'Perhaps we best get away from here first eh.' Then gently he led the boy out from his hiding place, noticing as they set off out of the derelict building and into the night that it was now getting perceptibly brighter. Jack Silver also noted that since the booming explosion all of the other screeching and wailing and night noises of earlier appeared to have stopped also.

Dawn was coming, and with-it Jack wondered what new reality might follow.

And the artefact rested for a time in the hands of the final carrier...but one.

Chapter Twenty-One
Telephone Line

Jack and Molly arrived back at the farm as the sun dipped into the early evening sky. Jack loitered until the sun went down fully and let Molly and Tully walk on ahead whilst he would sneak back in under the cover of darkness. He sat under a tree and fidgeted restlessly worrying about returning to the village, the one that they had visited that day. It would be tough during the darkness of full night, and where he might go from there was an open sore, an unanswered question.

He felt sure that Molly had been upset by the news that he intended to leave, and so suddenly, and she had said as much in her own child's manner, and yet with such mature expression she had added that she felt it was too soon, that somehow Jack Silver was not really ready for whatever was to come next.

So, Jack sat under a tree and tried to plan beyond that night's walk, all the while slapping at the summer greenfly that buzzed around his face. Hard as he tried he kept coming back to Molly, and as full darkness gathered around him doubts about all that he was doing began to creep in. He knew that the easy choice was to stay put.

Later that night under cover of saying good night to her beloved hound Molly had said she would return with a small pack of food and a water container. In his imagination, he saw her eyes lighting up at the news that in fact, Jack had decided to stay on for longer, that he had changed his mind. It would be that easy, and deep inside Jack felt that was precisely why it was both dangerous and ultimately wrong.

In his mind's eye, he held an image of both of the men that had killed the other friend that he had made on this continent, Caffee, and moreover a vision of those same bastards striding across the farm's dusty yard, double-barrelled shotgun in the hands of one of them. That image assailed him like déjà vu, and in that very second his mind was finally and irrevocably made up. He would set off tonight, and let the cards fall as they might, he couldn't bear to stay and in so doing make Molly or her aunt and uncle a possible target.

The child came as she had promised with food, and amazingly a small flask of coffee, he wondered how she managed such wonders. It was by then 8.30 in the evening, and the Englishman wondered yet again at the inventiveness of this young girl who had managed to secrete him like some latter-day Anne Frank these past weeks. She was a wondrous creature possibly the best person he had ever met he told himself.

There were many tears from them both at the farewell despite its brief and whispered nature. Jack found himself clinging to Molly who hugged him back equally fiercely, and for a time he felt certain that he would never be able to let her go.

In the end, though, a voice inside told him that it was time to go, and so he had let her go. Jack sent her back to the house, his voice hoarse.

She had walked away without looking back and Jack was almost glad that she hadn't, his broken heart clearly wrought on his face.

At the end there though, Jack had reinforced the message that he would come back, and Molly had turned to Jack and said, 'I know you will Jack, but you shouldn't.' That was the only time she had called him Jack rather than Mister Jack in all their time together, he hadn't noticed then, he did later.

An hour more and Jack was on his way. He had learned much during the past weeks and whilst he looked back on the farmhouse, now in darkness, with undoubted sadness, the opportunity to put his new orienteering skills to the test was a challenge in itself.

He felt somewhat more clear in his mind about what was to come than at any time since he had stood in the back alley behind a London eatery. If he was honest a part of him was excited to get going, he had decided to face his demons, and he wanted to get on with it, albeit he understood the what of not exactly how he would get to wherever he needed to go.

It felt a little strange to be alone again as he trudged steadily through the night.

The skies were clear and brightly lit and Jack covered at least a mile without incident, he stopped for a moment by a fence post, and resting on that post wondered at the stillness of the night and its unusual silence. He knew from the many walks with Molly that they were still on her in-law's land. He felt certain that when he had left the farm proper the usual range of night-time creatures, breeze-blown trees and other inexplicable clicks and chirrups had assailed his senses, certainly he had not been aware of the eerie silence earlier in the night that now seemed to pervade.

Jack Silver stood then leaning on a wooden fence post, and he listened into the night carefully, and in reply, he heard absolutely nothing. The night seemed to be holding its breath, and Jack began to wonder what for.

He was unarmed.

He had thought long and hard about whether he should seek to carry a knife or a bat or something similar if he could have got hold of one, but he was not when all was said and done a violent man. He had decided in the end that in all likelihood it would have caused him more harm than good should danger threaten.

After a few minutes, he began to walk again, still listening intently, feeling his heartbeat begin to thud in his chest, his footfall on the dry turf sounding off deep in his senses the silence that enveloped the night closed in.

Silver walked on, yet somehow the purpose he had felt when he set off seemed to be seeping away, swallowed up by the night's deathly quiet. Almost with each step, he became increasingly unsettled. At some point, absentmindedly, the Englishman reached into the pocket of his jeans and closed his hands around the small white stone, once again it felt warm to the touch, but unlike on previous occasions that warmth, that touch bought no respite from the feelings that were growing and beginning to churn internally.

He was about to speak out, to admonish himself out loud, for no reason other than to break the silence, but the words had not reached from mind to mouth when the night-time silence was torn wide open by a sharp and powerful crack, and a moment later another.

In spite of barely a second between the two sounds, Jack recognised them for what they were within an instant of the first report.

Gunshots he thought and had already wheeled around and begun running back towards the farm even before the second shot reached his ears. And as he ran, shouting Molly's name, Jack saw the folly in his departure, and desperation drove him to run like the wind back the way that he had come, struggling free of the small backpack he had carried without breaking stride, and praying that the desperate images that came unbidden to his mind were wrong.

This time he had no intention of running away, he hoped desperately that his ears were wrong, but really what he hoped was that Molly and her family were still alive, because he was certain that those shots had come from the direction of the farmhouse of Isaiah and Missy, and he was equally certain that Stevan Ciphers Stormtroopers were back.

He did the math in his head, leaping logs that lay in his path, barely slowing as he vaulted a low fence he had walked past not ten minutes previously. He thought he might have run then half of the way back, damn he thought why had he stopped wearing a watch. He wondered at how fast could he run in the dark, he wasn't an athlete, and he thought it would be a good few minutes, but he ran and ran, ignored the ragged breathing, pushed down the cursing and cajoling ignored the burning as his legs began to weary.

He heard no more gunshots, which he prayed was a good sign, and as he ran the Shaktar stone was clasped tightly in his right hand, burning hot, somehow imbuing him with some additional inner resolve. Not aid him physically, but it seemed to help him keep a clear head, a focus that allowed him to keep the emotions out and concentrate on what lay ahead.

He tripped on something hidden in the grass and staggered nearly losing his balance, his pace barely slowed, and he heard a hiss as he regained his full balance and charged on undaunted, a snake he thought, a sneaky fucking snake.

As he ran the hiss got him thinking about how he might approach the main farm, until that moment he guessed he would simply have charged in, but then as he ran on he began to think about what he knew.

'Got to be clever,' he told himself.

'Got to save their lives.'

'Be like the snake, slip in low and quiet.'

In the end, he came within sight of the farm within about six minutes and though that time felt interminably longer he was still in control and less out of breath than he feared as he slid up silently behind the barn.

He peered round the side and could see nothing out of the ordinary, and so he moved quietly down the dark side of the barn shadowed by the moon's bright rays, all the time watching unblinking for any movement either in the farmhouse or the yard out front.

He reached the end of the barn realising as he did that to get closer he was going to need to move across the baked dust of the yard, and that sprint would leave him outlined in the full glow of the night's bright moonlight.

That was when it clicked, bright light.

Two lights burned fiercely from within the farmhouse, one visible in the window of the room he knew was the kitchen and one that backlit the upper and lower windows that gave light to the building's main hallway and staircase.

He knew this despite until then never having entered the house.

And furthermore, he realised that it was all wrong, these people worked a farm, and in all his time hidden in the barn of Isaiah and Missy, they had always risen early and retired early. Farming life was seven days a week and three hundred and sixty-five days a year, and according to Molly this was the way of all farmers, two lights on at that time of night was out of step, impractical, and as realisation dawned on Jack Silver his nerves stepped up several notches.

He crouched down breathed slowly three or four times and forced himself to look at the yard and surroundings once more, slowly and carefully. He saw the old motorcycle that had been left there by the farm hands Chad and Stan by then over a week ago, remaining untouched where he remembered it to have been, right where the youngsters had left it. He saw the beaten-up old Nissan that Missy drove into town each day similarly in its regular space. As he watched the night darken, a cloud slid across the face of the moon, and without thinking Jack bolted immediately, scrabbling across the yard, none too quietly, praying that the moon stayed behind the stray cloud it had found for a few seconds at least. And more so praying he was not in someone's gun sites as the barrel rolled up behind the water well. He was then no more than twelve feet from the main farmhouse.

He risked a glance, low and fast around the well, and was rewarded at that moment with a shadowy movement across the downstairs hallway.

Nothing though was clear to him, the windows were covered with mosquito mesh netting, and so he remained uncertain as he darted back behind the shelter of the well. Somebody is moving around in the house he thought to himself, perhaps his mind retorted, and although it was barely midnight on the farm he understood that was the dead of night, as good as four a.m. in any other part of the country.

Any movement was without doubt out of character, his problem though was what to do.

Doubts began to set in, and he began then to wonder about the sounds he had heard.

What if they weren't gunshots?

What if they weren't connected to Isaiah and Missy's place at all?

What if he went charging into a house where he had never before been, awoke people he had never before met, and in so doing projected his mad paranoia onto others?

And worst of all, what effect might this entire disaster have on Molly?

What if somebody had just got up to use the bathroom?

'Christ,' he muttered to himself figuring he needed a sign.

The moon slid behind another cloud, and as Jack looked up he realised that the night was starting to cloud over, occasional sharp gusts of cold wind tugged at him, and he felt perspiration from the running drying cold on his face and hands. The weather was turning Jack thought absentmindedly.

He moved again hard, low and fast, running to the side of the house where he knew that there was only one window.

He needed to get a look inside he figured and that end of the house offered the most screening. As Jack Silver caught his breath, panting in short quick bursts he looked past the small copse of alders that grew amongst unkempt longer grass towards the front of the farmhouse, and for the first time got a clear view of the road that led up to the property.

Right there was the proof he had been looking for, and his heart hammered at the sight.

There parked askew across and just beyond the closed three bar gate, that stood as the property's boundary line on that side, was a jet-black sedan. It sat low to the gravel road like some fifties gangster car, and Jack Silver recognised it immediately.

He had seen one just like it weeks before, at least he had in his mind's eye, when he and Caffee had been running together. Though he could not have seen it approaching the house as he had through the yard to the rear, nonetheless there it was.

They were here, the Stormtroopers were here at Molly's house, the thought screamed inside his head and Jack Silver was suddenly very afraid.

A part of him wanted to charge into the house equal parts panic and desperation suggesting some illusion of heroism.

'Like in the movies,' a voice squealed on the verge of madness.

Smash the doors down and wrestle with the devil, fear or no fear. But deep down even in his wild panic he knew he wasn't the wrestle with the devil type. What mattered was saving Molly if he could, and her aunt and uncle too.

If that meant that Cipher or his goons got his hands on Jack, well then so be it, but he had no intentions of making it any easier than he had to.

He measured that he was about five meters from a doorway, a back entrance through a pantry Jack thought, although he wasn't sure. He moved forward carefully, sliding around the blistered wood panelling of the house like a skinny autumn breeze, whispering past with barely a sound. He thought he smelt something acrid in the air, blown his way on the night-time air, and as he sniffed the word "cordite" climbed up into his thoughts.

He tried the door, turning the ancient wood handle. It felt cold to the touch, his heart was hammering, and he was relieved when it did not screech. Instead turning once, and then with a single click, he opened the door inwards.

The interior was an order darker than the moonlit yard and Jack took a few seconds at the entrance to allow his eyes to adjust, flexing his hands into fists, trying to shake the headache that seemed to be building like a storm just behind his temples.

He wondered at the continued silence from within the house and quailed as he pictured all three family members lying dead on the floor. The vision was strong, and too much suddenly for Jack's imagination. As he stood there, in a hissed whisper, he said, 'No,' his voice coming out sounding to him flaky and panicky.

The mental image drove him onward when fear and determination could not, and so, head now pounding he stepped forward into the darkened house. It was quite probably the bravest thing he had ever done in his life to that moment, but the child, his friend, Molly was in that farmhouse, and she would not suffer the same fate as had befallen Caffee. God that had been less than a month before his mind offered unhelpfully.

The Englishman brushed against coats, work jackets, more of a closet than a pantry he thought, and saw ahead a modest increase in illumination, the windowed main hallway maybe six or seven meters in front of him. He shuffled along and all of a sudden, after so long a silence he heard a tiny sound, somewhere between a choked sob and a whimper.

It sounded bad to Jack not what he wanted to hear at all, but also, that sound indicated someone was alive, and that someone was close.

He crept to the end of the room decided to crouch in order to make himself a smaller target. And then after a moment, Shaktar stone back in his hand and burning white hot, he forced himself to peer round the corner.

There lying less than a meter from him, prostrate on the floor, covered in blood lay Tully.

He couldn't see where the dog had been wounded, but the amount of blood suggested that the dog had been shot, perhaps multiple times, and more, that the wounds were fatal. The Englishman saw no other movement, it didn't appear that Tully was aware of him at all, even when crouching low he reached out and gently stroked at the dog's flank. Tears pricked Silver's eyes as he understood the hound was wrapped now in a private battle to slow the life that ebbed away, a battle that the rasping short pants showed the animal was losing quickly.

Bastards, Jack thought, certain of course once more then that he had heard shots fired. He figured that Tully had collapsed onto the side where he had suffered gunshot wound, or wounds, and so he had no idea whether the dog had taken one or two rounds, but he was sure that he had heard two shots earlier, no more, and definitely no less.

Jack stood upright, his knees clicked with what seemed an unreasonably audible volume in the farmhouse silence, the only other sound remined the deteriorating wheezing of the slowly dying dog that Molly had loved beyond all others.

Jack realised something else then, if Tully was dying and Molly was not by his side then something very serious was standing in her way. She was a precocious and very smart girl. Panicking at the thought he almost called out her name.

It was moments later he heard voices; they came from upstairs. And though he could not hear the words, too far away, he heard distinctly two different voices and the voices appeared to be arguing.

The Englishman crept towards the bottom of the staircase looking about Molly's home somewhere that he had lived next to but never seen the inside of before that night. He was seeking something to grab hold of something to use as a makeshift weapon, anything. He saw nothing, just a heavy woollen jacket that Jack recognised as belonging to Isaiah hung from the banister post at the bottom of the staircase.

Jack noticed that though the hallway was carpeted, an ancient worn and green remnant, the edges of the hallway and indeed up the stairs for about a foot on either side the floor was still bared wood. Floor which had once long ago been painted white but was now an indistinct neutral shade.

Jack suddenly ducked as a door crashed into its frame on the first floor of the house followed instantly by a cry and a loud curse in a deep male voice with a London accent.

'You cunt,' he heard.

Jack Silver's hand had been reaching into Isaiah's coat pocket at that instant and as he ducked his hand closed around something small cold and hard, keeping low and close to the dingy painted edge nearest the wall of the main staircase he quickly moved up the stairs two at a time, heedless of danger, or sound, his mind clear as a bell one hand closed around the Shaktar stone burning hot, the other around the object he had grabbed in desperation from Molly's guardian's coat pocket only moments before.

He reached the landing about three seconds later noise was not at that moment an issue as a cacophony of sounds had broken out. Two men were shouting, and the shouts were followed by a series of repeated loud thuds. Jack looked around the moonlit landing. He saw four doors, three in a row, bedrooms he figured, and then a single door at the far end of the hallway which appeared to be the bathroom, all doors were closed.

It was not clear to Silver from which room the sounds had been coming. He had no time and so, before he could allow fear to seep into his thoughts, he slammed into the centre of three landing doors, the one closest to him.

He crashed through into a strange room, no carpet on the floor, merely dusty untouched floorboards. No furniture in the room barring only a small round dark wood table, with a small posy of flowers in a vase adorning it, and in front of that an old-fashioned finger dial telephone.

And as Jack skidded to a halt, realising that in his Russian roulette charge he had picked the wrong room, the phone began to ring…

The entity sought and found the one, and that one was to become its agent of purpose. Thereafter some small part sallied forth and became one with that agent, and far away that fraction of its being awoke to a different vista than it had ever before seen.

Chapter Twenty-Two
Secret Lives

The sun came up.

Jack did not notice it, the sky was thick with unbroken leaden grey cloud, but day dawned nevertheless and the scene before him was one of devastation.

Jack had learned some time back that the small underweight boy was Robbie Benedict, once of Wembley in London.

'Near the football ground, but I don't like football,' the boy told Jack straight off. The kid was twelve years old but even scruffy and covered in a good layer of the filth that smothered everything in that awful place Jack thought he looked undernourished and no more than nine or ten.

Silver learned a number of other things from the boy, not least that the shadowy creatures of the previous night, or "mentals" as Robbie had called them, apparently always disappeared during the daytime, sometime an hour or two after sun up.

'So not zombies then,' Jack said to himself.

'No...vampires!' a voice he called Caffee had replied in his mind.

The kid had no idea where the creatures of the night went during the day, where they came from at the outset of the night, but he had told Jack that as long as they were able to avoid the "killer cops" in the daylight hours then they would be all right.

'The days are better mistah,' he had announced unconvincingly.

Jack felt like he was learning things like an avid viewer of American T.V. soaps. The boy Robbie would change topic instantly, and so many of the things that Jack listened to came to him in fragments or in incomplete instalments, many never to be finished.

But the general picture was, as far as he could tell, that the world he had washed up in had gone to Hell in a hand basket. Perhaps as recently as a few weeks past. Seemingly from the boy's tale certainly no more than two months.

Frankly, Jack thought to himself, well he doubted that the young boy would have survived even that long.

At first the tale told of chaos taking the reins, and the boy early on had got separated from the grandparents that he lived with and so had found himself hiding out in the basement of a convenience store. He didn't offer many specifics about what had actually happened in the beginning, but he had said at one point rather chillingly when pressed.

'The bad men let a bomb, a terrible bomb off. Inside the grown-up's heads. The bomb exploded and everyone started to kill each other.'

Later in his disconnected way, the child had added, 'That bomb. It didn't go off in my head. It didn't go off in any of the children's heads.'

As far as Jack could understand whatever had occurred to the adults had not impacted the children, at least not in the same way. Silve wondered if that was all true how it was that Robbie knew so much about what had afflicted the people around him. It did seem to the Englishman that the boy had been fortunate, to have found himself hiding out in a convenience store, where it seemed he had stayed pretty much until the sweets and the fizzy drinks had run out.

As they walked it began to rain, small cold drizzle that did nothing to lift Jack's low spirits, he held the boys hand, and started to notice one or two other people moving about, always fleeting and always at a distance. Jack guessed that was how it was there, move low and fast, trust nobody, he truly was in a war zone.

With no real or particular direction to go in, Jack asked Robbie if he could find the place where he had hidden out before again. The boy answered affirmatively, and so they set off in a more easterly direction. Fairly soon they entered a more built-up sector. Jack guessed at one time this might have been a business district of the city, dressed with once smart office blocks of seven and eight floors. Though all of them now scorched and damaged, with broken windows and rent and twisted doors all around.

In several places, office furniture was strewn across the street, alongside computer terminals, derelict cars, and incongruous in this concrete edifice to humanity Jack saw, and turned away from, the rotting corpse of a horse.

In the instant, he spied it. Jack could see the beast had in life been a majestic example of its kind, but there, half eaten and with ribs showing through, the animal seemed even more tragic than the rest of the tableaux, and still everything was covered in that same layer of grey sooty dust that Jack had seen covering every inch of surface since he had arrived.

The boy still held the older man's hand, with fierce determination, and Jack was impressed that the malnourished kid kept up such a good pace. Within an hour they had travelled the best part of three miles, and Silver found himself walking through alien parts of an alien London that he admitted to himself he had never known, even before whatever had befallen the city.

He remembered watching a movie version of H.G. Wells's classic story *The War of the Worlds*. In particular, the part of the tale when everything became covered by some bizarre red vegetation, and he thought as he walked with the kid that this London was a little like that London. Though he corrected himself, except that instead of vivid glistening red here everything was a monotonous deadly dull grey. In that place, he figured in the mind of the author Mister Wells had been the red of an alien Martian vista, here Jack thought, well here the landscape just spoke of death.

No sound, barely anything moving, just Silver and the boy, crawling like ants across a wide grey carpet of death and destruction. And as they walked he wondered who out there was watching them.

By then, he had spotted a couple of dozen people. Every one of whom had kept their distance. And what he had seen of them suggested to Jack that all of them were equally malnourished, and furthermore most of them were young. He saw children, and he saw teenagers, perhaps fifteen or sixteen. And nobody seemed to pose any threat to either him or his charge, everybody darting panicky and afraid, moving from shadow to shadow.

In his free hand, he still kept a tight grip on the table leg he had picked up the previous night. His brain told him the people he saw were just the leftovers, the dregs at the bottom of the glass, the remaining few who were being drained away drip by drip, no threat to him, no threat to anybody, just waiting to die.

He wondered in this city, one he remembered once had a population of eight million people, where had all the people gone. If anyone else were left alive they were doing a bloody good job of hiding, and if they were dead, well where the hell did you put eight million corpses?

He pondered asking the kid but then decided that even if Robbie could furnish him with an answer that just wasn't the right question for one so young. Mostly then they walked on in silence hearing little and saying even less, conserving energy for climbing over the obstacles that they found themselves unable to walk around. And then suddenly after maybe four miles, and a lengthy period of silence, Robbie let go of Jack's hand and pointed.

'Over there,' he said. His finger was directed towards a ramshackle two-story building that stood low and squat, surrounded on either side by taller four-story properties.

It was more obvious than some Jack had seen that the place had once been a shop, not least because part of the original signage still clearly showed the letters "t o r e", an S in front was not a leap of faith. What Jack could not see right away was a way in. The place at first glance looked mostly like a huge pile of rubble.

'So how did you get in and out?' Jack asked.

'This way,' the kid responded, grabbing Jack's free hand again and heading towards a small indentation lower within the general rubble. Once there the Englishman realised that half buried in the bricks was a door. Though blistered and burned wood, it had once been painted a pleasant welcoming green. At first sight, the door simply appeared to be lying atop many thousands of broken bricks, bits of masonry, glass, timber and concrete. One in the pile of detritus just like everything else. So, Jack was surprised when the boy got a hold of the door and instead of trying to lift or push slid it easily round to the left and so opened up a hole about three feet by three feet, just big enough for someone to crawl in and out of.

The boy smiled and motioned Jack forward. 'Through here,' he said and proceeded to disappear into the dark entryway.

Jack was not entirely comfortable about crawling blindly into this space but convinced himself that the young boy appeared cheerful enough about crawling down the rabbit hole unchecked. And so with considerably more huffing and puffing he proceeded to slide down the angle of the dark hole head first, exactly as the boy had done, aal the while holding out the table leg in front of him like a baton.

In the end, the space was no more than seven or eight feet through before it opened out into the interior of a room, dim but not completely dark, about three and a half meters by four.

As Jack stood upright a dim electric light illuminated the darkness, and he saw that Robbie had switched on a small lamp, of a sort he didn't recognise but imagined might be something akin to a camping lamp. 'So, this is where you live then heh kid,' Jack said. 'Used to,' the boy replied suddenly sullen.

'You left. What when the food ran out, was that it?' Jack asked seeing that the boy's mood had changed sharply and wondering what in this hidey-hole might have caused that change.

'Yeah, when the food ran out,' the boy answered distractedly, unconvincingly. And then after a pause added, 'And when they started looking for me too. They can smell us you know, the metals. There used to be lots of people, enough to make it easy to hide at night, but then they caught them, a few here, a few there. Now there're only a few left. In the end, they come; they sniff you out,' he continued.

'So I ran; everybody runs, in the end.'

'I see,' Jack responded, seeing nothing at all. 'Well, let's see if there's any food left in here, shall we? What's through there?' he asked, walking through the one door visible in the small room. The Englishman looked around the space and realised from the plethora of wrappers on the floor, and the general detritus of cans and plastic bottles, that the boy had indeed eaten and drunk his way through everything he could lay his hands on in that Aladdin's cave. He guessed the place to have once been a newsagent or small convenience shop.

Jack had a theory upon hearing the boy's earlier tale, at the days beginning when first they encountered one another, and there and then it proved to be so. The child Robbie's definition of "run out of food" ran to the limit of that which could be seen by him, and that which could be easily got at, and got into. After a short period of scrabbling around, in what was evidently once the store's back room, fairly easily he found buried but unopened a hungry man's delight.

His treasure trove included tins of all day breakfast, dried almonds and apricots, and a dozen tins of long-life flavoured vitamin milk, covered in thick grey dust. It seemed to him amazing that this all lay about unfound, and untouched by the rats he heard chittering and crawling just outside the circle of light cast by the lamp. Best of all up on a metal dexion shelf still intact in one corner, complete with heavy plastic outer and cellophane sealing a box of one hundred and forty-four unopened bars of Bournville plain chocolate.

Jack whooped quietly to himself at this find, and in a short time, he had gouged openings in the milk concentrates and sat feasting with the boy Robbie on their find. Jack recalled the term "hangry" and looked on as the child's mood improved exponentially. After eating, the boy pulled up a small pile of dusty clothes, evidently once not too long past this had acted as his bed and so appetite replete the child promptly fell asleep.

'Well, I'll be damned,' Jack muttered to himself. Minutes later, he squatted down on the floor himself and decided this was an opportunity to take stock of the situation he now found himself in. He guessed it had been a day since he had found himself in this place. He knew he was in London, yet somehow this was any London that he had ever known.

First, there was the old man, at the beginning the fellow had seemed ok, but later, well later Jack realised the old boy had another agenda entirely.

Then in the night there had been another, someone or something, that had tried to kill him, tried and nearly succeeded.

Headlong flight through the night followed, and then as dawn broke Robbie.

Jack knew more now than he had twenty-four hours previously, and yet still he felt like he knew nothing, still, he was desperately short on the stuff that would see him out of the strange situation he was in.

'What happened to London?' he said to himself. 'And who did all of this?' he asked. His words were quiet so as not to wake the sleeping boy whose hand still reached out towards Jack. The voice of Caffee spoke in his mind and offered a sizeable question mark about the reality of that world Jack was inhabiting, but he told himself, however odd it felt entirely bloody real.

'What a fucking mess!' he whispered to himself.

And then about two seconds later all of a sudden he keeled over, his mind was assaulted for a second time in that place, attached by a movie reel series of appalling images of destitute agony and death. Silver was not prepared for this second subversive mind bomb. But he had been in the place for twenty-four hours, he was fed and somewhat rested, the images had visited him before, and most of all this time he put his right hand deep into his front jeans pocket and grabbed hold of the Shaktar stone. He landed awkwardly falling forward onto his knees but managing to miss hitting the boy. The imagery, the sounds and the metal scents revolted him every bit as much as they had before. Except this time he realised, with a considerable effort of will, he was able to force all of the filth that was assaulting him down. A supreme mental effort, one which seemed to him aided from without, allowed him to push the siren attack into one part of his mind, thus restricting the physical disgust and with it some at least of the overwhelming fear.

As a result of the supreme effort, the Englishman found himself able to retain a detached area within his mind, a place where the poisoned message could not seep in.

But this assault was different, the objective part of Jack's mind began to offer him. He watched as repeatedly the image of one man came to him, appearing like a signature upon a picture, an author's face on a dust jacket.

A slight man, indistinct with slightly receding mousy brown hair, a mediocre suit and a plain black tie. Jack Silver knew intuitively who the man was immediately. This was all the work of Stevan Cipher. And that part of his mind he had managed to fence off from the rigours of what he thought of as the filth bomb, bridged the gap, suddenly understood the link between two worlds, and so immediately the Englishman's unanswered questions and his unresolved fears grew exponentially. In his mind, he stared at Stevan Cipher, who stared elsewhere with cold dead fish eyes. The man appeared to stand motionless, in the centre of the carnage and clutched in one of his hands Jack saw was a woollen rag doll that ought to have belonged to a child. The doll had yellow straggles of hair that were poking out from between the man's delicate fingers. Jack felt that was significant but did not understand in the moment why. He wanted to articulate a scream, to roar at the vision in front of him.

'Enough.'

But nothing came out beyond a vague and virtually silent choke. And just as the vision reached a peak of clarity, so it was gone.

Clear of it Jack discovered he was on the ground, and he was leaning forwards on his knees. Amazingly the kid was still sleeping, lying wrapped in the pile of dirty coats he had dragged out earlier.

He wanted to wake him, to ask him what he might know of Cipher. To Jack all of a sudden, the boy's fears of "killer cops" and the like seemed somehow to perfectly line up with Silver's own encounters with the gangster Stevan Cipher's Storm troopers, albeit that had all been in some other world. He felt he might be able to pry crucial information from his young charge, but also wondered when the boy might last have felt safe enough to sleep, let alone as peacefully as he now was. And so the Englishman left him to his dreams, and he hoped that they were better than the images that danced among his own thoughts.

He sat down then crossed-legged on the ground, and thought to himself, perhaps, just perhaps, the secret was out.

He did not quite how he could exist in these two places at the same time, nor did they exist at all he supposed. But Jack saw in his understanding that somehow he and the man who had set himself as his nemesis were apparently a common factor in both places. Deep inside he felt a clear sense for the first time that the two were being inexorably drawn towards one another. Despite him struggling with all of his might, nonetheless in both worlds they drew close like magnets. It was crucial he learned all that he could if he wanted to survive the encounter.

Jack closed his eyes suddenly weary and somewhere at the back of his mind heard somebody answering a telephone.

The artefact could do no more, it had but one purpose, one instant of possibility, and that instant would depend on exacting attention to the passing of the moments. Henceforward there were just a few stitches in time's great cloth, woven down epochs beyond measure, and so attention would be required.

Chapter Twenty-Three
Ticket to the Moon

'Well, he ain't fucking here. You tell Mr Cipher his radar must've gone off the boil, yeah just some thick yokels. Yeah, farmers I think…course, we'll tidy em up.'

Jack heard the voice, angry, British with a sharp Scottish undertone. A second or two later he clearly recognised the sound of a receiver being banged back into its cradle.

Had he blacked out for a few seconds prior to that phone ringing?

He wasn't sure, but somehow the white fire of rage that had burned in him before, right up to the moment he had charged blindly through the door into this empty room seemed to have waned.

He decided he was thinking clearly but that did not help him to know what to do next. Somebody who wanted him was in the room next door, but crucially he could not tell whether Molly or her in-laws were in that room also. He crept across the room's bare floor and leaned an ear up against the dividing wall. He was able to discern what sounded like a quiet shuffling of feet. The sound suggested that the "telephone man" was now walking around the room, but Silver heard no evidence of other people.

He knew that once this man was aware of his presence he would not have much time. He might kill him, but he felt that it was more likely he would be looking to take him.

'Take us to your leader,' a voice like Caffee's spoke up in his mind, and despite everything, he smiled. His mind wouldn't budge and tell him over and over he was heading for an appointment with a certain Stevan Cipher, gangland overlord, and aggrieved sibling, and that was going to happen come what may.

But Jack Silver, who was now more in tune, accepting even of such an outcome wondered if in fact he was working towards some such himself. Despite that conjecture, he knew that then was not the moment to meekly hand himself over. There would be no trade-off with these psychopaths, especially once he had lost the leverage. And in addition to saving his friend, he now believed he needed to come to Cipher if that was an inevitability, in his own way, and at his own time.

The Englishman needed to manage an insane situation and so to achieve the best result possible figured he needed a plan.

'I need an imponderable,' Jack Silver told himself, and as he did, he opened his hand and looked at what he had grabbed in a blind panic from Isaiah's coat pocket. And as he looked down at his open palm he laughed quietly, and said, 'Well well…that'll up the ante.'

On the other side of a wall no more than three meters from where Jack stood in a bedroom furnished in what he would later think of as worn-out colonial lay a hunched body sat in front of a gaily covered pine bed and not quite matching faded pine dresser. The pale cream and blue of the double-bed coverlet was soaked with dark red blood and the body did not appear to be moving. The room's other occupant was pacing around the bed and then back again and appeared the cause of any remaining movement in the room. A brute of a figure, easily six feet four tall. Heavyset and dressed in a long charcoal overcoat and holding carelessly in his right hand a flashy-looking Colt 45 handgun the barrel dressed in polished chrome, a child's toy in the man's huge fist.

The man was scarred in the face, across the forehead and again down straight past his right eye trailing in a nest of crow's feet at the top of one cheek. Thunder was in the man's face, he had been told that he would find their quarry here in this shit hole, at the ass end of the world, tonight. And right then it looked like yet another fool's errand.

He and his two colleagues had driven a thousand miles through desert scrub and white trailer trash, one of them was waiting at some scrotal little nowhere town up the road.

He hated the whole damned continent, every meal he had eaten in America he had been greeted with, 'Have a nice day,' when he wasn't having a fucking nice day at all.

As far as he was concerned every day in Canada and the United States was a day that he wasn't back at home. The whole continent should just be flushed down the shitter.

He did not care either what happened to the scrawny little fucker they'd been chasing, all he really wanted to do was go home. Mind you he had to admit to himself the bastard they were hunting was either bloody lucky or had some inside information about when they were getting close. This was not the first time in recent months that he had got away by the skin of his teeth, and it all made Douglas Aitkin mad.

Just at the moment of that thought, and rather astonishingly, as he had begun to wonder where Tommy his companion had got to, the door to the room swung open. And stood there right in front of him was one Jack Silver, in the flesh.

The man had changed since the last time that Aitkin had seen him. Unkempt certainly, but as the newcomer let the door swing open stood feet apart staring back at Douglas Aitken he had a kind of contemptuous look on his face. Somehow the guy looked, well more whole, more capable to the gunman than when he had seen him before. The Englishman stood absolutely still, and he did not speak. His breathing was steady, and his eyes were unblinking, he was like the Matador, awaiting the charge of the bull.

Of course, Jack Silver had seen the gun immediately after the door swung open, he thought it looked like a toy in the hands of that huge evil-looking bastard. Silver was pretty certain he was facing down the very guy who had held a gun to a shopkeeper's head a month or so back. And if so then he knew he was in the company of at least one murderer tonight.

A half second later he saw the figure on the bed, and his legs very nearly gave out. But still, in those first moments, it was the gun that had held his attention, and it did so still, just. The brute lifted it and pointed it at Jack's face, and whilst it should not have made him feel better he quickly realised that the bundle hunched up and unmoving on the double-bed although partly obscured by the giant of a man, was in fact too big to be the body of Molly.

So it was that as the revolver was pointed at him a rather winsome smile washed across his features. He pushed back at the image of blood-soaked bed covers that were slowly dripping onto the room floor and focused on trying to read his opponent.

To that point neither man had spoken, Jack knew that timing was everything now and more, that his desperate plan needed to be paced just right.

'Dead?' he asked questioningly, nodding his head minutely towards the bundle on the bed.

'I'm fucked if I know, but if you move you will be,' the guy growled in his heavy English accent.

'I'm not going anywhere,' Jack continued, actually taking a step or two forwards, and so further into the room, allowing the door to drift back halfway closed behind him.

'Where are the rest of them?' Jack was fishing wondering now whether he had been a fool to walk so brazenly into the lion's den. 'Listen, you tell me where they are, and I'll cause you no more fuss,' Jack then offered.

'You ain't causing me nothing,' the giant replied, and before the Englishman could say more, he bellowed, 'Tommy, you fucking weasel, get up here n see what I caught me?'

Jack sniffed and caught the first acrid scent of burning in the air. So far this appeared to have gone unnoticed further into the bedroom. He girded himself and began to sidle slowly towards the bed.

'I've gotta see if that one's ok, if you gotta shoot me then you do your thing,' he said, still holding the gaze of the far larger man, who seemed to fill most of the room. He walked slowly towards the bed and as he got close he realised that the occupant of that bed was in fact a woman, and Jack realised straight away that it was Molly's aunt Missy.

He said nothing his mouth shut into a tight bloodless line. He sat gingerly on the side of the bed staying clear of the spreading blood stains. Jack was able to tell immediately that the woman was dead. Close too he saw a long blade embedded in her throat, and in fact, she was not wrapped up on the bed. Instead, it appeared she had just become caught up in another of the cotton bed dressings.

The look on the dead woman's face even in death was one of utter terror. Her eyes, glassy, were open. And as Jack leaned over her and gently brushed a strand of hair out of her eyes, before closing them, he decided that the man had to die there and then tonight, even if achieving that would probably cost Jack Silver his own life.

'Bastard,' Jack said quietly, 'you'll die for that.'

'Yeah, right. I'm petrified,' the monster replied. Jack stood again and stepped watchfully back towards the door. He understood that now everything came down to calculated risk. The gunman leaned back, twitching with his free hand at the room's one curtain, never taking his eyes, or the gun, away from Jack Silver, and after less than a minute calling out once again.

'Tommy, get up here you useless son of a bitch.'

It was at that moment that Jack saw his opportunity, and as the gunman lent back, fractionally off-balance for a second only, the Englishman suddenly bolted, stepping back instantly through the bedroom door and slamming it shut.

At the same instant, the gunman fired, and Jack winced as wood and plaster exploded inches from his face with a crack like thunder. He had banked on the fact that the gun had been aimed at his head rather than at his body and his gamble had paid off, just. The gunman off-balance had missed him by about three centimetres.

The door itself was made of heavy solid oak and even before the gunshot reverberated in his ears it had thudded reassuringly into the doorframe. Jack had spied the key sat in the lock on his way in, and in the moment of his exit had desperately twisted, hoping that his plan would hold and that the heavy door had a decent lock that might hold the monster for at least a few moments. A loud roar and a heavy thud on the far side told him that the gunman had reached the door barely a whisker after he had successfully navigated the lock. Jack was panting and darted his head to look around a third door on the first floor. He saw a bed and a few children's toys, Molly's room he thought, too few toys went through his mind, and he shook his head angrily as a tear ran down his face.

'No time,' he growled to himself and then almost an afterthought called out.

'Molly, are you in here? It's me Jack.'

No reply, nothing. *She wasn't in there*, he thought with instant relief. Moments later he heard another heavy crash and realised that the gunman was trying to smash his way through the locked door. The man was a scary physical specimen, but Silver was pleased that he didn't appear to have a PhD. He smelled burning in the air and wondered if the other man could also. The Englishman tore along the hallway, silence was no longer an issue. He saw smoke coming from under the door of the first room he had been into, and he knew then that the fire he had lit with Isaiah's Zippo lighter was spreading, wildly and quickly in the timber-built house.

Jack Silver figured he had maybe two minutes, and moreover, he needed to get down the stairs in about thirty seconds of that time. He checked the final door, looked beyond it and into a small indistinct bathroom. Once more he spied a mix of worn and tidy, a space in which nothing larger than a church mouse would be able to hide.

The gunman was bellowing and swearing, and Jack wondered briefly where the other gunman, the one he had called Tommy might be. There were too many factors beyond his control he thought to himself grimly, but he had no time. He jumped down the stairs three at a time, all the while calling out Molly's name urgently. His eyes had grown used to the darker less well-lit space upstairs but down here the hallway light now blazed, and Jack found himself squinting. He put his head in through a doorway and saw he had got turned around and that what he thought would be the kitchen was in fact the parlour, small and neat, and like the rest of the home everything in it was clean and presentable but just a little worn and weary.

That room too was empty.

As he stepped back and turned around he saw once more the dog Tully, who seemed finally to have succumbed, stopped breathing, and he felt both sad and yet relieved in the same instant. He saw Molly's loss, but he knew also that the hound's terrible suffering at least was over.

A second later he heard the crashing sound of a Colt 45 handgun, and a scream filled the air with rage.

'Fire, the bastard's trying to fucking burn me.'

Still, though the gunman did not appear at the top of the stairs, and Jack's hopes held, for just a few moments more.

He moved quickly down the hall and opened the final door in that house, the one that led to the kitchen. Jack felt in the shadows up the wall his hand searching for a light switch, one he quickly found and flicked on.

Bright radiance filled the room, this was the centre of that family farmhouse, bigger than Jack had envisaged during his long layup in the barn across the yard.

'Molly, Molly, it's Jack… You in here?'

Nothing. Jack walked into the room and looked around, his mind desperate, and in turmoil, he knew that his time was almost up. Where was she?

He stood absolutely still for about ten seconds; a long time given all that was going on around him. He simply breathed. And then finally, just as he was turning to leave, the door to a small cupboard immediately under the kitchen sink slowly swung open. And there huddled inside the child was crouched.

Jack stared at her.

He was astonished that in the face of all the horrors visited upon her home and family that night he saw still that same calm in her eyes that he had got used to.

'You OK?' he asked moving towards her.

'I'm OK, Jack,' she said. For a second time calling him simply Jack, and for a second time, it went unnoticed. 'Uncle Isaiah told me to hide out in here. Then he went outside. You shouldn't be here.'

'No time, Molly,' Jack said, 'the house is burning, and the bad men are coming.'

At that very moment, just as he waved her towards him, he heard the crack of another gun, deafeningly loud, the report different from the Colt he had heard twice in the past minutes. Glass smashed, and Jack realised that this gunshot had come inwards from outside the room rather than from behind him as he had feared. He dropped immediately to the floor, saw and scrabbled towards the large oval wooden table in the room's centre, reaching up he grabbed at a knife that was sticking out of a breadboard close to the table's edge.

Molly reached him a moment later, and she threw her arms around his neck in one further movement they both slid across broken glass and so under the table. The echo of the gunshot took a few moments to wear off and Jack had to shout twice before Molly heard and acknowledged his observation that the house was on fire.

'My uncle's outside,' Molly replied, 'but I haven't seen Aunt Missy...and Tully.' She trailed off at that, and Jack realised from her words that she had seen her beloved dog before the end. The sorrow of that was painful to her, but she could not face it right then, and Jack knew that was right, and reminded himself once again that they had no time.

A strange screeching sound of rending wood and steel from the upstairs of the farmhouse was followed by the electric lights flickering and dimming for a few seconds. Jack figured that the fire was reaching the point where the integrity of many parts of the property was becoming compromised.

But now there was another gunman to contend with. This one was outside of the property, and so had trapped them, and they needed to get out, get past him.

Beyond expectation, he had found Molly and now he was damned well going to save her. He stood up suddenly and shouted loudly, 'You, outside, I'm here in the kitchen. It's me Jack Silver. I'm not running. You want me to come in here and get me.' At the same time, the Englishman was urgently motioning Molly to stay put with his free hand and furthermore moving the bread knife down and out of sight behind his right leg.

The broken glass they had slid across appeared to have come from a pane in the back door and a few moments later that same door was angrily shoved open.

The man who had been within inches of Jack Silver just moments after he had murdered his friend Caffee a few weeks before strode defiantly into the kitchen. Pointing a gun at the Englishman he smiled and said, 'Bang bang you're dead.'

Jack held onto the knife, out of sight, loose in his right hand. He prayed the newcomer did not see Molly, at least for a few moments more. He expected to die in the next few seconds, but he realised he had made his peace with that fact, that he had made the decision he was going to give Molly every opportunity at life. Somehow that choice gave him a cool detachment from the fear and passion of the situation the like of which he had never before experienced.

'You can have me. But the house is burning, your buddy's done for. I get one of you bastards back at any rate.'

'You think I care,' the gunman called. Tommy said stepping forward and raising the hand holding the pistol to strike at Jack. He was also a big man, and he appeared sure he had the smaller man whipped, that he was in complete control of the situation. Jack was about to swing upward with the knife when in an instant everything changed.

The blade suddenly seemed to slip from his hands. In a blur, he could barely register and only much later comprehend a small figure shot forward. That figure grabbed the steel and jammed the flashing silver blade upward stabbing the bread knife deep into the groin and guts of the gunman.

At the same time, Jack registered another gunshot, and he could only look on in horror as a red rose instantly blossomed on the pale blue cotton pyjama top Molly was wearing. The gunman went down, writhing in agony, the gun had fallen from nerveless fingers. Jack stepped up to him and in the instant, before he crouched down to Molly he stamped with all his might on the gunman's throat. He heard a satisfying snapping sound followed by a weird gurgling and said, 'Shut up and die you fucker. That's for my friend Caffee.'

He crouched down next to Molly, and tears filled his eyes. He was then oblivious to the gunman and the fire. In fact, Jack Silver was close to the whole world. The Englishman gently reached his arm around behind Molly and lifted her head. The child was soaked in her own blood, and her voice was a sparse desperate whisper as she said.

'You shouldn't have come back, Mister Jack. I told you.'

'What have you done?' Jack said sobbing.

'What I had to,' Molly whispered pain creasing her features.

'I love you, Molly. You have to come with me now,' Jack sobbed, all the while cradling her close to him, pressing his hand over where the blood was pulsing. Deep in his mind, he wondered how one so small had so much blood in her body.

'I'm dying, Mister Jack,' Molly said. 'We both know that…and you gotta go.'

Two more gunshots tore through the night, followed by a scream of extraordinary pain. Jack looked up just for an instant. And when he looked back down, though only a second had passed Molly had closed her eyes, and she was gone. 'Molly, no. Please don't do this. I can't.' He sobbed unable to finish.

'Please open your eyes.'

Molly never opened her eyes again, but as Jack leaned close and kissed her on the forehead he heard her voice in his mind whisper to him.

'Go now and finish this. For all of us.'

Jack slumped on his knees for what seemed an age, all the while cradling Molly close to him. The lights fizzed and sparked and finally went out.

And so it passed that less than five minutes after he had walked bravely in on the first gunman Jack Silver stepped out through the kitchen door into a moonlit night, boots crunching on broken glass, carrying the dead body of Molly St Etienne. Jack didn't know then that her uncle lay dead also, not twenty metres from where he stood. And he did not even register the death screams of the second gunman, forgotten and ultimately who had been unable to escape the locked room. The man roasted to death, screaming horribly, as the house around him burned to the ground.

Jack carried the child across the yard and back to the barn where she had first brought him. He climbed carefully up the ladder and so carried her to the place where he had made a home, and where with her aid he had rebuilt himself. He thought then of her, of how he had found her, and yet he understood then finally that in fact, she had found him, astray, broken, lost and alone.

The Englishman laid her body gently down on the straw. He smoothed her pyjamas down as best he could, and then he covered her with a blanket that had been left thrown aside by him hours earlier.

Jack covered up the awful blood-soaked wound, knowing that the blood would soak through in time. He knelt looking at her for a long time, and he saw a peace in her face that he could not find in his own soul.

Jack stopped crying, and after a time he smiled wanly. He looked outward and up at the full moon shining through the open roof, and he said simply, 'I'm sorry, Molly.'

The Englishman Jack Silver disappeared into the night.

Death and madness went up in flames behind him, and in front, well his destiny lay before him.

And Jack Silver was heading straight for it like a bullet from a gun.

The thing had found hate as it had been meant to. It had ventured forth at first cautiously and then with greater confidence as its power and grasp of self grew. Self-aware and empowered beyond all it encountered the construct discovered existence in that form came at a cost.

Chapter Twenty-Four
Easy Street

Jack was clearer in his mind now.

He understood this world was not quite his world. He understood also that Stevan Cipher appeared, like him, to somehow exist in both places, here, and over there, where he came from.

He shivered, not sure if it was at the thought of Cipher or rather the encroaching cold that came with night's approach. Memories of the other place were jumbled and unclear to him though somehow he was sure this Cipher was a more dominant character, in this version, this world. Surely that had something to do with the hellscape he found himself in. Had Cipher bought him here? He didn't think so, but he could not explain why.

In fact, the Englishman felt sure he had been sent here, 'But by whom? And why?'

He asked himself, but no answers came, and he wondered too whether Cipher was looking for him in this world as he understood he was in the other. Jack drifted for a time, thinking about these things but not coming to any real conclusions eventually drifting into a sleep of dreams that contorted and twisted his sleeping features.

He awoke in pitch black, it was freezing cold, and the lamp seemed to have gone out. Jack came awake quickly and hissed into the darkness. 'Robbie are you here?' He felt in his pocket, and after a moment, his hand closed around a small plastic disposable lighter. Jack twisted the wheel three times before the spark took.

The darkroom was instantly lit by a lurid and flickering orange light. The space was full of shadows and dark corners places where that light did not reach. Where Robbie had lain there was no one, though the coats and covers lay in a heap the boy was gone.

'Damn,' Jack cursed, letting the lighter flicker out, both because it had burned his thumb, but equally because he had spotted earlier the fuel was almost completely gone. He reached blindly over to the pile of clothes and felt around until his hands closed on what seemed a lighter cotton fabric top. He pulled at it, and then reached down and picked up the teak table leg still sat only inches from his leg. Jack proceeded to wrap the cotton cloth tightly around the bigger end of the table leg.

A moment or two later Silver sparked the lighter and the cloth quickly blazed. After that, he needed only a brief time to spot the crawl way they had come in by, and feeling simply that he needed to get out he grabbed at his coat, whose pockets he had filled with chocolate bars and cans, and then crawled as quickly as he was able from that place.

As soon as he got outside, he shook off the burning embers of the cotton garment from the table leg stamped on them and then stood up tall stretching out his arms and legs. It was night-time again, though watching Jack was uncertain exactly how deep into night-time. Fires burned once again in the distance, although he thought the present district seemed a little less prone to the burning than where he had come from the previous night.

A distant howl indicated activity off to Jack's left but not close enough to be an immediate threat, but a stark reminder of the nerve-jangling night-time carousel. Silver was once again uncertain of what exactly he was to do. Firstly, he had no idea where the boy Robbie had gone. He had to assume the child had left of his own volition. He did not believe the child could have been abducted without him being awoken in the commotion.

It was a cold clear night and Jack shivered as he looked up to see a trail of sparkling debris high up in the night sky. The stars were plentiful and seemed to fill the black with an illumination he did not remember from his London. He pulled his coat tightly around him against the chill air. He understood intuitively that he needed to move away from where he stood, before the night denizens of that place, those that Robbie had called "the mentals" spotted him loitering.

Jack still had no idea really which way to head, but he had spotted about a half mile distant the glow of a fire that appeared larger than any other around and so decided he would go investigate.

Perhaps the boy Robbie would be there.

His eyes quickly acclimatised to the night, and as he walked, trading over the debris of all manner, he took several practice swings with the table leg in his hand, baseball style. As a result, he found just the right spot to hold it and then hoped fervently he would not find himself swinging in anger that night.

Jack covered the half mile or so in no time, but as he drew close to the glow, while obvious to him that something burned, from the dancing shadows on nearby walls. He was not able to see clearly from his direction of approach what he was heading towards. He had been travelling up a steady but shallow incline for the whole journey, and it was as he reached the crest of the hill that he heard a sound, which despite his short time in that place sounded entirely incongruous.

Laughter. Deep and booming, echoing laughter suddenly filled the night air. Men laughing, at least two, maybe more. Jack in the instant of hearing almost ran towards the sound, so desperate was he for some sanity in that asylum of a world, but caution was now an innate part of him. Instead, he crouched quietly down behind a burned-out hulk that had at one time been a small coach or van. After perhaps half a minute, the laughter gently died away. Distant voices drifted up towards Jack, and he crawled forward slowly, and as quietly as he could until he saw a sight in front of him as unexpected as the laughter he had heard.

Looking down from the brow of the hill he traced the outline of a road that led down to a square, perhaps two hundred feet away, possibly a city market square or the like. In the centre of that square, a fire burned, the biggest bonfire night conflagration the Englishman ever had seen. The fire burned twenty feet high and as wide again around its base, it lit up the surrounding night with leary dancing light and shade.

Sat around the base on a mixture of indoor and outdoor furniture Jack saw five, no six men, and in addition, in various positions of repose three large dogs. 'Wolves,' Caffee's voice corrected him cautiously. Jack Silver looked on and saw that all there were relaxed, enjoying it seemed, eating and drinking, and not fitting whatsoever the night denizens and pervading atmosphere he had encountered to that point.

He might have gone barrelling down there were it not for the fact that several of the men were openly sporting guns, advanced automatic rifles. And moreover, as he looked on, it became increasingly obvious that these were not the sort of folk you went charging into unheeded. He then spotted somewhat beyond the lurid burning flames of a building, unusual from all around it in that it was lit from within. The flames made it difficult to tell from his vantage point whether the windows shone back an electric gleam, but it certainly looked that way.

Realising he needed to move to get a better view he began to move carefully across to the far side of the road he crouched in. All the while being careful not to attract the attention of the "hoods" below.

'Do you know them already, Jack?' a voice piped up, but he was concentrating and quickly dismissed the thought.

After a minute or two, he hunkered down behind a half-lifted paving slab. Jack saw and recognised the lit building for what it was. He recalled seeing an old black-and-white movie, 'Metropolis,' his mind helpfully offered. A weird movie, but he had been hooked on that 1920s architecture ever after.

The Regal, as the sign above the door announced was a cinema. It was a building built in the same arthouse 1920s style, and whilst the light that emanated from the place appeared to pulse brighter and then dimmer every few seconds, still Jack looked on at the first evidence of modern technology intact he had yet seen in that place. A generator he decided. That's why the light is pulsing, cycling in time with a motor, not working to its peak.

He saw the shadows, shifting across a pair of first-floor windows, and finally, he knew he had stumbled upon a destination where he might fetch up some real answers to the many questions that burned inside him.

Looking left, the Englishman saw an alleyway that curved away into darkness and appeared to run down the slope parallel to the road that led to the square below.

He was about to set off when a commotion below brought his attention back to the gunmen "Stormtroopers", and their four-legged companions. Two gunshots followed an instant after raised voices, suddenly ringing into the night and reverberating off the surrounding buildings. Jack registered the muzzle flashes and heard a further voice shouting excitedly.

'Leave it you prick. Let the dogs have him.'

Just then a shadowy blur streaked across the square, darting it seemed in and out of the lurid orange light. A cat, or perhaps an urban fox, from where Jack looked on it was difficult to be sure. Seconds later four dogs were atop the creature snarling and tearing at flesh, the frenzy evident even from his vantage. Jack had only remembered seeing three dogs, but he saw then that a fourth had joined the fray, larger, more imposing than even they by far, clearly the pack leader had joined the fray, as the monstrous animal grabbed the blood-tattered corpse of the dead prey in its jaws and dared any or any of the others there to take it from him. The gunmen by now were once again deep in their own conversation and mostly oblivious to the animal byplay. Jack realised, though, that in addition to trigger-happy gunmen, visitors to this place would need to navigate a pack of guard dogs, one of whom, his mind nagged at him, he recognised. Based on what he had just witnessed, unwelcome visitors were liable to receive a harsh welcome.

He crawled away, rising to a standing posture again only once he was certain that he was out of sight of any prying eyes from the square below. He set off down the alley, which curved between tall buildings on both sides and darkened quickly, not benefiting from either the light of the fires or the light of the stars sitting deep between three- and four-storey, close-packed buildings. Jack trod warily, looking keenly about him and keeping his makeshift weapon tightly gripped in sweating hands. His heart hammered in his chest and the chocolate and milk cans filling every coat pocket suddenly seemed heavy and uncomfortable as they batted against arms and thighs.

Jack debated leaving them stashed as he continued his present errand but was unable to convince himself with any certainty that he would come this way again soon, even were he to have the opportunity.

He had walked for several minutes and was then far out of sight of the alleyway's entrance and was just beginning to wonder where he would come out when the noise began. A low, quiet growl, with a gurgling undertone and then silence for a moment. Then an answering growl, this one deeper, more feral. If Jack's heart had been hammering before, it practically went into overdrive at the new sounds.

'Why had he let himself become deluded enough to step into this alley?' he wondered to himself. The Englishman looked about him as best he was able in the darkness. He had no clue from where the two separate growls had come, and he could see nowhere obvious to go, other than forward or back the way he had come.

It felt like a trap, and for once Jack wished for one of those unchecked fires he had seen burning all about these past two nights. He thought of the gunmen, and the dogs, especially the one with the prey held casually in its yellow fangs, teeth more than able to rip through Jack's scrawny flesh.

That got him moving.

He knew that to stop then would likely bring death quickly.

Christ, this road goes on forever, he thought, and then Caffee spoke up clearly in his head.

'What if it turns out to be a dead end? What then Long John?'

Jack had no answer to that.

The growling sounds came again, and this time were accompanied by a heavy thumping noise. The sound was behind him and to the right. The Englishman glanced over his shoulder, still moving, but he saw nothing. There came another growl, this one closer.

'Agh, hell!' Jack said, in a frightened voice that sounded small in the night.

He rounded the last curve in the street and saw that he had walked into a dead end, he was after all trapped. The small alley had ended in a half-circle of four curved buildings originally on a terrace, now a huge pile of impassable rubble, twisted steel and ash.

The growling came again, and then again. Two, no three different makers of the sounds he thought. Sounds that were constant now, Jack turning and looking all about him, and up to the roofline of the broken masonry of those terraced buildings, club raised in one trembling hand.

Suddenly, in the night-time gloom, he thought he saw something. Against the darkness a man of sorts appeared, out of nowhere it seemed, about thirty feet from him, approaching warily, malice evident even at that distance, in that light, filthy, starved, vacant.

The creature reminded Jack of Dawn of the Dead, excepting only that this man did not have blank Zombie lifeless eyes; instead, even in the dark, and at that distance, Jack was able to see avaricious hunger drawn deep in the man's features.

He limped and was dressed – if you could call it that – in clothes reduced to little more than shredded, torn rags, and Jack saw quite clearly the man was mad. Another appeared, and then a third, Jack was indeed trapped, with no means of escape, either behind or ahead.

He shuffled a few feet to his left, hefting his wooden club, but none of the three "metals", that's what the boy Robbie had said, changed course, they were heading straight for him, slowly and steadily, three feet left or right appeared not to concern them one jot.

Jack saw that all three were making the growling sounds he had heard a minute or two before, the noise emanating from deep within each, hunting as a pack. And he spotted then also that one of the men, exceptionally tall, as much as six feet six, was gurgling rather than growling. Half of the lower part of that man's jaw was missing, and that part of his face was matted with filthy hair and dried blood. Not one of the creatures articulated a word, either to Silver or to one another. And yet they were acting in concert, drawing apart to create a net from which their prey would struggle to escape.

Jack Silver thought desperately.

Each of the approaching figures resembled something from a nightmare. The music to Michael Jackson's "Thriller" takes up frightening unshakeable residence in the back of his mind.

In the movies, he felt certain a swift whack or two with the hero's wooden club and three motley night denizens would be easily swept aside. But this was reality, well his reality, and this pack looked keen on killing. And furthermore, Jack Silver was no action hero.

'Cometh the hour,' Caffee spoke up, and the Englishman, speaking out loud said, 'Fuck off, Caffee.'

Just then he remembered the cans in his pocket that had felt so weighty. He had no idea why the thought should have come to his mind at that moment, but he knew well enough in an instant what he must do. I have six cans, he told himself, and it's me they're after.

As a boy, the Englishman had been a good shot, a lad with a good arm. He remembered fragments from another life, another time. A young boy, perhaps twelve, both his parents dead by then, him living with a foster family, and in that alley, he remembered the father. He had used to call him dead-eye Jack because of his innate ability to hit a set of cricket stumps time and again from forty or fifty feet distant.

Had he been a budding cricketer in another life, Jack wondered; but then, with "Thriller" buzzing through his mind and three growling metals thirty feet from him, he looked down at the heavy can he held in one of his hands, emblazoned with the words and writ in smaller letters underneath, 'Vanilla.'

Jack swapped the can with the club quickly, juggling between left and right hands, judging the rate at which the night people were closing the remaining distance. He lifted the can and, pointing with the other arm that now held the club, like a gunsight towards the target, he threw the can deadeye at the centre of the three men.

The man-creature was about his height, and looked thin and starved, though to Jack they all were. But in the case of this creature, he had evidently once been a heavier man. Silver hit him square in the face, he heard a bone crunch and instantly the guy went down.

Jack hissed, 'Yes,' into the night looking down momentarily to pull a second can from his coat pocket. When he looked up he was alarmed to see the downed man was rising to his feet once again. A little unsteadily for sure, and blood ran freely now from a fresh head wound, but it seemed the blow from Jack had slowed him only for a few moments. The Englishman took aim again and fired a second can equally straight and equally viciously, this one towards the furthest right of the men, the tall one with a part of his head left at home. The shot almost went wide, the creature was masked by deeper night-time shadows and Jack had jerked a little as he threw managing only to catch a glancing blow on the tall man's shoulder. The creature showed no reaction, pain apparently was not on the agenda, as far as he could tell.

'Dammit,' he cursed.

Twenty feet, he could see the whites of their eyes now. His heart hammered like a train blowing full steam ahead, his arm trembled as he drew another can out. He could not decide what to do, it would be like as not his last shot, perhaps one more if he was quick.

He thought frantically, and then in an instant without thinking he dropped his club, threw the first can, and in one movement drew another and threw again. This time he had aimed low at the middle of the three creatures again, but this time he had aimed at the legs. He hit the man quickly twice on the same leg, and he knew from the second satisfying crack that he had damaged the man's leg seriously somewhere around the knee or shin.

By the noise the second impact had made, it sounded like a break. In the same flowing movement, he then bent picked up the club and ran straight at the injured man, who, purely due to the laws of physics had gone down under the impact of the cans. Jack Silver swung wildly at the prostrate form in one motion as he hurdled the night man, catching him a crunching blow on the side of his head.

He ran and prayed that the remaining two would not run with him. It took only seconds, and he knew his prayers had been ignored. He heard thumping steps behind him and, in the still of deep night the earlier growling sounds rising then to a roar. The Englishman ran back the way he had come as hard as his legs and lungs would take him. Deep inside he felt sure he could outrun the thin broken creatures of the night, but then suddenly in front of him, he saw more, lots more of the same. A dozen had entered the alley and spread across its full width barring his way.

Jack stopped he realised despairingly that he had picked the wrong street, time was up.

Build it. Give it power beyond measure. Show it your enemy. Fill it with purpose. And finally, the gift of self-preservation.
Sally forth and do our bidding.

Chapter Twenty-Five
Without Someone

He travelled then for many days in a black fog. The Englishman walked. Skirting towns and communities, barely surviving, occasionally drinking from the abundance of fresh running water. And even more occasionally eating from fresh food picked up along the way, sweetcorn grown tall in the late summer and berries that grew abundantly.

During that time, he cared nought about his own situation. He no longer gave a damn about Shadowmen or police, good guys or bad guys. In his mind, all he saw over and over was Molly lying broken on her aunt and uncle's kitchen floor as death took her. His grief was inconsolable, his rage incandescent. Whichever way he cut it he should not have left and should never have allowed Molly to take the kitchen knife from his hands.

He cried often, swung wildly between letting go of what life he saw left to him and, as a counterpoint, an urgent, desperate will for revenge against Cipher and his men. For all who had brought awful death to his door once again.

During those long days and nights, he was destitute. Had anyone seen him during that time they would have spied madness dancing in his eyes.

Sleep came to him without dreams, in snatches, at moments when his conscious body became too exhausted to carry on. His waking hours on the other hand were a nightmare of image and horror told and retold, horror that left him drawn and forlorn.

The Shaktar stone was forgotten and lay dormant in his filthy jeans. He stank worse than the worst tramp, a mixture of his own soil and the unwashed filth of wild living that grew over him from head to toe.

On the eleventh day, he encountered a brown bear, a female full-grown, with two cubs in tow.

Jack walked upon them in the clearing of a wooded area he had been wandering aimlessly through, his mind caught still in the repeating loop it had been trapped in for long days. As he stepped out between the last of the shrubs and the trees he stopped dead. The bear had her back towards him at that point, and Jack, with no clear thought at all seeing the two young cubs at play, sat down on the dusty ground drew his legs up, knees tight to his chest and proceeded to watch.

Deep in his mind, a part of Jack's brain was fascinated by watching the cubs at play.

Like children, they showed neither fear nor plan, attention nor concentration. Rather, they ran and jumped and rolled, colliding with each other and their mother, everything linked by some deep natural instinct, and some part of Jack Silver's mind was able to tune into that. After a minute or so, mother bear turned around and, scenting the stink of an intruder, quickly sorted out and found the small, hunched creature rolled up on the ground, either by fate or fortune Jack was bundled in a most non-threatening posture. She ambled over to the thing and noted it smelled like nothing she had scented in the forest during her long years. In fact, the thing was not really like anything that she had ever encountered.

Mama bear saw no threat but proceeded to growl deep in her throat, raising herself up to her full height inches in front of the visitor, just in case, as mothers are wont to do. After a few moments, she seemed to bore, it was all just too much trouble, and so like weary parents before, and since she turned and went back to overseeing her young charges, with just a gentle sigh escaping her as she turned away.

This in itself might have looked strange to an onlooker, stranger still to the change that took place in Jack Silver. After watching the cubs for some time, and never having turned a hair at the brief but noisy attentions of their mother, Jack suddenly smiled and said, 'Yes,' in a voice no louder than a whisper.

And then quietly, without causing any further disturbance, the Englishman from the city stood up and proceeded to walk back the way that he had come.

Two days later Jack hopped a train. He had no idea where it was going, until some while into the long clanking journey a fellow non-paying passenger, one who stank of stale booze and yet fragrant next to Jack told him to settle in. Jack learned he had joined the freight train to Edmonton.

The journey was long and laborious, after little more than twenty-four hours the drunken man, by then sober became aggressive, and Jack with no compunction whatsoever stood, walked over to the man and kicked him hard in the face, watching blankly as the dried mud from his boots stuck in the bright red blood that instantly appeared.

Moments later, he forced the man to jump from the moving train as an alternative to being pushed. In another life, Jack Silver would have wrestled long and hard about the morals of such actions, even had he been bold enough to take them. And he had no doubt he would have been wracked with guilt after.

This Jack, though, was operating at a new level, alone, but he did not feel lonely, not with fiery revenge as his bedfellow. He thought about the phrase, *Revenge is a dish best served cold*, yet for him, it was a hot burning passion, and the only thing that kept him going during those darkest of days.

The drunk exiting summarily had left a dirty-looking rucksack behind, and the Englishman had been mildly surprised to find inside a change of clothes that, whilst not laundry fresh, were an improvement on his own. In addition, a bottle, only half-drunk, of cheap vodka lay at the bottom of the pack, seemingly forgotten in the man's drunken sloth.

The last accompaniment strangely was a New Testament bible, in which Jack discovered pressed and much worn, a photograph of a young and pale-skinned, freckled girl. She seemed in the image perhaps five or six years old, with ginger hair in bunches and a toothy grin given especially for the camera.

At the sight, he felt the smallest pang and fought for long moments to push down memories of Molly.

Sometime after, unexpectedly, and for the first time since the burning farmhouse, a voice spoke gently in his head, and the voice sounded like her.

'It goes on, Jack…you go on, too.'

He paid scant attention to the voice, proceeding to strip down naked as the train's steady movement rocked him to and fro. Using his own underclothes doused in the vodka he proceeded to methodically wash himself down from head to toe.

The vodka revealed a sea of cuts and bruises all over his body, and after a time Jack was forced to add his shirt and vest to the wiping-cloth collection as the filth continued to come off him unabated. He looked at himself naked and saw that the difficult weeks behind him had left his forty-something body lean and hard. The midlife fat war that he had been losing for the past few years had apparently been turned around, and his arms and neck, and presumably his face, too, though he had no means of checking, were brown as a teak.

Jack looked down at his manhood, saw grey in his pubic hair and wondered when last he had even thought about a woman in that way. Oddly then he considered masturbating, though just for a second, then realised as quickly that he just did not care enough anymore and so proceeded to dress in the tramp's clothes, that fitted him passably well. He then re-laced his own boots over the tramp's spare woollen socks, looked briefly at the small amount of vodka remaining in the bottle and poured it into his hands to wipe over his face and through his hair. The Englishman slept then. He had no idea for how long, but his old jeans made a pillow as feathery as ever he had lain on.

He awoke in the chill of early morning, slightly damp from the dusty wooden carriage floor, aware immediately the cumbersome beast was slowing as a loud clanking of carriages knocking together had got underway. Jack creaked as he stretched and, looking through the gaps between the wooden sides of the carriage, he saw that they were pulling into a more built-up district. Furthermore, he spied a steady drizzling rain falling.

Silver remembered his discarded jeans and turning away from the rainy suburban view went and dug into the pockets, where he found, all somewhat crumpled, his passport, a small roll of US dollars, and a Zippo lighter. He looked at the lighter for long seconds, remembering again the decisions he had made, and then put it, along with all the other items, into the pockets of the faded green denim that he now found himself wearing.

Last but not least was the stone, long discarded by his mind, he did not feel the former empathy he had with the object, it was a lifeless rock, and he sat then for close to an hour just looking at it. He wondered for some time about throwing it out of the carriage, tossing it aside to the hands of fate once more, whatever he hoped the small and oddly behaving object had hardly offered any help when he had needed it most, and he was filled with distaste at the world. Nonetheless, as the train lumbered slowly through the town and leaden skies tipped cold rain down on both it and the town's occupants, eventually, unconsciously he put the small rock into his new jeans front pocket and moved on.

The Englishman never learned the name of that small community the train chugged on through, it was information that was of no use to him. In the end, though, the whole diesel-driven contraption passed through the unnamed town and once more moved into unpopulated barren countryside.

And the Shaktar stone's journey continued with it.

Canada was a country of vast open spaces, and the three days of unbroken monotony that Jack Silver spent on the train, undisturbed by humanity, forcing appetite upon him leaving him hungry and dying of thirst, pressed him oh so slowly back into the world of the living.

He slept for more than half of the long journey and slowly his mind was put back together once more. And so, when finally, he jumped, near the end of the line in downtown Edmonton, though starved and parched beyond reasonable disposition his brain was as sharp as a tack.

But that mind was changed, maybe irrevocably. He walked for a time untroubled, pleased to be stretching his limbs, and shortly after dismounting, he bought a chicken wrap at a hot-food stand and a bottle of Sprite for company, both of which he consumed ravenously, only to have them revisit him violently less than an hour later.

That particular incident nearly brought him an encounter with local law enforcement. A patrol car slowed across the freeway from him as he was bent double and puking into the kerb. A scruffy drunk at any time of day was not readily tolerated in Edmonton. Fortunately for Jack, he didn't find himself answering difficult questions in a police station as, suddenly, the car's siren began to scream, and the vehicle shot off on a call of more apparent urgency. Jack remembered a car siren about a thousand years before, on the morning he had arrived in another city on this continent. And the Englishman admonished himself to be more careful.

He walked for an hour aimlessly, found a shopping mall, went into the first washroom he encountered and was appalled to see what gazed back at him from the mirror. He figured it was little wonder people looked at him strangely. Despite the vodka wash he had given himself a couple of days previously he had to admit he looked like a casualty from a war zone. Jack hadn't been aware that he had burned his face quite severely towards the end of his time in the farmhouse, and those burns, unnoticed during the days in between, had dried to leave his face masked with a purple hue that, along with the myriad cuts and bruises, left him looking nothing like the man he remembered.

'That's good,' he said to himself, pumping soap from the liquid dispenser, and pulling reams of paper from the hand towel machine. He proceeded to clean himself up as much as he was able. It was early in the day and Jack was lucky that no other soul came into the restroom during his ablutions. After washing, he drank sparingly from the tap water, which was cold but tasted flat and chemical after the spring and well water that he had his fill of in the previous weeks.

A short walk around the shopping mall introduced him to a sizeable discounter-style department store named "Zellers", in which he found a cornucopia of everything a modestly poor shopaholic might ever want. He picked out some unremarkable clothes, training shoes, a long black woollen trench coat similar to the one he had worn when he arrived in the United States, and lastly a medium-sized nondescript rucksack.

He saw large clunky mobile phones on a display, the new technology, and he knew they were all the rage. Jack Silver thought briefly about buying one, but then he realised that there was no one out there for him to call, even were he to want to. He gave the phones a miss, instead grabbing a sturdy-looking compass and a good-sized penknife from a nearby display. It was not until he reached the cash register that Jack suddenly remembered that he was in a foreign country, and, furthermore, with a small roll of US dollars, but no Canadian money at all.

In fact, as he thought about it, he wasn't even sure what the good citizens even spent in Canada, and just as he was pondering returning all of the items that he had fetched into a wire basket, he spotted with relief the shopper in front of him peel an American twenty from a small stack and pay for two packs of cigarettes to the apparent satisfaction of the uniformed old man parked by the till.

Jack took his turn, avoiding both the man's gaze and his pleasantries. As soon as he escaped the shop, he spied another washroom, went in and proceeded to wash and clean himself all over again, this time changing clothes in the bargain. The Englishman shaved the scrub of whiskers grown wild all over his face and was just washing his hair in the basin at the precise instant a father and son entered the restroom.

Both entrants to the room saw Silver in mid-rinse, and immediately they turned and left. Jack knew there was a good chance the father would head straight for the mall's security station. And so, he wrapped everything up quickly, finished dressing and then hurriedly left.

Minutes later, an inconspicuous traveller left the mall, jumped onto a city bus and headed away to nowhere in particular. Jack Silver was keen to get far away from anyone who might remember him in his previous guise. Barring the burns and bruises that were still visible, he figured he now looked mostly like anyone else in that city and so felt a little more at ease.

'Now to get back to the UK,' Jack said to himself grimly.

Later that day, he arrived at a busy tourist centre. And he found himself shocked as people and bustle moved around him in the largest numbers since he had arrived in Las Vegas some weeks before. A middle-aged native Indian woman in curious red plastic boots scolded him as he stepped down from the bus and almost landed atop a small Pekinese dog she had walked alongside her bright red footwear. Jack grunted and noted to himself that was the first acknowledgement he had made to another human being since cradling Molly's dying form in his arms. He didn't count kicking the drunk off a moving train whatsoever. He nodded to himself and understood that he had taken another small step on the winding road back from the edge.

Soon after Jack ate, this time being careful in both what he picked and the rate he consumed it, sipping iced water and keeping the food simple. An hour later, he had kept it down, and with it, he admitted to himself he felt considerably better. Jack searched out a phone directory at the entrance to the diner and sat with it open on his lap whilst eating. Inside the tome, he found, somewhat surprisingly, that there were three nearby airports. After further investigation, he found the international airport and noted with mild interest that it was the third highest airport above sea level in the world – this information sat next to an advertising slogan for whale-watching.

'Naught weirder than folk,' Jack mumbled to himself and looked up embarrassedly when the waitress passing his booth grunted her cheerful affirmation. He questioned her briefly, careful not to answer her enquiries with anything more than trivial utterances, and he discovered a nearby train station that would have him at the international terminal in about twenty minutes.

And so it was that an hour or so later he arrived at Edmonton International Airport on a train, albeit this time as a paying customer.

Revenge still burned hot through the fibres of Jack's being, but he found within himself at that time a cold and detached part of his mind never before in evidence. The Englishman was watchful, and he performed a casual circuit of the whole airport, ensuring he had exit strategies and boltholes in mind, careful not to arouse undue attention from the various security officers that were in evidence at that airport, like every other in those latter days.

Jack thought about how again and again the pathetic platitudes of extremist religion had reared up to intrude on the lives of ordinary folk: this had pretty much been the case since the dawn of humankind. Why was it, he wondered, that the vast majority of right-minded people, whatever their creed, still put up with the wild and unkempt patter of zealots the world over?

And the new Jack answered in himself in his mind, *Fuck 'em, just kill 'em all.*

Jack grinned in spite of himself, but he knew he still needed to safely negotiate a tricky time in the coming hours if he was to get out of Canada and find his way back to London in one piece.

After a time, having checked and rechecked the surroundings he approached Information behaving in the manner of a slightly befuddled English traveller. He soon discovered from a vacuous and disinterested gum-chewing clerk that Air Canada flew to London Heathrow via Calgary.

Jack thanked her, walked away and sought out the desk for Air Canada. There was no queue, so he showed his passport and, using almost the last of his cash, proceeded to pay for one economy-class ticket home.

Lots of good fortune so far, he thought, and no Stormtroopers to boot, he then added, keep it coming.

The Englishman went through Customs, dumping his meagre hand luggage in a washroom bin prior to joining the queue, and somewhat strangely found it necessary to offer a brief and ludicrous excuse about a present for his daughter when asked about the stone in his front right pants pocket when challenged that such could be deemed an offensive weapon.

Jack realised that had the rather inoffensive white rock been larger or heavier, it would certainly have been taken from him as said offensive weapon. As it was, the security agent gave him a long look up and down eventually sending Jack Silver on his way, having seen only the stupid British traveller that had been painted for him.

A couple of hours later and Jack climbed on board a 747 and noted the eclectic and rather noisy mix of travellers merging into the bright cloth and stark cabin colours. He spotted gleaming uniformed airline staff, and so he slid into his window seat and sought to slip immediately under humanity's radar. Jack plugged his seatbelt immediately, automatically smiled in a non-committal way at the overweight, hairless, mid-fifties Canadian salesman that planted himself next to him and decided his best course of action was to sit through take-off and as soon as possible thereafter cover eyes and ears and block the outside world till landing.

Watching a newscast on three hundred miniature screens he understood he had become detached from the rest of his former world. He felt though that he had no affinity whatsoever with the actions of that rest of the world, and so shortly after persuaded himself back to the private darkness that he filled with his own horrors.

In that dark cocoon, intruded upon only by the drone of the jet engines Jack slipped quickly into the torpor of his own despicable thoughts, in the middle of which shone a new and particular determination.

'Whatever it takes.'

He saw the faces, of those that had died, those that he had killed. And he heard their voices, too.

At first, the voices just added colour to his recollections. And, tortured as he was, Jack found a small part of his mind that wondered how he would ever be able to break free of the vice-like emotional grip the horror of the events had on him.

As time passed, the voices increased, in volume and in determination speaking about him, to him. Recollections of the two Stormtroopers that died in the farmhouse bought a variety of vitriolic outbursts. In his imagination, those two characters appeared to have enough life in them still to threaten his sanity. They had been scary guys, and the analytical part of Jack's brain, the bit that knew he was no cowboy, looked back in some wonder, and realised that whatever the ultimate outcome had been, somehow he had managed to put pay to two murderers.

It was the voice of Caffee that pointed out he had killed men that killed for a living, and furthermore that it was good he felt no remorse whatsoever. Still, it did not matter his act of murder was cold comfort. Molly had gotten killed, and whichever way he sliced himself up, he saw no way in which that wasn't entirely his fault. He had effectively caused innocent people to die in a little more than a month, and Caffee had been his friend, and Molly, well, thoughts trailed off.

A voice, nebulous in the space between thought and feelings, cut through the pain and darkness.

'You knew it was time to go, Jack, but you came back.' The voice was that of Molly and the Englishman gasped, unable to respond, and the ethereal Molly voice continued, 'I know it hurts, Mister Jack, but you gotta understand, I knew what I did back at the house, and you know what you have to do. You have other things to attend to.' And then, after a brief pause, 'It was my time to go I understood that, and another thing Mister Jack.' And then to Jack's utter astonishment, Molly's voice was joined by another. And in stereo, he listened, and he looked inward, as Molly and Caffee spoke as one. 'Jack, we're here. Many things are changing for you, but both of us are right here.'

Jack watched carefully, looking at what he thought must be the first tendrils of madness trickling down and into the edges of his mind. And yet at the same time somehow he found that his two friends, dead as they were, was the nicest thing that he could have imagined.

In fact, it was better than that.

And there and then Jack decided that if that was madness, however fanciful, then bring it on. He had no place left in his heart for a world without Caffee and Molly. As he drifted towards sleep he found himself wondering how the two of them might have got along if they had really met.

Sleep took him, and the thought that drifted past and barely slid through the closing door of his consciousness whispered, 'Met, we have met. We're all together here. You don't you understand. Not yet, but soon.' The hairless whale sat next to Jack looked up briefly from a copy of Time magazine and frowned as the sleeping stranger grunted. 'No... I don't.'

The makers, fearing for its safety in the millennia of years of dormant watch, had been wary about placement. Thus, the thing awoke and found itself born, if such a term can be appropriate, right on the edge of the vast and fast-expanding wilderness of the omniverse.

Chapter Twenty-Six
Send It

Jack stared at the array in front of him, men and women of all ages and types.

One woman, at least sixty years old, stood feet apart and was staring hungrily towards him, torn dress around her waist, breasts hanging loose and filthy over sagging, creased flesh.

Next to her stood a man of obvious Indian descent, neat still after all the apparent deprivations of that place, dressed in a black gown and turban, staring, again with equal hunger towards Jack Silver. Yet both of these individuals, like all of the night people that barred Silver's path, despite all the obvious differences between each of them, had one thing in common.

Each one of them bore eyes like silver fish. Reflecting the small amount of night light each had eyes that held nothing more than feral hunger. He spied no gleam of intelligence in any one of these creatures that he was barely able to articulate as human. It appeared that connection to their humanity had been long since extinguished, and, despite the terror that he felt Jack was overwhelmed by the utter sadness of seeing the creatures brought so low.

In one small corner of his mind, he saw images. World War II detainees at the prison camp in Auschwitz, he had watched fascinated once, on film but still utterly gripping as a younger man. Even then decades after that war had ended, flickering movie-tone images in faded black and white.

As a result, Jack the writer had gone on to prepare a biography on behalf of the family of a Polish internment camp survivor. He remembered the meetings, the notes, it had all been just a few months after the man had passed away.

The Pole, Victor, like every one of those tortured souls, despite all the deprivations suffered, despite many having been broken by starvation. Despite many more being sent across the bridge of madness by loss and grief. Still, Jack had seen some grain of humanity in each of them.

These creatures were different.

'Not people,' Jack mumbled out loud to himself and, then in his mind, added, 'Yes, the flesh and bone were there, the opposable thumbs, seemingly more human than those prisoners of his memory. But nothing else went on inside these people. The light switch inside each one had been permanently flicked to the off position.'

It was a grim thought and following behind it he had a pretty good idea who was responsible for that. So, hunt or be hunted was the order of the night, and he appeared to be the prey.

A thought arrowed through the murk of indecision and fear and right to the front of his mind, and a voice that sounded vaguely familiar spoke, 'Do you remember the moment when the house that you grew up in stopped being your home?'

Jack was confused, what the hell was that about, he had spent half of his younger life living in institutions.

'These poor souls have no home any more, can you see, everything has all been stripped away from them. They are lost Jack, you are not. Show them how to go home.'

He stood uncertainly, looking still at the approaching hoard, but his hand had drifted to his front pants pocket, where he felt for the comfort of the Shaktar stone. The stone once more felt warm in his grip, and an image of sleepiness, quiet and restful, next to a warm brightly burning hearth, grew swiftly in his mind. He looked up at the night folk now only twenty feet in front of him, had something changed?

Jack thought that as he had grabbed a hold of the Shaktar stone that a glimmer of light like the first spark of a campfire had begun in the eyes of the nearest of the sad creatures slowly shuffling towards him. He looked then at a scrawny and skinny man of indeterminate age, scabby ginger beard matted with blood and some kind of white powder that looked like talc. A moment before, the same skinny man had been staring blankly towards him like all the others, blank and yet vaguely feral, yet in an instant Silver saw that something had indeed changed, something had registered. He understood that he Jack Silver, appeared, remarkably, somehow to be, he thought for a second and then came up with, broadcasting.

He looked at them all then, and each in turn sparked as thoughts of home and rest burned red-hot from his imagination. He watched as the half-naked woman that had slowly but menacingly begun moving towards him, hesitated as the glimmer sparkled in her eyes. Jack saw a huge, black-skinned man, twenty stone at least, and in poor physical health, and he also, in turn, ceased his slow, lumbering, limping approach.

Silver had no idea what was going on, but he stared at each of the souls in front of him in turn; stared and sent out as strongly as he could a message of home and hearth, and then stood and watched as all of the people that he looked on stopped and then, after a few moments, like children in a nursery class awaiting story time, one at a time they sat down upon the ground.

The Englishman was astonished, overwhelmed in fact, he had no frame of reference, but then he figured he had been getting by on bullshit for some time in that nightmare land.

He heard a rustling from behind him and, having forgotten momentarily his pursuers from that direction, turning quickly he saw an empty plastic bag being tossed and blown by the night-time's gentle breeze across the debris-strewn landscape, and there sat, not five metres behind him, two of his pursuers.

Even the seriously injured soul that he had smashed in the skull a minute previously was sat down on the ground with a kind of beatific look upon his broken features, blood slowly congealing around the wound to his skull.

But Jack was no fool, and so he turned away from the three original pursuers and ran back up the alley the way that he had entered quick as you like, stepping carefully between the prostrate forms all then sat upon the ground. The stone was clamped tightly in his right hand, and his brain willing to think the right thoughts.

'No, Jack,' the inner voice told him. 'You can't make this happen. If you force it, the light will dim.'

He had questions to ask of that voice, that inspiration in his head that had instilled in him such a moment of life-saving invention.

That would come later, he shot out of the alley like an arrow, and he hit the ground an instant later. The crack of an automatic rifle tore apart the brand-new silence the night had so recently found. Jack Silver's scream further upset that quiet, he knew instantly he had been shot, and about three seconds later his brain, overloaded, shut down his nervous system, and to the watching mind everything turned to black.

'Stay dark…keep your eyes shut…keep your breathing slow.'

Over and over the voice ran on like warm water through his slowly waking mind. As Jack drew up towards consciousness he heard other voices, at first distant but as he became more aware, careful to follow the instructions in his head, those voices resolved into clarity.

He lay immobile, eyes tight shut, barely breathing, and he was listening to every word. He heard a woman's voice, deep and sensual. In fact so deep and so sensual that Jack Silver felt a stirring in his groin, for the first time in longer than he could remember.

The luscious deep voice reverberated gently around him.

'Something's happening out there. They brought one of the boys in. Apparently, the boss didn't like what he had to say. Then the dogs got skittish, and the short one, Shrimp, he took a shot at. Well, at nothing.' Mister Cipher was not pleased.

'Sister, it's all unravelling. Don't ya think?' a male voice interposed. Jack heard it, hard and flinty with a husky antipodean undertone.

'Why do you say that Harvey?' the husky voice replied. 'Don't let the boss catch you talking like that. He'll be here soon.'

Silver heard nothing then for what seemed to him an age. After a time, he decided to crack an eye open, certain the voices had come from behind his body hunched on the ground in the foetal position. He held on for long seconds, suddenly reminded of the rifle shot, the blinding pain that had followed. Then nothing until the insistent voice that had brought him cautiously back.

As he lay there, no pain assailed him. In fact, he felt nothing at all. His whole body was numb, and so with that realisation, he cautiously opened one eye, just for an instant, and immediately clamped it back closed again. In the fraction of a second that his right eye had been open, he took in everything he could. He saw a room that he thought he recognised, though he could not place where.

A fire burning in an open hearth, a decorative mantel surrounding that hearth and lit luridly by the flickering light cast by the flames. Sat atop the mantel, a china figurine, a lion seemingly growling and yet cowering before the trainer's whip.

The room was dimly lit, and Jack spotted that he was not indeed foetal on the floor but upon a sofa, olive-green, and dark with age and wear.

But in the microsecond, his eye had been open, that which had held his attention had been the door. Shut, in its frame, and yet apparently ill-fitting. A sickly green light was bleeding through the gaps. More precisely around the edges, the small inch or so space between the closed door and its surround. The sickly light seemed somehow to be stretching and crawling over the blistered wooden panels at the door's heart.

Georgian Jack thought suddenly scared as to who that door might admit.

He grabbed at his fear and pushed it forcefully back down.

He was in a place not of his choosing, with people that weren't likely to be amiable, and he was trying to understand why he couldn't feel the gunshot wound that he knew he had suffered.

But most of all, he was petrified by that door.

Dammit, he thought, continuing to choke the fear back down. What was it with that fucking blistered old door? He risked and looked again, quick and furtive eyes shut within a half-second. And that second time he saw a substance like, yet also unlike, varnish that was peeling away from the door's panels. That was peeling also along the seams and around the black ironwork of the handles. In its place, on the woodwork a repulsive yellow sticky substance that looked a lot like syrup.

After what seemed forever but was probably no more than ten seconds, a flinty voice spoke again.

'No, you're on the money, but nothing feels right any more. I mean, who's this bastard? Where did he come from? I thought they said that the normals were all dead.'

'Harvey, I am certain that when he wakes up we'll find out whatever the boss wants us to.'

Despite his tightly shut eyes, Jack was certain that as the woman had spoken, she had pointed at him with one long arrow-straight finger, undoubtedly tipped with a blood-red fingernail that was sharpened to a point.

The one called Harvey laughed, and seconds later Jack's brief flirt with consciousness was done. Darkness closed in once more and clamped down on the cocktail of fear and revulsion that stirred in his mind and body. The darkness came and took him away from his anxieties once more. 'Dark is safe; don't go back to the light just yet,' said the voice in his mind. 'Yes, I must,' another voice replied.

'It is time to face the devil, I think,' the second of those two voices suggested. Jack came to, woke and without hesitation this time opened his eyes.

He remembered the room that had been disconcerting, and in that same second Silver became reacquainted with the pain of a gunshot wound. Hot lead burned like the sun in his right shoulder, and he groaned involuntarily. The Englishman sat up, and he immediately realised two more things a moment after.

Firstly, he was not tied or bound. And secondly, there appeared to be no other people in the room.

The deep growl that followed seconds after his own anguished howl told Jack that, despite the absence of humans in that weird, dated lounge, it did not mean that he was the room's only occupant.

He saw that, sitting absolutely still, slightly behind a tall leafy palm in the furthest corner of the parlour, was a dog. It was the very same huge bastard of a hound that he had last seen ripping flesh to pieces outside the front of the theatre. The animal stared at him, and Jack understood why there had been no need to tie him up, escape was not an option.

The dog made no move towards him, but the beast held Jack's gaze, and he was sure that the creepy Hound of the Baskervilles dog was whispering, inside of his head.

'Go on then…you can see the door, run for it. Look, I'm right over here in the corner. Can't catch you, Jack Silver. You slip through everyone's fingers.' This began repeating in his head, six or seven times, like a child's nursery rhyme, and Jack was sorely tempted to bolt.

Despite the agony that burned in his shoulder he knew it was not a place he wanted to remain in a moment longer than he had to. But then another voice spoke, cool and calming, tiny, a child's voice.

It spoke in barely a whisper at the back of his mind, quiet and yet clear and resolute. That voice seemed to him like a sharp morning gust catching him on the step moments before he had finished buttoning his coat, a puff to remind him winter waits just around the corner.

And the voice told him to batten down the hatches, and Jack did just that.

He closed his mind off from the louder and intrusive voices and instead focused on the tiny female child's voice. He let that voice lead his mind to a calm place, and with that calm, unexpectedly, came some release from the terrible pain of the gunshot wound.

Sometime later he looked at the wound, pulled carefully at his cotton top noting the matted blood that had caused it to stick to his arm and torso. He levered it away patiently and stared at the blood-congealed mess that was his shoulder. The Englishman thought for the second time in that room that he might be sick, but he held onto the bile and instead merely gazed at the wound, brushing at the scabbing blood with his fingers. Tentatively at first and then more firmly, fidgeting until he elicited a small yelp from within as he found the wound's centre.

'Twat!' he admonished himself and then feeling around the back of his shoulder and finding a similar exit wound he decided that whatever type of round had struck him, it had exited the other side.

The pain was pain, but in the place where he now found himself, he was damn sure that if by some miracle he did escape his current situation, then infection wrapped around a bullet would probably ensure a grizzly and painful death, he felt grateful for small mercies.

Jack sat up fully on the green baize sofa and looked around the room. He was becoming aware of an undercurrent of sound from beyond the room's perimeter. Voices rose and fell like the sound of a television in another room, and there was also an additional humming. A sound deep and throbbing, mechanical; an undercurrent of power.

Jack recognised the second sound was almost certainly that of a generator, and a big one if the deep bass sound was anything to go by. He looked around and saw floor-to-ceiling heavy drapes along the wall immediately behind him: they were blood-red in colour and Jack pictured the Georgian sash windows that stood tall behind those weighty curtains. The fire burned low and sullen, and Silver felt the close, sweltering heat that had built up in the room.

He looked again at the beast and wondered if that creature, too, felt the suffocating warmth that had him tugging at the neck of his top, suddenly tight and constraining. He thought about his situation and felt certain that he must have been shot by one of the crew he had seen loitering outside the front of the theatre. Of course, he had no idea how long ago that had been. But logic suggested, as did his personal guard, that he was holed up somewhere near that theatre, very probably somewhere inside of it, captured.

Jack Silver felt he was close to, if not now within, the inner circle of Stevan Cipher's domain, that this was the freak-filled place. The kid that he had earlier managed to lose painted a lurid picture of a world destroyed, a place where only a few held tightly on to the reigns of some final authority, but over who and for what purpose?

He wondered at where that poor lost boy might be now, where all the poor lost souls of this world gone mad now were. He thought that Robbie Benedict the child had been pretty close to the edge and barely surviving when he had stumbled upon him, balanced on a precipice of terror that looked beyond his understanding, and surviving by only wits and luck.

As such he had been like a representative for that whole mad world, broken down and sliding inevitably towards hell. So it was that Jack Silver had woken one day and found, like Rip van Winkle, a world changed beyond comprehension.

The images of death and depravity that had earlier twice assaulted him, seemed to him now more like newsreel, amplifying all that he feared or understood.

Somehow, somebody had taken the world, this world, and twisted it with deeds most foul, leaving it rotting and slowly dying in the hands of a few remaining scavengers.

The Englishman mused about this, and he wondered too about escape.

Voices spoke up from beyond the door. Jack heard a high, fluting tone that for a moment he thought might be of a child, then corrected himself as the voice continued, and he realised it was a man speaking. He closed his eyes and tried to concentrate all of his will on listening to what that voice was saying, and within he heard the words.

'One step at a time,' and that gave him the seeds of a plan.

It had issued forth an essence of itself and found an agent of purpose. In order to slake a burning thirst for malice, the entity needed to bring itself to the heart of the action, the midst of the living clamour. Faster than thought, and beeline straight, it set forth.

Chapter Twenty-Seven
Last Train to London

The persistent electronic beeping of the overhead display announced it was time for seatbelts, and Jack awoke.

He found that he had slept for most of the flight and supposed that was good. His creaking joints paid testament to the discomfort of having been in the same small square of space for so many hours, and he was desperate to piss but realised that he would have to hold himself for a further twenty minutes or so.

He watched as a heavyset man, a thug if looks were anything to go by, and not the sort to cross, stood up in spite of the seatbelt light, right across the aisle from Silver, walked down to the block of toilets immediately past the pretty blonde stewardess, entered a cubicle and shut the door with a thud. Jack unclipped his own seatbelt, and after nudging the passenger next to him and eliciting no reaction, barked.

'I need to piss, move?'

The rotund man looked at the passenger who had lain asleep next to him for more than ten hours and was about to make some acid pronouncement of his own about the seatbelt light until he saw the fury raging deep in the man's eyes and that frightened him so much he was out of his seat in about half of the two seconds available to him.

'Sorry' is the single word uttered by him in a sullen, scared tone.

The pretty stewardess looked across the space between her and Silver and also seemed about to speak, but Jack stared at her with gaunt unblinking eyes as he stepped into a washroom and slammed the door shut behind him. He stared at his reflection in the tinted glass.

Bruises yellow and black ran across his face, he knew he was returning to the country of his birth in a worse condition even than when he had left. But, as he urinated hard and long, washed his scabbed and bruised hands, found no paper to dry them on and chose the front of his top instead, he reflected that this time he intended to kill before being killed.

He looked again in the mirror at the grim, gaunt and unshaven face that stared back at him, lit by the intensity that burned in his eyes. That face seemed full of a fierce determination that frankly he found a little scary.

He had flown one way across the Atlantic in order to escape the clutches of a psychotic pursuer, but now he returned to exact revenge.

No, not revenge, Jack corrected himself, this was retribution. He understood that he had found his children whilst on the run; not the seed of his loins, but certainly each one had opened the door to his soul. And each of them had fallen into his care, and twice now they had been ripped from that care.

Jack Silver understood in order to exact retribution he must become that which he had dreaded, a more dangerous man than ever he had been.

Sometime later the plane landed and, after the usual irritating wait, engendered by only three staff working in passport control, Silver slipped through the airport without incident. He had his collar turned up against prying eyes and a cap pulled down low. The Englishman had no luggage to wait for, and so he stepped out into the cold of a British autumn morning.

During his absence, he had forgotten what home felt like, the taste in the air, the feel of rush and scurry from the people around him. And, despite the fact that this country, and this city in particular, had been home to him for more than four decades, as he stood there wondering at his next move Jack felt the world surrounding him right then was alien indeed.

He had thought about flying onward again, ultimately he was heading for Edinburgh, he knew that much about where the heartland of Stevan Cipher was based. Jack knew that on home soil his opponents would be watching out for him, and these bastards that had found him in the woods in Canada, wouldn't let home turf be a cakewalk.

No, he thought to himself, *he needed to be like The Sandman, now more than ever, slipping between the fingers of any and all pursuers.*

He decided, as he watched his breath white in the morning air and stamped his feet, that what he needed was to slide below society's radar.

As Paul Weller had liked to sing a decade before, he too was "Going Underground".

He looked towards the coach park waiting area and saw, among a multitudinous variety of people loitering in the hope of a bus showing up, two teenagers in zipped-up sweat tops, both of them smoking and whispering earnestly, hoods pulled low over the head like latter-day monks buried deep within the folds of their cowls.

Jack could see neither one's face, could only guess at their ages and demeanour, and decided on the spot that was the way forward.

He looked for the route to the tube terminal, saw a sign and decided his journey would start with a more literal trip on the underground than perhaps Paul Weller had meant.

Unknown to Jack, as he walked back onto the moving walkway in order to re-enter the terminal, Stevan Cipher knew full well that his enemy had returned to the land of his birth, and he no longer needed spies nor Shadowmen to feed him such titbits.

The steps of Jack Silver were now to Stevan Cipher lit incandescently bright. And so as Jack Silver's plane touched down at London Heathrow, so bright was the light around him as to hurt Cipher's eyes. So white as to brighten further the rage he felt burning inside him.

That brightness made Cipher squint, and so still somehow Jack Silver seemed to find the dark places to slip into, and so continued to avoid Cipher's Shadowmen for a little longer. But Cipher knew the enemy had returned, and so he too prepared for the coming of the endgame.

Twelve hours later, Jack found himself on a sleeper train to Edinburgh.

He had changed his remaining forty-three dollars to sterling and felt some vague humanity in him still at the disgust felt at the lousy rate he got.

At Euston Station, he saw a gift shop and bought himself a large grey hooded sweatshirt emblazoned with an overlay of the best of London's tourist attractions. The large nondescript top presented Nelson's column, Tower Bridge, Buckingham Palace, The Natural History Museum, and like an arc behind them all, The London Eye. Jack bought it because he hated it. It was ugly, and he decided on exactly the kind of cheap tacky tourist wear that made people look the other way.

Also, because he had got all of that for precisely £15.99, leaving him with the princely sum of £6.37 in the world.

After he ate a sweating overpriced burger and fries at one of the station's franchise outlets, got onto the train as soon as the platform was announced, and achieved it without a ticket.

The Englishman travelled quickly to the back of the rearmost part of the train, moving past each of the sleeper carriages with a series of one and two-bunk cubicles. He peered into each one warily.

When he got to the last carriage he scrunched himself down into a seat in the rearmost corner. Above him, the light was failing, and he was sat next to a grate which gently blew out a warm flow of air that smelled vaguely of diesel.

The carriage was empty, and he figured other passengers were making a grab for the available bunks. No one else entered the carriage until about two minutes before the train was due to depart. He prayed the ticket inspector wouldn't reach him until the train had departed deciding he would cross that bridge when he had to.

Soon after drifting towards a napping sleep unexpectedly a metallic clunk followed by the quiet swish of the electric doors opening, brought him back to wakefulness.

A young couple came into the last car, both no more than early twenties. He looked up from under the grey hood he wore then pulled low over his head.

The couple stepped aboard hand in hand, dressed like fashion victims from a 1980s wedding in matching soft pastel colours. And they both entered the carriage obviously the worse for drink.

The couple saw the hooded man only as the doors swished back closed, and in that instant both stopped laughing. He appeared to them strangely indistinct. The light above him flickered slightly and the pair saw dirty jeans and a grey sweatshirt too big for the wearer, pulled down fully over the man's head.

Even in the dim light, the Englishman looked the sort that couples in wedding guest clothes ought not to sit close to on a nine-hour train ride to Scotland, nor even the first two hours to Birmingham.

And so, after a kind of telepathic glance at one another that transmitted that all in a nanosecond, the two turned away from the grey man, walked quickly to the opposite end of the carriage, and without any subtlety whatsoever opened the interconnecting doors and were gone.

Jack smiled to himself and nodded approvingly as he thought that at first the whole sweatshirt hood thing had done exactly what he hoped.

He needed space, and the relative security space might accord him.

Night came quickly, and Jack gazed out through the windows. He did not see the countryside as it sped by, instead, alongside his own disembodied ghostly reflection he saw a series of images in the glass of the window. He thought back upon all that had happened to him during the past few months.

He saw again a vision of a man killed in a dark alley. Murdered in cold blood, he stood by and watched.

He asked himself for the thousandth time why he had stepped outside of that bar; if only if only, he thought wryly.

In that moment, he had stepped out of his old life, safe and sterile as it had been, and into some alternate universe. Now he found himself in a world governed by the devil and his minions.

And in that new world had spent many months running and hiding, scurrying from shadow to shadow, a hunted animal.

As the train rumbled on he recalled how in a frail and random moment of chance he had met Keith Kirkcaldy. A young roadside vagrant who had been getting by on wits and not much else.

How quickly Jack reflected they had grown to be friends. For his part, he thought that he'd been struck by a young man pressed hard by the difficulties of his life, yet who would live still by such a clean and honest moral code?

At the time he had been in a mess, and Caffee's mere presence had shown him those first steps on the road back to some kind of personal redemption.

They had crossed borders both geographic and personal, and in the end, despite all that he had learned about moral code and honour from the young man, Jack had been willing to break his promise.

Before the end.

He stopped short then for long moments as the vivid image struck him once again of Caffee lying on the hardware store's floor, life ebbing quickly out of him.

Had Jack stopped then because of the memory of Caffee lying dead or was it in fact because he carried the guilt still? His conscience reminded him over and over that, however much he had sought and found redemption nevertheless he had been on the verge of letting Caffee down, running out on him, breaking promises made.

And then flight. He had been blind, lost in the darkness of his own fear, and he had run.

At this point, Jack fished the Shaktar stone out from his jeans pocket and scrutinised it closely. It looked like nothing more than a seaside pebble. There were millions on Brighton Beach alone, yet this stone had come to him in the woods when Caffee had been vibrant and alive still.

Passed to him by a strange old man.

'Ageless Jack, not old,' Caffee's voice spoke up in his mind. He knew now that this stone, however much it appeared like so many others was unique.

But he still did not understand the gifts the stone might possess, nor its purpose if any. But he understood that stone was in his care for a time.

The Englishman's thoughts turned then to Molly; she too had saved him. Despite the fact he had found her unconscious and alone, and moreover had never found exactly how she had ended up like that. 'You may know before the end, Mister Jack,' she spoke up quietly at the back of his mind. Jack thought he was saving her, a child he had found in distress. Yet in the end, he understood she had saved him.

From himself as much as from his pursuers.

That girl had rebuilt him.

In the dusty peace of her aunt and uncle's rural life. And the clean country air and summer sunshine of a world he had never before known, Molly had understood instinctively that, however complicated life became it was those simple things that we all fall back on, safe ground in times of pain.

Jack reflected that she had often appeared to possess insights and maturity far beyond her young years. In many ways, she had become more than a friend to him, she was his daughter, as Caffee had become his son. And she spoke to him inside his mind still.

Jack felt her guiding hand even in the days that followed her awful death. He had learned so much from Molly St Etienne, and he loved her and all that she stood for.

Caffee and Molly were the best people he had known. And yet, in the end, he knew he had failed her too.

She had died because he turned away because, in the end, he left.

The Englishman looked again at the reflection in the train window and saw tears running freely down his cheeks. He blinked a couple of times and as he did he realised the train was slowing.

"Birmingham Central" was announced on the intercom, and a minute later the train pulled to a halt at the only stop between London and Edinburgh.

He sat up straight in his seat and pulled the hood that had fallen from his face during the intervening hours back fully over his head. The train made a series of mechanical pops and hisses as it sat motionless in the station. The noises were accompanied by a cacophony of lesser clicks as heat bled from the vehicle's mechanical systems, and people noisily disembarked and joined the fray.

The long iron beast sat at the station for precisely seven minutes, and despite the hubbub in that time, Jack saw only two people walk past his window. He checked anxiously for a ticket collector.

It was approaching ten o'clock in the evening, and so he reasoned that not so many people would be out without somewhere to go on a cold autumn night. He was ruminating on this and whether he thought it might be safe to step from the carriage and seek something to eat and drink when a whistle sounded, and he understood it was time to get moving.

Jack was pushing back into his seat when, once more he heard a clunk swish, and the doors to the carriage opened again.

This time the opening admitted a single person. At first, look at a mirror image of Jack himself. A scruffy man in baggy low-hanging jeans and a black hooded sweatshirt, similarly, pulled low over the wearer's head.

The whistle blew once again, and the train clunked and started to ease slowly out of the station. The new arrival, without appearing to look up at all began to move towards Jack, wobbling slightly as the train picked up momentum.

Before Jack Silver could even consider the carriage's new passenger, a voice emanated from the black folds of the sweatshirt's hood and asked, 'Mate…is this the train to London?'

The artefact appeared dulled as much by the long years as by the burden of its not random journey. It needed one thing more before the appointed moment, one thing only in order to make it right. Yet at that instant, it appeared to seek nothing, merely waited and watched.

Chapter Twenty-Eight
Tightrope

As hard as Jack tried, he could not break down the rumble of voices he could hear into distinctive words. He looked across at the beast impassively sitting behind the tall palm in the room's corner.

He heard a woman's voice, and a higher reedy voice, a man's though more feminine than the luscious-sounding woman.

He waited for one or for both people to enter the room, to seal his fate. Yet as seconds turned to minutes nobody came. Jack had assumed, mistakenly it seemed that his capture would be the first order of business in this strange world of nightmare.

But for whatever reason after some minutes the voices receded, and Jack was alone again except for the damned dog.

Christ he hated dogs he thought to himself, looking balefully across the room at the animal. He for a time unmoving, knowing he was in a precarious position but unable to think of any logical way out of the situation.

His sensory awareness had increased during the time he had spent in this "other world". And so, piecing together what little he knew, or at least thought he knew, from the mixture of hypothesis, distorted memories and nightmare, he tried to formulate an escape.

His shoulder throbbed horribly, but it did not hurt as much as Silver thought a bullet wound ought to.

As best as Jack and the insistent voices in his head seemed able to put things together he was caught, most likely by his chief persecutor.

It seemed, just for added value in that place of unremitting awfulness that said persecutor appeared to have effectively reduced humankind to a rag-tag starving band of tortured and broken souls, at least in the locales that he had been privy to. Folk with no dignity, no future, and in most cases, as far as he could tell most had gone completely insane.

Of course, Silver had no real idea whether any of those thoughts were true. But it "felt" to him like what had happened. It all felt right to him.

The whole wrongness of the place clicked into a warped kind of logic when he put the pieces together in just that certain way.

He considered more and found he didn't understand how or why a child had been spared.

Though he had met only the one boy, somehow even one sane child running around trying to survive in a world populated by the mad, under the yoke of Cipher's tyranny. Somehow that "felt" even worse.

He had no idea what part he might have to play in this drama, but the Englishman was convinced he could not fulfil that part sat in some Victorian sitting room awaiting the fall of fate's axe.

He peered again at the dog and then looked towards the mantel.

He had glanced around the room previously, searching for a weapon. Everything seemed hopeless to him. He remembered the small night creature torn limb from limb in seconds, the killing beast's dull yellow fangs, incisors longer than the fingers on his hands. And even as he steeled himself to attack the dog and suffer the inevitable vicious response Silver looked desperately round the room a second time, hoping to spy a weapon, something to give him a fighting chance.

Atop the mantel sat a China figurine in two parts, he vaguely remembered spying it before.

A highly glazed China scene depicting a lion sitting low to the ground on all four paws, head lowered between its front legs. The eyes, even in the dim flickering light from across the room, showed a kind of sullen servility, no kingliness inhabited that lion's features.

The eyes told everything, the beast had met its match, and more. Across from the beast stood the lion tamer, dressed in a dark blue coat with tails and a red-striped waistcoat showing from beneath.

The lion tamer seemed to hold a whip in his left hand, and in his right a little incongruous now that Jack thought about it, the figure held a small lantern.

The lantern was lit, and at the back of his mind Jack could almost make out the hushed whispering of the crowds, the distant voice of the ringmaster still entreating all comers.

'Roll up, roll up, good people. Just a penny buys you miracles and magic.'

He imagined the entire scene taking place just outside the circle of light cast by the lantern, and Jack suddenly understood it was the lantern that held the lion's gaze and not the whip.

That was the trick.

You couldn't beat down a lion with a whip, because inevitably it would one day rear up and tear your heart out.

'But, hey, you can trick anything, anyone into submission, if you can just out think 'em.'

Silver thought about it, still gazing intently at the scene on the mantel.

Lions (dogs) were dumb animals. One was king of the jungle, and the other was man's best friend, but neither was awarded the cleverest dick in town.

Oh no not by a country mile, even in a town like this, one that seemed to have had an intelligence bypass.

Jack thought maybe he might be able to deal out the whip-hand.

His hand strayed down to his jeans, and he pulled the Shaktar stone out from its hiding place. The stone felt warm to the touch once more.

He remembered that feeling from another time and place, and as he looked it seemed that the stone glowed a mild milky white, as if it were somehow lit from within.

'Lantern bright,' a chirpy voice piped up in his mind.

Without thought or plan Jack lifted the stone between thumb and forefinger and held it up over his head, kind of presenting it to the animal. The gesture appeared to grab hold of the animal's gaze.

And then said, in what sounded to him like an incredibly slow and sonorous voice.

'Here, doggy.' Then after a second or two again, 'Here doggy. Look at the stone, isn't she beautiful?'

And to his surprise, the dog looked. In fact, not only did the animal look, but it stared hard and unblinking at the stone, and Jack Silver felt excitement building. The creature appeared to gaze in rapture at the milky white apparition, sort of expectantly.

Silver thought to himself the dog was a huge dumb vicious monster of an animal, yet it stared rapt at the pulsing stone in the hand of the person who only seconds before had been the prisoner. And he realised as the beast looked towards his outstretched hand, the prisoner had become the master, the dog was at that moment no more threatening than a babe in arms.

The Shaktar stone continued to get warmer as he held it up, and his shoulder throbbed with holding that arm above his head, and the gunshot wound on the other side for company. He understood instinctively it would be a mistake to lower that arm, or even to swap the stone from right hand to left.

He was the ringmaster now, and he was taming his lion. Not with brute force. No, Jack was using his brain or so help him, he hoped that he was. He sat up straight and continued to hold the stone up, arm arrow straight.

The dog stared at it, at him, for a long time. But as each minute passed Silver thought the animal became less and less aware of the stone's holder, less interested in anything that was not the pale white pulsing glow.

The animal had been named Dagger. Big as a puppy when he had been found, sharp teeth and trained by evil masters in malice and cruelty, fed him on flesh and nothing else. Those men had taught the dog to fight and to be obedient too. The hound had responded well and started to climb his own ladder within the greater hierarchy that existed, till eventually in the four-legged world the animal held sway.

In the yard and the kitchens and all of the low places, a dog might come to.

This animal ruled his pack in his way. Dagger did not know why his masters wanted this particular piece of meat, this white-skinned man so weak and afraid.

Nevertheless, it was his job to watch and keep guard.

Yet somehow, as the light grew inside the animal's mind, a new instruction came, born on some breeze within the beast's own imagination.

More time passed, and that new guide simply repeated over and over, round and round, in time with the rhythm of each pulse.

After a time, the dog laid back down on all fours, held still by the luminescent glow, paws out in front. Slowly, inch by inch, Silver watching as still as a stone gargoyle, the animal's gargantuan head drooped and dipped until, finally, it lay between those two front paws.

And at last, beyond any expectation, the animal closed its eyes and drifted into sleep.

Jack held the stone up for a full minute longer, though noticing how immediately the dog had fallen into slumber the glow that had so beautifully lit the scene only moments before began to diminish. He stared at the big dog and felt without looking as he placed the stone gingerly back into his front pocket, all the while attempting absolute silence.

He was moving at a snail's pace, though inside he was exultant at such an unexpected and spectacular triumph.

In the distance, he heard music and was able to piece together the words to Glenn Miller's *At Last* crooning out in muted tones with a big band backing.

He climbed to his feet and immediately toppled forward and almost fell back onto the floor. He had lost blood and lots of it. Pins and needles assailed both his legs, the movement to upright had shocked his previously recumbent body. He looked at the Hound of the Baskervilles unmoving in slumber and, after gathering his wits, and ensuring that his body parts were all in some kind of working order, he moved towards the door.

Once he was upright the previously daunting panelled door appeared to hold a little less threat. Jack understood that whatever the Shaktar stone had done with his canine jailer, seemed likely to be short-lived, and he needed out of the sickly and overwhelmingly odd room as soon as possible, and that meant going through the door, whatever lay beyond.

'Are you sure about that, Jack Silver?' a voice asked in his mind, and he thought he was.

Jack moved to within inches of the door and listened. He heard the muted big-band music, IT had moved on from Glenn Miller to a melodic track Jack half-recognised but couldn't place. No one sounded close by and so, with a final backward glance at the still-sleeping animal, he stepped boldly around the door and out into a passageway of sorts. It bore no resemblance whatsoever to the room he had been in.

Grey-floored, the space was lit by some type of fluorescent light that shone evenly throughout. The corridor was perhaps fifty feet long with white walls that appeared to be made from some kind of plastic.

Sterilised, ethereal, Two Thousand And One A Space Odyssey, it screamed at Jack. It's all mad, I'm in a dream, and with that he stopped dead, only having taken two or three paces into the strange hospital "morgue" corridor.

There were several doors further down the space, spread evenly on both sides, at least a dozen as well as he could figure.

Eleven were closed, and one stood ajar.

Jack looked hard at the door, squinting in the brightness of the luminescence, and as he did any thoughts of dreaming disappeared as he was hit by gut-wrenching fear once more.

In the next breath, a pulse of pain from the gunshot wound bent him over double, and he vomited violently.

Hurtling together like a pitcher's ball into a catcher's mitt.
Created only with and for this single purpose.
Aware and yet not, the arc of a single throw random chance or the result of all its creation had wrought to that moment.

Chapter Twenty-Nine
Honest Men

Not only was it bright in the corridor, furthermore Jack realised it was cold, freezing cold.

'Deathly cold, the kind you found in a place where the dead lay their heads down to rest,' so spoke up a stark voice in his mind. Jack was looking at the steaming content of his guts quickly cooling on the floor. He felt a little better, though reflected that his arm and shoulder hurt like a bitch. It appeared somehow as if he had stepped through a portal into another place, yet another world.

The fetid warmth and sickly yellowing lights of the parlour were here replaced by white walls, white light and white breath from his puffed-out cheeks.

He crossed his arms and shivered, and then looked at the series of evenly spaced doors, eleven closed and only one open. Neat he thought to himself, a little too neat. He turned quickly and was less surprised than he might have been that the peeling Georgian panelled door he had moments before stepped through was gone. Behind him now was just another closed door, an exact match for the other twelve.

'Thirteen in total that figures,' Jack mumbled to himself. Then he added, 'Unlucky for some. Still, I guess that sorts Rover out.' He shivered again and wondered if it was the cold or the ominous silence.

The pervading sense that all of a sudden he was even further away from anything that resembled home than he ever could have imagined, further than anyone had ever been away from his or her home he thought.

Just when he could have done with a reassuringly glib riposte from one of the new friends his brain seemed to have been gathering, everyone it seemed had gone suddenly very quiet. Jack noted that the muted big-band music had vanished in the moment he slipped through the portal from scary Sherlock Holmes parlour to…well whatever this place was. A voice whispered urgently in his head, 'You gotta get outta here,' and in the same moment, he thought to himself, Arkham Asylum, it feels like Arkham Asylum in Gotham City.

Memories of all those Batman comics he had read over and over as a kid when he needed a place to escape to whilst in the care homes. Recollections of Tony Stark, industrialist; Matt Murdoch, blind keeper of justice; and, best of all, Bruce Wayne, millionaire philanthropist and caped crusader of the night. Batman the uber-warrior.

Back then all those mighty and yet flawed men were all that he had to cling to, honest guys that went into battle time and again, and that won, kind of. But as he grew older he hadn't really stopped reading comics, rather that comics had stopped looking for him. Up. They had helped to tune his imagination and make it sharp and intuitive, but they had shown him Arkham too.

There had never been more than a dozen titles at Hillside House, where he had spent more than two years after his father had expired. And the issues had been random and dog-eared. You walked into the middle of a story latched on for forty or fifty panels and then got off breathless and hopeful for more. Jack remembered and understood why he liked Batman the best. Always the villain held the whip-hand matching up to the hero. Somehow Batman had always stood apart, not because he was a badass himself, but rather because all of his archenemies, every single one of them, had hailed from that same awful place, from the Batman villain-making factory that was Arkham Asylum.

Jack figured he had landed in his own Arkham Asylum, and he was no Batman.

'Ahh, shit!' he whispered to himself. 'Never a superhero around when you need one.'

Jack looked all around him; his head was darting from side to side like a hunted beast, and like the song said he thought panicked, 'Nowhere to run to nowhere to hide.'

He figured his options at somewhere between zero and a fraction less, yet as a buzzing screech began to brow about him he really had no clear idea what he thought was coming.

Suddenly, the open door, the one furthest from where he stood slammed shut with a loud metallic clang.

A moment later, the corridor was plunged into darkness.

To the Englishman's eyes that instant dark was absolute. Where moments before he had been squinting against the stark unvarnished white light, it was in an instant so dark he could not see any part of himself.

The voice came again, whispering urgent and hard, right at the front of his mind, 'You've got to go now, get out of here, right now. No delay.' He was all turned round, but the furious desperate whispering in his head got him moving.

He couldn't tell which way to go but took two or three paces and smacked hard into a wall. Juddering pain bolted through his injured shoulder and that pain brought him back, His eyes shed sudden tears, but they were adjusting. He saw vaguely the line of one long wall and, reaching out with his good arm, he began to feel his way along that wall. He noticed the temperature was rising. Not exactly soaring, but it had gone from freezing to passable in maybe ten seconds.

He started to creep along the corridor, hand sliding along the wall. It felt damp. In fact, it felt like the wall was sweating. In no time, he reached the first door.

'Go, Jack. Go now. Here is not for you.' He heard the insistent voice pushing at him. There appeared ahead something like a small window or porthole in the door, with something like and yet not like that wired safety glass synonymous with schools and other public buildings.

He stepped past the door and did not look in. Inside he was desperate just to glance. He knew there would be something to see, but the voice inside pushed at him, cajoled him, kept him moving and kept him off-balance. Still, it took every fibre of his being not to look. He was human, that's what humans did, wasn't it?

The sound that had begun was a wailing which he imagined coiling up and down, a small auditory boat tossed about on some stormy soup of silence, it frightened Silver. Something about that sound was not right, sounded bad, grating like cat claws on a chalkboard. No worse he thought, more, well revolting he decided. The Englishman thought he might lose his guts again, but he held out and moved on, fighting almost physically the horrible intense buzz-saw wailing. He knew at a level more guttural even than instinct that when the thing responsible for that awful sound found him any opportunity to escape that place would end abruptly.

He reached the second door that sat on his side of the space. His eyes had adjusted somewhat, and from his vantage point, he saw the outline of yet another door opposite, a door width further down.

'They do that so the inmates can't communicate,' a voice suggested to Jack's frayed nerves. 'So that they can't disturb one another in those cold dark cells.'

He looked at the door opposite and saw the same small peephole window three-quarters of the way up the steel-like construction still too dim to make out more. Silver slid past the second door, again managing not to look. As he did abruptly, the wailing stopped, and as he slid along the sweating wall, perspiring freely now in the heated-up atmosphere, something brushed against his face.

It felt like nothing more than a wisp of cobweb, but Jack was certain no spider survived in that sanitised place. He yelped, unable to stop himself, deep within he felt his insides twist as terror took hold.

'Fucking hell, get a hold of yourself,' he said to himself violently, out loud, desperate to keep any sort of hold upon his sanity, yet even more frightened by the shaky sound of his own voice.

The next two doors were easy; he was so frightened that he had no desire to look at anything, let alone through or beyond. He tried as hard as he was able to actually look at nothing.

He wasn't moving quickly, but he was moving steadily. He had now negotiated four of the six doors on that side of the wall, effectively eight of the twelve, he figured. The silence was complete again, and Silver felt it enveloping him. 'Wrap you up and choke you, sweetums,' a new and unwelcome voice whispered nastily in his mind. And whilst he didn't like the tone he knew it was right.

Jack felt the atmosphere, the silence itself was malevolent, and it swirled around him with eddies filled with hatred and vitriol. Compared to that silence the wailing of before now seemed peachy, he thought.

His arm throbbed up and deep in his shoulder a burning that grew and bled into his torso. He felt in his front pocket and found the Shaktar stone there. It sat deep at the base of the pocket, wrapped protectively in the cotton lining of his jeans.

But where before the stone had exuded light and energy in the face of the menacing hound, it sat then chill and lifeless. Silver thought it felt all used up, something about that place was different.

He thought it wasn't actually a place at all, at least not in the sense that he understood such things. Where he found himself he figured was more akin to a gap, a space existing between places, the dark damp bit between the plasterboard and the brickwork.

Through the doors, Jack thought would be the world's where the likes of him were supposed to exist, where the moon moved through the sky and followed the sun. Where people were born and lived and died.

In that dark and sweating space, the likes of him were not meant to be. His instincts told him that things existed there that were from, if not the other side, at the very least another side.

Jack did not know what that meant precisely, but from the other side seemed exactly right.

Mind you he considered, thus far he hadn't encountered any living thing, and he hoped that would continue.

He realised that when he had walked through the door from the Sherlock Holmes parlour, he somehow had gone elsewhere from where he should have. He wondered if maybe the Shaktar stone had slipped him in here.

The Englishman had no idea, but as he moved up close to the penultimate door on that side of the corridor a feeling overwhelmed him that he had only moments more before someone, something found him.

He stepped past the fifth door, peering across the gloom briefly at the offset door opposite. He wondered at that last door it was closed now, and it had been open. Jack wondered whether that was an invitation or a warning. He figured he could do with a lead from those voices in his head.

The door slammed shut. He wondered was that closure shutting him out or tempting him to try his luck and join those within.

His instincts offered him nothing.

The fear was cloying, the heat the darkness and the atmosphere, all closing in on his anxiety. The Shaktar stone remained dead and cold in his pocket, and time felt as if it was hurtling much too quickly through some countdown to doom that he felt much too clearly.

Once again he found himself unsure what to do. His hand reached the edge of the door. Did he push through to some Promised Land, or did he wait on the precipice of doom, he simply did not know.

'Shit! It'll probably be locked,' he said to himself spying the faintest gap between door and surround close up. His fingers brushed at that gap inadvertently, and he broke the silence again with a small yelp. The gap was only a couple of millimetres. Yet the cold air that blew through that space felt like some version of absolute zero and only amplified how hot it was becoming there in that dark black place.

It had felt so cold on his hand as to make him jump, his body instantly covered in goosebumps, cold enough even to have hurt him.

He stepped away from the door without any conscious thought as to what he was doing. All of a sudden he was away from the relative safety of the wall he had been sliding along. He immediately discovered a disconcerting sensation akin to vertigo, he was spinning in an inky void that was the middle of the corridor. Everything began to whip around him, faster and faster, very quickly reaching an incredible rate. His head swam, his whole body clenching and releasing with uncontrollable contractions. The Englishman staggered and almost fell, staggered again, took a step, and then a step more, and then with a dull painful thud, he smacked hard back into the wall.

'God!' Jack choked. The sound of his voice was loud, too audible in the silence. The single word cut through the atmosphere like a knife in a way his earlier utterances had not, and Jack reached out with his arms and felt the sold wall, all the while coughing and retching, trying to wrest back control of his body.

His guts had ceased to tense and release only as he hit the wall, yet it still felt to him like he had been trampled on by a herd of rhinos.

Jack threw up, suddenly and unexpectedly, spitting at hot burning bile in his throat; spots floated in front of his eyes, miniature jellyfish swimming across the ocean of darkness that surrounded him.

He was doubled over and felt the throbbing in his arm and shoulder as a deep solid pain that told of difficult times to come if he survived!

He had bent as he threw up, become once more disoriented, and as he stood upright again found himself directly in front of a door.

The Englishman gazed at the spots that swirled and eddied slowly clearing as his vision closed on the view panel in the door.

He looked part-eyed through the porthole; at the same time, part of his eyesight caught the reflection behind him, visible as a back-to-front, an inverted reflection between the two places.

What Jack Silver saw on the other side of the door made him scream, his voice breaking and hoarse.

In the darkness beyond, he saw hundreds, maybe thousands, maybe even millions of pairs of eyes. And all of them staring back at him.

Still, pale white, unblinking and passive dead eyes stared straight back at him. How could that door, any door, offer him escape when what lay beyond was a world of eyes?

The eyes of those that would be left after.

There was no escape in there he thought bitterly.

Except that, in the same instant he saw the staring eyes of a sea of lost souls, he saw something else. Something that was turned towards him. Jack saw a reflection, and it was close and stood in the uniform inky darkness behind him.

The thing was huge, sinewy black and glistening, a creature from a nightmare.

Dripping with some awful bright yellow venom, rancid with a stench that assaulted Jack Silver's nostrils with a putrescence that brought fresh bile up into his mouth again. The thing was utterly inhuman, and it was vile and filthy in a way that repulsed him more than anything he had ever imagined possible.

A voice deep within called the thing out and named it apocalypse. That ancient evil incarnate all humankind had been brought up to fear.

Silver heard the voice but felt it viscerally, instinctively.

And so, in only one instant, he saw the ocean of eyes and the appalling reflection both.

And worse, he understood the thing saw him too and wanted him for itself. Something within compelled him to push at the door he was up against, to step through into the ocean of eyes. Yet in the moment before he shoved, he felt a deep and awful throbbing in his shoulder, a pain worse than any that had gone before.

And so it was that throbbing, that bullet he had taken – forced him to his knees at the last, pushed down rather than pushed through the door.

Instead of opening the door, he found himself scrabbling desperately across a wet and slippery floor.

He never opened the door, never dived into the cold dark place. Instead, Jack slid, scrabbled desperately feeling his mind unravelling, babbling, and spinning out of control desperate to avoid the nightmare behind him.

But an instant later he realised trickery had been at work. The thing wasn't reaching for him, it wasn't reaching for him because it wasn't really there, at least not in a physical sense.

Jack understood it was a creature born in his mind, fed and nurtured on his, on all humankind's fears that had been reaching into him, a representation of all of the fear made real put there exactly to push him through that portal, into…

He shuddered and dared himself to think no further.

Despite then knowing there was no monster there, not in the biblical sense at least Jack still felt his mind sliding towards the edge. His thoughts were like jelly. He kept grabbing mentally at them, but just couldn't get a hold.

He didn't have time to think rationally but scrambling to his feet he reached the door diagonally across from where he had seen the eyes, amazed and thanking any god that would listen for the bullet wound that had proven to be the only thing that gave him a grip.

That wound had reminded him of his left and his right and had made him aware, in a pause so brief as to be instantaneous, that he was about to step through the wrong portal. And so, standing once more he jabbed two fingers hard into the soft tissue where the bullet had entered, screamed loudly and pushed.

In one motion, the door opened, and he slithered, and the Englishman dived blindly through into whatever lay beyond.

A second later something cold and hard hit Jack in the head.

Darkness closed around him, and unconsciousness took him once more.

Time passed.

Jack came round feeling dazed. He found himself slumped on a hard floor. It was dark, the black was absolute, and he couldn't see a thing. There was no scent the air was still, the temperature neither warm nor cold.

He felt no urge to move and was unsure whether something had hit him, or he had hit something. He had no inkling how long he had been unconscious, and he thought that in the darkness it was impossible to know anything for sure.

'Saved by a bullet, who would have thought it,' Jack said to himself, sensing that maybe he wasn't alone, but finding it difficult to be certain.

'Just the two of us, I guess,' Jack said, pulling himself into a more upright position and crossing his legs.

He let the silence draw out, hoping to garner something more from or about the disembodied place he was in, as well as trying to confirm the presence of another that he thought he sensed.

Before he had been diving through an opening, praying for his life.

Sometime before that, and it concerned him he wasn't sure how long before, but some time before he remembered a room and a very big dog.

Jack found that he had no pain. He prodded at his shoulder, at first gently then more aggressively. It felt numb, but not painful to the touch. He didn't know if that was good or bad, but it didn't hurt, he thought that was at least something.

Changing tack Jack spoke out into the inky blackness.

'Do you know who I am?'

Silence.

He shrugged, then yawned and closed his eyes. His heart rate was slow though he was undeniably suspicious. The place did not evoke the terror of those other destinations he had moved through.

'Are you able to give me answers? Do you understand? Do you even hear me?'

And then as he yawned once again following a lengthy pause a voice replied.

And in Douglas Bader's best English, said, 'Well, not exactly correct, sir. A good fist I'll grant you. Good enough, I think. Yes by Jove, good enough for today.'

Jack jumped at the voice. He had just begun to think he could not trust his senses as much as he thought. The new voice whilst neutral had features and inflections that Jack was trying hard to grab hold of. It seemed to him that the voice was neat and articulate in a way different to Jack's own.

He had taught himself to speak, as a youngster he'd drilled himself over and over, finding an inherent ability to apply the right tone and the right language according to the company he found himself in. It had proven to be a skill that had served him well throughout his life. He was mildly surprised that someone had spoken despite the sense there was someone lurking there and moreover at the tones of formal education, at the smattering of accent, which he could not quite identify.

'Who are you? Have you been here for long?' Jack asked, hoping to gauge where the voice came from, and how close the speaker was.

There was no reply for a long time, and just as he was about to speak again, a voice, different from the last spoke up. It sounded just inches behind his left ear.

'Do you want to play at honest men?' the whispered voice asked enthusiastically, Jack could hear excitement in the tone. Turning his head quickly he swung his arms outward in the direction he thought the voice had come from. He connected with nothing.

He didn't reply, the Englishman was trying to keep his own feelings in check, and at some level, he felt like the voice was inviting him into some sort of game. And right then a game seemed to him like a trap. He was certain of nothing, and so decided to hold himself. To keep quiet and see what occurred.

A minute passed in silence, and then another. Jack heard nothing barring the steady thudding of his own heartbeat. He thought for a moment longer, shrugged and finally replied.

'Yeah, why not? It's as good a place as any to start. You sound like two, but you feel like one. How about you tell me who you are? Where you are? If you want to take this conversation any further.'

Without a pause this time a disembodied voice responded.

'We are your flip side, to use your vernacular. You might say we are the opposing side of the coin that is you, if you will. I am where you are, and I have only been here for as long as you have, Just for good measure, I will not stay here one instant after you are gone.'

Once again all proffered in best Douglas Bader.

Jack felt somewhat confused by the answer but thought that no deception was apparent. He was eager to find out more. Certainly, some things weren't quite right, that much was obvious, but he felt no threat, and it was the first time he had been able to say that for one hell of a long time.

'Now I get to ask you something. And do remember this is honest men. Tell me the truth we move on, tell me a lie and,' the voice trailed off.

This time, Jack noted that Douglas Bader had been replaced by what he now thought of as Mister Robertson, his old Maths teacher. Whilst the other had been speaking, he had been reaching out, exploring with his outstretched hands silently wafting over the floor in expanding circles, feeling the smooth neutral ground under him.

He encountered nothing and so, as quietly as he was able, shifted a few inches across the floor and reached out again. All the while awaiting the question and trying to compose a more telling question for his own next turn. He felt certain there had to be an agenda. On the one hand, the clock appeared to be running; on the other hand, the voice appeared to be cajoling him to ask the questions that it welcomed answering.

'All right then,' the voice said after a minute. 'Here goes, something I really do want to know.' And then, 'Can you stop me?'

Jack Silver had no idea what it was he was going to be asked, and once asked no idea what the question meant. And so, no idea what the correct answer was supposed to convey. He realised that it was a multiple-choice question, three choices realistically.

Yes
No

Don't know, not sure. He thought and, however, confusing he must try to answer anyway. It felt like he was in a high-stakes poker game and the only way he could continue the game was to answer the question. And just like poker, he guessed he would need to bluff.

But which answer?

He left the deciding of his answer until he began to speak. Thus, finding himself in the hands of an imperative. And he didn't notice his hand closing around the Shaktar stone in his pocket.

Something deep in the root of his mind took over, and the answer that came out, in voice myriad and many, neither his own nor alien, both and more besides, answered loudly and clearly, 'Yes.'

A pause.

'Then you are our enemy, you keen-eyed cunt,' the voice replied, in an instant grown hostile, sharp-edged, flinty with fury.

'We wondered if you were. We never did quite believe you would understand.'

The voice broke into a cackling laugh, and between gales of that laughter began to repeat one word over and over.

'Good,' said the voice.

'Good, good.'

And Jack understood the voice meant it most sincerely.

'Good, good good.'

In the moments that followed, he remained in the hand of other than himself, so allowed his voice to be led, though it didn't feel like much allowing in the process.

'It is my question now. Will you tell us the truth?'

The voice barked back immediately, even harsher, and brogue with an accent so thick that Jack barely got hold of the words, sensed rather than heard the meaning in them.

There was a stink in the air, putrescent cloying. It smelled to him like filth in a sun-warmed sewer.

'Aye, I'm yar enemy, and I'll bay the finish of ya. Damned, yar will be. But I answer them truthfully enough. Tis honest men we play tarday.'

Jack shivered and noticed finally his right hand clenched tight around the stone, his left hand digging deep into the opposite pocket, searching.

What was there to find, he had no idea.

The voice screeched again.

'Your tairn, your question. Yar want tay know more, truth be the only choice. If yar lie, then today is done.'

'Do you know what I am going to ask?' Jack asked quickly, and he heard the glee and sensed the awful horror-filled joy that shared the space with him.

He knew then that the voices lied. This voice was a mere trickster, but what was it they wanted?

The voice spoke once more, close up, back under control, with almost no inflection.

'Our answer to the question you meant to ask is that we come to finish what we started. You want to know what we bring, when we come, how we intend to finish what we started, where we will find, or even why, then answer truthfully one last question, and we shall reveal. Answer with a lie and our time here is done?'

Jack's nervousness was still in the hands of some other force. The dialogue seemed to play out at varying levels. His hand clenched the stone tight.

'What's your question then?' he blurted out.

'OK then. Yes or no. You say you can but will you? That's our final question, will you stop us?'

Of course, Jack didn't understand.

He twitched his hands in his pockets, he felt strangely sure he wasn't going to be answering that question.

Mostly because he hadn't a clue what the hell the voice meant, though a whisper deep within suggested some part of him did.

He felt like he split into two.

One part of him, the half that connected to the Shaktar stone understood intuitively what the voice was asking, what it desired to know. Jack felt that half compelled towards truth. The other part, the fraction of his free will that was fishing around, clutching at something small and hard in his other jeans pocket didn't have a clue.

Yet he, the Englishman, realised something that neither half appeared aware of.

Jack understood implicitly when the time came it did not matter which answer he gave, either way, the voice would have what it required. Tell the truth, and it would know. Tell a lie, and it would know anyway, as the questioning would cease, in that way, the whole game was a contrivance.

He tried to get the attention of the rest of himself, but Jesus…how did you get hold of yourself? He wanted to shout, but that made no sense. He tried to think loudly, but that seemed immediately pointless. He felt an answer on his lips, a single word forming.

Both his hands slipped out of their respective pockets, in one he held the Shaktar stone cold and lifeless, still behaving like a pointless bit of rock. The Englishman felt a sound beginning at the back of his throat.

They wanted to know more and demanded truth, but all answers here led to Babylon, and that truth would spell the end. He understood what was in his other hand, and so he put his thumb on the small metallic wheel.

The sound that had been building broke through from his oesophagus. He pushed, and in that instant, the word finally expelled from his mouth, and simultaneously he struck the lighter pulled from his other pocket.

One chance, one try, everything on the turn of a tiny wheel.

It turned, the heat seemed to travel faster than the light and yet, a moment after his thumb pulled back from the metal scalded, a circle of brightness blazed around him. Jack saw the shape of a person and a part of him expected to see what he saw. Jack closed his eyes against the sudden brightness and inside of his mind, in that place where nothing else could break through, Jack heard an old man's voice.

'You got to know where you bin in order to know where you goin,' that voice said.

And once more he was in some other place.

Whilst hurtling faster than thought can be processed, this thing that was now an entity in its own right covered millions of light years in moments, and yet still there were so many trillions to cross.

Chapter Thirty
Wild West Hero

Ah hell, Jack thought to himself. The last thing that he needed was some drunken teenager giving him grief for the next five hours.

The train pulled out of the station picking up momentum quickly, power thrumming steadily over the rails, causing that quiet clunk every second or so that sped up incrementally and gave some small clue of the speed the mechanical behemoth was beginning to generate.

Silver knew his next planned stop was Edinburgh station.

'London, you say,' Jack replied, all the while keeping his own hood up and shadowing his face.

'No, if it's London you're after, well you've made a mistake. This is the train to Scotland. Well, Edinburgh in fact. I think you might be stuck here for a bit son, find somewhere to sit?' As he finished he looked up from under the folds of his own hood. The kid because that was what he was Jack thought. Seemed little more than a pre-teens child. He pushed back his own black hood and grinned at Silver.

'Got ya,' he said and burst out laughing.

'Is this the train to London? Good one, eh?'

Jack peered back and appraised the carriage's new arrival. He figured him at maybe fourteen, a narrow face topped with a mop of unruly curly dark hair, so dark as to be almost jet-black. The kid had a roguish look about him. He was as Jack imagined a pixie might look, or perhaps one of those dark elves.

Slight of build, but carried with a confidence that suggested, at least thus far, the boy had not been busted up too much by the nastier aspects of the world in which he lived. And more, that in a pinch, Jack thought the kid looked like he would do all right.

'Are you old enough to be out alone?' Jack asked. The kid's joke had been kind of funny he figured, but it had grated a bit as well.

Part of him was still recovering his poise from the prospect of over-powering some nasty teenage drunk who had invaded his home.

'Er, yeah!' said the kid.

And before he could say anything more, Silver jumped in as quickly as the boy had before and said, 'Got ya.'

'Yeah, well I guess you did, mister.' The teenager sat down opposite Jack with a thud. 'So, then, what makes you a tail-rider?'

'I don't know,' the Englishman replied pulling back his hood. 'If I knew what a tail-rider was, well then I might tell you.'

'I might though I wouldn't be too sure.'

'Tail-rider, hah. A tail-rider's someone who's sat in the last seat of the furthest back place of any fallooking where. You know, whether bus or plane or like tonight, you here on a train.'

'Reckon it's usually someone looking to be invisible, no shilling n' swerving trouble.' An then after a pause.

'Or looking for it! Is that what you're doin tryin to be invisible?'

'Yep, that's it,' Jack replied. 'I'm a regular Sue Storm.'

The kid laughed again, Jack laughed and any tension there might have been between the two of them slipped quickly away. The young man introduced himself as Harry Hood, known as Houdini or Hoody at least according to him.

Jack liked him straight off, and in particular liked the name Hoody which he figured unusually appropriate, mindful of Jack's own views on that most teenage of modern fashion accessories.

The kid was, much to Jack's surprise nineteen years young, at least according to his own protestations. He had to admit the more that he spoke the older the lad seemed to become.

He introduced himself, pointing out he was known as Jack, or sometimes in a pinch Sue Storm, getting another laugh and a nickname into the bargain.

Harry told Jack he was on his way home to Scotland, although if accent was anything to go by the lad was certainly not Scottish.

No one came into their carriage. After an hour of undisturbed travel, during which time, they swapped stories and anecdotes, Jack careful about what he said, the lights without warning dimmed, and the train slipped smoothly into night-time sleeper mode.

'You tired?' Jack asked his fellow traveller.

'No, not a bit of it. Too much sleep ain't so good for you. I don't sleep much, specially at night, you?'

'No, sleep brings out the demons.' It was the first hint Jack offered as to anything like trouble in his reality. The kid Harry Hood looked mildly surprised and raised his eyebrows. And if you had asked Jack Silver, he could not have told you what compelled him to blurt out such a line.

'So you got troubles? Listen we all got demons man,' Hoody said peering keenly at Jack in the carriage's new half-light, his blackcurrant eyes twinkling. Asking yet not asking questions of his companion.

Jack looked back, holding the boy's gaze for a long moment without speaking, then offered.

'When we arrive at Edinburgh station, you and me, we're going to go our separate ways, right?'

Jack didn't wait for an answer.

'We can sit here and be friendly for an hour or three, but when we get to the station, that's it…we're done.'

'OK?'

Hoody squinted, looked back with half a smile playing across his lips.

He saw the deadly serious expression on the Englishman's face and so replied affirmatively, continuing to stare at the man opposite who seemed such a curious mix. The lad who knew a thing or two about surviving under the radar decided the guy sitting across from him looked, well sort of like he didn't belong. And so though different from him, still exactly the kind of guy who might just be sliding around underneath society's radar.

He had already spotted cuts and bruises, faded but still visible on hands and face. The guy was cautious; but the younger man figured older people were. But also, there was something else, some other air about him.

It had taken a while for Hoody to put his finger on it; the guy at first look appeared more hunted than hunter. Not scared exactly, but on the lookout, wary of all comers.

What Harry Hood saw as he looked straight back into his travel companion's face. Beyond the eyes, the bruises and the scars. What he saw was desire, and it burned white hot. He saw a man looking for a foe, and the young man, tuned in to the edges of those people he met understood the indefinable something in the

Englishman's nature that gave that fact away. This man intended to do harm when the time came, despite clearly not being the type.

Still, the hooded youth had a robust self-confidence, one that demanded that he didn't take a backward step. He understood the traveller was in the hands of some imperative, and as such he either floated with him for a time on the other man's terms, or he floated away.

He considered for a few moments, already knowing there was something in the fellow that frankly he just liked. And then he said.

'Yeah, we'll be goin' our own ways I guess. In the meantime, we're just a couple a guys sittin' on a train together chewin the breeze…ain't we?'

Jack nodded in turn.

And so, for a third time he found himself in the company of a younger person.

He was a changed man, both from and since those previous encounters. He spoke now with great care, as the two men talked their way deep into the night. The train rolled on throbbing and thrumming its way across the English countryside towards its land-locked northern neighbour.

Jack, early in the conversation, brought up the man at the centre of his troubles, and was less surprised than he might have expected that Hoody had not only heard of Stevan Cipher, but he was somewhat acquainted with both his reputation and indeed one or two of the more infamous parts of his operation.

Elements of that operation apparently spread their net through the length and breadth of Edinburgh, Glasgow and Aberdeen.

Silver did not tell of all of his adventures, and certainly did not suggest openly that he was on the hunt for Cipher and his entourage. He did ask many questions, and as darkness drew night towards its centre learned from his companion that Stevan Cipher had a growing influence in Scotland. Moreover, to the boy's knowledge, was becoming known by more than just reputation in London, and in other places further afield.

It seemed this gangster's activities impacted even the likes of Harry Hood and his ilk, those teenagers that generally survived below the tide line of mainstream society.

It seemed that Cipher's Stormtroopers as Jack called them, a title which Hoody immediately adopted, held a stranglehold on eateries, security and shopping malls; as well as the more traditional unions, drug dealing and prostitution.

Cops and judges too, apparently fell under the Cipher spell. Hoody suggested there were regular reports of shady beatings, stabbings and even shootings associated with the coercion methods of these suited Shadowmen.

Hoody knew some of these older villains, meatheads he called them and whenever possible gave them a wide berth. It seemed that Cipher's industry of crime and deprivation was growing, spreading far and wide. And whilst the lad had no real view on other aspects of Scottish life Jack Silver learned that the fingers of Cipher's poison were delving into many areas of that Scottish life.

As he listened, internally Jack reinforced the message to himself he must remain wary, of police, local government, hotels and hostels. Indeed, the more he listened the more he realised he would not be able to just waltz into town like some proverbial marshal bent on revenge.

'Did I ever think that?' he mumbled to himself during a break in Hoody's sermon on the evils of the crime lord.

The boy stopped speaking and looked at him quizzically. After a minute of silence between them, Silver found himself telling Hoody the story of his evening at a London restaurant. And more importantly what he had witnessed there, and what followed after. And it proved easy to do, seemed even quite natural to him.

The boy's reaction opened new understanding within Jack.

Harold Hood, who had spent the summer in Brighton working a fish and chip van, living hand to mouth, suggesting, without ever quite saying, that he too was avoiding some other conflict, just nodded and pursed his lips.

The teenager had had no idea about the death of Cipher's brother Cedric, when Jack finished with his tale of witnessing the callous murder the teen expelled a long-held breath and said.

'Well, it explains a lot. I been gone for a long time, and I guess some way away, but d'ya see. Without his brother Stevan's always been a frigging nutter. Cedric, that's his brother. Well, at least it was.' He paused and then said, 'We used to call him Vincent. He looked like Vincent Price outta them horror movies. He was the one that could stop him, the only one. We used ta hear stories of him cutting up people just for kicks an' stuff. Stevan's a regular Jack the Ripper, if the stories are true. See it was Vincent kept him in check.'

'Worst of all, and reckon everyone knows it, he hates children. The most, if the stories are true.'

Hoody took a long breath and then continued, 'They nick'em off the streets, those, what did you call'em, Stormtroopers? And then, well then no one sees'em any more. An what does that tell you?' Hoody continued now in full flow.

'And he loved his brother. I have heard it said that he never loved no one cept his brother, and I've heard lots of other black stuff about that one, too. So, if you got trouble with him, then you'd do well to stay out of the way.'

'Going to Edinburgh, well, it don't seem smart to me.' Harold Hood stopped speaking and looked pointedly at Jack, then continued once more.

'If his brother's dead, there's no telling what he's gettin' up to; wouldn't be nobody left to stop him.'

'That bastard, from what I've heard he would kill everyone if he took a fancy to it. You gotta be mad even sittin' on this train. He finds you; he'll kill you, for sure.'

Hoody finished and sat and stared hard at the carriage's only other occupant.

Jack looked back, said nothing, perhaps understanding why Cipher and his men had been able to come after him so fast and so hard. Of course, you would come after your brother's killer. And if you were some big-time gangster, then wiping him out wouldn't faze you one bit.

Jack thought back, remembered in the first days after, when he still harboured visions of setting things right. Sure, he'd been scared. Those blokes that had stabbed the other Cipher, they were really scary creeps; and they had seemed to be everywhere that he went.

Outside of his home, and then the police station, his publishers, time and again. He remembered phoning the cops anonymously the first night that he had spent away from his flat, and what had the guy said?

'Come in sir, there's nothing to be afraid of. We can look after you here. Yes, we do want information on the killing last Friday night…blah blah blah.'

But when he had arrived, stepping cautiously within the vicinity of the police station, some hours later. It too had appeared to be in the clutches of the killers.

In fact, in those first few days, everywhere he had turned he saw the two men from the alley. The BMW too, sat parked at the top of the road or just around the nearest turn. Jack wasn't stupid. He figured out quickly that him staying alive wouldn't be any part of the killers plans. What he didn't know just then was that they had made such a good job of turning him into the culprit.

And then, on the second day after the killing, still unsure of what might be best he visited his editor's offices in Barclay Square. Tom Billings, long-time friend and boss had told him that some men had been in and asking questions, had shown ID, said they were cops. Apparently, they made no secret of the fact that they were looking for Silver in relation to a killing, and worse still, as he had been sat in his friend's office nervously drinking black coffee they had come back.

He remembered how he had run and fallen, charging down an iron fire escape staircase, strangely American in the heart of London, but thank god it had been there, right outside Tom's office window. It had saved him, and by the skin of his teeth. And though there had been many reasons why he had run, as he sat there remembering that was truly the moment he thought that his long exodus began.

For a time, Jack deluded himself he could swerve away from what he had seen, from what he had failed to do upon seeing it. Cipher wanted him dead because he believed him the killer of his brother, although only Christ knew why that man thought he would have done such a thing. And as much as he was in the hands of an imperative, driven towards some apocalyptic final conflict with his opponent, it seemed increasingly in his mind that was the case for his opponent as well.

The BMW men, well a dead Jack Silver presented them with an alibi, alive perhaps not so good.

He came back to the present, still thinking about Cipher. Both men it seemed were driven now by the cold hard desire for revenge. Both men were in the clutches of magicks the like of which Jack Silver frankly did not understand. And beyond even that Jack had glimpsed within his mind's unconscious eye another place, a world like and yet unlike, that which he called his own. A shadow-world, or more correctly perhaps a mirror world.

In that world, Stevan Cipher had managed to drag civilisation back down into some kind of desperate Dark Age. To a place where the rule of law, the freedom to live at peace was utterly usurped, and in its place an empire of chaos. Oiled with the blood and the pain of innocent millions apropos to satisfying some all-consuming need for revenge in the heart of evil.

In Edinburgh, Hoody had spoken of dark deeds, and as he had Jack's fears for the future, for more now than just his own skin began to grow, to take on a momentum fuelled by the dark dream world just behind his eyelids.

No matter, Silver wanted Cipher dead, and that was revenge pure and simple.

Despite all his fears, and in spite of the decorum of his formerly civilised life, he would see Cipher's corpse laid out on a slab, punishment for the murder of his two friends, and he would be damned if he cared any more for the rest of it.

But, and it was more than passing strange to him, a looming feeling within. He also believed now destiny was sending him a message, telling him that the crime lord of this world needed to be dead for other reasons. Before this world, his world, the one of his waking mind followed lockstep the path towards that other place. Could that be possible, he wasn't sure. After the last few months, he was unsure about so much that somehow the effect of Stevan Cipher being greater than the sum of his parts would come as no great shock.

'We're all just folk,' Jack said to himself, drawing another curious look from the carriage's other occupant. And it dawned on him that if Stevan Cipher proved to be a catalyst for events greater than he himself envisaged. If in fact, he by his existence might precipitate catastrophic change, then was it not true also that Jack Silver might be pivotal in his own way?

However freaky those thoughts seemed to him under the dim flickering electric lights of a train carriage heading to Scotland, he felt certain he was treading destiny's path. He was beginning to feel other movements, other turns of the wheels that tie souls together.

Wow, where did that come from, he thought; and though it sounded strange, still it felt right. He saw more clearly now the direction from where he had come; and looking forward he began to resolve into clarity where it was his destiny might take him.

He reached into his pocket and pulled out the Shaktar stone, looking at it long and carefully.

'Do you believe in magic?' he spoke up, looking across at Hoody.

The teenager gazed back at him, scratched his ear and pushed back long lanky curls that dropped over a swathe of his face.

'Magic, you say. I remember someone told me about magic once. Can't remember the words exactly, but it went something like.'

Magic is just the stuff some people do that others don't know how to. I mean, if you was floating down the Amazon on a boat and then some native guy jumped on. Some bloke with a spear, never seen a Westerner before.

'An' say you got a bit scared at his big sharp spear, and you saw all his mates on the bank. And say you shot 'im with your gun in front of all his people. Would they call you magician or murderer? Kinda hard to tell, don't ya think?' Hoody asked, winking and looking sagely across the carriage.

'Yeah, I believe in magic, and who knows, maybe we'll stay together long enough ta see some.'

Jack thought about what the young man said and realised a truth. His mind was busy doing flips and somersaults, and maybe that wasn't a big surprise, considering how long he'd been running and what he had seen during that time.

But maybe this whole thing wasn't about magic; maybe Hoody had it right. Maybe after all, in fact, it was simply about knowledge. And if that was true, then quite clearly he did not have enough of it. He had been stupid right from the beginning.

Another part of his mind protested.

'Dammit, why was everything so confusing?' What he had seen what he had dreamed, everything felt on the brink all of the time, and it had shown him only one thing for certain. When people abrogated their duties to those around them, when society became driven by the needs of the one as opposed to the needs of the many, that was when people like Stevan Cipher were able to sneak up, to grow and spread their cancer of rage and hatred and death. Being scared of something, or indeed someone, ought never to be reason enough to turn and run away.

Jack Silver had turned away once, and he had been running ever since. And God knew how many people had paid with their lives for that single moment of cowardice.

One, two, a whole world?

He understood it could never be righted, there was not an acceptable price, and yet now he would attempt to put things right.

This was not going to be about revenge after all, this would be a reckoning.

Many things were at play, and he accepted he didn't have a handle on nearly enough of them, but he was heading to Scotland in order to walk down the main street with his pistol cocked.

He intended to look the bad guy in the face, to draw and fire.

And then after, he would find out if the good guys did ever win in real life.

Putting the stone back into his jeans pocket without further comment Jack decided he needed to focus on what was directly in front of him. In order, he told himself, first get to Edinburgh, then get into the city without bleeping Cipher's radar, only then go find the man, find a way in. And then finally find a method to help him go and join his brother.

In his mind's eye, Jack Silver saw himself standing over a shadowy blood-covered corpse, and he was smiling. He could not see the dead body; all he really could see was an indistinct black and vaguely red blob. That's okay, he thought to himself: if I make it that far, then that will be okay; and he felt certain that the black shadowy corpse would resolve into a far more distinctive form when the time came.

Returning to the present moment, and to Harry Hood, he smiled and said, 'You know, I think whoever told you that might just have something. I guess I'm just one of those spear-chucking savages.'

They both laughed, the lights dimmed further, and the thrum of the engine deepened as the train charged unblinking into the darkness of a tunnel that ran long miles under the Pennines.

Sometime later the engine tugged its carriages into Edinburgh's main railway terminus at Waverley Station. It was the early hours of a chill Scottish morning, and few people were about. Both Jack Silver and Harold Hood had stayed awake throughout, talking of many things. Jack remembering long conversations with another young male, a travelling companion from a lifetime before. It seemed very different, and yet so much the same.

He told Hoody much more than he planned; found the young man mature beyond his years, easier to engage with than he would have expected, and that seemed to him possibly because both Hoody, and he were painted onto the same canvas. Or perhaps it was just because, despite his young years, Jack found himself looking into the boy's hard face, seeing there some of the courage he had not sought but somewhere along the road seemed to have stumbled upon in himself.

He admired the kid and felt a wisdom pulsing from the lad that reminded him that such had never been the private province of the elders.

To Jack, the boy seemed like some latter-day Jesse James, an outlaw somehow just a bit too good to ever be the bad guy. And he liked that, he liked it a lot.

As the train slowed to a halt they both stood. Jack pulled down his small carry bag from the overhead rack. Hoody peered out of the nearest carriage window and down the platform, and he didn't reply when Jack said.

'Chilly! Is it always this cold in Scotland?'

He turned to ask again and the look on his companion's face stopped him dead.

'What is it?'

'Cops, there are cops on the platform, cops and no people, worst kind of mix Jumping Jack. Can't go that way. I guess this is gonna be where we go our separate ways.'

The train was grinding to a halt, losing the last of its momentum as Jack in turn looked out of the carriage windows towards the ticket barrier, the heart of the station still a little distance away, the world beyond suddenly unreachable as what he saw froze the blood in his veins.

'Ah, damn it!' he cursed spying three uniformed police. Their outfits were slightly different to those he had gotten used to during a life in England, but he didn't dwell on that as he stared at them, each one outlined starkly under the bright neon that was supplementing the first dregs of early-morning daylight fighting to break through the station's glass roof.

There was one other person stood talking to the coppers, back turned, and Jack saw a black overcoat. He felt panicky immediately, they were onto him, they knew he was coming.

He looked at Hoody.

'It's me they're after, Hoody.'

'Shit! How stupid have I been!'

'Even after all of it. After all, that's happened.'

'Listen Jack. Maybe they're after you. Maybe they're after us both. Either way I gotta split. If you need to disappear, then come with me. It's your call.'

Jack looked at him, and he saw no fear in the young man's eyes just a youthful intensity. Looking in those eyes he believed absolutely that Harry could keep him free, would keep him free.

Hoody looked back. And lifting his hood up and over his curls he smiled tightly.

'Right, we need to wait. Until the absolute moment that the train stops. Got it? Then we move quickly. Put up your hood and just follow my lead. Quick and close. Right.'

Jack agreed. Every part of him was tense, and he watched closely as Hoody stepped back from the carriage windows and moved quickly back to the rearmost part of the vehicle.

Then, at the precise moment that the train finally ceased to move, pulled to a halt with a dull thud as the gentle impact into the buffers shuddered down the length of fourteen carriages, Jack heard a simple click.

Realisation dawned on him.

At the moment momentum had ceased the train's system unlocked all the doors. And that included the doors between the carriages.

And also apparently included the door Hoody was now opening.

That being the absolute last door to the very last carriage.

And why not Jack thought as he scrambled after Hoody, who was waving him through.

After all his mind piped up in a slightly crazy and excitable voice, 'It's a safety-conscious world. Who knew when a locked door might bar a necessary exit.'

Outside the cold was instant and bit sharply. Jack smiling followed as Hoody moved quickly, low to the ground, down past the popping clicking mechanical beast. Both men were half-crouching, heads moving left and right peering about them searching for interested spectators.

After no more than thirty feet, Hoody suddenly leapt across the tracks to the platform opposite the one their train had pulled into.

Jack realised that they were still covered from onlookers on the original platform by the train's own bulk. Mentally he applauded the young man, the door, the timing of the whole thing. For not charging back the way, they had come and so becoming inadvertently visible.

The boy was both resourceful and clever, and as Jack panting pulled himself up onto platform six, he looked up into Hoody's face. It was still covered by the black cotton sweat top.

And instead of thanking him, between breaths Jack said.

'Magick huh. You're very good Harry. Very, very good.'

Hoody smiled briefly and said nothing. Instead, he pointed and sauntered off towards an unattended ticket barrier. Jack expected a further sticky moment in about a hundred feet. That would be when they walked past the last point where the train covered them from any watchers on Platform Seven.

But he followed Harold Hood's lead, pulled his own hood down over his head and hoisted his pack high onto his shoulders. He dug his hands deep into his jeans pocket and ran to catch up with his companion by then six or eight feet in front of him.

'What about the cops?' Jack hissed as he came alongside. The boy replied amiably enough, 'Listen, don't look or talk to me. This is Edinburgh's Waverley Bridge Station. And it's huge. And even at this hour it's full of teenagers just like me.'

Half of them are dealing drugs. All of them are using drugs. And the cops can't get rid of 'em.

You just gotta be one of them for about thirty seconds. Can you do that?'

Jack said he thought he could, all the while trying to hide his anxiety by looking down at his feet, breathing in and out hard, steeling himself to step across the space ahead.

Ten seconds later still looking down Jack shuffled across the open expanse, staring hard at a trodden-in piece of gum embedded into the platform's concrete just beyond the gate that led onto the main concourse.

The Englishman heard voices drifting on the chill early-morning air, and he was sure he recognised one of them.

Hoody was speaking to him. At first he didn't hear, but he concentrated as he walked.

'Don't look, Jack. If they speak to you, don't look. And don't stop. Just keep going. Steady does it.'

His invisible companion was whispering, and suddenly Jack felt certain he was about to get nailed. He visualised coppers pushing and pulling him roughly into some porter's side room. Dammit why had he come here? This wasn't the way to get back at Cipher. He had known Cipher would be looking for him. Why the hell had he just walked straight into the lion's den?

He found himself looking up. The chewing gum, where was the bloody chewing gum?

The vague sound of voices speaking now resolved into words, and Jack wanted to glance, just one quick look. And so he peered up and across, and at that very moment the two hooded men passed through the old-time iron trellis at the terminus to platform six and into the station proper.

Jack Silver saw nothing and the weight in his mind lifted. He expelled the breath he had been holding. In the end, there he had heard something he was certain. A low voice, something distinctive in the mumble and grind beyond railway-station patter.

He knew he had been concentrating hard on trying to glance casually, on moving past without being seen, but he had heard something, of that he was certain. Silver was convinced he had heard a light, almost flamboyant, tone floating barely above a whisper on the morning air. 'He's here now. Find him,' that voice said. Leastways that was what his mind told him as the two hooded figures scurried across the main terminal's tiled floor like ants moving across an expanse of kitchen lino.

As it had turned out at the precise moment they walked through into the station proper the policemen and the black-coated individual had begun to move down the train's carriages, peering into each one. Certain the quarry for whom they searched lay finally within their grasp.

The artefact waited, for it had nothing now left to do but wait, and, if moment allowed, then act.

Chapter Thirty-One
Four Little Diamonds

Jack did not know where he was.

He stood on a plain of dusty reddish brown that ran endlessly towards a horizon, one that did not seem quite right to his senses.

The sky above his head was blue, a deep dark hue that seemed again just a bit off from all that he knew.

Small, scruffy scraps of cloud raced across the sky, dark grey and mustard mixed, fairly whipping across the expanse.

Then Jack put his finger on a strange thing. As he looked around him, turning a full three-sixty, the one thing absent within that deep dark blue sky was the sun, any sun.

And yet the scene was as brightly lit as the brightest summer's day.

He had already made connections subliminally his senses weren't quite able to give voice to.

Things were off kilter. The horizon was further in the distance than the millions of years of human-race memory instructed him it ought to be.

'It isn't Earth,' Jack said, and even his voice seemed deeper, hollower than he had ever heard.

'La…la…la. Crap, that sounds weird,' Jack continued, raising his voice at the last, yet noting little change in the volume that escaped his lips.

He looked down at his feet and noticed the layer of red-brown dusty top that appeared to be clinging fulsomely to both his shoes. And more, to the lowest two or three inches of his blue jeans.

'Oh well,' Jack said, gazing wide-eyed all around. 'Looks like it's just me, me and me. Soooo, eenie meenie miny mo,' he continued pointing his left hand out horizontally towards what he believed were the four points of the compass.

At the last of the four he began to trudge in that direction, the one that Mo took him in. 'Can't stay here. Shit, I don't even know where here is! Boris Vallejo art and then some,' he mused out loud, oddly enjoying the unusual sound his voice made in the subtly different atmosphere.

About two miles distant as far as he could tell a small rocky outcrop marred the clean line of the horizon.

'Well, Mo, looks like you beat Eenie, Meenie and Minie hands down,' he said.

And then in his mind added. Well, at least I have something to head towards.

He remembered where he had come from, all that had gone before. Somehow, though, in this place he was detached from it all. His mind had received a news report outlining the events of some other person's life and the Englishman had merely stored it away, filed it for other later uses.

Where he walked now instinct told him all that other stuff was irrelevant. And so, he trudged on. Heading towards the low rise, not anxious particularly.

In fact, it was possibly the most relaxed he had been for as long as he was able to remember.

Soon after he began to whistle. At first tunelessly, then after a time, enjoying again the fact that it all just came out a bit differently the aimless sound of his whistling resolved into a tune, one it took him a few bars to recollect.

'Well,... Gilbert!' he said to himself, then returned to the whistling. It was a song called 'Alone Again,' and he smiled as he thought, naturally.

He walked for an hour and then noticed that he wasn't any closer to the rise than he had been at the outset.

He thought perhaps he must have got things a bit wrong, in this place where everything was a bit different. He wasn't tired or hungry or thirsty, the only change seemed to be the creeping red dust, now inching up towards the knee of his jeans. Jack thought it must be very fine dust because he didn't appear to be disturbing any, visibly as he strode along.

Another hour at least he decided. Hard to tell without a watch, and without even a sun to chase across the sky. The Englishman had gone from whistling to singing: David Bowie and his messed up Major Tom. Jack decided he was enjoying the walk though he understood at some deeper level that two hours or so at the steady pace he was trudging ought to have begun to remind him of his forty and some years, and yet it didn't.

He was walking, and it was not wearing him out, and he was not getting anywhere.

Jack had begun to notice other things, too. Though the clouds above were fairly racing across the sky down at ground level where he made his way not a puff, the air remained absolutely still. He had whistled, sung and shouted, but barring that not a whisper had disturbed his senses. And one other thing. Soon after finding himself in what seemed to him his personal Narnia, he had passed wind. He remembered wrinkling his nose at that, and as far as he could remember that was the last thing that his nose had smelled.

The place appeared to be sense-neutral, whatever that might mean. More than that he wasn't anxious, and he knew he ought to have been. He was in a very strange place, and he didn't really understand how he had got to that place or why.

Perhaps the place is neutral for a reason, Jack considered. And if purpose came into the equation then Eenie and Meenie and the rest ought not to have been offering him a guiding hand, he thought coming suddenly to a halt.

'Dammit!' Jack said. 'I'm buggered if I'm going to walk all the way back.'

He turned a complete three-sixty again, as he had done two hours previously. And he realised that the vista looked the same. In fact, everywhere looked exactly the same as it had done before.

What to do Silver thought.

He had walked and got nowhere; he had thought and got nowhere, either.

He tried hard to decide what other positive action there was he might take. He thought about digging a hole but looking around there was nothing he might use as an implement, and he did not fancy his hands and arms going the way of his legs and footwear.

He was now covered halfway up to his thighs with the reddish-brown dust, which for the first time was beginning to prompt some vague consternation deep in his psyche. He might have wondered how it was that the dust, if indeed that was what it was, in an unmoving atmosphere, with neither breeze nor evidence of disturbance was inching slowly up his person. He might too have questioned how he had walked for two or more hours across that eternal plain and yet left not one single footprint. But in that place where everything was different such issues seemed minor, too small to be concerned with…yet.

Standing still he bent his mind towards how he might change the environment he was in, get to wherever it was he was supposed to go. He believed that the place's neutrality served some ordained purpose, even if that purpose escaped him. As hard as he tried he could not think of what else he must do.

And then, when he'd all but given up, was when it came to him.

Caffee spoke up in his mind.

'If you cannot go anywhere, if there is nothing else you can do, then assume that you are where you need to be. It's an Ockham's razor moment.' And that did seem correct, at least as far as it went.

He didn't fancy sitting and didn't welcome covering himself in any more of the clinging red dust, so he stood there, and he closed his eyes.

And moments after when he opened them again he saw that he was indeed precisely where he was supposed to be.

Opposite him stood two more travellers, two more visitors to that strange land. Jack looked in fascination at what his mind told him could only be an extraordinarily anorexic St George, and a huge but really shabby-looking dragon.

The Englishman stared unblinking, first at the pale-skinned man who stood a good six inches taller than he, in bare feet wearing only a pair of red silk shorts with electric yellow bands running vertically down either side. Above he wore a faded brown leather hauberk.

The tall, emaciated figure had an ancient-looking sword tucked none too securely into an equally age-battered leather belt cinched around his waist. And that all did nothing whatsoever to disguise the incredible thinness of the man, who nonetheless looked back at Jack equally enough.

In any other circumstance, he was absolutely certain that the incredibly tall and astonishingly thin man would stand out a country mile. Except only that here, in this place, where everything was just a bit off. Standing next to the thin man was a twelve-foot-high raggedy dragon.

Black leather reptilian hide hung loosely over a hefty frame. Wings Jack felt certain would span at least fifteen feet apiece extended, each with evidence of rents and tears across their breadth. The dragon's eyes held Jack, and in their bejewelled red he saw a deep fire that looked to him like a window into the dragon's soul.

He gazed in frank wonder at the two newcomers, the tall man put his hand out in a rich and sonorous voice that made Silver think of the scent of vanilla and of a beautiful French woman struggling with the vagaries of English.

'Good day. You are Jacque yes?'

The Englishman looked at the tall man and then at the dragon, and finally replied.

'I'm dreaming, right? This, all of this is a dream?'

A different voice answered. It was slow and heavy, as a dragon speaking might be expected to sound.

'Well, actually this is a partial aphasic reality dysfunction.' And then 'Sympathetically clouded for ease of flow. So, I suppose you might describe it as a dream. At least you might if you were pushed for time. I am McKenzie, of the House of McKenzie, of one and of four, and K and one again. You may call me Mac, he does.'

The dragon finished, jerking a stubby articulated forepaw towards the skinny man.

The creature had short front-mounted arms which disconcertingly reminded Jack of the pair of small front limbs he remembered seeing in a movie full of Tyrannosaurus Rex some years before.

'He's Shorty,' the dragon then offered.

'Easy for you to say,' said the tall man, and to Silver's consternation both chuckled.

'We just wait on the fourth then,' said the one called Shorty. Silver looked at him. And as he did so a voice spoke up behind him in high fluting tones.

'No need to wait on me. Here again? I thought we were done with here,' that voice said.

Jack turned away from Shorty and Mac and right there, stood no more than six feet from him, with a broad smile painted across his face, stood Stevan Cipher.

'Hello,' he said in a slightly effeminate tone.

'You two I know…but you?' he asked questioningly looking at the Englishman. 'Who are you, then?'

'You know me, Cipher,' Jack replied drily.

Ignoring Jack's riposte, the other man continued.

'Listen, you can call me Tokyo Rose.'

This did nothing to allay Jack's confusion.

'Perhaps you have me mixed up with another,' the new addition finished.

It all seemed odd and a bit convivial to him.

The three, each one at least a little, and mostly a lot, weird in their own unique way, were looking at him, looking to him he corrected.

He also noted that Cipher, the one that called himself Tokyo Rose now, stood before him wearing his trademark neatly tailored black suit with a white crisp-collared shirt and simple straight up and down black tie.

Jack looked down and saw with an ounce of satisfaction that Cipher/Rose seemed to be suffering from the creeping dust syndrome also.

'So, what happens now?' Jack asked. 'Seems as like you guys all know one another. I'm guessing you've all been here before, right?' Mac replied, slow and steady, Jack thought operating at a slightly different RPM than the somewhat smaller companions, 'We are four disparate and yet the same. We are here certainly to make some things clear, and to leave some things in the dark also. Linear time is limited, as it has been for, well some time.' He puffed a small laugh at his own joke and then added, 'And now the square has its four corners, so we should begin.' Tokyo Rose eyed the other three in turn and facing Shorty said, 'You like to speak. In fact, you usually love to talk, jabber jabber.'

'Hell, we struggle to make you stop so why don't you begin.'

Shorty looked at Tokyo Rose, a smile creasing the corners of his mouth. 'Well, yes, perhaps I should begin.'

'Ugh huh, well why not, OK.' 'I think it is safe to say we all now understand this is a forum for debate.' 'A place where we may ask and learn and share.'

'Or not share as the choice may provide.'

'And all this in peace.'

'I shall begin with a few words that I have found, what should I say, appropriate.'

And then he began to recite, and his voice, beautiful and quite melodic in that still place, rose and fell.

'This is a war. But since these play, before they die, like puppies with their puppy. Since a man, I did as these have done but did not die. I will content the people as I can and give up these to them. Behold the man who may become.'

He stopped then and internally Jack understood these words were but a part of a whole, a window into the tall man and all that he was, that he represented.

'You understand both of you,' the one called Shorty continued looking at Jack and Tokyo Rose.

'My brother Mac and me. We walk now on a different path to you.'

'And yet it is a truth that all of our paths are in the end the same.'

Then after a long pause Mac spoke, and he too it seemed had a verse to offer. And so, Jack listened to that slow sombre voice, deep and bass.

He could almost feel the vibration way down in his chest. 'Once, near to the starting my nose crawled like a snail on the glass. My hand tingled, and I wished to burst the bubbles drifting from the noses of the cowed, compliant fish. My hand has drawn back since then. I often sigh still for the dark downward And for the vegetating kingdom of the fish and reptile.'

Jack felt there was some meaning, but that it floated just below his consciousness. He felt more than clearly appreciated that Shorty and Mac were not entirely as they seemed, though the seeming was already a difficult reckoning.

Something inside of him suggested that they were more like outlines, pencil sketches, echoes of some other selves.

But before he could think any further on what he had heard, of what his senses told him, Tokyo Rose began to recite.

In perfect cadence, high-fluted tones perfectly formed the words that emerged.

Fantastic grow the evening gowns
Agents of the Fisc pursue
Absconding tax-defaulters through
The sewers of provincial towns.
Private rites of magic send
The temple prostitutes to sleep
All the literati keep
An imaginary friend.
Cerebrotonic Cato may
Extol the Ancient Disciplines,
But the muscle-bound Marines
Mutiny for food and pay.
Caesar's double-bed is warm
As an unimportant clerk
Writes
I DO NOT LIKE MY WORK
On a pink official form.

Cipher's verse, spoken with careful patience proved to be the lengthiest yet, inside Jack it evoked feelings of tragic choking loss.

He felt a sense of sorrow, both for the speaker and for them all.

That last verse awoke in Jack a feeling that terrible events awaited him, and Tokyo Rose too. Events that stood still for a moment only whilst they stepped out to the debating table. Perhaps their path too was written, like the words to each of the verses spoken.

The three looked towards him and then waited for him to speak. He had no idea what it was that he should say. The relaxed sensation that had followed him around this strange land left him, instead he began to perspire. His mind went blank.

He looked down at his feet and choked back a cough as he saw the reddish-brown dust covering his jeans right up to the waist.

How could that be?

He had simply been standing there, it seemed like the stuff had a life all of its own.

He again noticed it had climbed up Cipher's suit also, and was sat somewhere between knee and thigh, and he noticed also a bead of sweat that ran down the centre of the other man's forehead, to drip a moment later off the end of his nose and onto the ground.

That Shorty and Mac seemed untouched by the devil dust was more than passing strange, and where did the name devil dust come to his mind from, he wondered.

In the moment of reply, which came from far down inside of him, came his verse; a tiny voice spoke up and said to him.

'Well, this place is hardly Xanadu now, is it?'

'Thank you, Caffee, and you, too, Coleridge,' Jack said out loud and then, looking at all three of his companions in turn, he too began a recital.

'In Xanadu did Kubla Khan, a stately pleasure dome decree: where Alph, the sacred river, ran through caverns measureless to man down to a sunless sea.'

Jack stopped for a moment, searching in his mind. But he needn't have worried, Caffee took him by the hand, and together they walked the path.

'So twice five miles of fertile ground with walls and towers were girdled round. And there were gardens bright with sinuous rills where blossomed many an incense-bearing tree and here were forests ancient as the hills, enfolding sunny spots of greenery.'

Silver trailed off and looked again at each of the three in turn.

And in their eyes, he saw his face reflected, and there, tears ran free.

He was at that time uncertain of the value and meaning of what it was he had said. But these other three, most mysterious apparitions all he reflected, seemed to have been affected by his words.

Jack smiled to himself, for the first and only time in that strange desert landscape.

Nobody spoke for some minutes each in his own world. After a minute or two, Shorty moved away from the other three and appeared engaged in some heated mumbled debate with himself.

Mac seemed suddenly uncomfortable, fidgeting from one massive hind leg onto the other, shuffling about in an area of about six feet by six, as if somehow, for the present at least, he was hemmed in, tendrils of smoke slowly escaping the dragon's maw.

As Jack watched, something became apparent to him, and that was that Tokyo Rose was as much in the dark at that moment as he was himself.

His discomfiture it appeared, was born of the same concerns and curiosities as those Jack found himself engaged in. That at least, and the clinging red dust that covered the two men exclusively, and now covered him from the neck downwards.

Jack's thoughts were interrupted as Shorty turned from a spot he had taken up about forty feet distant. His tall, emaciated body clanked as the various parts of his anatomy and its covering swung around in some kind of retarded slow motion that only seconds later caught up with the initial movement.

The look on his face told Jack that others had come to a decision, and before he had a moment to contemplate further the tall knight of some strange unknown realm began to speak.

'In all the times, we have come to this table of debate,' he commenced, a seriousness in him that had not before been evident, 'stretching back all the long years of my life.'

At this point, he stopped and pointed one long narrow finger towards the dragon creature that looked down on proceedings with twinkling red eyes. 'He and I have only ever had to make choices that had regard to ourselves. Now, so it seems, we must do more. And though we have no template from which to draw, no experience with which to paint this new day, I feel that it is right that we should tell you some things.'

Again, he stopped.

No longer pointing at the dragon he looked long then at each of the two men, continuing his slow, careful monologue. 'It is time that we speak to you of your death. You,' he said, now pointing at Jack Silver. 'And you too,' using a second long bony hand to aim at the other.

Jack looked involuntarily towards Tokyo Rose, to him still an articulation of Stevan Cipher; a man seemingly interminably intertwined in his destiny.

Only once, for all that he had learned of him, had Jack Silver laid his own eyes upon Cipher and as Shorty continued, he found himself adrift and remembering when…

He had been sat at a small corner table in the pub. He didn't remember where – something about a sign above the door poked at the back of his mind, but it didn't resolve into clarity; it didn't matter.

He remembered nursing a half-pint of some thick soupy real ale, and the atmosphere of the bar had swirled with cigarette smoke.

A darts match or some such had continued in one corner, the combatants, maybe ten in all, dutifully ignoring the scruffy out-of-towner wrapped in his own gloom across the room from them.

Occasionally, the door to the side of Jack's table would swing open, admitting a short and slightly dumpy teenage bar girl, who Jack had figured as quite pretty in an obese society kind of way. She would somewhat laconically complete her round of empty glasses collection and ashtray cleaning as he looked on.

Back then, he still carried a pack of Marlboro and a lighter, despite not smoking.

In those early days of his flight, it had not been some scheme to cultivate more attention, nor indeed better service, certainly not in the venues he found himself.

No, Jack left them out on the table and sat on a beer mat, seemingly discarded, for precisely the opposite reason.

It appeared right.

It just seemed to him to be a natural part of the uninteresting pub customer disguise that he had so assiduously cultivated.

Uninteresting, that had been a look Jack had developed early on.

When you're running away, the worst two things that you can do is to look like you might have some money first.

A no-no on the streets, a place where he had found that there is always some poor sap that will want to beg, borrow or steal it from you.

The other thing, which when you are aware of it negates the first problem, is never to look interesting.

There are Jack figured for every poor person twenty at least are lonely. And then at least of those twenty perhaps ten who would be looking for your company if you appeared even remotely interesting. At the outset of his flight from pursuit, he had made the mistake of assuming that disinterested, as opposed to uninteresting, was the solution to the many that happened upon him at one rest stop after another.

Christ he thought as he recalled one guy who had started a conversation about his dead spaniel in a public toilet.

He had learned, and piece by piece, step by step, had turned himself into one of those people who fill all the gaps in the modern world and yet the rest of society try their hardest to turn away from.

He came to understand the reality of lonely, needy folk. They don't really care whether you're interested or not, only that they can jack into you, and into your energy, your life force to draw off a little of whatever it is that they need to get through their reality for a little while longer.

As he had fled from his old life and the danger that had lately invaded it, Jack knew he needed still the occasional hearth. Jack had sought freedom to move underneath the radar of people, and the way in which he found that had been to become as uninteresting as possible, to as many people as possible, as often as possible.

He was like a sepia-tone image in a world of digital colour. He tried, and mostly succeeded, in not causing ripples in the consciousness of the majority; and at the very least he avoided eye contact with the rest.

And it was this that had saved him as he sat there nursing a beer that he did not want even when he ordered it. The Englishman had been loath to return to the cold night, the drizzling rain outdoors, uncertain as he had been where he might be going next.

A bell had tinkled shrilly as the main door to the establishment had been pushed open. He remembered hearing the heavy door thud back into its frame, and moments later as a second inner door was pushed open, and all the other patrons of the establishment looked up to observe the newcomers to the bar.

All that was except Jack who instead hunched his shoulders, picked up a pencil stub that lay in front of him and began to doodle, apparently absentmindedly, onto a beer mat.

His torso was turned about three-quarters away from the new customers, but he still managed to register two people, both men he thought, as he watched off the side of one eye.

A second later a thrill of pure fear and all-consuming adrenalin shot through him as he took the quickest of half-glances, before turning his back fully.

The man from the alley!

His mind screamed at him.

Murderer…and he came close to screaming out impulsively.

The other instantaneous reaction Jack felt was an overwhelming desire to bolt.

They must have known he was there.

He considered that three weeks had been no mean feat. To have kept running from guys like these, connected guys, for three weeks. Hell, he deserved a medal.

But he wasn't done yet, was he?

He managed to stay put.

He didn't bolt, practiced as he had become in the art of, 'I am uninteresting, and therefore, I am invisible.'

To any onlooker, he continued to scratch idly at the beer mat.

He took a short gulp of the ale in the glass and then looked studiously at the sediment as it resettled into that glass's bottom.

The two men up to the bar, twenty feet from Silver himself, and he could overhear only bits of what they were then saying, in apparently earnest conversation with the young server, and then with the manager of the place.

A few moments later, he felt another huge surging shot of fear and adrenalin when he clearly heard the one who was called Dickie, in a quiet tone that required Jack's hearing to be operating right at the limit, proclaim.

'Mister Cipher will be needing somewhere quiet.'

Less than a minute later, both men walked past Jack without a sideways glance and pushed on through a pock-marked door. Above an unadorned sign proclaimed somewhat grandly.

'You are leaving the public bar and entering the saloon bar.'

Jack was for long moments too astonished to think.

He ought to have upped and left as soon as the two men had let the door swing shut behind them, instead something within him persuaded him to try and figure out why they were here.

They walked past him no more than six feet distant, close enough to touch had he reached out an arm and tried. 'Close enough for government work,' a voice spoke up in his mind.

Neither man had looked down, nor potentially more dangerously, back over a retreating shoulder.

Had they done so Jack knew that would have been all she wrote.

He would not have made it to the door.

They were here, and he was here too, but they apparently did not seem to be appraised of that latter fact.

The pub had a central serving bar that allowed one staff member to keep an eye on both rooms when the place was not so busy, a common design in smaller rural pubs; and Jack realised that the two men having moved away from the darts match into the saloon bar had in fact improved his acoustics, and he could hear somewhat of their conversation.

He could hear quite well the clipped and fluting tones of the one and the more gruff bass of his companion. Not only could Jack hear the men speak, but by a curious quirk of fate he was sat in the one place where they would not see him, even should one or both stand again and seek service from the bar.

He was safe, at least as long as neither man decided to step back round to his side of the public house he had thought.

Initially, the conversation between both men proved boring. Accounts and airline delays, complaints and procedures.

After a time, Jack's senses dulled despite the undercurrent of fear. He had even become a little bored.

Both men seemed careful in how they framed their various conversation topics, and at one time Jack wondered if perhaps they were speaking in codes. But then he dismissed that particular flight of fancy as ridiculous, not least when he considered they had chosen to enter that particular establishment freely and might have held the same conversation anywhere they wanted and in confidence, had that proven important.

After some while, perhaps as much as an hour, the conversation slowed, and the Englishman realised both men had been served some food and had fallen to eating together in silence.

His mind had spoken up then, 'Mr Cipher does not like anyone to speak at the table during his dining.'

Jack wondered at the voice that offered that particular insight; it was like he had had a flash of mind-reading, a moment of telepathy, and as he sat there mulling things over, something about that strange, seemingly unimportant fact bugged him.

Banishing the voice, he thought of dinner himself and slid further into a lulled sense of well-being, cautiously beginning to plan another exit from right under the nose of his pursuers.

A telephone had rung behind the bar, and Jack had drifted further into his relaxed state as he fell once again to listening, this time to half of a conversation between the young bar girl and at the other end of the phone someone he guessed to be a boyfriend.

'No see. I never get off before half – eleven. An' darts is on, so prob'ly nearer twelve,' he heard the girl say. Followed by, 'You gonna pick me up? Go on I'll make it worth it,' followed by a salacious chuckle.

He had imagined the twinkle in her eye, and an equally persuasive twinkle in the man's groin. Men were so bloody predictable he had thought. He remembered wondering at his own recent abstinence from sex and understood it was circumstance. Fleeing for your life will do that to you he had thought grimly. And he recollected that moment when he had realised suddenly he had been listening to the wrong conversation.

The two men speaking again. This time in heated tones, voices raised. Jack had missed what had been said.

Dammit pay attention or get out.

Do you want to get caught?

'Four o'clock, I spoke to 'im, aye. And he said he would see us before nine.'

Somebody cheered and shouted, "One hundred and forty", from the far corner as the darts match had taken another twist, but Jack was then fully re-immersed in the conversation underway in the other bar, he had no time for the other staff or patrons of the establishment.

He had strained to hear above the sudden din and was rewarded when he heard once more the fluty tones that seemed to him in keeping with the nasty delicate little bastard that pursued him. 'Dickie, he's near. I can feel it you know. Him I mean. You may think that sounds strange, Dickie, but it is indeed the truth.

I can feel the heartbeat of my brother's killer and right now I tell you, I am close to him.'

A number of thoughts had shot through Jack's mind as he rose from his chair, swaying ever so gently on legs still uncertain whether they intended to support him or drop him like a stone.

One part of his mind had driven him on despite the unsteadiness. Any onlooker would likely have passed it off as mid-evening inebriation.

Another part of his mind weary with the travails of the previous weeks had wondered at the fleeing panic that drove Jack Silver onwards; wondered whether with the security of witnesses all around him the time might be right.

Had that been the moment to confront that Mister Cipher? And to confront the real culprit for his brother's murder. He remembered, the verging chaos, the let the damned cards fall as they might.

His tormentor had been right about one thing Jack thought grimly.

Fate, or something more had delivered the two men to the very venue where Jack was currently attempting to skulk in the shadows.

And right there lay a whole hunk of the problem he had realised as he continued his short journey towards the pub's exit.

Cipher was head honcho that much was clear, but the man Dickie, well he was a murderer.

And Jack had no doubt that the Shadowmen would kill him given the slightest opportunity.

These weren't the bad guys in the movies. These were really bad men.

Men of no conscience, cold hard killers both.

And so, if such were possible, these were men capable of far worse.

Though back then Jack had had no idea what worse might be.

And as clearly as Stevan Cipher believed he could feel Jack Silver close by, so the Englishman in turn had felt the evil intent that bled from the man's very soul.

'Run,' Jack's mind finally shouted at him.

Go, and find a deep dark hole and hide yourself away for a very long time.

And maybe one day this man will find out who it was that killed his brother. And maybe, just maybe mind, you can come blinking back out into the light.

Until then get gone.

And with that, he had opened the inner door pulled his coat close and half a second after had collided with the big man coming the other way at precisely the same moment, driving rain and wind adding to inward velocity.

Jack remembered issuing a gruff.

'Sorry,' as their shoulders thumped and were being rewarded with an unpleasant, 'Fuck off,' for his troubles.

He remembered looking up at the man attempting to push past him about to respond, some tension at the moment forcing some kind of self-destructive adrenalin rush through his system that demanded attention.

Deep inside he had felt thrilled. He knew he was about to get into it with the foul-mouthed guy.

'What did you say?' he had asked, attempting to put some steel into his own tone.

But in that same instant that he looked at the other man's face, a series of mental connections had also clicked.

He had remembered the thug Dickie speaking earlier something about somebody meeting them before nine.

His body clock warned him it was not far past that hour.

The big man looked down on the smaller man in the tight space and said with menace, 'What I said was fuck off, you fucking squirt. Get out of my fucking way before I make you really sorry.'

He was caught adrenalin had been forced through his system, and though he felt certain that was another of Cipher's Stormtroopers, at the same time something compelled his mouth to speak.

He had replied, 'Listen, mate. I'm not looking for trouble. But you're not talking to me like that. There's no need.'

He had slid past the bulk of the man as he had said this and was reaching for the exit door's main handle when suddenly he was violently shoved and had found himself outside and on the ground, cold water seeping instantly through his clothes, driving rain pelting him as he slowly got to his feet, shock dawning on him.

He looked into the face of the man and saw sour disinterest, a look that quickly froze any courage he had felt moments before. On one knee, he stalled as the man spoke again. 'Yeah, y'see, me I'm looking for trouble. I'm always looking for trouble. Stay down, cunt, or I'll fucking give it to you. Big time.'

The man's face was heavily scarred. One particularly ugly example divided the left side of his face into two severe halves. Both the man's fists were clenched, and to Jack he looked like some grizzled ancient prize-fighter, backlit as he then was by the pub's ambient interior.

The Englishman had stayed down, sense and reality reasserting some control. He realised that the man had shoved him out of the pub door six or eight feet across the gravel car park.

He had seen then the qualities that it took to make a bad guy, the simple indefinable hardness that set someone like scar-face apart from Silver himself, the absolute freedom from moral conscience. To Silver, any such inconvenience had bypassed that one early in life.

He reflected that he had got his first proper look since that terrible first night at one of those who came to be known as Shadowmen. Or as he had by then begun to think of them, Darth Vader's Stormtroopers. God knew mind, he was little enough any kind of Luke Skywalker.

The guy had glared down at him for long seconds, seemingly enjoying the cowed aspect. And then in slow motion, Jack saw the beginning of recognition in his eyes. He realised that luck had been about to run out.

He remembered scrabbling to his feet and backing quickly away; his voice frightened even to his own ears.

'Leave it, all right. I already said I didn't want any trouble.'

Turning he had begun to run, out into the wind and rain of the cold winter night, picturing giant cogs in the other's mind clicking into place as the thug realised he had just had his hands on the boss's prized prey.

And more, that he had let him go.

Momentum had come to Jack and, as he ran through the gates of the car park he had heard, could still hear in his mind the anguished howl from behind him.

He never looked back, and the Englishman had run and run ever since.

Unknown, guessed at by the other, each side sought a final solution. The Vistarens built the greatest engine of destruction any living thing might yet comprehend. They saw their great work and were certain nothing could stop it from fulfilling its purpose. For had more powerful destruction existed than their own, then surely that instead would have been the construct they built. The Hive made the Shaktar stone, small and insignificant, hidden from view through the aeons. Soon then came the final test, the reckoning for each of these creations.

Chapter Thirty-Two
Twilight

Jack meant it when he said on the train that he planned to separate from Hoody. But in the event without Harold Hood, he knew he would have most certainly found himself in the clutches of Scotland's police at least, if not Cipher and his henchmen.

Not only had he got him off of the train and past the watchers at the railway station, but he had succeeded in being pretty darn cool about the whole thing whilst doing it.

They walked briskly away from the station and then kept on stepping for a good couple of hours. Harold Hood led the older man through Edinburgh's early-morning streets with accomplished ease.

Eventually, they stopped at a back-street café, full in the early morning with tradesmen and labourers. It seemed to the Englishman that everyone there was dining on steaming fried food and heavily sugared tea.

Sat at a table close to the eatery's main window Jack came back to his own hot tea from daydreaming about a waitress called Dolores and a food stop far distant in Nevada.

He was amazed when he heard Hoody at the counter speaking to the heavyset female who stood there with the broadest Scottish accent he had yet heard.

The lad mastered the accent perfectly, and if Jack Silver had not listened to him speaking for the previous twelve hours in "good auld London" would have believed that he was listening to the most Scottish of Scotsmen.

When Hoody came back to the table, a few moments later, he watched his new friend carefully as he leaned over the table and then whispered to him.

'I'm impressed. How Scottish was that?'

One or two other patrons turned and looked at the two of them curiously, but most of the customers remained focused on their copies of the Daily Record spread atop bangers and beans.

The young man flicked his eyes left and right, suggesting to Jack that some other might hear the wrong thing and Silver nodded imperceptibly, returning to his tea. He looked out past the grease-stained net curtain hanging from a point halfway down the single twelve-foot window at the café front. The window was steamed up, and he struggled to see clearly beyond it.

At that precise moment, crawling past so slow that it seemed to him to be not really moving at all, was a big car, a Bentley or perhaps a Rolls-Royce. The car appeared full, and despite the impediments to his view Jack was suddenly certain the four or five occupants were about town looking for him.

He twitched his eyes back and forth furiously. Noticing the anxious gesture Hoody turned, apparently unconcernedly to any onlooker, and glanced out beyond that same steamed window. After a count of perhaps ten seconds during which time, the slow-moving car moved out of view he turned to Jack and said.

'De ya need a piss?'

He got a nod and both men rose from half-finished refreshments and headed out towards the rear of the eatery. They found themselves in a tight passageway running directly past a squalid kitchen full of eggs bacon and bubble frying loudly under the gaze of an unshaven hulk of a man with a cigarette hung loose from his disinterested mouth. Silver turned to his younger companion and said, 'Listen, I've got to get away from here right now. It's me they're looking for. I'm sure of it. Do you get me? This is like the station. Only worse.'

He raised his voice over the sound of a woman blaring from the radio out back and battling with the frying pans and general mishmash of sound from the café kitchen.

He was closing in on panic once more. The sudden change in tenor had caught him off-balance.

After events in Canada for a time, Jack felt like he had taken control and overcome his liabilities to fear. The panic that blindly cleared every obstacle in the way of his desperate charge to escape for so many months had gone, finally. Instead replaced by fury and the cold dark desire for revenge. That beast had driven him forward. Pushed him, shoved him in fact, straight to this moment and this place.

He figured once again he'd been stupid. That if he was not careful, or more importantly, really lucky during the next hours, perhaps the next few minutes, then he would end up delivered into the hands of his enemy and revenge would mean nought. Hoody looked at him and said sagely, 'So you want ta get out a here?'

His accent was still broad Scottish, now a permanent fixture in their new surroundings. 'Listen, they may be after yay. Or ya may just be some paranoid ninny. But I like ya. There's a place, cairn't be but fifteen minutes from here. If yer game.'

Jack looked at him hard, his mind in turmoil.

'Caffee, these people aren't messing about, you know.'

'What did you just say?' the boy replied.

'Who or, more precisely what is a Caffee?'

'Sorry,' Jack replied. 'You reminded me of someone for a moment there. Friend of mine, one of the good guys.' He paused to collect himself and shuffled a bit further down the passageway to ensure he couldn't be seen nor heard by the cigarette-chomping chef. 'Listen, I'm sorry. I've been a bit surprised. These people are all around me, and I didn't expect that somehow. Cipher's people. And I can't explain to you how, but I'm not mad. And I know with absolute conviction they are out there looking for me. The simple truth is you should get away from me. Run as far as you can. And when you get there, run some more. These guys want to kill me. And won't hesitate at piling the bodies up in front of them to get to me.'

Even as Jack spoke, he knew already Harold Hood, sometimes known as Hoody or Houdini, understood only too well people like Cipher and his Stormtroopers.

He was young, yet in many ways, he was light years older than Jack himself, especially when it came to people like that.

And so, after all the protestations were duly completed, Jack Silver scurried out behind the teenager into the back alley behind the café.

'Where is this place we're going?' he enquired as they slipped quietly through several alleys that backed onto the gardens of row after row of semi-detached houses. 'Well, aye, I might a bin exaggerating a bit when I said it was close. But I know a girl, and we are friends. Well, sometimes we are friends. It's more…' He trailed off for a moment. 'Anyway, her name is Rosie. You make sure an' call her Rosie. And naught else, or there'll be hell to pay.'

As they walked, five minutes turned to ten, and then ten to twenty. The two moved steadily and the day drew forth, crisp and bright and clean. Hoody kept them away from major intersections, walking through a series of back streets and alleys separated by communal grass areas until they reached what Jack could only describe as the seedier part of town. In the space of minutes, the houses became markedly shabbier, paintwork blistering, a burned-out car standing before one small front yard.

Few people were about. Those they saw were wrapped up against the cold and paid no heed to two more men out and about with their hoods up against the inclement season. Jack noted all of this, his breath a white smoke in the chill morning air.

After a time of looking down, he discovered he was staring at a small kid, no more than five years old. The child scowled at him whilst sitting on a three-wheel bicycle too small for him. Jack saw no adult close by and guessed that was the way of it in places like that the world over. Edinburgh might just as easily have been Calcutta Beirut or Mexico City.

'If not for the sodding cold,' Caffee spoke up in his head.

The homes whilst tatty were also older than he might have expected, and despite the obvious neglect each was slightly different to its neighbour.

Eventually, after most of an hour, Hoody pushed a screeching wooden gate inwards and the Englishman figured they were going into number Seventy-Four.

Not by virtue of numerals on the door or gate, but instead because he had noted the number Seventy-two houses earlier, painted in white paint with a child's writing skills.

Hoody produced a key from a pocket secreted somewhere inside his hooded jacket. He put it into the front door lock and Jack looked around noting ironically that the front yard was actually the worst of those he had seen thus far. Few cars were parked thereabouts, he guessed they might end up on bricks if left unattended for too long.

As he stepped off the street though he did notice a dark blue Ford Transit van parked a couple of hundred feet up the road that seemed unattended and intact. He shrugged to himself pictured a decorator or plumber home for lunch, or more likely playing away.

Grass and weeds grew all about the small yard up and beyond both men's knees and the twisted metal frame of some long-discarded appliance sat front and centre like a proud lawn model. As he stepped in he wondered if it might once have been the undercarriage to a pram though age and rust had sought to fudge the item's identity. He considered that it could just as readily have been a microwave.

At that moment Hoody grunted and pushed open the door with a shove. Silver pictured the junk mail piled up on the door's far side.

He walked inside and smelt mustiness in the air that suggested the windows had not been opened in a long time. Alongside the piled-up mail reassured him no one had been there in some time. A prerequisite for paranoid folk looking for a hideout he considered.

It was dim inside the house, and he blinked as he followed his companion down a short passageway, dust motes floating in the air, eddying around as they pushed through them.

Hoody called out.

'Rosie, you here?'

His voice sounded strangely flat in the dim disused building.

There was no reply, nothing, not a sound. The house appeared to be empty.

'I'm guessing your friend Rosie. She doesn't own this place, right?'

Jack said, brushing at a cobweb he had inadvertently walked through, and looking at Hoody with some doubt. 'Nay, it's, well I guess that ya might say it's a commune. A squat, to be exact.'

'A squat!' Jack replied.

'Well,' he started seeming momentarily confused. 'Well, so we have no right to be here. Do you know who does owns this place? And how come you have a key to the front door? They just give them?'

Jack never finished.

He heard a loud woody-sounding creak, followed by a burp and a foul-mouthed curse. And then about a quarter of a second later the door in front of him fairly exploded. Three men crashed through, instantly filling the narrow space. Jack registered timber and hurtling bulk as suddenly everything changed.

Something smashed him hard, he went down, and at the same moment, he heard a naked scream as it sounded like Hoody suffered a similar fate. Agony flared like white fire inside Jack's head. He realised in an instant all his plans had come to nothing as the air escaped his lungs in a sudden forceful burst. Even then, down and defeated, he was forced to smile.

He heard a young man's voice shout and a loud metallic thud followed by a guttural scream. Jack figured Hoody had got a lick in for the good guys. Then suddenly an instant later his balls swelled up like a blossoming atomic explosion. They seemed instantaneously to have grown to ten, his mind amended crazily, a hundred times their normal size. He might have managed to figure someone's boot had gone in had he not been prostrated and mewing puke with the astonishing agony suddenly visited him.

Then, as suddenly as moments before silence had become noise, so light went to darkness.

And as it did Jack faded away. The voice within his mind that trailed him into the black asked, 'How did they ever find me here?'

Interlude
Dark City

He stood in a room that was ink-black and looked out on a vision of a primeval storm. Lightning tore at the fabric of the sky and thunder rumbled mercilessly, loud and menacing.

The earlier news had carried reports of strange events happening, out beyond the moon among the stars. Reporters murmuring urgently about something major, as far as he could tell. If the curious and nervous uncertainty of the newsreader had been anything to go by seemed like big news.

The television was off now, he never had been a fan.

No, he persuaded himself he was learned in the old ways. Didn't mess more than he had to with technology, understanding that for him it was best not to cross the streams.

At times, going right back to his earliest days, he had known intuitively that the world flowed through his mind. And over the years, and most especially at those times he had learned that the technology of the modern world sought only to interfere with the clarity of that signal, that broadcast. Down many years as the broadcasts came, the small man had concentrated and practiced holding wild and wide-ranging imagery in his mind. In time learning somewhat about its type and its nature. Through long years of watchful study, he found ways to engage, to embrace, and finally to slip something in, because from the outset he saw the route to power, and power was what he craved.

Stevan Cipher learned to pull apart those signals just a fraction, in his imagination like separating a garment's stitching.

Ever so slightly, ever so slowly finding a route. And at some point a way to add to the mix, to subtly alter the broadcast. Eventually, as his early manhood turned to his middle years, he believed that he made that world within his own personal territory. Separated and adjusted the signals had brought knowledge, wealth and power, but had brought other changes to Stevan Cipher, also. At the outset, he was little more than a huckster. A circus hypnotist, a charlatan conman who had some small influence over weak-minded people. Had he known that had been mostly through the force of his personality? Nonetheless, as he had crafted his talent, the actual ability to see beyond, to look into, to alter perception, his influence over those minds around him had grown.

People had begun to gather to the banner of the brother's Cipher. Drawn first by his more charismatic brother, by the image of wealth and power, and then as time passed by his own drive and instinctive dominating influence. He drew folk to him and then held them like a religious cult leader. None of it mattered to him as he stood and looked out on the world enveloped by the storm busily spewing naked fury. He felt empowered, uplifted in a way that all of the bludgeoning blood-curdling power-crazed trip to the top of his particular pile had never achieved. Lightning cracked again, and he felt current surge into him, through him.

Out loud he recited the names of the seven princes whose learning had beaten him bloody. In a time so long past that it was barely recognisable to him any longer, other than as an indistinguishable part of his core being. They existed like a black-and-white photograph forever imprinted on his brain. There was a time long ago when he had been a victim, and not certainly as he now was.

A time when the devil had been white and not of the night. The time when he found learning in the Dark City, at the feet of the King of Destruction…

'No matter,' his mind whispered.

'You command now.'

'Here, in this place, the time of your kingdom is upon you.'

'First on the lists of course The Master of Rituals.'

'And he is named Baal-Beryth.'

'That one will watch over the carnage to come.'

'Cipher knew he would smile at the chaos his chosen one upon mortal Earth brought to the small people and their best-laid plans. And Baal-Beryth will come only to pick through the bony remains at day's end, for he is the mover prime such is his right.'

'Second is Dumah, commander of the demons of Gehenna.' And as Cipher spoke the name reverentially he felt it was indeed him that sat at the head of a horde astride the fiery demon steed. Out among the stars just beyond the electronic eyes of mankind, awaiting the moment.

Cipher felt him, felt the ecstasy, and it invoked a great part of his reverence.

'Third comes Meririm, and he is The Prince of Air.'

Cipher stood staring out, and he imagined that Prince of the Black Blood conjuring the night's great storm with the majesty only one such as that might hope to command.

'Then is Rehab, Prince of Oceans, his time comes later, as will that of Sariel, Prince of the Moon, the fifth. Sixth are you my Lord Mephistopheles.'

And though he would not articulate it Stevan Cipher felt that one most like in kind to himself.

For a while in life, he perceived his departed brother one to and with Lucifer Rofocale, Minister Prime, controller of wealth, the seventh and not the least of those great princes. Still, Cipher himself lusted after destruction was driven by the need for vengeance, seemingly upon all things. It was the purpose that he had built his life upon, and for its sake only.

He like the sixth gloried and gorged upon the most heinous suffering, and so he had always sought oneness with Mephistopheles, who was legion, and forever the destroyer.

And as he stood watching the storm Stevan Cipher understood two most momentous things had happened to him that very evening.

Firstly, and by no means the lesser of the two events of the day, he had finally caught and scratched an itch, one that had crawled and gnawed at him and eluded his grasp for too long a time.

He acknowledged that the strange link, the one between him and the man called Silver had brought much confusion. For a time, he had begun to believe somehow that destiny might keep Silver from his grasp, keep him just out of reach, while close enough to dig and knead at the deepest parts of his psyche.

Then unexpectedly, at the eleventh hour even that one had been brought to heel, now held securely in a stone cell far below where he stood.

In time, he intended to watch Jack Silver kneel.

And then wail.

And then finally emit his dying screams laid out before him.

And then secondly, had he not felt the arrival, the divination of the seven great princes, those with whom he had formed his alliance down the smoky darkness of the years?

Any lingering doubts had been cast aside, certain that he stood as the chosen one. That he alone was each and all of The Four Horsemen of the Apocalypse.

And he wished fervently to visit all four, be they plague, famine, war and most of all death, upon all mankind.

He would fulfil his destiny. Given to him by the voices that had spoken to him since boyhood, forever whispering through the mist and mirrors in his mind.

And whilst he was not certain of the how, soon would come the ultimate destruction, the revenge that would be the culmination of his existence.

The small, neat man saw with the absolute conviction of the true believer. To him, his empowerment was not spiritual humbug, not the false hope and empty rhetoric dished out by the church of the weak and the meek. He felt real power course through him, and it was akin to the electric current that lit the night's darkness.

He saw then images beyond the ken of man and felt no compassion whatsoever for those he intended to smite. All now were just blight upon that he beheld.

He was in the thrall of destruction and trembled with ecstasy as the names of the demons of hate and dominion, vengeance anger and war, danced and ran wildly about his mind.

Amducious, Andrus and Abbadon. Baal, Nebiros and Sargatanas, Agaliarept, Satanchia and Fuerety, Belphegor and Svengali.

Names of power all, each, in turn, fanning the white fire of madness that ran unchecked through the mind of Stevan Cipher.

He stood at a portal beyond which raged storm and destruction. And, with no hesitation his mind opened that doorway wide and invited all through.

His first order of business was Silver. He had sent men down the seven stories between him and the itch.

How long ago had that been?

An hour or two.

He wasn't certain.

The mundane had certainly become increasingly muddled in recent times.

He turned away from the beauty of the night's storm and quietly slipped out of the room.

'Pennywise is pound foolish,' the small man mumbled to himself and started down the long winding staircase towards the castle proper and its lower levels. And he thought about how, in the end, he had to sort everything out himself. How in the end everything was down to him.

He and the weak-minded fool Jack Silver.

The makers had remained concerned, despite their utter scouring of the omniverse. Life would sprout again, and so the purpose of the thing they built. Awakened the construct, their great final solution, might quickly engage itself with great engines of destruction, bastions of offence made down the long intervening years. Aeons to prepare while opposing life crawled out into the light to multiply once more.

Chapter Thirty-Three
Your World

'You need not speak to me of death, I know all that there is to know of that demise.'

Jack looked round at Tokyo Rose and realised the statement was some tacit admission that he was at least in part Stevan Cipher. The man that Jack Silver had crossed paths with in another place. The reference to Tokyo Rose escaped him, but he believed now that the generally sanguine persona portrayed to date in that place was indeed no more than that.

Jack had begun to understand that the Mac and Shorty sideshow, whilst more colourful was actually less important. And whilst he did not clearly understand the verses and the deep meaning of many things about which they had spoken, he did understand that his destiny was entwined with that of Stevan Cipher.

So as Tokyo Rose was about to speak again Jack interrupted. Timing the interruption to ensure maximum frustration.

'I too have learned about death, more than I might have wished in recent times. But speak to me as you will, I at least want to hear what you have to say.'

Cipher glowered and Jack inwardly smiled knowing he had scored a hit in the strange mental poker game that appeared to be developing.

Shorty and Mac remained seemingly unaware of the small byplay between the two men, and after a moment the thin man Shorty's voice proceeded to reassert, as if he had never been interrupted. 'Invested in you both is the nexus of our solutions, being two. Millennia past us. I suppose you might say we fell out. Disagreed at a fairly. Well, at a grand level.' At this point, the other interrupted with a snort, followed by a small gout of smoke and flames from a blackened snout, exploding. 'Fell out, fell out. It was a bit less trivial than falling out, old man!' 'Yes, yes, OK. Well, we had a sizeable disagreement. Is that better? Would you like to tell them?'

At this, the dragon looked down balefully at the emaciated speaker and shook his head. Jack wasn't sure which question the shake of that bony skull was meant to address, but it appeared sufficient to allow Shorty to continue his narrative. 'So, we found it difficult to get along. Mac and I ended up having quite a big squabble. Anyway, that was a long time ago. I guess you could say that we've both moved house since then. We don't see so much of each other these days.'

Jack noticed that Tokyo Rose was starting to de-dust. The red that in Jack's case had elevated to his collar was slowly sliding back down the other man's clothing as surreptitiously as it had earlier climbed.

Nobody else appeared to notice.

Jack figured the small man's previous outburst had led to a quantity of the dust falling away from his person, and he wondered as it settled even lower whether this too was offering him an insight not otherwise apparent.

'We were both pretty angry back then and spiteful to boot.'

Shorty stopped and looked at Mac who gazed into the distance and appeared to be trying to ignore him.

'Can we get on with this?' Tokyo Rose interrupted.

'I thought you said you were speaking to us about death, not your interminably tiresome bloody squabbling. Who's in charge here, for God's sake?'

His ire appeared to rise another notch; the red dust was holding steady just past the knee of his trousers.

'And anyway, what the hell are you talking about?' he finished in exasperation.

Jack watched him carefully throughout and did not think he needed the dust to tell him this time that the angst was feigned. The small man had hidden his anger before, and now he pretended emotions that were not there. Tokyo Rose, or Stevan Cipher, either one, was playing some kind of game, and Jack thought must have known more about what was going on than he did.

He remembered what Mac had said before about this being a place to make some things clear, and to leave some things dark. He had also said time was limited, and Jack wondered at whether things were proceeding too slowly for some, or for one.

Shorty shrugged his shoulders and said, 'I'm doing the best I can here.' And, looking again pointedly at Mac, he continued.

'I am trying to fulfil an obligation that was made a long time ago. I don't know if I agree with it or not And I am certain that there are other places that I could and probably should be right now. Nevertheless, I am endeavouring to make some things clear. It is of course entirely up to each of you whether you choose to stay or indeed choose to listen. Shall I go on?' Shorty looked at all three of his companions, and whilst nobody appeared to offer consent, neither did anyone leave.

Jack smiled.

He felt like there were invisible lines of alliance. And if so, that he was most closely tied to Shorty, who in ways he could not put his finger on appeared most similar in outlook to himself.

He couldn't deny that from the outset he had liked Mac too.

But Mac was enigmatic, alien, entirely impossible to read. And Jack thought, being frank with himself ultimately he was a dragon.

There was something dangerous in the nature of dragons.

In spite of all the courtesies and kind words the fire and the teeth, along with the sheer stature and imposing presence of Mac must be an issue.

As time passed the dragon felt increasingly like an impostor in that strange land. There was at the very core a disagreeable part to the whole Mac caricature. A shadow of malice wrapped around the creature Jack was uncomfortable being that close to.

Something else increasingly evident to Silver was the conditions around them which were starting to change, to deteriorate.

The deep azure blue of the sky was darkening, the neutral temperature had begun to rise. In fact, by paying attention, it was quite considerably heating up, and he felt uncomfortably warm. He noticed a breeze, and it began to push at him. His trousers flapped, and the red dust started to fall away, but the breeze was hot. Shorty had begun to speak again, Jack missed the opening stanzas, distracted as he was by the changes taking place around him. All of a sudden, just as he was dragging his attention back to Shorty's speech, all hell broke loose. Without any warning whatsoever Mac, the raggedy dragon roared.

Jack heard, 'Time's up!' as the great dragon spread his wings wide and let loose a deafening ear-piercing screech that ripped apart the previous quiet. The creature rose quickly to over a hundred feet into the air, hung static for a moment and then dived straight at the tall, emaciated man called Shorty.

In the next instant, faster than Jack could comprehend, the thin man changed.

Where before he had been attired in a poor man's fancy dress of leather and iron, coloured boxer shorts and a tattered scabbard, pale and weedy. Of a sudden not thirty feet from the Englishman stood a warrior. Glimmering scale armour rippling from the ground upwards over a six-foot-ten frame filled out and pulsing power. Helmeted too, smooth chrome lines broken only by two slits. Eye sockets that shone forth in vivid neon green.

In the warrior's left hand, a small round battle shield, shining black and reflective like some new plastic toy. Not in keeping with the armour at all, nor nearly as impressive as the four-foot broadsword of glittering deadly polished steel brandished in his right hand and swung aloft.

The warrior that had been Shorty till moments before emitted a battle cry. And it was as guttural as anything Jack had ever heard.

A moment later the two were joined in terrible combat.

The din was astonishing as one of Shorty's arms pumped and the sword clanged mightily against the dragon's heavy hide. The creature blew enormous gusts of death-dealing fire that washed over the armour and apparently bounced right back off the round black shield.

In those first seconds, the dragon's attack appeared ineffective.

But then the bulk of the creature, with arms and legs smashing and gouging, settled its full weight onto the far smaller glittering warrior, and he instantly disappeared from sight.

The whole incredible change happened quickly; Jack had not moved an inch. The wind rose, the sky darkened, and the two combatants screamed venomous war cries, as Jack thought of escape and started to turn away. His senses were a moment behind the rest of him and suddenly felt a needle of white fire shoot through one side of his body.

He stopped mid-turn and looked down at a blade stuck hilt-deep into his shoulder, at the blood pulsing down his front. The Englishman smelt Cipher and knew the man was mere inches from him. Under expensive cologne, Jack caught a whiff, and the smell was foul, utterly rancid.

In spite of the pain flaring exactly where in some other place, he had been shot, and the utter confusion about the sudden dramatic change in that strange desert land, he reached up with both hands, and he grabbed with all his might.

He closed both hands around the other man's throat.

At the same instant Cipher's hands closed around his neck also. But Jack Silver intent on squeezing the life out of the insane murderer barely even registered the fact. Indeed, no more than he then felt the white fire of death as the hilt-deep knife wound emptied his lifeblood.

He squeezed using every ounce of strength that remained, and beyond the shoulder of the man he was trying to kill, he stared at a strange parody of the killing embrace between him and Cipher as the two inexplicably alien creatures also sought mutual and utter destruction in their own strange tableau.

The sky had darkened to an ink-black night. Stars a distant panoply spread across the sky as far as might be seen. The breeze had become a wind, a storm that swirled increasingly violently around all four. Though the storm whipped hard into his face Jack didn't blink as he choked with his hands and as he looked on at a knight warring with a dragon.

No air was going into his lungs, he like the other three was in a race to death. Jack watched as the knight Shorty stabbed the great blade upward in a vicious arc. And for the first time, the long steel came back in its downward arc bloody.

Silver's vision began to waiver, the fire in his shoulder was numbing and his senses began to shut down. The great dragon opened its wings wide once more and with a roar like thunder swept one great forepaw down into the midriff of his smaller opponent.

Even as he faded Jack heard the rending of metal, as bright red blood sprayed yards from both alien combatants. Suddenly, he felt the weight of Cipher sag, and a moment later they were both pulled down to their knees, still holding, still squeezing furiously.

Jack saw that Shorty had dropped onto one knee also. He thought perhaps the tall warrior was almost done. He watched through fading eyes as the knight raised the gleaming red and silver spike above his head one last time, in his exhaustion letting the black shield drop.

He wearily beckoned the dragon forward. And the small "come on" gesture with the warrior's free hand, despite everything, was almost comical.

As the last of Jack began to pack up and leave, a word climbed into his mostly vacant mind.

'Propaganda.'

It had all been in the name of propaganda. And in the end, he thought, like Neville Chamberlain's "peace in our time" the propaganda had failed utterly.

Deep in his psyche Jack thought the four had been brought together to proffer some acceptable future vision, some kind of workable solution. But there was none, in the end there never would be. All there were mutually opposed, and so as the clock had spun down to the zero moment each of them had pursued their own agenda.

Like Tokyo Rose broadcasting to Yankee soldiers at the end of World War Two, all the rest was simply propaganda, nothing more.

Had Cipher known this throughout, thus the parodied name, the poker game, the whole façade? Each one is present following a path ordained by their nature. And now all or at least some would die, Silver understood that and more, that from the off death had been Stevan Cipher's only ambition, and the dragon Mac's too.

The Englishman went blank, came back, and then blacked out again. He swayed and discovered a final vague moment of consciousness; aware his life was leaving him too. His grip on the other man was loosening as his own life ebbed away.

Jack caught sight of the winged dragon trembling in mid-air, like a dog on hold, awaiting an instruction to go, hanging on the precipice of the killing thrust. The knight though had risen to both feet, dropped the shield to the ground, and stood legs apart his defences downed, yet still he did not take a backward step.

The Englishman thought he understood; and as that understanding dawned, so he gently dropped his own hands from his opponent's neck and, with the last of the life in him, pulled the thin blade from the wound in his shoulder and thrust it outwards with the last of his strength he connected solidly with something.

And everything faded to black.

The Shaktar stone knew the time had come and understood it needed to be somewhere other than where it was. Saw that place and sought one last twist of fate. Asked one last favour from the purpose that had served it so long.

Chapter Thirty-Four
Tightrope

Jack came to.

He was bound to a chair; one whose back was tall enough that they had been able to bind his head around the top and firmly to the seat's back. He could turn neither left nor right, merely stare ahead and to the limits of his eyes' vision within that constraint.

They had beaten him, and he was hurt. Yet as he sat there, he was amazed at how little harm had actually yet been visited upon him. He looked about as much as he was able and saw he was in a large room, a hall of sorts. A room with a vaulted ceiling and high windows that ran lengthwise as far as he could see along two walls.

The room was perhaps sixty feet by forty and seemed a little like a chapel, he thought, and yet not quite.

Jack thought the room was more austere and stark than any religious hall he ever remembered.

No invocations to the Lord adorned the walls, nor pictures or drapes of any kind. Candles burned all around the room. Jack saw there were more than a hundred blood-red candles flickering in various embrasures and iron stands of twisted black, and no lights hanging from the ceiling, as far as he could see. As a result, eight or nine feet above the room's floor, the space became dim and shadowy. The hall as a whole, thought Jack, resembled something from the mind of Edgar Allan Poe.

He shivered.

It was not warm in the cavernous space, and they had stripped him of his clothing. He had been pushed into what he understood to be a dungeon, deep below. In the darkness of the hall, he sat quietly and remembered how as they took him he had tried to hold his nerve, all the while wondering and worrying about his young companion.

It had been pitch black and icy cold, and he had been awfully afraid.

For what had seemed a long time, nobody had come, and the only noise he'd heard was his own breathing, that and his calls to Hoody, to his captors, to anyone.

The time had stretched out, elongating to a point where each second lasted a minute, each minute an hour, and in the black, his mind had drifted slowly on the eddies of his cares. The Englishman had begun to reflect, to look again at events as a whole rather than in disconnected parts sitting on the cold stone floor.

He thought back and wondered once more at his long journey. He considered the people he had met, and those he had lost along the way. At the pursuit of Cipher and his henchmen.

He thought again of the night in London, and of the days that followed. And he understood he no longer was the man he had been back then.

He had been an archetypical product of the West, arrogant in the security there was always another meal, another warm bed, another buck waiting around the corner. But he also saw that as a growing picture of fractured humanity in a greater context, not an issue of one, nor of nation-state, nor race or creed. He understood it was an issue of perception and of the whole.

Jack saw that like himself it had all gotten back-to-front, and in that cell deep below the castle proper he began to see the evidence of the cracks that had long been appearing in the human race as a whole.

Fault lines that would soon be irreparable.

There was harm to the Herd, he saw that.

To the Herd, to the Hive.

His vision continued to grow and became an epiphany in his mind, and he spied that change was needed.

As it had been needed to mend him despite not knowing he had been broken until that instant. Jack realised the greater truth in that dark space.

The same was true for humanity as a whole.

Would though change arrive before his world, his herd were broken beyond repair? And if so would the pill be one too bitter to swallow?

He had imagined all his life that events just unfolded, without choice on his part, fate, or some kind of universal script. Yet he saw then that actually, it had all been about his choices, as it had all been about humanity's choices.

There he squatted, held in the trap of his enemy with no hope of escape, and liable to die in the very near future, probably after a period of extreme pain.

As his vision broadened though the Englishman discovered a kind of peace. And unbidden came the words of Christ passed down from Psalms.

'And the meek shall inherit the Earth.'

He saw it clear in his mind that in the end only the meek could inherit the Earth. In any other direction, the outcome was destruction for all, mutually inclusive.

He considered, meek, being humble in spirit and manner, patient with self and others, or it was nothing. And the voice that spoke to him then had been Molly's.

And so, in that dim place where he had begun in terror, and become resigned to his fate, at some point in the deep velvet blackness he had found answers, and both peace and a modicum of fortitude. The two things that had eluded him for so many months. And should he live long enough he guessed he had found a clue to his destiny, too.

Finally, he understood he would stand before his persecutor, and that revenge whilst it flowed through his veins, was not the thing that would put him there.

Like Shorty and Mac, he and Stevan Cipher were diametrically opposed.

It did not matter what had gone before, they ultimately were but a part of the eternal conflict. Good versus evil, darkness versus light, heat versus cold, order versus chaos…and on and on.

His plans, like his efforts to elude capture, had all come to nought, but that no longer mattered.

At that moment, his mind lit up like an operator's switchboard.

Unknown to the Englishman Jack Silver during that unguessable passage of time, his mind had been opened, used much nearer to its capacity. Whether preordained or a result of the peculiar circumstances he had no clue. And yet quietly, like an Aston Martin idling for a time and then remembering its own smooth power accelerating away, Jack Silver thrilled as he began to thrum with the pure clear mental energy that was within him.

Instead of the mundane, the angst of the insane, he found himself walking paths of deeper meaning, in a place below conscious thought, far from debate. Away from all that he had been. He found again each and all those voices that had guided him. And he found more besides.

Within him they sang, and Jack Silver caught a glimpse of that which was the Hive.

A million miles beyond among the stars, yet close enough to the trifling cares of humanity to worry those with eyes to see events were unfolding that dwarfed all humankind.

A machine, a product of the minds of the most powerful beings in time and space had yet born into existence. A final solution to the spreading survival, the weed-like growth that was the Hive had begun to count down. The lighting of that final of fuses.

So one man squatted on the stone floor of a cell within an ancient Scottish monument to feudal futility, naked and alone. He only saw within his mind the hope of the Hive. And sat primly right by the side he saw also the doom of all.

The door to the cell creaked open, a bright light shone down upon the small naked form curled up on the floor, and three men looked in, craning their necks to see, expecting to see, should have seen, a broken man, a man pleading for his life. They did not, and for that alone, each one was astonished. The man rose from the ground to a sitting position and blinking looked back at them, at peace.

The man for whom Stevan Cipher had sent his Shadowmen chasing all over the world had been found and brought back. The same man that had skipped past them time and again. The terrified rabbit scampered hither and thither, eluding them severally by the skin of his teeth. For a time so elusive, it had seemed he might drive their boss to the brink of madness. And here he was, sitting naked in a cold dark cell, deep in the heart of his enemy's lair, and he was unafraid. Each man knew this would mean trouble, but even when the deep voice echoed off the stone walls, 'Pick him up, the boss wants him in the big hall,' and each man bent to comply, still none of them had any idea just how much trouble lay ahead.

Jack came back to within himself, came to now in the hall of his enemy. He told himself he was not afraid, and he thought that was true.

At least till he heard the footsteps, understood that, finally he would stand before his nemesis.

At the base of a long winding flight of stone stairs, Cipher was overcome by a wave of, what was it?

He was not certain.

Something akin to the broadcasts he himself had used to influence those around him washed suddenly and unexpectedly over him.

But this had been different than Cipher's understanding. Somehow huge, and a child's voice whispered, 'Frightening.'

He banished that thought instantly. He was Stevan Cipher, he dealt in death and people feared him.

Moments later the sensation passed. He tried briefly to categorise it, to tell himself it was akin say to a bout of low blood pressure, or dizziness brought about when standing too quickly. And so swiftly he shoved it forcefully from his mind.

The small man pushed open the heavy oak doors to the great hall and felt a chill draught as he stepped from the passage, the smooth worn runner onto the bare flagstones of the imposing room. He stood framed in the doorway and looked around the cavernous space, the dim light baffling him momentarily.

And then he saw him…and he smiled witheringly at what he beheld.

The entity arrived. It appeared and became instantly inert and so invisible to anyone watching, floating silently in the dark eternal night above one small blue globe spinning idly around a young parent star. The entity was prepared for every eventuality its makers could imagine and so waited to see which might now come to pass.

HOLD, HOLD, HOLD, HOLD, HOLD, HOLD, HOLD, HOLD, HOLD, HOLD, HOLD, HOLD, HOLD, HOLD, HOLD, HOLD,
GO.

Chapter Thirty-Five
Fire on High

The men had come to take him, and Jack had closed his eyes again and drifted to unconscious.

Sometime later he awoke to a vague scraping sound.

At first, he thought perhaps it was his imagination at work. He wanted to open his eyes but found that he couldn't. He wondered if he might have been drugged, but then bound as he was and already in the clutches of his enemy, what would be the point?

He heard whispered voices, and he strained as hard as he could but wasn't able to make out what they were saying or who they were. Two at least, but there might have been a dozen.

He heard scraping and clanging, sounds of iron.

Fear coursed through him at a biological level, yet his body was otherwise completely numb. He couldn't help that, but his mind remained crystal-clear.

He knew he was in a predicament, and while his mind had receded from the earlier high, he was operating still at a raised level of perception.

The sounds went on for some time, an hour, and still, he couldn't open his eyes. Still, no one came to him nor spoke a word to him, and he realised he was not able to speak also, and that he hadn't even tried.

He remembered the cell he had inhabited earlier; and much of what and where his mind had walked during those last hours. He felt a scrap of cloth on sore flesh and realised someone had dressed him in the moments between the turns of the page. And moreover, some small part of his vanity was grateful: no man wanted to go to his death naked, that was a privilege saved for birth he figured.

And at death's consideration, suddenly, he remembered.

From the cold and dark cell to the great hall, and then Cipher had come. They had all come, and they had brought Hoody with them.

In the same hall then as he was now, he felt that. He had been peaceful and yes they had allowed him to dress. Even untied his bonds for a brief time, so certain were they of their supremacy in that place.

And he had sat meekly as a lamb, believing perhaps there was nought more Stevan Cipher could now do to him, resigned as he was to death's slow and tortured passage.

Stormtroopers stood around the room in ones and twos. Jack Silver saw the London pair had been conspicuous by their absence. He had watched every man flinch, then cower at the entrance of the quiet, unremarkable man that was Stevan Cipher. He remembered thinking how history had painted such ordinary folk black time and again.

At first and for some time Cipher ignored him, preferring it to minister the business of his lieutenants, offering a quiet authority that would have not been out of place in many boardrooms across the globe. Jack had watched as best as he was able, by then once again tightly bound to a chair. And he had admitted internally he had been both surprised and impressed at the calm, efficient way his enemy dealt with his world.

However, mad the man in his mind had been, at that time he had seen evidence only of a controlled and competent administrator, a leader of men. And somehow he had hated him more for not having proven to be the stereotypical psycho.

All that changed the moment they had brought Hoody into the room. The boy was bound also, tied tightly to a seven-foot rusty iron pole, nothing more than an oversized spike. He was gagged and Jack saw the boy's eyes, spied the terror in them, thew he saw also he had some mastery of his fears still, and he felt a great pride in that.

Harold Hood had struggled against his bonds and so, at a small wave of one of Cipher's hands, two of the Shadowmen had laid into him, punching him to the face and gut mercilessly. Jack heard the boy's jaw crack and break after one severe blow. He saw blood spray time and again, and Harold Hood was quite literally able to do nothing, so tightly was he bound.

But Jack Silver never looked away.

Throughout he sought out and found and held the boy's eyes. Trying to impart something, some inner resolve, anything to help him beyond the moment until whatever moment came next.

A time came when the beating the boy's face had closed both eyes, and Jack could not see any more through the tears that streamed from his own.

Even had he not been gagged he was mute, beyond the pale of sickened horror for this latest attack on an innocent soul, one who had tripped over nothing more unfortunate than Jack Silver himself. The boy had struggled against his bonds and for that was beaten nigh to death.

And Jack wanted to say "enough", but he understood that when it came to Stevan Cipher, it would never be enough.

During the beating, the dapper little man had not even been looking, preferring instead to focus on the organisation of some strange iron and wooden contraption in the room's centre.

As Harold Hood hit the ground with a thud, out cold, or dead maybe, Cipher finally spoke.

'Stop,' he mumbled distractedly looking only momentarily away from the unusual iron and wooden wigwam that had taken up residence in the room's middle. Jack only then noticed this new thing. A knot grew in his gut, and he blinked furiously trying to clear the tears from his eyes to see more clearly. That blinking appeared to catch his enemy's eye and Cipher turned, beckoning a big man that was next to him to join him as he walked over to where Silver was sat, bound and gagged.

'It seems something has upset our guest,' Cipher said, addressing his comment towards the man with him, another six-and-a-half-foot giant.

Christ, they're all monsters, Jack thought with a shudder. He didn't get to expand this any further as Cipher continued quite equably.

'Stop him crying. You know how I hate weakness.' And half a second later, a fist slammed into Jack's face.

He saw it coming but was unable to do anything other than admire the perfect arc the mass of bone and gristle took as it arched in towards his face. And then closed his left eye with an explosion of white agony.

'Yes…yes, that's done it,' Cipher continued unable to conceal a small chuckle as he spoke.

'Now, shall we give him something to sob about, heh?'

Gruff voices assented from around the room.

Jack was unceremoniously dragged still bound to the chair and planted maybe five or six feet from the eight-foot lattice of wood and iron.

He tried to struggle within his bonds. And he thought he was about to take another sledgehammer blow to the face, but instead heard Cipher announce, 'Leave him be plenty of time for that later. I want him to see this.'

The big man who had single-handed bodily moved Jack and chair across half of the great hall's length stepped away from the prisoner, rebuked.

Jack saw a flash of lightning in his peripheral vision, counted "one elephant" twice and was rewarded by a monumental roll of thunder.

It sounded like the end of the world outside, yet he would have given much to be out and in the centre of that maelstrom at that exact moment.

But another part of him, the evolving man understood that he would stay and see this through to the end even were he unbound and free to go, whatever that might prove to be. The lightning had brought a lurid glow to the scene for a few moments that seemed to hang in the rooms still air.

In that glow, Jack could no longer see the prostrate form of Hoody and hoped desperately the room's other occupants had forgotten the boy also.

He peered once more as best he could at the strange construction Cipher had so admired. The poles of iron did not stand free upon the grey flagstones of the floor but appeared to have slotted into iron sleeves, apparently specially prepared for the contraption now erected. The latticework of heavy wooden struts over the three metal posts that joined at a point eight feet above the floor was horizontal and tied into a preordained arrangement with heavy hide ties.

The whole thing seemed to have been built over a ring of stones, in the middle of which sat a pile of black coals with a powdering of white where before had been something burned.

Jack had seen all of this in the flash of lightning. His stomach turned and, despite the gag pulled tightly across his mouth the Englishman tried to shout out, 'No.' Once again his attempt to speak attracted a reaction from Cipher. The small man at once walked away from him and picked up a small three-legged hardwood stool. He walked back and placed it carefully just three feet away from the prisoner. He looked left and right and then, in a confidential, only for my friend's tone, began to speak.

'This…no, no, not for you, Jack Silver. This is for your little mousy cunt mate over there.'

At this, he nodded over Jack's shoulder seemingly rather disinterestedly before continuing.

'You wouldn't know this, but as a boy, I used to read about cowboys and Indians a bit. Perhaps you did, too?' He framed the statement like a question. Then appearing to realise that Jack could not reply continued.

'I disliked those cowboys, prancing around on their ponies, shooting everything with their bloody guns, poofs the lot of them. And do you know what's more than passing strange about all of that history? No, well I shall inform you. It's all a load of poppycock. The Mexicans, The Indians, all of the indigenous peoples that had always lived there. Well, the simple truth is they had been fighting among themselves for, well forever.'

The small man was drowned out by another roll of thunder and then lit at the moment in stark detail by the lurid lightning. He frowned at the storm, looking as if he expected that, too, to bow to his will.

'What was I saying? Oh yes. The peoples of that continent had been more than capable of inflicting pain on one another since long before the advent of Europeans and their killing technologies.' He paused and smiled at Silver witheringly.

'Do you know it took more than fifty years for three hundred thousand invaders to pacify twenty-five thousand Apache Indian braves? I guess that's the kind of fact you won't find in the winner's schoolbooks.' Cipher looked out at the growing storm and then continued.

'The Apache Indian was the most heartless and cold-blooded adversary in the history of humankind's conflict. Had it not been for both overwhelming numbers And one or two fortunate twists of fate, alongside rather advantageous fighting equipment the Apache's skill in killing their enemies would have wiped out even the overwhelming number of marauders.' He paused as more thunder rumbled noisily.

'And do you know what, Jack Silver? Even then it was a close thing. I consider myself like the Apache. I learn lessons where I must. The Apachean taught me your enemy is nothing, merely an opposing force once he enters your realm. As such he is already a dead man.' 'So, you see, unfortunately, you are my enemy, and this world is my realm. Those Indians devised methods to kill that warned all others of their status as a warrior first, foremost, and only. You know a scholar would understand that is why the white Americans put the Indian nations into history's greatest prison. Ultimately, their descendants have been forced to live out nearly 200 years in a concentration camp of the most exquisite design: one that appears in its glamour to give back at least some part of what was once taken from them.'

Cipher stopped then and thunder and lightning filled long moments. Jack saw that the man was fey. In the grip of his own masters.

Or demons perhaps.

The Englishman understood it was all bad now.

He wants me to watch, he thought, *to know my fate and to be broken by the knowledge alone, to torture my mind every bit as much as my body, to take me low and make me beg.*

And then Caffee spoke up, 'That is when he will deliver the killing stroke.'

He could not help but see the comparison between Shorty and Mac, with the great panoply that had played out between the Vistarens and the Hive. It seemed to him they were somehow playing out the great galactic soap opera in miniature.

Hoody was going to die. Christ maybe the kid was dead already. A part of him hoped that was true.

Stevan Cipher stepped away and made a gesture Silver couldn't see, and then he listened and heard the unmistakable sound of his friend's prostrate form being lifted closely, followed by a retching cough that confirmed Hoody still lived.

Jack thought of the superheroes that accompanied his youth, remembered the years he had dreamed of being like them, the years he had wished for the power, the nobility, the cape…hell, even the good looks.

He understood now that it was none of those things that set heroes apart. Instead, he realised it was a whole lot simpler. It was being able to sit, bound to a chair in a room full of degenerate evil men intent upon inflicting an end to life. And to watch with your eyes wide open as they slowly take away that life from a good man. Little more than a child murdered for no reason other than because they can.

And so, in spite of the bonds he pulled himself up a little straighter in the chair, and with his one good eye he marked the men in that room one at a time, finally resting upon Cipher's macabre grinning visage. He then looked unwaveringly towards his friend. Behind the gag that covered his mouth he smiled at Harold Hood, and maybe that small gesture helped the lad as he met his death, and maybe not.

Nevertheless, Jack Silver sat up straight, and he watched the awful tapestry unfold. And he showed nothing, neither flinch nor tear to the men that did their terrible killing.

There was nothing in the entire universe that remained, with power enough to stop the construct, except perhaps the construct itself. Between slim and no hope sat self-preservation. And that was the hope of the makers, of the Shaktar stone.

Chapter Thirty-Six
I'm Alive

Pain assailed him from all quarters.

He remained bound tightly.

Below that pain, he felt pins and needles as his circulation struggled against the bonds that held him firm.

A moment later he discovered one eye could not focus, and though his hands were tied in front of him any movement caused a sensation like molten fire burning in his ribs.

The bastards broke my ribs he thought, followed immediately by Molly's admonishing voice of reason.

'But you're still alive, Mr Jack.' Nothing from Caffee, he at least appeared to understand that Jack was in a predicament. He tried to peer around the room with his good eye and recognised the bleak stone backdrop of what he had come to think of as Castle Cipher.

Though his judgement felt off Jack was sure the room was cold. Condensation on the stonework suggested as much, but his nervous system had overloaded on pain and his senses couldn't properly tell. Light burned brightly from the ceiling's centre. It hurt his good eye when he tried staring at it.

So don't look came the thought, unbidden and tetchy.

Jack tried to laugh at that irritability, but he succeeded only in croaking. This in turn began a coughing fit that left his senses reeling in further pain, spots of blood-red floating beetles in front of his eyes.

He wasn't able to get up and didn't feel inclined to even try. But a moment later he shuffled his prostrate form a few millimetres on the stone floor in an effort to discover a fractionally more comfortable position for the agonies of his damaged frame.

The Englishman remembered before, though he didn't know how long before, and didn't speculate. He no longer felt fear or horror at the pain that had been visited on him, despite the vivid reminders each passing moment brought him.

Jack Silver thought instead about Hoody.

He had made three friends whilst out there, running both from and finally to the megalomaniac psychotic that now had him securely in his clutches. And three friends in this world were not something to be sniffed at, even though the last of these he had known for only a very short time indeed.

Now, each one of them was dead. And that was directly or indirectly at the hands of Stevan Cipher. Equally, Jack was absolutely certain that they were dead as a result of knowing him. And though to him they existed still in some strange Freudian way within the confines of his mind, he understood they were still most assuredly dead. And he was still most assuredly caught.

In the end, he supposed they had all got screwed. And despite all the stories the bad guy looked like in the real world, he would be victorious.

Jack reflected, it felt like one of those moments in the movies when the lead character would sigh and look heavenward, and then the credits would start to roll.

But he was no leading man.

And moreover, he was in no fit state to do anything even as dramatic as sigh. And so, he just lay there, and he believed finally he had nothing left to give.

His body had been broken by the tortures Cipher's Stormtroopers had visited upon him. And his mind somewhat too, at the least by the appalling vision of his companion's brutal murder. Here, at last, he was to truly be a broken man.

Jack drifted for a time and thought about the dreams, and the other places. He wondered, too late perhaps, if he should have paid more heed to the many clues that evidenced themselves during his time in those dream spaces.

Warnings.

Hadn't it all been about warnings?

Well, that and subterfuge.

Those other worlds.

The other characters he had met.

That had proven to be the phoney war, the propaganda war.

Stevan Cipher was a creature bent on destruction, out of control and in the hands of some imperative greater than he. A creature with no goodwill towards man or beast. Jack had seen in his dreams how such as him would grow and consume. A thing that kills all it comes into contact with until finally, at the very end, it turns inward and consumes itself in one final act of heinous self-immolation. A Vistaren he thought thinking of Shorty and Mac. But then was Cipher not in fact Tolkien's Shelob. Skulking in his lair with a will to devour the world.

Some part of him deep inside, far below the voices that echoed in his mind felt great movements during these last hours, both waking and sleeping. Jack felt wheels turning and recently figured he had begun to understand that the life of him, and Cipher, and every single living thing in this world, his world, swung and dangled on threads pulled by distant and greater things. But similarly, his greatest wisdom from Mac and Shorty was that those threads were maybe not so great, and not so distant as he might have thought.

In the end, when those two strange beings, combinators they had called themselves, grappled and grabbed at one another by the throat, seeking to destroy whatever the other was, Jack had seen that they too were simply sitting riding upon the carriage of existence.

They too were every bit as blind as he.

Live, thrive, die.

Though Mac and Shorty had been ancient, yet still neither one had been able to see where in the cycle they were sat. And so each had apparently learned little despite all the millennia of their existence.

Silver wondered then, how might he hope to know whether humanity approached some final doom or just a first summer of race adolescence.

Cipher had been his target, and he had lost that one. Now what he was left with was to try and die with dignity. Because when everything else went away from you that was what you did.

Wasn't it?

The Shaktar Stone had given him glimpses of magicks that were beyond his preconceptions. But the movements he now dwelt upon were he thought deeper still. And whilst he had not been able to pinpoint them or their meaning, nor to find an explanation to that state of mind he found himself wrapped in, still, he realised some small part of him, some spark deep inside that his core hoped still for an epiphany, a path beyond the moment he found himself in.

Silver realised it was not a religious vision he sought, rather, if he had at all been right then all the paths had been determined since the first moment.

Free will had not been the precursor but rather the distraction.

The destiny of certainty had driven him forward to this moment, dogged his every step from that first instant when he had stepped out back of a London eatery about a thousand years ago, indeed from the first instance of anything, ever.

He hoped even as the end approached that should this prove to be true Jack Silver might still hope for luck whatever his view of determinism, luck to still be a part of the plan.

He fanned that spark, held out his hand like kindling wood and beckoned lady luck's unique indulgence one more time. As he lay there figuring this all and making his final farewells he heard the sound of heavy-shod feet approaching.

'Shadowmen, Stormtroopers,' the voices in his mind cried in unison.

And so it was that they came for him a final time, and the endgame began.

The Hive had made a mirror, and nothing more clever than that. The Shaktar Stone was that mirror. All but indestructible, placed before the entity. An invitation to see itself, its purpose, its outcome. The all-consuming end that must follow is so destructive an outpouring.

Final Chapter
Showdown

He stood on trembling legs, fated, baited, slated, utterly wasted. Alone yet not alone in a room that stank of piss and the rancid odour of rebellion. He knew that nobody there would stand with him now, and finally, he understood he did not need them to.

He was Jack Silver, and he had awoken that which sat deepest inside of him. He was communing with the omniverse.

Cipher stared at him, utter contempt writ on his face.

'You have run as far as you are going to Silver,' he said, in a voice that dripped ice and poisonous vitriol in equal measure.

'Indeed, I have,' agreed the Englishman pulling himself up a little straighter, coughing badly and speckling his lips with fresh bright red blood. He winced at multiple injuries that included broken bones, a ruptured spleen and no small amount of internal bleeding.

Though he hurt seemingly beyond redemption he had found his purpose, and so he told himself the pain was not ever going to be enough to divert him from that path. Cipher's Stormtroopers had inflicted the injuries, but Jack had noted with less relish as proceedings had continued. More curious still to him not one of those physically imposing thugs remained in the room now. At the crucial moment, it was just Cipher and him.

With trembling broken hands, he struggled to reach into his pocket, his fingers felt lifeless and without the strength to grip. As he did so Cipher snapped… 'This what you're after?'

A savage grin revealed boiling emotions as Cipher held up his right hand. There clutched delicately between thumb and forefinger was a small shimmering white stone. Jack tried not to react, but he knew that at that moment, his eyes had opened a fraction wider. Just a fraction, and perhaps for only half a second, but it had been enough, and of course, the man Cipher had seen it. In order to mask his anxiety and in spite of the overwhelming pain, Jack reached for the only ally he had left, and so began to talk.

'So, I guess you're gonna kill me. That much has been obvious for a while.' He opened none too carefully, in a tone deliberately filled with scorn, each word spaced evenly. It took a lot out of him, and he began to swoon. Even without the Shaktar stone, in his hand, he had begun again to feel those alien movements deep inside of him. As his internal exploration had become more attuned, so he had begun to understand how it was he felt the shifting of rhythms far out and in the darkness beyond the castle walls, in places beyond his imagining. What he felt was the shifting of power, cogs turning again in some long-still behemoth. This all was happening out in the deeps of cold black space, eddies in his mind equating to the most enormous turns of an omni-galactic wheel, and somehow if his understanding was right his connection with the small stone held up in Cipher's hand was simply tuning his dial to that particular frequency.

The Herd had awoken within him, and the Englishman saw things clearly.

'One more time,' a voice whispered in his head. And though he did not understand he knew what to do, and he continued, 'You know, don't you? Know I didn't kill him, your brother. And I think you've known for a while now. You…your brother, it isn't about that. He paused and coughed bloody and wet. I was there all right and looking back I should have tried to stop them. But.' And he faltered for a moment, staggered and then recovered himself as dizziness assaulted him. After a minute, he continued, 'I was a different person back then. I think we both were.'

He stopped and looked closely into Cipher's eyes. The small man stared hard at him, and it was long seconds before he replied.

'Yes, I know you didn't kill him. Anyhow, that doesn't matter.' Cipher's words stumbled no longer clipped and as efficient as previously, and then simply halted. He frowned and looked momentarily confused. Jack realised he too was feeling those same shifts and eddies of power. Hope glimmered within him. It seemed there was some other connection, between him and the psycho-crazy man, or at least between them both and the Shaktar stone.'

'Between him and all the other crazy stuff,' his mind whispered.

He wondered once more and did destiny still had a card to play.

If he saw at a level beyond galactic things that were moving into some long-perceived position, to his failing mind like a room full of ballroom dancers waiting for the orchestra to begin, then how, he wondered, did Cipher see such?

Was he too one of the players looking in, and about to discover how the sands of destiny might choose to settle upon their small backwater rock orbiting around the edge of nowhere?

Jack shook his head and attempted to cuff at the sweat in his eyes. He decided that was all beyond his reckoning. Cipher, he had to focus on the Cipher here, in this room, now.

'But you're gonna kill me anyway…right?' he suggested in a hushed voice. As he spoke he tried to hold the gaze of Cipher's cold blue eyes, forced himself not to look at the Shaktar stone, still visible in his peripheral vision and growing steadily brighter.

He felt pain throughout, but he tried still to hold steady understanding events were hammering along, "moving at the speed of light" came the chorus in his mind. Life moved at a pace and the Hive now showed him glimpses of the Forever Expansion.

Though he and Cipher headed pell-mell towards whatever dramatic conclusion of their own.

While everyone else headed towards their own equally dramatic conclusion.

While possibly even an ending to everything that had ever been to what was in favour of what must come after.

Still, the expansion would continue, untroubled by what befell within, watching forever from without.

Jack wondered whether this deterministic reality planned for him to live beyond the next moment, guessed it mattered not much in the scheme and understood there were no actual choices. There had been the first choice, and all else was simply the infinite expansion that came from every preceding moment that blossomed from that moment. But still, he could hope.

Cipher looked back at Jack, his skin seemed to Jack pulled pale and tight over a crazy man's features. Hours previously the small man had instructed the systematic beating and breaking of Jack both physically and psychologically. And he had made Jack watch as they killed Harold Hood.

Then, after appalling deeds, the man had sought to bring Jack Silver past desperation. Stevan Cipher had gloried in those hours, never once leaving, staying to watch every ounce of the horrors inflicted upon his opponent. He never touched Silver himself, instead instructing his thugs. Guiding and cajoling them to ensure they never slacked and never let an ounce of humanity get in the way. And despite those men being rogues and murderers of the worst kind Jack had seen at the end, felt in the room's atmosphere, that those Shadowmen or Stormtroopers or whatever they were, they would have let him be. They would have let him live.

Or at the least let him die with some small remaining dignity intact.

Even men such as those could see he had taken enough, that he had earned the right to just let go. But Cipher held them all in thrall. He had made each one continue even then. Until he was ready to call time, and not one second before.

The men had broken his hands and his feet, made him look at his busted and bleeding fingers. They had lit long moist Cuban cigars and sat smoking them, laughing and joking before turning towards him again. Burning then his palms, deep and wet with the red embers of each of those cancer sticks. Jack had soiled himself, and he had screamed. His voice is raw. He had been no longer fearful of what was to come, merely fighting the battle between brain and body. On the one hand, his mind's desire to hold on, at the other end of the scale with each breath the chance to fulfil his body's wish, and simply let go.

Stevan Cipher didn't make things complicated; didn't bother with technology.

'Pain, the old-fashioned way.' Silver had heard the words repeated time and again. And after pain heaped upon pain, torture after torture, finally he had drifted from consciousness when that pain got too much when his overwrought nervous system shut down.

Still, no respite. Cipher had instructed his men to pour sachets of salt into open bloody wounds. Apply smelling salts prodigiously, to hose him down with ice-cold water.

And so, he was brought back from the brink again and again, screaming over and over. And they never let up, not even for a moment.

They had wanted to though; he saw that in the eyes of hard men, though never even once in the eyes of their master.

Cipher instructed his minions to break the Englishman's body with a bat fist and hammer. All the while he ensured his men were clever enough to deal excruciating pain without ever quite dealing the death blow. Jack wavered in and out of consciousness. And they had left his eyes, for reasons to him then unknown. And with those eyes, he watched a madman.

Towards the end, the whole sick tableau appeared to him as a series of vague perverse images painted upon his tortured imaginings. Movie-tone stills of horror visited him in some other world.

Jack Silver watched Stevan Cipher glory in the pain and the promise of uncompromising death he would visit upon him. He saw him revealed fully at the last like some giant blister of swollen disease. A puss-filled sack of living evil for whom all of what took place could only ever be a momentary release from whatever poison assailed him from within.

Deep inside a voice spoke to him, explaining how Jack falling to inevitable death would act as a trigger, a springboard allowing madmen to bend others to his will, more and more. Allow the virus that was him to explode into an orgy of crime, rape and death that would spread like a tidal wave and eventually engulf the whole of the world.

Once released from this life Jack would have been nothing more than a failed bung in the dyke, forgotten in the huge tidal surge. The voice told him to hold on. Made him understand that once burst there was no going back. That is the way of things, no going back, ever.

And a lingering thought deep in his amygdala wondered, 'Would humankind survive long after? No going back there either.'

Jack pushed back to the present and told himself to concentrate on Cipher telling himself. 'You can't change the rest.'

'Keep him alive and hurt him.' Those had been Cipher's instructions.

Silver thought that at some point, maybe even at many points, he had wished for death's blessed release, the eternal peace that would follow.

But he didn't wish for it now. At that moment he craved life more than at any other moment in his forty and some years. He had seen into the depths of his opponent's madness and looked beyond the limits of his most mortal life. He understood the game was afoot and destiny shouted that he had his part to play.

'C'mon, Jack,' Caffee's voice echoed deep in his mind, 'keep the dude talking, find the moment and damn well take it, we're relying on you.'

Jack felt more than knew Caffee in his mind was right, but he was growing weaker as every moment passed, it seemed time ran desperately short.

The Englishman had learned many lessons from the triumvirate of friends he had made along the way. The young people had shown him that fear and old father time were cancers both.

The biggest difference between youth and maturity Jack had come to understand was that the younger version of you is likely more often to just follow instinct uncluttered by all of the other junk. Jack had learned from Caffee Molly and Hoody that there is magick out there. That he every bit as much as they breathe and swim and move around in it every day. That the magick is us, and we it.

He remained uncertain whether all things were determined, within his new expanded understanding of reality, or whether the choices he deemed able to make could yet change the path of events, it did not matter, and so he spoke.

'I am young still, and this is my leap of faith,' And his voice was strong and recovered in spite of all. 'You know Cipher I've been inside your head too. I know as much about you as you do about me.'

And as the words released realisation revealed. Both he and his opponent had glimpsed history, the Hive, the Vistarens, the birth of the universal path they both now trod. Neither man he realised understood it, neither could. Jack struggled to hold onto concepts which only a short time before he felt certain he had complete mastery of the madman who stood before him and did not want the concepts, he sought a different mastery.

Both men had played out a chase across half of Earth's northern hemisphere born out of a slight, a crime which never existed. Stevan Cipher's brother died, but so many people had died. Jack understood then that though two men stood in a room, diametrically opposed, hating. One battered and broken, the other arrogant and certain of his supremacy, only one saw that there was a bigger picture, that the other thought he was the bigger picture.

Strictly speaking he, Cipher, both were tools of the echoes of long-departed races. Of beings that long ago left the universal battlefield behind who themselves were nothing more than patterns within the great tapestry.

He forced his bowed head up, looked again at Cipher and squinted at the stone which then shone bright as a star. 'I am your mirror, and you mine. We are the product of destiny. Like Mac and Shorty Mister Cipher, we two are representations of ideologies. Yet still we are simply marionettes. I wonder if somebody has been playing the most monumental cosmic joke on us both. What do you think?' He stopped, exhausted, tottering on the edge.

He had no rage now at the man opposite him and had begun to understand they played their part in the galactic chess game, pawns in the hands of determinism.

'Must be,' he croaked.

Whether all things were determined or whether some fraction of free will remained mattered not, the gateway was the same for both men. The gateway was the same, but the heritage of the men was unique Jack Silver thought, and he raised his head and stared wide-eyed at Stevan Cipher.

'That which once made the Hive strong still makes the Hive strong. They ultimately are all one. Together, mortal, flawed, individual, but yet ultimately collective, they, and me, and him.'

So spoke a voice that was in turn one and at the same moment all of the voices in his head made audible in that room. He saw that he was the Hive. Alive or dead was meaningless, each was part playing their role in the whole.

The Vistarens had proven nigh on immortal, each living for millennia, untouchable striding effortlessly, arrogantly around their garden of stars. They had wiped out the Hive in the trillions. Yet the Vistarens were long gone. 'The Vistarens are gone,' myriad voices chorused in Jack Silver's head, and apparently in Ciphers too as he grabbed suddenly and desperately at his temples and dropped moaning to his knees.

The Hive was here, and it had grown vibrant right then before both men.

That was what being a part of the Hive meant. For all his rage, Stevan Cipher was a creature alone, but he was not Vistaren; he was as human as Jack Silver, a part of the whole. Jack sucked in a lungful of air his throat whistling, pulled back his shoulders as best he could and smiled at the man standing opposite him.

'Shaktar stone's no good to the likes of you Cipher.'

'What do you know fool?' the other responded panting pushing up from the squatting position he had taken when trying to shake off the voice in his mind.

'I don't need magic to sort you and this whole damn day out once and for all.' The small man's voice rose. Jack saw he was letting his anger boil up like filthy seawater filling the bowels of a sinking tramp steamer. Stevan Cipher was letting his fury overwhelm him, trusting it to compel his next move. Perhaps he felt the Vistarens' burning cold fury, the contradiction they had been in life. Perhaps he was placed in the hands of that animal instinct exactly as Jack himself was weakening, fading, dying he supposed.

The Englishman staggered forward and laughed suddenly croaking like a crazy man. He charged drunkenly on awful broken limbs straight at his nemesis, at the matador that had pursued him relentlessly. Cipher screeched with glee at his enemy's pain releasing one hand from his forehead he beckoned Jack Silver forward and suddenly cold steel was revealed glinting in that hand. 'I'll kill you. I'll kill the whole fucking world. Do you hear me Silver? The whole world?'

The Englishman saw black around the edges of his vision, not now he thought. Spots floated in front of him, and he began losing sight of Cipher. He felt himself stagger and tried to squint. Something shone brightly before him, but he couldn't tell if it was the glint of steel or the white of the Shaktar stone. Thunder crashed outside the room, and deep within a storm raged too echoing from the universe beyond.

Cipher he thought was screaming.

Silver heard words, heard ecstasy in the voice.

He heard it not before him but within him.

The voice was alien, not English, barely even human.

'We are Vistaren.' 'We hate you.' 'You are nothing. Less than nothing to us.'

'Thought you were dead.'

'Killed you once before.'

'Now will kill you again.'

Silver could see nothing but then heard Stevan Cipher's voice inches in front of him.

'Starting with this one.'

A deep booming reverberated from deep underground, far deeper than the foundations of that place, deep in the bowels of the world. At that moment, people from many miles around awoke from uncertain dreams to crouch and hide in fear of humankind's waking nightmare carried down through the generations.

Hunched and in desperate pain, Jack sought to stumble one more pace forward. There was a thrumming sound, some monumental build-up of power assailing his hearing from all sides. It was like being in God's own power station. The deep thoom, thoom, thoom he felt more than heard as it built up speed. Revolutions of unimaginable power as whatever was that thing grew quickly to an unimaginable capacity. Jack dared not think about it; instead, he just forced and tried to push one foot out in front of the other.

Cipher lunged forward, sudden and deadly, and in the same instant Jack Silver felt a stunning, searing new pain. It all happened in less than a heartbeat and in that exact moment, Jack had closed one hand around the Shaktar stone.

Cipher rammed the long sharp-edged steel blade he held deep into Silver's body, and twisted it viciously, grinding through Jack's ribs and straight into already-damaged lungs. The small man was dealing the death blow.

Silver closed his eyes and inside of his mind he called on Caffee, and Molly, and Hoody, and upon the Hive that had spoken in his head, and that could hear him in that second. Jack Silver did not ask that they save him or protect him. Instead, he asked them to remove one of their own, one of their number. For that was Jack Silver's ace. He believed, at least hoped, that in the end, whoever Cipher might think he was, whomever Cipher might represent. At the death, and death was what they were dealing with, he was a human being: He had been born, like Silver himself, as a member of the human race, simply as one more of the Hive.

Stevan Cipher carried malice and method, and evil too. And though he had turned away from the main body and grazed alone, nevertheless Jack now called on the Hive to judge Stevan Cipher. The Englishman hoped that they heard him, hoped fervently they would find his enemy wanting.

All that he then could hear as his own life ebbed from him was the deep bass thumping vibration, like some earthquake presaging Ragnarok, drowning out everything else.

Inside of him, in that sacred place where he had found the answers to all of his questions, Caffee, Molly and Hoody were silent. It seemed at his approaching death they were gone… Jack Silver felt waves of astonishing heat, his ears hurt from the awesome noise all around him. He fell abruptly to his knees, blood spraying lively from the deep killing wound inflicted by his opponent.

'Have mercy,' Jack croaked, his words lost in the din.

Cipher screamed out a cackle of rage, it sounded to him like some viscous alien animal scream that, could be heard even over the raging nightmare that surrounded the two men.

Everything was going grey; he figured that Cipher had won. At the final tally, he had asked for the Hive, but when he had needed them most of all they had not come to him. He had things wrong, the twin engines of destruction from the two most ancient species in the universe going toe-to-toe one final time, Stevan Cipher and Jack Silver, the Hive, all in his mind.

And as the darkness finally took him still Jack whispered, 'Help me,' and fell in a dead heap on the room's cold stone floor.

Epilogue

The Vistarens had built the omniverse's greatest weapon. For when its work was done, they had been sure to build an off switch. A thing of such power did not have a switch to turn it off, rather function complete—it must die. That was the only way to be certain such omnipotence could not turn upon its maker. Hardwired into its soul, destruction is absolute by destroying yourself utterly.

In the end, the artefact simply showed the entity itself. It beheld reflection saw its own destruction and so understood that to survive itself required that life abound.

Given a choice the construct moved on, and so lived.

Doomsday did not come that day, except only to one small finger of malice, one vanguard of evil purpose discarded.

On the edge of a spiral galaxy, several thousand million light years from the centre of the omniverse, a small rocky sphere circled serenely around a class three yellow star. Six billion souls worked ate slept and continued the industry for countless years.

Somewhere in that world deep in the lowlands of an ancient country named Scotland one man lay dead while another rose shaking to his knees.

He coughed out ash and dust, and he smiled, finally triumphantly.

Jack Silver struggled for a moment, realised he was not quite able to climb to his feet and allowed himself to fall forward and rest his hands flat upon the now-cold stone floor.

Two feet from his own resting hands Stevan Cipher lay dead. Tendrils of smoke were rising lazily from his corpse. And there, inches from one of Cipher's outstretched blackened and burned hands, lay the Shaktar stone, again small and indistinct and beside it also blackened a long slim knife blade.

Jack was not sure what had happened and realised as moments stretched into minutes that something had changed inside of him that was as dramatic as anything that had happened around him.

Jack spoke to his mind.

'How did this happen?' He grabbed them at his temple with both hands as a cacophony of images, replies flooded into him.

But a few seconds later a single voice seemed to break free from the mass of data, from the sounds and images, the voice was a young girl's.

His dead friend Molly showed Jack then how to tune out. Showed the Englishman how to dial down the Hive voice he had finally awoken to.

And at the same time to hear that voice and acknowledge and understand that this world, his world, was no longer the one he had been born into.

He smiled at the sound of Molly's voice tears pricked at his eyes. Despite all that he had suffered the Englishman was sure now he would live beyond this day because those boundaries had moved too. Jack had changed, and humanity had changed. And never again would the world seem quite the same.

THE END!

Story Synopsis

Jack Silver's life changes in an instant after witnessing a brutal killing outside a London eatery. Pursued relentlessly by the psychotic brother of the victim, Silver finds himself falsely accused and on the run. Darting from shadow to shadow, he finds allies and understanding in unexpected places…

In the cold black of space, an ancient artefact of immeasurable power wakes and instantly rockets towards Earth.

A chain of events is set in motion that may bring about the downfall of not only Jack Silver but perhaps the end of all humanity.